The WEST TEXAS MURDERS

A Morgan Crew Mystery

The WEST TEXAS MURDERS

A Morgan Crew Mystery

Arthur A. Lee

Leeward Publishers, LLC
Winter Garden, Florida

The WEST TEXAS MURDERS

By

Arthur Lee

This is a work of fiction. Names, characters, places and incidents are either the product of the author's imagination or are used fictionally, and resemblance to actual persons living or dead, business establishments, events or locales is entirely coincidental.

Silver Cat Press
An Imprint of Leeward Publishers, LLC

This Book Is Dedicated To

Harry Winslow
The Bounty Hunter I Knew
A Long Time Ago, In My European Days.
He Was Former OSS And
A Really Good Hunter of Really Bad People

Other Books by the Author

The Morgan Crew Mystery Series

A Storm In From The Sea
The Las Vegas Murders
A Deadly London Fog
The Four Seasons Murders
The Hawaiian Sunset Murders
The Spy Who Would Not Speak

www.leewardpublishers.com

The WEST TEXAS MURDERS

By
Arthur A. Lee

Contents

CHAPTER ONE – SAN JUAN DE CRISTO 1

CHAPTER TWO – THE BIRTHDAY PARTY 11

CHAPTER THREE – BETSY'S STORY 23

CHAPTER FOUR - A SWAMP FULL OF GATORS 35

CHAPTER FIVE – TOO MANY MAYBES 45

CHAPTER SIX – GREAT MEXICAN FOOD 55

CHAPTER SEVEN – YOU'RE GOING HOME 63

CHAPTER EIGHT – HOW DID YOU FIND ME? 78

CHAPTER NINE – ROCKER AND EDGY 87

CHAPTER TEN – TO SAVE BETSY CONCANON 95

CHAPTER ELEVEN – MORE GUNS THAN PEOPLE 106

CHAPTER TWELVE – I'M NOT SURE WHAT I'M LOOKING FOR 113

CHAPTER THIRTEEN – FIGHT FIRE WITH FIRE 121

CHAPTER FOURTEEN – FISH 132

CHAPTER FIFTEEN – ROSITA 144

CHAPTER SIXTEEN – COLONEL MAX 162

CHAPTER SEVENTEEN – I'M SICK OF ALL THE LIES 175

CHAPTER EIGHTEEN – THE KILLINGS 193

CHAPTER NINETEEN – COME HOME WITH US 201

CHAPTER TWENTY – SANTOS 221

CHAPTER TWENTY ONE – THE TRUCK 234

CHAPTER TWENTY TWO – GETTING CAUGHT 245

CHAPTER TWENTY THREE – NOW WHAT 253

CHAPTER TWENTY FOUR – YOU KILL HIM, I CAN'T 260

CHAPTER TWENTY FIVE - HOGTIED 277

CHAPTER TWENTY SIX – WE'LL GO TO TRIAL 284

CHAPTER TWENTY SEVEN– THE PARTY 297

The WEST TEXAS MURDERS

CHAPTER ONE – San Juan de Cristo

West Texas is desert. There's not much else you can say about it. Oh, there are a lot of people who like it and live there happily. They are for the most part cowboys and their women; people who scrape a living from the desert raising cattle and a few horses. But West Texas is desert. There are cactus plants of several varieties; there are clumps of sage; a few trees struggling for life, and in the spring, after a little rain, there are millions of beautifully colored flowers that turn the desert into a magnificent painter's pallet. There are snakes to be steered clear of; there are lizards big and small; there are coyotes that howl at the moon and hunt the smaller creatures of the desert. But basically, West Texas is desert.

There is a small, ramshackle town in the desert of West Texas, at the foot of dusty and rocky hills. The Town was named, a hundred and sixty-seven years ago, San Juan de Cristo. The Mexicans who migrated from the south built the town. They wanted the little spring that flowed slowly from the rocky hills to quench the thirst of their sheep, their goats, and their children. Life was slow and small back then. Life was good.

They slapped together a handful of adobe buildings that still stand after all these years. They are now randomly mixed with wooden structures out of a 1930's cowboy movie and a few more modern buildings of stone and steel. The Mexican population of 23 people in 1845 has grown to 86 today.   In each generation, too many of the young men drifted north and west to work the farms in California and Colorado.

San Juan de Cristo has a general store that stocks mainly canned goods and liquor. There is a Post Office that is open only when someone needs to mail a letter or once a week to pick up mail. There is a small bank that barely stays afloat. There is a diner run by old Millie Perkins that was supposed to attract truckers but is too far off the main highways. A few old men spend their mornings there swapping lies of lives they only wished they had lived and drinking Millie's coffee, often for free when their meager Social Security checks run out before the next arrived.

And there are two roughneck taverns – 'The Last Stand' and 'The Mustang' – that sell beer and greasy hamburgers and Tex-Mex food. Cowboys spend their off hours at The Last Stand, drinking beer. The Mustang is nearly never open for business. Nearby is Justin's Western Wear that sells all the clothing the locals need by way of jeans, boots and big Stetsons. And at the edge of town, in one of the old, original adobe buildings there is an un-named little place that sells Mexican beer, cheap tequila and good food to the Mexicans who aren't welcome at The Last Stand and The Mustang.

At the northern edge of San Juan de Cristo there is a school house where the few local children get an education sufficient for them to read, add and subtract, and know something about the history of Texas. High School means an hour and twenty minute school bus drive to Balling, the nearest town to San Juan de Cristo. At the other end of town is a feed and grain store owned by Jorge Martinez. Jorge has a small livery stable and coral in the rear where he keeps a few horses he has bought, hoping to sell them for a profit which is only a hope, as few people in the area have the cash to buy another horse. Out front is a one pump gas station and small auto repair shop.

And there is a sheriff's office where Sheriff Matt Kronk spends his days smoking Mexican Cigarillo cigars and drinking bitter, often burnt coffee in spite of the heat. Sheriff Kronk likes to talk to whoever will listen about his adventures in the jungles of Viet Nam. Sheriff Kronk's wife, Martha, knows that Matt never left the warehouse in the suburbs of Saigon where he was a U. S. Army supply clerk who never made it to NCO rank during his four year enlistment. But Martha says nothing to anyone because all she has is Sheriff Kronk, her little house with the flower garden she struggled to keep alive, two children who left West Texas as each reached eighteen years of age, and Sheriff Kronk's small salary. Keeping quiet means she can keep what little she has.

San Juan de Cristo is divided into four sections by two streets; Main Street is County Road 8, and it runs north and south. Santa Maria Street runs east and west. Where the two streets intersect, the town widens around a traffic circle. The inside of the circle is surrounded by brown desert rocks with a mound of dirt in the middle. There is an old breach loading canon with thick layers of black paint against the rust and decay. A tall white flag pole is centered on the mound of dirt. On it a big American flag hangs above the flag of the State of Texas. And on the pole itself, at shoulder height, someone has pasted a decal of the Confederate battle flag.

Outside of the City limits of San Juan de Cristo the roads are rutted and dusty, and for the most part unpaved. Three years ago the two streets of San Juan de Cristo were paved for the first time, thanks to the thousands of dollars donated by Harry Perkins who owns the Bar H Cattle Ranch.

The Bar H is a sprawling 36,000 acre ranch twelve miles south of San Juan de Cristo. The ranch is the big employer in the area and without it . . . well, San Juan de Cristo would turn to dust and blow away to be spread across the West Texas desert.

It was quiet that Saturday afternoon. It was mid-August, and it was hot. Dust was blowing in from the southwest, covering almost everything in town. It hadn't rained for two months. In five hours some of the ranch hands from the Bar H would drive into San Juan de Cristo and fill up The Last Stand to drink beer, eat, and dance with a woman or two, if any women decided to dance with them. But at half-past one in the afternoon, only a sad looking, skinny, yellow dog was outside, and he was asleep in the shade of a rusting pickup truck that had died a long time ago and had been left near Jorge Martinez' feed and grain.

San Juan de Cristo used to be a ten minute stop along a short hall bus route, until the bus company went out of business nine years ago. Now it was unusual for anyone except locals to drive into town. Sheriff Kronk heard the car before it crossed into his town. He had been trying to stay awake by reading once again a three month old copy of 'Deer Hunter's Diary' magazine. He pulled his scuffed and well worn brown cowboy boots on and, because there was nothing else to do, he stepped outside his office letting curiosity take up some time in his boring day.

The big red Cadillac was kicking up a cloud of dust behind it as it sped – too fast, as far as Sheriff Kronk was concerned – into town. As the car got closer he recognized it as a really old Cadillac, one with big fins on the back, and a top down convertible at that. The color was what he remembered everybody calling 'candy apple red'. But as it started to slow and continued past him, he saw something even stranger. It was driven by a big black man. There hadn't been a black man in San Juan de Cristo for a long, long time.

The Cadillac slowed when it reached the pavement along Main Street and came to a stop in front of The Last Stand. The driver turned the wheel and pulled the big car to the edge of the street, parking next to the battered and dirty, blue, 12 year old Ford pickup truck he was looking for. Sheriff Kronk stood on the wooden porch of his office and watched the driver struggle to get his huge frame out of the Cadillac.

The man brushed the dust off of his scarlet colored jacket. Under it he wore a pale blue silk shirt, open at the collar. His blue jeans fit tightly over his muscled legs and covered his soft leather Italian boots to his ankles. The man was big, Sheriff Kronk saw. Maybe the biggest person he had ever seen.

Matt Kronk was 5'9" tall and too fat. But San Juan de Cristo was a small town. All he had to do was roust a couple of drunken ranch hands on a Saturday night and locked them up in one of his two jail cells until they sobered up. He didn't need to be a muscle-bound weight lifter to do that. But this stranger was big and he looked like he might be dangerous.

Jimmy Dyson stepped up onto Sheriff Kronk's little porch. He wore a plaid flannel shirt that was torn at the elbows and down his back. It hung loose over second hand jeans that had seen better days. Jimmy was a part-time handy man around town who was also a professional, fulltime drunk. "You gonna' do sumpthin' 'bout that, Sheriff?" he asked. Matt Kronk could smell the booze on Jimmy's breath.

"Do what about what?" the Sheriff asked.

"You gonna' let that big city black som'bitch just walk around town?" Jimmy asked.

"Go someplace and sleep it off, Jimmy," Sheriff Kronk said.

Jimmy walked away, mumbling under his breath as Sheriff Kronk stepped off the porch and crossed the street. The big black stranger saw him coming. He smiled, turned, and walked into The Last Stand. Sheriff Kronk picked up his pace and quickly walked into the bar behind the man. He stood with his back to the open door and watched.

The Last Stand was a dark, dank saloon, filled with mismatched tables and chairs that had seen better days. The walls were dark wood and held the heads of once hunted animals, old saddles, rusty antique rifles from the old west, several wound lariats, and framed photos of people, men and women, dressed in flamboyant cowboy outfits.

There were two pool tables in the center of the room that seemed to be well maintained. The cowboys liked to play pool to impress whatever ladies might be in the bar. There was a lit up jukebox at the back of the bar, but there was no music playing. The air carried the odor of stale urine and beer. The floor was sticky under well walked on sawdust as the stranger walked to a stool at the far end of the bar and sat.

Behind the bar the wall sported a big mirror with bottles of whiskey on shelves lining either side. Most of the bottles as well as the shelves were dust covered from lack of use as the patrons of The Last Stand were more interested in beer than liquor. There was a sign hanging by a thin cord on the left side of the mirror, on the wall in front of the black stranger that read, 'WE RESERVE THE RIGHT TO REFUSE SERVICE TO ANYONE'. Pasted next to the words on the cardboard sign was a small Confederate flag, similar to the one on the flag pole.

The stranger sat on the barstool and looked around. There was only one other patron in the bar that afternoon; Billy Winders. He was new in town having arrived three months ago. Billy made a few dollars doing repairs and pumping gas at Martinez' little gas station. There weren't many trucks and cars that needed repairs but Billy made enough to buy food and an occasional beer. He slept in an old, rusting, 15 foot camping trailer that had been sitting idly next to Martinez' corral for a couple of years.

Burl Evans, the owner and only employee of The Last Stand, stood behind the bar, at the opposite end from the big stranger. He was roughly wiping glasses that didn't need wiping. He glared down the bar at the big, black stranger but didn't move towards him. Burl was short, not more than 5'6", and very heavy at almost 230 pounds. His hair was a tangled mess of mousy brown and grey, early for his age of only forty-eight. His round face sported a big scar across his right cheek, the result of a drunken Mexican's knife when Burl tried to throw the bigger man out of the bar.

The stranger looked at Burl and asked, "Can I get a cold beer, please?"

Burl didn't move but continued to wipe the glass he held. He stared at the stranger angrily. "We don't serve your kind here," he said.

"What kind am I?" the big stranger asked. He smiled broadly showing off perfectly white teeth.

Burl looked the other way, at Sheriff Kronk. "You gonna' do somethin', Sheriff?"

Sheriff Kronk had been given a gun by the town when he was appointed Sheriff. It was a third hand purchase by the town; a Smith & Wesson .38 Combat Masterpiece, a former military weapon from the 1950's. He left it hanging on the wall of his office, in its old leather holster. He took it out once a month to plink tin cans for target practice and then spend an afternoon cleaning it. It was hanging on the wall that afternoon; he wished he had it with him.

The Sheriff looked across the room and said, "What do you want, mister?"

"I want a cold beer," the stranger said. "I'm thirsty."

"Give him a beer, Burl," Sheriff Kronk said.

"I ain't gonna' . . . Burl started.

"Give him a beer, Burl," the Sheriff said again.

Burl tossed his towel on the bar and bent to pull a can of Bud from a cooler under the bar. He walked slowly down to where the stranger sat and slammed the can down hard on the bar. He pulled the ring to open the can and beer spurted out.

"Can I have a glass, please?" the stranger asked, still smiling.

"Get it ya'self, boy" Burl snarled.

The stranger lost his smile and said in a loud, deep growl, "Boy? How big are men in this damn town? Give me a damn glass or I'll rip this place apart."

Sheriff Kronk said, "Give the man a glass, for God's sake, Burl. No sense in asking for trouble."

Burl reached below the bar and took a dirty glass from a plastic pan filled with dirty, soapy water. He put it on the bar.

"Wash it," the stranger demanded.

Sheriff Kronk said, "Give him a clean glass, Burl. Don't be stupid."

The Sheriff looked at the big stranger and asked, "You gonna' pay for that beer?"

"Of course I will," he said. "And I'm in the habit of leaving a big tip, too." The man's voice was deep; the words were spoken slowly but without an accent. He pulled a thick wad of cash from his pocket. It was held together by a big gold money clip with a ring of small diamonds on it. He peeled off a twenty dollar bill and held it out for Burl to take from him.

Burl hesitated but he reached out and grabbed the bill. "Keep the change," the stranger said, smiling once again. Burl gave him a clean glass and walked to the other end of the bar.

Billy Winders was watching all this using the big mirror to see everything. He was smiling. He found this whole thing funny. Billy was young, maybe twenty-three, and he found racial hatred to be stupid and old fashioned.

His father – damn his soul, Billy thought – was a bigoted idiot. As far as Billy was concerned, everybody was equal and hatred was a waste of time. If the big guy had money and the money was good, why not just be nice and take his money?

Sheriff Kronk decided that there wouldn't be any trouble, but it might be a good idea for him to go get his gun . . . Just in case. He turned and walked out of The Last Stand.

The stranger filled his glass with the cold beer and then drank it down in one swallow. He was alone in the bar with Burl and Billy. It was what he had been waiting for. He didn't want trouble and evaded it as much as possible, considering the work he did. He eased himself off the barstool, turned toward the door, and started to walk slowly. Burl was happy to see the man leave.

But as the big stranger neared Billy, he pulled a chrome plated .45 Colt 1911 from under his scarlet jacket and held it against Billy's temple.

"I believe you're William Winders," he said. "Please stand and don't give me any trouble, Billy."

Billy knew what was happening. It had to happen sooner or later. He couldn't hide forever. He slid off the barstool and turned his back to the stranger.

"Walk slowly," the stranger said. "Outside."

Billy did as he was told. The top of Billy's head came up to the stranger's barreled chest. He wasn't about to argue with the stranger. Outside, on the wooden plank sidewalk in front of The Last Stand, the stranger said, "Put your hands behind your back, please. I'm going to put handcuffs on you. No trouble now, Billy. Don't be stupid."

Again Billy did as he was told and the stranger closed the chrome plated handcuffs on Billy's thin wrists. Burl Evans was at the door watching all this. As the stranger put Billy in the back seat of the big red Cadillac, Burl stepped outside and yelled for Sheriff Kronk who was about to walk into his office.

The Sheriff turned, saw the stranger and the big gun, and called out, "Hey you! What the hell's goin' on here?"

The stranger stood at the open driver's side door and called back, "I have a bench warrant for William Winders. He skipped out on his bail in El Paso. I'm bringing him back."

"You're a damn bounty hunter?" Sheriff Kronk yelled.

"I prefer civilian assistant to law enforcement," the stranger called back. "But bounty hunter will do if that's what you want."

He pulled himself into the car and started the engine. He pulled the car away from the curb and drove slowly north, back out of San Juan de Cristo the same way he had come in, past the Sheriff's office. He drove slowly and stopped next to Sheriff Kronk who was standing on the office porch. He held out a piece of paper towards the Sheriff and said, "This is a copy of the warrant . . . For your records if you want it."

Sheriff Kronk took it and asked, "Who the hell are you?

"My name is Gandalf Finch," he said and drove away with Billy Winders.

CHAPTER TWO – The Birthday Party

It was Caroline's second birthday. Sandy and Betsy had spent weeks planning a blow-out party for her at the San Marcos Country Club. We live in the house I designed and had built in the hills above Harborside. We can sit on the rambling three story deck at the rear of the house and watch the sun set in the Pacific past the harbor. Cool breezes from the ocean ease the heat even in the hot summer months.

Betsy had come into our family and was Sandy and my daughter's nanny. She was a troubled, rebellious young lady who was just steps from jail when we took her in. She dressed in black 'Goth' style, dyed her hair sometimes green and sometimes fire engine red. But she and our daughter Caroline took to each other quickly, and Betsy turned out to be a doting nanny.

I guess Sandy and Betsy got carried away with planning the party because they had reserved the largest of the four banquet rooms at the Country Club. And they had hired a very expensive professional party planner from all the way down in Los Angeles to overly decorate the room and plan the feast that would be served.

There were games for the children to play, and six ponies tearing up the driving range for the children to ride. There were three clowns making asses out of themselves and a magician who couldn't even fool the kids with his "tricks". But the children were in heaven and they had a good time. Caroline, not absolutely sure of what was going on, laughed and waddled around as best she could, taking in every new sight available.

There were two bands hired; the first a four piece group with long hair that specialized in "bubble gum rock" for the 26 children who were invited. They arrived at two in the afternoon and played until six. The second band, which arrived at half past six, was a better dressed dance band for the adults.

A second banquet room had been reserved and converted to a play room for the children. Enough beds and cots were brought in for the 26 children to sleep the night away while their parents danced and made good use of the open bar. A staff of nurses was hired to watch over the children, who had enough toys and cookies and milk to keep them happy way past their normal bedtimes.

It turned out to be quite an eclectic group of people at the Club to celebrate our daughter turning two years old. Sandy had invited all our friends – Bob Sommers was at the top of the list of course. Bob is a college friend of mine. He had a rough time of it after school, his marriage ending in divorce. He was a Los Angeles detective and had turned to booze to ease the pain of life. It didn't take long for him to be fired from the force. I took him in and sobered him up.

When he was ready, I used my family's influence to get him a job on the small San Marcos police force, as the only detective in town, not that we needed a detective necessarily. A few years later and he was in charge of the whole twelve man city police department.

Every fisherman and boat crewman from Harborside was at the party. I knew all of them since going out on a boat for a day of fishing is second only to a day on the golf course. Well maybe third. A day with my wife, Sandy, and our daughter Caroline is always the best of days.

A few disreputable characters from North Harbor,

friends of mine who were not friends of Sandy, were invited at my insistence. North Harbor used to be a nice area of town where middle class people lived. Times changed, and North Harbor is now mainly destitute and abandoned homes interspersed with strip bars, cheap liquor stores, and decrepit boarding houses. The people from North harbor seemed to mix – albeit uncomfortably – with the many well dressed Country Club members at the party. But a good time was had by all.

Betsy Concanon, our tattooed biker chick nanny, was showing signs of growing up. She was 19 years old and carrying a full load of pre-med classes at the local college, with a 3.4 GPA. She had let her hair grow out from the bright red and green she had colored it, to its natural light brown. It hung softly to her shoulders. I think she may have been influenced by Sandy's wonderful hair.

Her wardrobe of black t-shirts, ragged blue jeans, and studded motorcycle boots, had gradually been replaced with the more 'current' style of today's young ladies of college campuses. She and Sandy had been taking a lot of shopping trips to the better stores, filling Betsy's closet with expensive clothes even though Betsy seemed to appreciate tight fitting jeans and T-shirts.

Her black leather, studded motorcycle jacket had been donated to the Salvation Army, along with most of the other accoutrements of her past wild life. The night of the party she had worn a really nice pale blue dress that covered all her tattoos except the thin band of barbed wire on her left arm. I had to admit, she was learning how to be more attractive than rebellious.

The young Country Club men apparently found her attractive, too. I think the exposed tattoo was working as a suggestive come-on. She is something unusual amongst the Country Club elite, as was Sandy when I first brought her to the club. Sandy is tall and well put together; so different than the skinny anorexic look so common at the Club.

Sandy has never liked the San Marcos Country Club. She refers to the members as phony elites and a few other four letter words when necessary. But we go there for dinner and the dances the Club puts on. She even tried to play golf with me once and swore she would never try that again.

Betsy spent most of the evening at the party, after the children were 'put to bed,' dancing with one son-of-the-rich after another. Following that lead, Sandy dragged me off to the dance floor multiple times, too. Dancing isn't my thing, as the young folks say. But I never refuse an opportunity to hold Sandy close to me.

The party finally broke up around three AM and the four of us arrived home at a quarter to four. Sandy and Betsy carefully laid the sleeping Caroline in her crib while I showered and crawled into bed. I was asleep in minutes.

At eight-thirty the doorbell woke me. Someone must have had their finger super-glued to the bell, as it was ringing over and over again. Sandy rolled over, pulled the blanket over her head, and mumbled something about me going to the door. I think there were a few four letter words thrown in.

So, I pulled on my bathrobe and slipped my feet into my old, worn out slippers (I keep hinting that I need new slippers but birthdays and Father's Days and Birthdays go by with no new slippers), and started out of the bedroom. It was immediately apparent that I was consumed with a really good hangover. The house seemed to have been transported out to sea as it was rocking back and forth on heavy waves. I walked into a wall or two on my way to the front door. The bell kept ringing. I yelled, "OK! I'm coming! Stop with the doorbell!"

It was a lot of work, but I finally did reach the front door. I held onto the wall as I unlocked it. I pulled it open and standing there was the biggest man I had ever seen. The Black man standing there was head and shoulders taller than me . . . And I stand six foot two inches tall. His hair was cut short, he was clean shaven. His eyes were bright and clear but I could feel the palpable danger behind them. He wore a bright electric-blue suit, well cut and not inexpensive looking, and there was that all too obvious bulge under his left arm that I was familiar with. Over the years I had come to recognize that bulge as the gun really dangerous people and cops carry. This guy was carrying a really big gun and he wasn't a cop. My immediate thought was, "I ain't gonna' fool with this guy".

The man's voice was deep but not harsh. He spoke without any accent. He said, "Is Elizabeth Concanon here?"

"Why?" I asked. I stood in the doorway, one hand on the door and the other on the wall. But I felt a little foolish because I knew I couldn't stop this guy from bursting into my home.

The man smiled, almost laughing, and said, "Because I need to see her."

"Why?" I asked again.

"Look, little man," he said derisively and grinned a little. "I know who you are. You have no idea who I am. But I'm a peace loving kind of man. I deplore violence. So I'm going to be up front and truthful with you. Elizabeth Concanon has been charged with murder in the State of Texas. I hold a warrant to return her to that State. So, please let me in and I will take Ms. Concanon with me. No trouble now little man, alright?"

"Ms. Concanon is my employee," I said. "This is also her home. Before you do anything, I need to see your badge and the warrant."

"I am sorry, Mr. Crew," he said. "I don't have a badge. I'm going to reach into my right hand jacket pocket using my left hand. My gun . . . As I'm sure you are aware . . . Is on my left side. I am going to slowly retrieve the warrant so you can see it."

He slowly pulled some folded papers from his inside jacket pocket as he said he would and handed them to me. I opened the papers and had no idea what I was looking at, but they looked official and legal enough.

"You don't have a badge?" I asked. "You're not a cop?"

"I am not a cop," he said.

"How much are you being paid for this?" I asked.

"Ms. Concanon has left the State of Texas while on a quarter million dollar bond. When I bring her back I will receive $25,000."

"So you're a bounty hunter," I said. It wasn't a question. I knew the kind of work this man did but I wanted him to admit it.

"I prefer civilian assistant to law enforcement," he said and smiled at his little joke. "But you can call me any name you want. I am not easily offended. I'm too damn big to get offended very often. If I did, too many people would wind up hurting very badly."

Sandy had walked to the door and was standing behind me. She was wrapped in a fluffy white bathrobe. Her hair was uncombed; her feet bare, her eyes were still full of sleep.

"What's going on here?" she said in a raspy voice.

"Mrs. Crew," the man said. "I am very sorry to have awakened you. I have a warrant to return Elizabeth Concanon to the State of Texas. If you will just allow me to come in and speak with her, I will be gone and out of your life very quickly."

"Look," I said. "I don't know who you are and I don't know if it's legal for you to do what you want to do."

He smiled again and said, "My name is Gandalf Finch. I can assure you it is constitutionally legal for me to take Ms. Concanon back to Texas."

"Well, Mr. Finch," I said. "I think I'll let my attorneys make that decision. Come back in an hour and we can talk about it."

Sandy had walked away while I said this. Gandalf

Finch had watched her walk away but I was still too hung-over and sleep deprived to notice his eyes leaving mine. Maybe it was just a man watching a beautiful woman in motion. Maybe it was the man's natural suspicion and caution when doing the work he did. Either way, his eyes didn't leave Sandy and his right hand moved slightly toward the gun under his left arm.

"Please do phone your attorneys," he said, looking down at me once again when Sandy had disappeared from sight. "I know what they will tell you. But I'm not leaving here. May I wait inside while you phone them?"

I was getting frustrated and a little angry. But that was caused by the hangover. My head was full of clouds and a headache pounded in painful rhythm. If it weren't for that I would probably be bowing and scraping to the very tall and very big Mr. Finch.

"Mr. Finch. You may have a warrant of some kind for my employee, but you don't have any legal right to enter my home. Come back in one hour, please."

"You are wrong, Mr. Crew," he said. He took a small step closer to me. It wasn't much of a step, just a small movement, but there was a threat implied in that half step. And without thinking I flinched and took a step backwards. I mean, I may have been sleepy and a little hung-over, but I wasn't stupid. The man was big enough to snap me like a twig.

He went on, "I have every legal right to enter any premises to take into custody a fleeing felon."

I looked up at Gandalf Finch. His eyes were clear and sharp, but behind them I could sense impending violence when violence would be necessary. I felt small standing in front of this man. I swallowed hard and said, "You may be right, but I still want to speak with my lawyers."

Gandalf looked away again, over my shoulder, at something happening behind me. I turned and saw Sandy walk back to us once again.

"Where have you been?" I asked her. Actually, I was hoping that she had found some big, bad gun somewhere and was about to stick it in Gandalf Finch's face.

"I went to Betsy's room. I wanted to hear from her what this was all about."

I waited for her to say something else and when she didn't I asked, "So? What did she say?"

"She didn't say anything," Sandy said, she smiled uncomfortably. She pulled her bathrobe tightly around her and looked up at Gandalf who wasn't smiling anymore. "She appears to be gone," she said with a nervous shrug of her shoulders. "The window in her room is open. A few of her clothes are gone."

Gandalf laughed broadly and loudly. It was a laugh that only someone his size could own. He started to turn and walk away. I stopped him.

"Wait a minute," I said. "Come inside. I want to talk to you."

He stopped and turned slowly. There was that smile again, and to be very, very frank, it scared the hell out of me.

"You mean *now* I can come into your house," he said.

"Now that Betsy is gone, you can come in," I said. "I want to know just what the hell's going on."

"Alright," he said. I stepped aside and the big man walked past me, ducking to get through the doorway. He stopped inside our house and looked around. One would think he might be checking out the interior decorations, but in fact he was checking for traps, escape routes, and places people might be in hiding. A man like Gandalf Finch did not take chances

We settled in the living room, Gandalf's great bulk taking up a good portion of our imported, handmade Italian leather couch. Caroline had climbed out of her crib and waddled into the living room. She stopped at Sandy's feet and hugged her knees, holding her hands up, reaching for Sandy, who lifted her and held onto her.

"What a beautiful child," Gandalf said. "I have two adopted sons back home. Of course they're in school. And I have another son. Of course . . . Well, let's not talk about him now."

Sandy, once again taking control as she does so well, forced a smile and asked, "How old are they?"

"Eight and eleven," he answered. "They attend St. Francis Boy's Academy . . . That's near El Paso. It's a fine school . . . A very good curriculum, sports, horses, everything the boy's like."

"So you and your wife live in Texas?" Sandy asked. I knew what she was doing. I'd seen her do it many times before. Find something that Gandalf Finch wanted to talk about, to brag about, that made him feel good. If she could keep him happy, then he might be reluctant to hurt anybody.

"No, I've never married. The boys are orphans," he said. "St. Francis is a boarding school. My life and work is not conducive to a good home for children. But I'd rather talk about Elizabeth Concanon. You, of course, warned her and helped her run. Now we are here, talking about my children in order to give her time to get far enough away."

"Of course," Sandy said. There was no sense trying to fool or manipulate the man. Listening to him, even for such a short time, Sandy and I both knew he was educated and literate and smart.

Sandy swallowed hard and said, "You are . . . sort of an imposing figure. Betsy is very close to us. We care about her and we don't want to see her in trouble."

"She is in trouble already, Mrs. Crew", Gandalf Finch said with as much patience as he could muster. "She has been charged with murder. She skipped out on her bail. She's running again, and you good folks are trying to delay me going after her. So you think by me sitting here and talking about my children, Elizabeth will have time to run and hide."

"That's ridiculous," I said. "Do you really think my wife

and I can stop you from leaving here and chasing Betsy down? No, there's some other reason you're sitting there and talking to us. I don't believe for a minute that you're a stupid, two bit, flat foot. You want something. So tell us what you want."

"OK," Gandalf said. He pushed himself up to sit straight and leaned forward, his elbows on his knees. His bright blue suit jacket fell open enough for us to see the big Colt .45 in a shoulder holster. "I've read the police reports. I've read the court filings. I know some of the people involved. Your . . . Betsy as you call her . . . is charged with killing a young man whom she met in a bar. I don't believe she killed him. I think she is being framed for the murder."

Neither Sandy nor I knew what to say. Betsy had become a part of our family. She had become close to us, and there had been a bond formed there. Of course, we knew something of the life she had lived before she came into our life. There were motorcycle gangs. There was her life as a pick-pocket and purse thief. There was the rebellion when she was a teenager. And there were probably things we didn't know and maybe would never know. But here was a bounty hunter, come to our home, sitting comfortably on our leather couch, with the intent to take Betsy away where she would be tried for murder. That . . . Well, I just couldn't accept that and I wasn't about to let this man take her away. Just what, exactly, I would do to stop him was as yet not clear to me.

Breaking the silence, I said, "So you think she's innocent yet you want to take her back to stand trial? I don't get it."

"Actually, it's quite simple," Gandalf said. "My job is to bring her back. It's up to a judge and jury to determine her guilt or innocence."

"And you get paid to do that?" Sandy asked. Caroline, sensing that something serious was happening, had stopped giggling. She was looking from one of us to another, hugging Sandy tightly, maybe a little frightened of the big man.

"Yes," he answered very simply.   "There is a $250,000 bond on her.   I will get ten percent to bring her back."

Money. Now that's something I know about. I may never have met a bounty hunter before, and I try as best as I can to stay out of courts and legal trouble. But money I can deal with. It has been my experience that almost all the trouble I have been in, all the trouble my family and friends have been in, all the close calls with death Sandy and I have experienced, are directly related to money. Greed and never knowing how much money is enough is all too often the cause of the trouble I've seen all my life. So I thought I might try using money to get Betsy out of the trouble she seemed to be in.

"Tell you what," I said. "I'll give you $25,000 to go away. How about that?"

Gandalf looked into my eyes and smiled, but said nothing. He lowered his head and almost imperceptibly shook his head, I thought perhaps in sadness. I guess I had disappointed him.   Or maybe I was just doing what he thought I would do.

"OK, how about $50,000?" I asked.

Still he said nothing. He stared down at the floor. Was he waiting for something? Or maybe just holding down some rising anger inside of him? I hoped the former rather than the latter.

"So how much will get you to go back to El Paso alone?" Sandy asked.

Gandalf's smile was unbroken. He was thinking and that, I thought, might be a good thing or maybe not.   It depended on what he was thinking about.

Finally, he said, "Mrs. Crew, I know you and I know your husband. I know all you've done over the past few years. I always do in-depth research on the jobs I do before

I do them. What I want are two things. First, get one of your very expensive attorneys to represent Elizabeth. Second, Mr. Crew, I want you to help me find whoever really did kill that boy. And I want to take her back for the bounty."

CHAPTER THREE – Betsy's Story

I was on the phone, speaking with Peter Jascro of Harper, Harper, Jascro and Nettles. I like to describe them as Lawyers Extraordinaire. Others have described them as a pack of damn wolves. Peter Jascro is a friend of my late father and like an uncle to me. I was explaining the problem and asking that one of their criminal attorneys meet us in El Paso, Texas when Sandy returned to the living room. I hadn't seen her leave but when she returned Betsy was with her.

Gandalf laughed deeply and then said, "I figured she was still here."

"You're saying you knew I was lying?" Sandy asked.

"Certainly, Mrs. Crew," he said. "I'm not stupid and I've been dealing with people for a good number of years. But I'm not angry, just amused."

"Then why didn't you just search the house?" she asked. "I mean, we certainly couldn't stop you."

"I want your help," Gandalf said. "If I had played it rough . . . Would you have agreed to help me?"

Betsy was standing nervously in the arched entry of the living room. She spoke softly, "I didn't kill him."

Sandy, still holding Caroline, took Betsy by her arm and led her to a chair. "Sit down, Betsy," she said in a soft voice. "How about you tell us all about it? Start at the beginning."

Betsy was scared, the color had left her face and she was twisting her hands hard enough to turn her knuckles white. Tears filled her normally bright eyes. Even little Caroline was upset and reached out to Betsy to comfort her in some way.

Betsy's Story

It was a week before Betsy's fifteenth birthday. She was at home, suffering through a two week suspension from school for fighting with three girls who had been making fun of her old blue jeans, torn black T-shirt, black finger nail polish, and bright green hair. Although the three girls needed medical attention after the fight, the school police did not file charges against Betsy.

Betsy's father who, drunk or sober, either ignored Betsy or yelled at her for everything and anything, told her there would be no birthday celebration because of the suspension. Her mother was too drunk to care. Her latest Country Club boyfriend had just broken up with her when his wife found out he was sleeping with Betsy's mother. Betsy had had enough of life at home. She was sure that somewhere, life would be better for her. She ran away in the early morning hours of the next day while her parents slept off their drunk, her mother passed out on the living room floor. Florida sounded like fun and far enough away from California. She had heard of Disney World and thought that would be the place for her.

She hitch-hiked south out of San Marcos to Los Angeles. She made it across the desert to Las Vegas with an old couple who were excited to get their hands on some of those penny slots in the casinos away from The Strip. They were sure that they would come back rich or maybe with one of those expensive sports cars anyone could win.

In Las Vegas she found a trucker who had hopes of some sex with the young girl. Betsy was able to fend the trucker off with promises until they reached Salt Lake City. There she told him to screw off and continued on her way.

She fed herself by stealing food from convenience stores along the way, and when necessary, she did dumpster diving behind fast food restaurants, but she never begged on street corners. Despite everything she still held her pride. She told us she would never do that. She would hold on to her pride even if she lost everything else.

Once, a family of itinerant Mexican farm workers drove her twenty miles down a side road in a rickety truck that struggled to move at thirty-five miles per hour. The father was thin and leathery with days of beard unshaven. The mother was old at middle age, wrinkled and tired after a hard life working farms where work was available. There were five children with them; the oldest barley nine years old; all skinny and none had ever been taught to smile. But they felt sorry for Betsy, a young girl on the road to nowhere, and gave her a five dollar bill to buy some food.

She told us she didn't have a plan, nor did she have an idea where to go once it was apparent that Florida was too far away. She just wandered wherever rides took her, without purpose or even caring where she would be the next day. It took half a dozen rides with strangers but she soon found herself in Dallas, Texas, searching for some food and a safe alley to sleep in.

Walking along a dark street away from downtown, she heard music and turned a corner and walked into an unlit alley lined with dumpsters and over turned garbage cans. Deep into the alley she found a club and the heavy metal, punk rock music she liked streaming from it. A red neon sign hanging over the closed door to the club flashed SAL Y'S – the second L was not lit but Betsy knew it meant Sally's.

She walked inside and found young people dressed

like her, in black with shaved heads or brightly colored hair, and makeup out of a cheap horror movie. There were black leather and chrome chains everywhere. They welcomed her into their world.

The young people in the club were dancing wildly and laughing loudly. Betsy danced and drank beer and laughed and felt good for the first time in a very long time. Sally, who was a tattooed lady of fifty-two years, saw Betsy and took the very young girl under her wing. She could see that Betsy was too young and probably a runaway. She had seen runaways too many times before and always felt sorry for them because she knew their future was bleak. When the club had closed and the last young people drifted away into the early morning sunlight, she took Betsy to her small apartment above 'SAL Y'S', fed her and gave her a place to sleep.

Ignoring Betsy's obvious young age, Sally gave her a job serving bottles of beer from behind the bar at the unlicensed, underground club. Every now and then the City Police would raid SAL Y'S, arrest a few patrons on drug charges, and then empty the place and padlock the door. The next night Sally would cut the padlock off the door and her night club was again filled with young people dressed in Goth black.

Betsy soon had her first, second and third tattoos, and she was happy for the first time in years. Sally also taught her how to pick pockets in order to make a living and have some kind of future. Betsy turned out to be a quick learner and was very good at it. Sally spotted the well healed guys, often Goth imitators who came to her club looking for sex, and Betsy took their wallets before they left.

One night . . . The days and nights were all blending together, one to the next, as Betsy quickly lost track of time and really didn't care anymore . . . One night a young man wearing a big white Stetson cowboy hat walked into 'SAL Y'S'. He was young but older than Betsy. He was slim but he had muscles tugging at his red plaid cowboy shirt. He wore fancy cowboy boots, brown and red, and reptile skin. He was handsome with a square jaw and bright blue eyes. He was completely out of place in 'SAL Y'S'. Sally nodded, a signal telling Betsy he would have a fat wallet. But Betsy didn't lift it. She went to him and offered him a bottle of cold beer.

He told her he was just curious when he walked into the club. He heard the booming music and it led him into SAL Y'S He told her his name was Jimmy Perkins. They spent the night together in the small bedroom above the club, in the small bed Sally had given Betsy.

Betsy had never been with a man . . . or boy . . . before. Although sex was a new thing to her, and wasn't nearly as pleasurable as she thought it would be, she found herself wanting more and more of young Jimmy. His young, strong body was a magnet to her hands and she searched every inch of him in the dark of the room. Sleep evaded them as she experienced things she had only dreamed of before.

As they lay in bed next to each other in the early morning hours of the fourth day, exhausted but happy, Jimmy said he had to go home. At first Betsy was panicked. She jumped up in bed, letting the sheet fall from her teenager's breasts, and came near to bursting out in tears. She bit the side of her hand to keep the tears from bursting lose. She was going to lose the boy, and she didn't want that to happen.

As tears began to fill her eyes, Jimmy said, "Why don't you come with me?"

At sunrise, Sally cooked a big breakfast for them, and then she hugged Betsy goodbye like a mother seeing her child leave home for the first time. "Take care, honey," Sally said. "Come back if you need to." She slipped two twenty dollar bills into Betsy's pocket without her knowing, with all the skill of a good pick pocket.

Jimmy and Betsy drove west on Interstate 20, onto Interstate 10, and then turned south on a lonely two lane highway in Jimmy's brand new, bright red, Dodge pick-up truck. There was a gun rack in the back window but it held no guns. And below the empty rack was a decal of a Confederate battle flag in one corner and the lone star flag of Texas in the other corner.

Jimmy smiled and pulled Betsy close to him as he drove. She put her arm around his neck and rested her head on his shoulder. She liked being with him, she told us. It was comfortable being with him. She felt safe with him. She felt loved and hoped he did love her. But the words had not been spoken yet.

They drove on into the West Texas desert. They stopped several times in the heat of the middle of the day to make love in the back of the pick-up. They stopped twice to eat at out of the way little places that served greasy food and cold beer, but neither of them cared what they ate, so long as they were together.

They stopped at the side of a lonely road that night and slept huddled together in one old sleeping bag against the cold desert night air. It was mid-day when they turned off a dusty, pot-holed road onto the long straight drive, rutted by frequent use and lined with sun burnt weeds on both sides. A tall gate made of poles from twisted desert trees spanned the dirt road. On top of it was a wooden sign with burnt on letters announcing they had arrived at the Bar H Ranch

Cattle roamed freely along the four and a half miles of unpaved, bumpy road that was the driveway to Jimmy's home. The hills, far off on the horizon, were of a burnt-brown color in the afternoon light. Betsy remarked that there were no trees, just cactus and brush. Jimmy just smiled and patted her on her knee.

The big Perkins' home came into view finally. It was two stories tall, white, with windows everywhere. The front of the house and both sides were lined with a big porch, covered to protect it from the desert sun. Betsy was impressed, and she had high hopes of living there forever with Jimmy. He pulled the now dust and dirt covered pick-up to a stop in front of the house, at the bottom of the five white painted wooden stairs leading up to the wide porch. At the top of the stairs Betsy saw the seven foot tall, double glass front doors. 'These people have money', she thought.

As they stepped out of the truck, the big front doors of the house swung open and Jimmy's mother and father greeted them from the porch.

"Jimmy!" his mom said happily. "You're home finally! And who is this beautiful young lady with you?"

Betsy followed Jimmy up the steps. She was uncomfortable, uneasy, but hopeful that they would like her.

Jimmy said, "Mom, Dad, this is Betsy Concanon."

"Well, ya'll just come on up here so I can give you a great big hug, darlin'," Mrs. Perkins said.

While Jimmy shook his father's hand, Betsy was hugged tightly by his mother. "Why, you're just the cutest little thing I've seen in a month a'sundays," Mrs. Perkins said. "Ya'll come inside outta the heat, darlin'. I've got a big ol'pitcher of sweet tea. Ya'll like sweet tea, darlin'? An' we haven't had lunch yet. Why you're so tiny you look like I need to fatten ya'll up, darlin'"

For the next two days Betsy was in heaven. They liked her! They actually liked her! There was laughing; there was kindness; and there was food without her having to steal it. The Perkins family was actually interested in Betsy and spoke with her like she was special.

The morning of the second day Mrs. Perkins drove Betsy into San Juan de Cristo in her brand new Mercedes GLK. She bought her too many clothes at Justin's Western Wear. There were tall cowboy boots; there were tight fitting blue jeans; there were plaid shirts and striped shirts and skirts and dresses and big, puffy crinolines Mrs. Perkins said she would need when square dancing. And Mrs. Perkins bought her an array of lacey, sexy underwear. They were not the clothes Betsy was used to, but they were new, and they were gifts given with love and kindness. She was experiencing a life she had never known before; a life of love and acceptance and kindness.

On the evening of the third day, Jimmy took Betsy into the little town of San Juan de Cristo. They ate too much Mexican food and drank too many Mexican beers at The Mustang. Jimmy introduced Betsy to everyone there, and they danced to the western music played on the brightly lit jukebox.

Betsy was wearing her new cowboy boots, a red, white, and blue full skirt over the stiff crinoline and an embroidered blouse bought for her by Mrs. Perkins. No one commented on her tattoos, and her bright green hair seemed to go unnoticed. She drank beer after beer, more than she had ever had before. All the young cowboys in The Mustang – there were six of them – wanted to dance with Betsy. She was thrilled at the attention. She danced and was spun around. She laughed, and as the full moon hung above the bar in the dark night, she was exhausted. Jimmy sat and watched, clapped his hands to the music and when the men got too close, he stood and separated them from Betsy. But he didn't dance with her. And when she had drained one bottle of beer, he brought her another.

There was one man, Edward Hands, he said was his name, but everybody called him Edgy, who seemed particularly interested in the young girl. He was tall, very muscular, and in need of a shave. His hair was cut short and his eyes were dark and piercing. When their eyes met, it was hard for Betsy to look away. Oh, he let other men have their turn dancing with her, but he seemed to be there to twirl her around more than the others. And when he got close to Betsy, Jimmy didn't interfere as he did with the other cowboys.

As the evening turned into night, Betsy was drunk from the beer and the dancing. Her head was spinning, her stomach was turning, and she felt she had to sit down, but Jimmy and his friends kept pulling her to her feet to twirl her around and have "Just one more beer darlin'".

At some point in the night Betsy said she fell into blackness and had no memory of what happened next. Hours passed with her head spinning out of control. She was falling into a deep, dark hole; the noise surrounding her was deafening. She tried to grasp at something, anything that would save her. But the black hole swallowed her.

Betsy was awakened early the next morning by Sheriff Matt Kronk. She was huddled in a corner of a back room that was full of the stink of urine and death. A mop and pale for cleaning up The Mustang stood in the corner. There was a set of metal shelves that held bottles of bleach and a few cleaning supplies. There were a few empty cardboard boxes that smelled of mold and age and rotting paper. There was a rusting metal cot with sagging springs and no mattress. And there was the body of Edgy Hands lying on the floor next to the cot with his own bone handled knife with the eight inch blade stabbed into his chest. There was an empty scabbard hanging loosely from his wide leather belt. He lay in a pool of his own blood that was turning dark and coagulating after hours of death.

"Get up," Sheriff Kronk growled as he shook Betsy roughly. "Get up, I said."

She was lying on the springs of the cot, her clothes stained with vomit and blood. Betsy tried to open her eyes but the fifteen year old girl had never experienced a drunken stupor or a hangover before. She tried to lift her head but the splitting pain was like electricity shooting through her brain. Her stomach turned and she vomited again, painfully. Her head was spinning; her stomach was twisted in painful knots. Someone was standing there but she couldn't focus her eyes to see who it was. The earth was spinning around, out of control, all around her.

"Young lady," the Sheriff said. "You are in big trouble. You done killed a man."

Betsy was carried by Sheriff Kronk and two other men down Main Street to the little jail. She was all but thrown on the rusty cot with the stained mattress in one of the jail's two cells. She passed out once again and slept for ten hours. When she did wake up it was late afternoon and the cell was like an oven. Her head was bursting with pain and her stomach knotted violently, she was quickly and roughly fingerprinted and charged with the murder of Edward Hands who had seemed so interested in the young girl the night before.

There is no court house in San Juan de Cristo. Sheriff Kronk wanted to call in an El Paso County Judge to have Betsy arraigned and tried quickly in his little desert town. Twice before, over the years since he had been appointed Sherriff, the same had been done for the only two serious crimes committed in San Juan de Cristo, both by Mexicans. Serious crimes by whites were handled locally and quietly. But Harry Perkins, the most influential citizen for hundreds of miles around, quickly reminded the Sheriff that Betsy would not receive a fair trial in such a small, rural area where everybody knew everybody. That night and the next day she was alone in the cell. No one came to check on her, no water was given to her, and her screams for help went unanswered. The next morning Harry Perkins, with Sheriff Kronk along as a passenger, quickly transported Betsy to El Paso.

That same afternoon Betsy stood handcuffed in front of the judge, in the same filthy dress she had worn for the last two days and nights. A female Courthouse Marshall had to hold her up or she would have collapsed onto the floor. Words were being spoken but it sounded strange, like people speaking foreign languages all at once surrounded by the buzzing of a million bees.

Evidence was presented at her arraignment. The knife that was found in Edward Hands' chest was the damming evidence. The knife had Betsy's finger prints on it. The Sheriff testified that there were multiple stab wounds on the body and there was Edgy's blood all over Betsy's clothing. The other five cowboys at The Mustang had given rough, short statements to Sheriff Kronk that they had seen Betsy and Edward Hands dancing, kissing, and then leave the dance floor for the back room around one AM. Jimmy Perkins did not give a statement.

Betsy was still too sick to understand most of what was happening and what was said. She kept repeating, in a weak and faint voice, "I didn't do nothin'. I didn't do nothin'". A county Public Defender was appointed to represent her, but he said nothing during the arraignment, except to say that Betsy would plead not guilty.

Mr. and Mrs. Perkins were in attendance. Mr. Perkins posted ten percent of a $250,000 bond in cash. He spoke in defense of the girl and said he was willing to be responsible for her until her trial. And Betsy, considering that she was a minor, was released into his custody. Without asking the court's permission, the Perkins family took Betsy back to the Bar H Ranch. They fed her, let her soak in a warm bath for an hour, comforted her, dressed her in clean clothes, assured her everything would be OK, and they allowed her to rest for the rest of that day.

That night, when they were alone, Jimmy told her, "Look, Betsy. You're gonna be found guilty. They're gonna put you away for a long time. Hell, they might even put you on trial as an adult and that could mean they'd kill you. I don't know why you left me for him, but you ain't got a chance back there. Now, I like you . . . I like you a lot. So I'm gonna' help you."

He reached into his jeans pocket and pulled out some money.

"This here is three hundred forty dollars. It's all I got.

Now you get outta' here tonight. After everybody's asleep. Don't argue. Just go and get outta' Texas."

Betsy did run. She dressed in her old clothes and took nothing of the things Mrs. Perkins had bought for her. She had told Jimmy and his parents she had been on her way to Florida, so she reasoned that would be the first place anyone would look. The Mexican border was very close but she was afraid of Mexico; she had heard too many stories of the gangs and of people disappearing down there. She knew California; it's where she had been born and raised. That is where she returned to. She tried L.A. but it was too big and too rough. She settled into the street life of San Francisco where she could become invisible. Soon she was taken in by the Hell's Guardians motorcycle gang.

Sally had taught her well. She made good money as a pick-pocket, and that money bought her safety with the gang. There were no demands for sex as long as she brought money in. She tried some of the lighter drugs but was afraid of them. The gang protected her, and she was happy.

CHAPTER FOUR - A Swamp Full Of Gators

By the time Betsy was done telling us what had happened . . . At least what she remembered of what happened . . . She was sobbing freely. Sandy put Caroline on the floor. She sat on the arm of her chair and put her arm around Betsy's shoulders. The baby pushed herself to her feet and toddled to Betsy. She hugged Betsy's knees. Betsy picked her up and held her lovingly on her lap. When her tears subsided, I asked, "Did your lawyer talk to you at all?"

"I really don't know," Betsy said. "I was so sick. I mean, I've had too much to drink before, but I've never been that sick. He may have talked to me . . . I just don't know. I just don't remember."

I turned to Gandalf and said, "I know nothing of Texas law. Could they actually sentence her to death? I mean, she was a juvenile at the time."

"It's been done before," he answered. "Of course, she would be in prison for years before that could happen. Look, I know something about this case. There are holes in it that a good lawyer could drive a truck through."

"Like what?" Betsy asked hopefully. She had calmed down and her tears had subsided. She prayed for that ray of sunlight that would burn away the spider web surrounding her. Caroline was having fun sitting in her lap now that

Betsy was feeling better. "I mean, I don't remember a damn thing . . . I'm sorry. I mean, I don't remember anything about that night."

"How many beers did you have?" Gandalf asked.

Betsy thought about that for a moment and then answered, "I don't know . . . Maybe six or eight. I lost count and they kept handing me one bottle after another. I didn't want to say no . . . I guess I just wanted them to like me. I mean, I was just a kid, and I was scared."

"Have you ever had that many beers in one night before or since?" he asked.

"Sure," she said. "Down in San Fran, when I was with the Hell's Guardians, all they did was drink beer and party. Of course they did a bunch of meth but I stayed away from that."

"Did you ever get to the point where you blacked out after eight beers?" Gandalf asked.

"No," she answered. "I mean, I might have tossed my cookies once or twice. But I never blacked out."

Gandalf looked knowingly at me. I understood, of course. He didn't need to say anything. It was very likely that Betsy had been drugged. If so, someone wanted her unconscious, someone didn't want her to be awake when the murder occurred.

Gandalf then said, "Some other things bother me. The body was cremated quickly after an autopsy by a County Doctor. He's an old time Doctor who treats as many horses as humans. I got my hands on the report. It could have been written by a first year medical school student. The witness statements were almost word for word alike. They each used words such as: 'She was hot for the guy'. And I can't believe that Jimmy Perkins, who is a typically young guy, would watch his girlfriend go off with another guy and not at least get angry. According to the reports, he did nothing."

I sat forward and said, "So Betsy was set up? Why?

Who?"

"I don't know," Gandalf said. He reached into his coat pocket and pulled out a packet of French Gauloises cigarettes. Sandy shot him an angry look that would have knocked out an elephant. Gandalf smiled and slid the cigarettes back into his pocket. "I don't know why she was set up," he went on. "That's why I asked you to help her."

"It's obvious we're going to do all we can for her," Sandy said. "She's part of our family now. But other than getting good attorneys, what can we do? Do you think the police will just let us walk in and prove them wrong?"

"In Texas I have to be a licensed Private Investigator to collect bounties. That's the law. I am licensed, but I'm not a cop, and my skills at investigations are limited. I mean, I can find people, but beyond that . . . I'm afraid I'd be splashing around in water that's too deep for me. As far as proving the police wrong . . . Well, you've done that before."

Sandy and I looked at each other. We didn't need words. We knew exactly what was happening; it had happened many times before. We were being thrown into a swamp full of gators once again, to get someone out of trouble. Sandy shrugged her shoulders to say, 'What the hell'. And I agreed. Betsy had become something special to us. And besides that, Caroline would never forgive us if we let her go to jail.

I turned to Gandalf Finch and said, "OK. You and I will go to Texas. We'll see what can be done. I'll have some attorneys there to dig up some facts."

"That's fine," he said. "I'll take Miss Concanon back and meet you there."

"No," Sandy said quickly. "Betsy stays here until we find out what's going on. She'll take care of Caroline, and Morgan and I will go with you."

"That can't happen," Gandalf said. "She will have to go back with me."

I asked, "Why? Why not leave her here if you think

she may be innocent?"

"Two reasons," he answered. "First, I want my $25,000. Second, there are at least two other people looking for her for the bounty. They aren't as nice as I am. They'll hurt anybody who gets in their way. They'll hurt you without even thinking about it. They're old school . . . They make a living doing the dead or alive thing. Do you really want that to happen?"

"Mr. Finch," I said as I sat forward to let him know I was serious. "When I phoned my attorneys they told me something very interesting. California law allows people like you to . . . I guess you say hunt for bounty . . . But it doesn't allow you to take the person out of the State. You have to turn the fugitive over to the police for extradition."

"I'm well aware of the law, Mr. Crew," he answered. Gandalf was relaxed. He sat comfortably, crossed his legs, and the smile never left his dark face. I waited for him to tell me that he would turn Betsy over to the State for extradition proceeding. He said nothing more.

I asked, "So that's what you intend to do?"

"No," he answered. "I intend to bring her back to El Paso."

"And will the State of Texas just keep her? Will Texas ignore the laws of California?" I asked.

"I have a hunch that is exactly what will happen . . . In this case anyway," Gandalf said.

"I don't get it," Sandy said. Of course, I knew she did get it. Sandy is just about the best person I've ever known at sensing a situation and putting everything together.

"Mrs. Crew," he said. "I've said I think Elizabeth . . . Betsy . . . Is innocent. I think she's being framed for this murder. Why? I don't know that. But I think, as they say in the old movies, the fix is in. I believe there may be money and politics behind this. No, she will be held in Texas and California will not get her back."

"And if we say she'll stay here?" I said. I know, I know

. . . It was a stupid question that I already knew the answer to. But I had to ask.

"Mr. Crew," he said. "I *will* return Betsy to Texas. With all due respect to you and your wife, who's going to stop me?"

The three of us sat silently. I guess even Caroline sensed something bad was happening because she shot an unhappy glare at Gandalf and started to cry.

Gandalf turned to Betsy and said, "Please go pack a bag. Take a few things that you'll need. Don't take any jewelry or expensive clothes. Take your makeup if you want. Leave weapons of any kind here. We'll leave as soon as possible."

"I don't wanna' go, Morgan. I don't wanna go." Betsy was crying again and Caroline was crying. I hadn't seen Sandy cry in years, but a few crystal tears were filling her eyes and spilling over.

There was nothing I could do. Gandalf Finch was too big for me to even think of anything physical. I could try to phone the police, but I knew that would only lead to more violence, and I had to do what I could to protect Betsy. So as a last resort, I said, "I'm going with you."

****

We left Sandy and Caroline standing at the door, watching as we got in Gandalf Finch's bright red 1957 Cadillac Eldorado Biarritz convertible. The white top was up, and the windows had been replaced with dark glass. No one could see inside. Gandalf tossed Betsy's small suitcase and my garment bag into the trunk. I noticed on the floor of the trunk was a short barreled pump shotgun and an AK-47.

Gandalf told Betsy to sit in the back seat. "If you promise not to do anything stupid I won't handcuff you. Do I have your word?"

Betsy looked at me and I nodded. She said, "OK, I promise."

I waived to Sandy as I slid into the front passenger seat. We pulled away from the curb and drove slowly down the hills and out of San Marcos. Gandalf drove carefully and slowly. He never broke a speed limit nor failed to stop at a traffic light or stop sign. We made it onto I-5 and started south.

It took two days to cross thru California, Nevada, Arizona and into Texas. Gandalf wouldn't stop to spend a night at even the cheapest motels. He did pull into drive-thru fast food places to get food. He agreed to stop at rest area restrooms when needed. Betsy slept fitfully in the back seat. I tried to stay awake but sleep did overcome me occasionally. Gandalf seemed able to stay awake and alert for the entire drive.

I tried to keep Gandalf talking, both to keep me awake and to learn more about the man. It seems Gandalf's grandfather was a semi-famous South Chicago pimp. He ran a string of hookers, from the mid-thirties until he was murdered in 1959 by the Chicago mob because he wouldn't "pay up". Paying up, Gandalf educated me, was tribute a criminal pays to bigger criminals in order to stay in business.

Gandalf's father was 13 years old at the time. He inherited his father's 1957 bright red Cadillac convertible and his father's hookers. By the time Gandalf's father was 16 years old he had killed seven members of the Chicago mob who dared cross the line into South Chicago.

Gandalf Finch was born in May of 1969. His mother and Father were not married; his mother liked to read and named the child Gandalf after J. R. R. Tolkien's character. She instilled a love of books and reading in her son, teaching him to read by the time he was three years old. In 1987 Gandalf's father was killed in a drunken knife fight one night in a dirty little bar. Gandalf inherited his father's hookers and the 1957 bright red Cadillac Biarritz convertible.

After the funeral, Gandalf took $1000 in cash from a skinny, pimply faced, foul mouthed pimp for his inherited hookers, got in the bright red 1957 Cadillac convertible and left Chicago. He left with a few thousand he had managed to save up plus what he got for his father's hookers. He wandered around aimlessly for months and when he had run out of money he found himself in Austin, Texas and flat broke. He was spending his last five dollars for a beer and a hamburger at a dingy bar. An old man, sitting in a booth at the back of the bar, noticed Gandalf Finch. He was an imposing figure, well dressed, wearing a big diamond ring and a white rose in his lapel. People stepped aside for him as he slid from the booth and walked in unhurried and measured steps towards Gandalf. Gandalf saw him coming. He turned and felt for the .38 pistol he carried in his jacket pocket.

The old man was a bookie and sometimes bail bond agent. People owed the old man money and Gandalf looked liked just the right kind of guy to collect those debts. The old man paid for Gandalf's meal and offered him 3 one hundred dollar bills as an advance of what the man promised as a job. In fact Gandalf became an excellent collector of debts. It was rare indeed for anyone to say 'NO' to the big man.

He also learned how to bring fleeing bail jumpers back and found that kind of work was more profitable than strong arm debt collecting. Soon, he was in demand by bail bondsmen throughout the State.

The last thing I wanted to do was to get this guy angry with me. So, I held back asking too many personal questions. I figured if he wanted to tell me why he spoke without an accent, for instance, he would. He spoke slowly and the closest thing to an accent he had was the suggestion of an Ivy League College professor.

The drive was long and he told me enough about himself, on his own, for me to respect him, perhaps out of a little fear for what Gandalf could do.

It was pressing 3 AM when Gandalf pulled his big Cadillac into the parking lot of the El Paso County Jail. I was asleep in the front seat; Betsy was asleep in the rear seat. Gandalf woke us. I slid out of the car and stretched, yawning. Betsy sat up in the back seat, hesitated and then crawled out.

"Miss. Concanon," he said as she pulled herself from the back of the car. "I'm sorry, but I have to handcuff you now. They require it when I take you inside."

I was out, rubbing the sleep from my eyes. Betsy was sobbing again. She pleaded, "Morgan, do I have to do this? I didn't kill nobody."

"Betsy, this is the only way. You'll be safe inside and I'll get you out as quickly as possible. I promise. Don't say anything to anyone. I have a lawyer here who will see you in the morning. We'll get you into court and I'll post a bond. I'll try everything, Betsy."

I stood in the parking lot and watched Gandalf take our biker-chick nanny into jail. The big question rolling around in my mind was, 'What the hell do I do now?'

Fifteen minutes later Gandalf walked out of the tall, sand color stone building and leaned against his Cadillac. He pulled his pack of Gauloises from his jacket and lit one. He hadn't smoked during the long drive from California; he drew deeply on the strong cigarette.

When the cigarette was nearly gone to ash he turned to me and said, "I suppose you're going to go to San Juan de Cristo, aren't you?"

"That's where all this happened isn't it?" I asked. "So I guess that's where we're going. Do we start now or can we get something to eat and put on some clean clothes?"

"*We* aren't going anywhere," Gandalf said as he crushed out the stub of his cigarette under his heal and lit a second. "I'm not exactly welcomed company out there. I've had some unpleasant dealings with the Sheriff back there. You're going to have to go there by yourself."

"I thought you said we would work on this together?" I said. I moved a step closer to Gandalf, hoping to get a few breaths of the smoke. I was about to bum one off of him when he said, reading my mind, "Your wife wouldn't like it if I gave you one of these, so forget about it."

"OK, but what do we do now?" I asked.

"I take you to a hotel where you can get rested up. You rent a car . . . I suggest a good off road four wheel drive . . . and you go to San Juan de Cristo. Find the Bar H Ranch. Start there."

"And what do you do?" I said as I took a deep lungful of the strong cigarette smoke. It made me choke and cough, but I enjoyed it anyway.

"First, I collect my $25,000 bounty. Then I have a hunch I'd like to follow up on. I have some friends . . . Believe it or not, I do have friends . . . I want to talk to. I think there's more to all this than might be obvious."

"Like what?"

"Think about it, Mr. Crew," he said. "Why frame a young girl for murder? What is there to gain? No, I think there's more to this and I want some background information. So, I'm going to talk to some friends of mine. Your cell phone won't do any good where you're going, by the way. It's too far out in the desert . . . No cell phone towers. But I'll find you when I need to. Now get in the car and I'll take you to a place you'll like."

Gandalf drove to The Ironwood Mansion Resort. It turned out to be a wonderful, 5 Star resort. I had never been there before but a quick view of the championship golf course made me make a mental note to come back some day. The resort itself is 18th Century Spanish grandeur with cactus gardens and fountains and walking paths through manicured gardens. Gandalf waited while I booked a suite. I figured I needed some kind of headquarters, and The Ironwood Mansion would be the best HQ I could think of.

After I finished registering, Gandalf walked with me to

the suite.   "Yeah," he said, "I've never stayed here but I heard it's a nice place."   I ordered breakfast for both of us from room service.   A T-bone steak and four eggs for Gandalf; two eggs and bacon for me. Between the two of us we drank a gallon of good coffee. He left shortly after.

CHAPTER FIVE – Too Many Maybes

With the help of the resort's front desk manager I managed to find a rental car company that had a small supply of Mercedes G Class four wheel drive SUVs. I rented one and set off for West Texas. I drove east on Interstate 10 out of El Paso. Gandalf had written down directions that would take me onto unpaved dirt roads that were bumpy and potholed and caused a cloud of dust to rise behind me as I drove slowly. The roads would eventually get me to the little town of San Juan de Cristo. Once there, "Anybody there can tell you how to get to the Bar H," Gandalf said.

I found County Road 8 and bounced along headed south, trying to avoid as many pot holes as I could. In the distance I saw what I thought would be San Juan de Cristo. It was hot in the desert; the car's air conditioner, even turned up to MAX, could barely keep the sweat off of me.

I was kicking up a lot of dust behind me as I approached the little town. Suddenly, less than a mile outside of town, the road became paved and smooth as I slowed along Main Street. The town was something out of a really bad cowboy movie from the 1940's. The sidewalks were wood; most of the buildings were wood and weather beaten. There were a few adobe buildings here and there, each looking as old and tattered as the wooden buildings. I could see no one; it could have been a deserted ghost town except for an old yellow dog that was asleep in the shade under the wood sidewalk in front of one of the adobe buildings. He raised his head to look as I drove by, but was totally disinterested and went right back to sleep.

I was thirsty, and all I saw was a bar with a big sign hanging in front that read: THE LAST STAND. That seemed like a place I could get a cold beer and directions to the Bar H Ranch. As I pulled to the curb in front of the bar, I saw signs in the front window indicating beer was in fact available inside.

Inside it was barely cooler than outside. I guessed air conditioning had not reached San Juan de Cristo yet. It was a dark, dank saloon, filled with mismatched tables and chairs, all beaten up and old. There were two pool tables that seemed to be well maintained. There was a jukebox at the back of the bar, it was lit up brightly but there was no music playing. The air carried the odor of stale urine and beer. The floor was sticky, and there were only two customers - one at the bar and one asleep, leaning back against a wall in a chair at a small table at the rear.

I took the first stool at the bar and wiped the sweat off my forehead. The bartender walked up to me without a smile and asked what I wanted.

"How about a really cold bottle of beer?" I said. I tried a friendly smile but he didn't return it.

He reached under the bar and retrieved a bottle of Coors, opened it and laid it on the bar in front of me. I am familiar enough with cold beer to know that a cold beer has condensation outside the bottle and feels cold to the touch. The bottle I was given had neither; it was easily at room temperature which inside the bar was easily over 80 degrees.

Saying nothing, the bartender walked away and started wiping down the other end of the bar in front of the man sitting there. They exchanged knowing looks and sly grins. I guess they didn't like my white golf shirt and tan cotton pants. And my soft leather loafers covering my sockless feet must have looked pretty funny to them.

I drank the beer down quickly – even a warm beer was good when thirsty – and asked for a second, "Maybe a cold one this time?" The bartender came back to me like it was a big job to do so. He opened the sliding top of a refrigerator and reached in, pulling out a bottle and put on the bar. This one was well frosted. "That'll be ten bucks," he said.

"Five dollars a bottle?" I said and laughed. "That's pretty expensive."

"Yeah," he said. "Costs a lot to truck stuff in."

I pulled a twenty dollar bill off my money clip and handed it to him. He turned, rang up $10.00 on an old cash register, slipped the twenty into it, closed the drawer and walked back to the other customer. They smiled knowingly at each other and nodded at the big joke. I guessed I had just given the guy a big tip.

I drank half the second bottle and called down the bar, "I'm looking for the Bar H Ranch. Can you tell me how to get there?"

At the other end of the bar, the bartender and his customer looked at each other, looked at me, and then looked at each other again. The guy sitting at the bar, dressed in faded blue jeans, a wrinkled pale blue shirt, scuffed cowboy boots, and a big, dust covered cowboy hat sitting on the back of his head, asked, "Why?"

"Why do I want to know how to get to the Bar H?" I said. "Or why should you tell me how to get there?"

They looked at each other again, sharing some confusion. The bartender said, "You ain't from 'round here, are ya'll?"

"That's extremely perceptive of you, sir," I answered, using my best college educated words. "The query you have proposed may contain some surreptitious mendacity, as I doubt you have ever seen me before."

They looked at each other once again, and then the cowboy said to me, "What?"

"I'm sorry," I said. "No, I'm not from around here. Do you know how to get to the Bar H?"

The cowboy had this sort of confused look on his sun burnt face. He asked again, "Why?"

"Look," I said. "I just want to get to the Bar H. I have business there. I don't have a map and it doesn't show up on the GPS. Can you help me, please?"

The cowboy slid off his barstool and walked to the back of the saloon. He pulled a quarter from his jean's pocket and dropped it in a pay phone. I couldn't hear what he said but I waited. It took less than a minute until he hung up and walked back to the barstool. He drank some of his beer and turned to me. He said, "Go back north . . . The way ya'll came. 'Bout five miles or so. You'll see a big red rock on the right side. Ain't nothing else there but the rock so you can't miss it. Turn onto the dirt road there and stay on it 'till you get there."

I finished the beer and said, "Thanks." To the bar tender I said, "Hey, keep the change from the twenty."

Back in the rental SUV, I drove out of town, to the north. I kept track of the miles, and when five miles went by I thought I may have been lied to. But then I saw the big red rock the cowboy had said would be there. And there was, in fact, a rutted dirt path just past the rock that I guess a lot of people would call a road. I turned onto it and I was thankful I had the four wheel drive as I bounced along as slow as the big car would go. I tried to avoid the bigger rocks and deeper potholes while staying in the ruts.

A mile further on I saw a sign for the 'Bar H Cattle Ranch' and an arrow telling me to turn right again. I turned off the dusty, pot-holed road onto the long drive entering the Bar H Ranch. The road was better, still dirt but not as many pot holes. There were cattle standing and watching me curiously along the four and a half miles of unpaved driveway to what I assumed would be some kind of headquarters for the ranch. The hills, far off on the horizon, were burnt-brown in the afternoon light. There weren't any trees to be seen anywhere, just cactus and brush, and lots of cattle that eyed me suspiciously. Betsy had described the ranch very well.

Finally I saw the big white house off in the distance. As I got closer I could see three big, green trees trying to shade the house in the desert heat. I slowed to take in the view of the big house. There was a large red barn to the right and a corral in which three horses stood, hanging their heads over the railing, curious to see who was coming. A good looking hound dog was asleep under one of the big trees. He looked up, howled faintly to give an alarm of sorts, and laid his head back on the cool ground.

I stopped the car at the foot of the stairs leading up to the front doors of the house. A man was standing on the porch at the top of the stairs, watching me pull myself from the car. He stood, arms crossed, with a questioning look on his face.

I started up the stairs, smiling, holding my hand out to him and said in as friendly a voice as I could manage, "Hello, I'm . . . . ."

"Stop where you are," the man commanded. I did as he said, waiting on the second step. "I don't know you," he said.

"I was saying . . . I'm Morgan Crew. I wanted to speak with you about Betsy Concanon."

A woman walked out of the house and stood by the man. She smiled warmly and said, "Little Betsy! Why, ya'll just come on up here, Mr. Crew. Are you a friend of Betsy? We all here are so worried 'bout that little girl. Do you know where she is?"

"Yes," I said reaching the porch. "She's in jail. In El Paso."

"In jail!" the woman said. "Why Harry, we just have

t'do something for that poor pretty little thing. You just go ahead and send a lawyer out t'take care of her, you hear?"

"Are you Mr. & Mrs. Perkins?" I asked.

Mrs. Perkins said, "Oh my lord! I am so sorry. Yes, this is my husband Harry . . . Who apparently has forgotten how to be polite", she said in a scolding voice. "And I am Mary Lou Perkins. I am so glad to meet you . . . Was it Mr. Crew?"

"Yes, Mrs. Perkins. I was wondering if I might talk to the both of you about Betsy."

"Of course," she said with Southern grace. As I took the last two steps onto the porch, she stepped aside and took my arm, leading me into her home. "You know, we just fell in love with that beautiful child. We were just so upset about the trouble she's in. How is she? It's been years."

It was cool inside the house. We took seats in an expensively and professionally decorated, and large, sitting room. The furnishings were elegant 19th Century European. Mary Lou delicately picked up a small gold bell from an intricately carved side table. She rang the bell quickly and seconds later a woman stood in a doorway on the far side of the room. She was a dark skinned Mexican, she looked older than she was, and she looked tired, too. She stood stiffly, saying nothing and looking down at the floor.

"Rosita," Mary Lou said. "Something cool to drink, please. Lemonade if we have enough lemons left, please. Quick now, girl."

Rosita turned and left the room, carefully closing the door behind her quietly, without saying a word.

Harry Perkins had said very little since my arrival. He was not happy; the scowl on his sun burnt face told me that. He said, "So you're here to talk about Betsy. What do ya' wanna' know? We ain't seen her since she skipped. Cost me a lot of money."

Before I could say anything, the phone rang. Harry pushed himself to his feet and walked to a beautiful and intricately carved desk on the other side of the big room. I listened as he spoke into the phone: "Hello . . . Yes, this is Mr. Perkins . . . You're who did ya'll say? . . . I never heard of ya'll . . . You did what? . . . Why exactly did you do that? . . . You a real son'a'bitch, ya'll know that? . . . What did ya'll say? . . . Ya'll joking with me, ain't you? . . . Tell ya' what, you go t'hell an' get your money there."

Harry slammed the phone down and returned to his chair. He asked me, "Do ya'll know somebody who calls his-self Gandalf Finch?"

"Yes," I said. "He's a bounty hunter. He brought Betsy back to Texas."

Mary Lou was shocked. She said, "Why would he do somethin' so terrible? That poor little girl."

Harry said, "What that son'a'bitch wants is for me to pay him $25,000 for bringing the girl back. Can you believe that? I already lost me a quarter million. Mr. Crew, are ya'll a friend of this son'a'bitch?"

"He's not exactly a friend," I said.

Before I could say anything else Rosita returned with a tray holding a glass pitcher of lemonade and three tall glasses filled with ice. Mary Lou stood and served the cold drinks as Rosita held the tray. Mary Lou was frowning. When each glass was filled, Mary Lou pointed to a glass topped coffee table and said, "Leave the tray on the table, Rosita. And I think Mr. Crew will be joining us for dinner. Now go back to your kitchen, please."

"You were sayin' you ain't no friend of this son'a'bitch," Harry said.

The lemonade was too sweet but it was cold. I sipped some and smiled my approval. I said, "Mr. Finch came to my home and took Betsy . . ."

"Ya'll just let this man take that poor little girl?" Mary Lou said disapprovingly.

"Mrs. Perkins," I said. "Gandalf Finch is about 6 foot 6 inches tall and he must weight close to 300 pounds. There's no way I could have stopped him. Besides, he believes Betsy is innocent."

Harry and Mary Lou looked at each other. I caught the look; I had seen it many times before. They were hiding something. They were lying about something.

Harry looked at me and said, "Innocent? Then why bring her back here?"

"He's a complicated man," I said. "I think it's a combination of wanting the bounty and believing in the legal system. I'm not really sure. But I don't believe for a minute that Betsy killed that guy. And that's why I'm here. I want to find out if she really is guilty or not."

They looked at each other again; that look of secrets shared.

Mary Lou said, "And we believe that same thing, Mr. Crew. Didn't we put up a quarter million dollars as bail? Didn't we lose all that money? If we thought that pretty little thing was guilty, would we have done that?"

"Of course not," I said. There was no sense in alienating them, at least until I found out what was going on. "So we have that in common. And I think you may be able to get your money back now that Betsy's back in jail." I added.

"Just what do ya'll want from us, then?" she asked.

"Well, first I'd like to speak with your son, Jimmy. Is he here? Can I talk with him about that night?"

"Jimmy ain't here," Harry said quickly, anger behind the words.

"Will he be home soon?" I asked.

"Don't know," he said. "The boy's a grown man and he comes an' goes like he wants."

"I appreciate that," I said. "How about the other men at The Mustang that night? I understand that they all work for you here on your ranch."

"Let me get somethin' straight here," Harry Perkins said. "Are you tryin' to get that girl off by blamin' my son or one of my hands?"

I said, "Let me get something straight, Mr. Perkins. Do you believe Betsy Concanon killed that man?"

Mary Lou said quickly, "If we did . . . Why would we put up that bail?"

That was the second time she reminded me of that fact. It was a really good question that I was determined to find an answer to.

Harry wasn't happy. He stood up and paced back and forth in front of me. When he stopped he looked down at me and said, "Ya'll tryin' to pin that killin' on Jimmy or maybe one of my ranch hands." It wasn't a question, it was an accusation and there was a threat not so deeply hidden in the accusation.

"Now Harry," Mary Lou said. "We don't know that. Please just sit back down an' let's find out what's goin' on here."

She looked at me, smiled sweetly, and said, "Mr. Crew, when our Jimmy brought that sweet young girl home that day, we just fell in love with her. She was just the sweetest little thing. Why, when she was arrested for that terrible murder, we were just heartbroken. Now, I'm gonna' tell you the truth here."

"Mary Lou!" Harry interrupted but she would have none of it.

"No, darlin'," she said. "Mr. Crew has to know the truth." She turned back to me and went on, "Me and Mr. Perkins and our Jimmy, we couldn't leave that little girl in jail. We were all just certain she didn't kill that man. So we posted her bail and brought her home. Our Jimmy really liked her . . . Maybe he loved her . . . I don't know. Anyway, without telling us, he gave her money and told her to leave. If he had asked us we would have said 'no'. But he didn't ask; he did it all on his own. That's all we know."

"Did Jimmy tell you where Betsy was going?"

"As I recall, she said she was goin' to Florida."

"Did she ever tell you about what happened that

night?" I asked.

Mary Lou stopped her husband from saying something when she said, "That poor little girl was so upset, all's we could do was feed her and comfort her. All's she did was cry. I assure you, Mr. Crew, that's all we know."

"That's fine," I said. "Thank you for that." I forced a smile and hoped it was convincing enough. Maybe, I thought, the secret was that Jimmy told her to run? That would be a serious crime. Maybe they were just trying to protect their son? Maybe?

But I have this little voice that sits in the back recesses of my brain. It's quiet most of the time, but screams "GET OUT OF HERE! . . . RUN AWAY! . . . RUN AWAY!" whenever I'm inches from trouble. I seldom listen to that little voice; most of the time I ignore it and wind up in deep trouble.

I heard that little voice screaming away right then. Mary Lou and Harry were lying to me. I knew that. I could see it in their faces and hear it in their words. They may have taken Betsy in and bailed her out of jail, but there was more to it than they were telling me.

So, I ignored the little voice once again and told myself I was going to find the truth, regardless.

CHAPTER SIX – Great Mexican Food

I didn't stay for dinner at the Bar H Ranch after all. The Perkins' made it apparent I wasn't welcome anymore. So I started the drive back to San Juan de Cristo. I was hungry and I needed a place to sleep and I didn't feel like taking the long trip back to El Paso. I was fairly sure I could get some food in the small town, but a place to sleep was another matter.

I'd been inside The Last Stand, and the thought of a meal there wasn't very appetizing. As I drove slowly into town, I saw The Mustang, where Edgy Hands had been killed, and I guessed it wasn't any better. In fact, it was dark and looked locked up.

At the edge of town I saw what looked like it might be a restaurant. There were two beat up wooden benches out front, under a sagging porch roof. The old yellow dog was still asleep under one of the benches and a few people were sitting on the benches eating what I thought might be tacos and burritos and other things. As I stopped in front of the adobe building and rolled down the car's window, it all smelled spicy and terrific.

So I parked at the edge of the wooden sidewalk and went inside. It turned out to be a small restaurant. It was filled with the most wonderful smells of onions, peppers, grilling meats, and strong spices. My mouth was watering by the time I sat at a very small table in a far corner. The table had four legs, one of which was shorter than the other three; the table rocked back and forth but I didn't care.

An attractive, olive skinned woman with long, silky jet black hair walked slowly to my table. She wore a brightly colored embroidered dress that was full and flowing, and fell to her ankles. Her blouse was white and puffy at the sleeves. A string of polished black stones hung around her neck and matched her eyes. There was a look of confusion on her face. I think she was surprised that I was there. She said in a nervous voice, "Senor, que' puedo conseguir para usted?"

"I'm sorry," I said. I tried to smile enough to make her know I was not going to be trouble, if that was what worried her. "I don't speak a lot of Spanish. Do you speak English?"

She smiled a little and called out "Jose!"

From a back room a young guy walked quickly to us. He was wiping his hands and was wearing a dirty apron over an aged grey T-shirt. He looked to be maybe 25 years old. He was slim and walked lightly on his feet. His dark eyes were partially hidden behind longish strands of sweaty hair. The waitress said something to him and he turned to me.

"She speaks about as much English as you speak Spanish," he said. There was an accent there but very little of it. "We're not used to seeing gringos in here. Cowboys go up the street. But you ain't no cowboy. You want something?"

"I was hoping to get some food . . . And maybe a cold beer or two," I said.

"Sure," the young man said. "You know this is a Mexican place, don't you?"

"Well," I answered. "I'm not looking for German food. It smells wonderful in here. What's good?"

He grinned and said, "Everything's great. I'll tell them to bring you some special stuff? You like it hot?"

"You bet," I said ignoring what Sandy would have told me about eating that kind of food. "And don't forget the cold beer . . . Better make it two."

For the next hour, plates of the most wonderful food was brought from the kitchen and placed on the table in front of me. There were dishes of beef, pork and chicken, all spiced like I had never enjoyed before. There were dishes of all types of beans. There was rice. There were warm, freshly made corn tortillas and flour tortillas. There was a whole lot more than I could even think about eating. So I started to wave the few Mexican customers in the restaurant over to share the feast with me. They quickly sat at the table with me and dug in.

The word got around quickly and soon the little restaurant was full to standing room only. Children were dancing around, and old people were laughing as they ate. A couple of men brought guitars and music started. What a party! I was having a good time when the town Sheriff suddenly appeared standing in the doorway.

The music stopped instantly. The children ran to hide behind their parents. People backed away to hug the walls. Silence crashed all around me.

"What's goin' on here?" the Sheriff asked.

No one said anything. The nervous silence was deafening. I stood, cleared my throat and said, "I guess I started all this, officer."

"I'm a Sheriff," he said. "Lot's a'noise coming from here."

"I'm sorry, Sheriff," I said. I started to walk towards him but he stopped me with a raised hand.

"This here's a small town, Mr. Crew," he said. "We don't take to riots and such."

"You know my name," I said, surprised.

"'Course I do. You come t'town just to cause a riot?"

"We were just enjoying the food, Sheriff," I said. "No one's causing any problems. We were all just having some fun."

"We here 'bouts don't think riots and such is fun," he said. He stepped inside and started walking around. The middle of the little restaurant was empty; everyone was pressing themselves against walls. A few brave folks quickly disappeared through the kitchen.

Everyone there was obviously very scared of him, yet he wasn't a very imposing man. He wasn't tall, and he had a good beer belly hanging over his big silver belt buckle. He wore a big cowboy hat, not a new one, covered with a fine sheet of desert dust and dirt. He didn't carry a gun. Yet the aura of fear that surrounded him was palpable.

He stopped in the middle of the room and said to the Mexicans there, "Ya'll better go on home now."

His words opened a flood gate and the couple of dozen people there all but ran for the door. Jose, an old couple who owned the place and the waitress who didn't speak English were left standing at the door to the kitchen. The Sheriff walked slowly and threateningly to them.

"Jose," he said. "Ya'll tell Francisco and Carmelita there that I done warned you folks 'bout this kind of thing."

Jose translated. The old man, Francisco, said something and Jose spoke to the Sheriff, "Mr. Vargas said he's sorry. It all just sort of happened. It wasn't planned. It won't happen again."

I stepped forward and said, "Look, Sheriff. It's my fault. It all just got out of hand. I was the one ordering all the food and telling everyone to eat."

"So you paid for all this?" he asked.

"I was about to do that," I said. I pulled my money clip out and peeled off three one hundred dollars bills. I walked to Francisco and handed them to him. "Is that enough?" I asked. Jose translated and Francisco nodded, saying it was enough.

"OK," the Sheriff said. "Then all this crap is over and done with. An' if I gotta' do this again, I'm gonna shut this

God damn place down. Ya'll understand that?"

Jose assured the Sheriff it wouldn't happen again. The Sheriff then turned to me and said, "Now, ya'll got your fill a'food, I suspect. That bein' the case, I suppose ya'll gonna just drive outta town, right?"

"I was hoping to spend the night somewhere," I said in as friendly a voice as I could manage. "Is there a motel in town?"

Sheriff Kronk laughed, spit on the floor, and said, "Only thing close to a motel is one a'my jail cells. Ya'll wanna' get locked up there over night?"

"Thanks all the same, but I think I'll find something else."

"Then, as I said, ya'll get outta' my town, hear?"

"Sure," I said. "You got it. I don't want any trouble, Sheriff. But is it OK if I use the restroom first? I have to go really bad. Too much beer."

"Ya' gotta' go, ya' gotta' go," he said. "Be quick."

The Sheriff turned and walked out. When he was gone, Jose and Mr. and Mrs. Vargas started talking in animated voices. I needed to find out what was going on in this dusty little back-road town, and I hoped maybe they could tell me. So I stepped next to them.

Jose said to me, "Out back. It's a one holer."

Using the restroom was just an excuse to get rid of Sheriff Kronk. I asked, "What the hell just happened," I asked.

Jose said, "Sheriff Kronk don't like Mexicans a whole lot. He lets this place stay open but we gotta' be careful."

"So he's sort of a little dictator in this bright little town?"

"You can call it a town, if you like," Jose said. "Sheriff Kronk doesn't answer to anybody . . . Except Harry and Mary Lou Perkins, of course."

"Harry and Mary Lou Perkins!" I said, surprised. "You mean the Bar H Ranch Perkins people!"

"Sure, Jose said. "You know them?"

I told him I had been to the ranch earlier that day, but I didn't mention anything that we had spoken about. "Look," I said. "It's late. Is there a motel or something nearby? I need a place to sleep."

"You're kidding, right?" Jose laughed. "You never been here before, have you? There ain't no place to sleep except the back seat of your car. And good ol' Sheriff Kronk ain't gonna let you do that."

"So what do I do?"

"You gotta drive about an hour and a half to Balling," Jose said. "They got a couple of motels there. The food ain't so good but it won't kill you. Drive south outta' town. About a half hour out you'll start seeing signs to Balling. It's down near the border."

Not having any choice, I decided to drive to Balling. I thanked everyone there and apologized again for causing trouble for them with the Sheriff. As I drove slowly out of town, I saw Sheriff Kronk standing on the tattered wooden sidewalk in front of his office, smoking a little black cigar. His eyes never left me as I drove past. He didn't look happy either.

****

Balling, Texas was a little bigger than San Juan de Cristo, but not much better. As I drove in to town the first thing I saw was The Tick Tock Motel with a sign under it declaring they had rooms available for $19.95 a night. I figured at that price, still having rooms available as night was folding around town wasn't something to brag about. So I drove on. I saw a passable looking place called The Balling Diner and figured I might get some food there.

I sat at the counter and a woman the other few customers called 'Aunt Mimi' filled a cup with stale coffee and asked what I wanted. The menu was limited to fried stuff, which was alright with me as long as Sandy wasn't there to tell me to get up and go somewhere else. So I enjoyed a big, sloppy cheeseburger and spongy fries that I soaked in ketchup. I followed the meal up with a big hunk of two day old apple pie and some passable vanilla ice cream. That meal was one thing I would never discuss with Sandy. She'd have my head if she ever found out about it.

There were a few small stores, all closed for the night, and three gas stations, two of which were still open and the third looking as if it had been out of business for a long time. I passed a Post Office and a bank, and a couple of seedy looking taverns. Then I saw a fairly nice looking motel, The Garden Inn it was called. So I quickly pulled into the parking lot, got a room on the second floor, and in the room I phoned Sandy.

"You wouldn't believe this place," I told her. "Talk about small towns . . . And they have this Sheriff who is something out of the old west. He has everybody scared."

"I believe it," Sandy said. "I got my hands on a map of Texas and I couldn't find San Juan de Cristo on it."

It was nice speaking with the woman I love so much. I lay back on the bed that wasn't too lumpy and we talked for an hour. I told her about my trip to Texas with Gandalf and Betsy, my visit to the Bar H Ranch, and my day in San Juan de Cristo. She told me all the amazing things our little daughter, Caroline, had learned to do, including reaching up for breakables on tabletops and breaking them.

"Look," I said. "Do you think Caroline would like an airplane trip?"

"Just what do you have in mind, darling?" she asked with a little snicker behind her words.

"I've got a nice suite at The Ironwood Mansion in El Paso. It's got a really good restaurant and a golf course that looks pretty good."

"Forget the golf course," she said laughing.

"I think it might be a good idea for you to be in El Paso and check in on Betsy regularly. I've got a lawyer to represent her, but I haven't met him yet. And I think it would be good to keep track of Gandalf Finch, too. I don't fully trust him, yet."

"Good," she said. "I was hoping I could do something. And I think C needs to get used to traveling. I want her to grow up seeing the world."

"You called her C. Is Caroline her name or not?" I asked.

"I just miss Betsy, that's all," she said.

We stayed on the phone until half past midnight, talking like a couple of teenage kids experiencing their first love. When we finally said 'good night', I fell asleep quickly and had uncomfortable dreams about cowboys chasing me. Looking back on this experience, I think those dreams were a premonition of the dangers to come.

CHAPTER SEVEN – You're Going Home

The sun was peeking in behind the heavy orange and brown drapes of the motel room when I woke up. It wasn't eight o'clock in the morning yet and the room was hot and still. I checked the A/C unit and it was working but not doing much to cool the room.

I showered and shaved quickly. Stopping at the desk, I told the day manager that I would need the room for seven days and paid for it with the Black Amex Card that is billed to Harper, Harper, Jascro and Nettles, the Crew family attorneys. I didn't know if I'd be back to the motel again. Hell, I didn't know what I'd be doing six hours from then.

I walked to The Balling Diner and found breakfast to be a little better than dinner. And since Sandy wasn't with me, I decided to cheat once again and enjoyed a tall stack of hotcakes, fried eggs, sausage, a couple of buttery biscuits with a couple different jams and mounds of butter, and of course a lot of coffee that was as stale as the coffee was the night before. I tried the OJ, but it was out of a can, and I pushed it aside.

I needed to talk with a lot of people and I assumed that almost all of them were back in San Juan de Cristo. The drive back was longer than the drive to Balling the night before, not in miles but in fear and anticipation. Truth be told, I really wanted to get on a plane and go back to San Marcos and my family. I wanted to go to the Country Club, play some golf, have a couple of bourbons, trade bragging rights with some friends, and go home to play with Caroline, and later that night lay in bed next to Sandy and hold her close to me. But Betsy was sitting in jail, oblivious of what was happening, facing life in prison or worse, and she had become an important part of my family.

And there it was again. I had to step out and put myself at risk for family and friends. It never changes. Time and again, it never changes. Sandy was nearly murdered; I'd been shot; I'd killed people; and the nightmares were frequent and never ending. Yet I had to put everything at risk once again . . . For Betsy who couldn't help herself.

San Juan de Cristo appeared on the sun-burnt brown desert horizon. Without thinking about it, my foot eased up on the gas pedal. I was reluctant to go back there, but I knew I had to overcome that reluctance . . . the fear if the truth be known, and do what had to be done for Betsy.

It was just past noon when I parked at the curb of the wooden sidewalk in front of The Mustang. I stepped out of the car and walked up to the front door. It was locked tight. The windows to the right and left of the door were blocked by old, stained, faded window blinds. There were no lights inside.

I got back in the car and made a U-Turn, parking in front of the The Last Stand. There was a faded sign hanging by a thread bare string on the front door that said, 'CLOSED'. So I waited. I rolled down all the car's windows and tried to find some good music on the radio. I went through the entire AM and FM dial and found little worth listening too on the few stations receivable in that desolate area. I turned the radio off and reclined the seat back to wait for someone to show up.

I was the only human on Main Street. There was that old yellow dog lumbering along from one spot of shade to another, hoping to find a place to sleep the heat of the day away. The desert heat was beginning to burn. I began to doze when someone reached into the car, shook my shoulder and woke me.

"What the hell ya'll doin' here?" Sheriff Kronk growled. "Thought I got rid ya'll yesterday."

"I'm not bothering anybody Sheriff," I said. I forced a smile and sat up straight trying to conceal the nervous tremor I felt riding up my spine.

"You done caused some trouble t'other day, Mr. Crew," he said. "I thought I done made it clear you ain't welcome 'round here."

I thought about it for a full minute, making the Sheriff wait, bent over to see inside the car. I swallowed hard and decided to play it tough. "You know my name," I said. "So you obviously know who I am. I am not breaking any law by waiting for that saloon to open. If you want, I'll have a few of my lawyers here in the morning and they'll drag your fat ass into court for harassment. Now go away and leave me alone."

At first I thought he was going to pull me out of the car through the open window and beat the crap out of me. Sheriff Kronk was shorter than me and he had a bigger beer gut than I have. He was maybe ten years older than me. I figured I would have a 50 – 50 chance of taking him. He wasn't carrying a gun again and that was in my favor. But then he stood up straight and just walked away. Five minutes later, the doors to The Last Stand opened and the 'closed' sign was taken down.

Burl Evans stepped outside and stood in the open doorway, his arms folded in front of him and a very angry look on his round red face. I got out of the car and edged my way past him, careful not to touch Burl, who didn't move but kept his eyes on me as I stepped into The Last Stand and looked around.

It was a dark little tavern as taverns go. It had eight

wooden tables and mismatched chairs filling the floor space, and there were a couple of pool tables that seemed in pretty good shape, compared to the rest of the saloon. And there was a dark jukebox that had not been turned on yet that day.

There were mounted animal heads hanging on the walls, a few old saddles hanging next to them and a couple of moldy lariats hanging from nails nearby. Everything was covered in dust and cobwebs. Above the bar were two old, rust covered rifles from the cowboy era a hundred years ago. And a cardboard sign was hanging predominantly and askew from a thin cord that read, 'We reserve the right to refuse service to anyone'. Next to it on the cardboard was pasted a small Confederate battle flag. The shelves behind the bar were almost empty, carrying only a few bottles of whiskey, brands I had never heard of before. Here and there were cheaply framed old photos of people in garish cowboy outfits out of a 1930s cowboy movie.

I sat at the bar, pulling myself onto the first stool near the door, and waited. Burl walked behind the bar, leaned against the cash register, and stared at me, arms still folded in front of him. It wasn't any cooler inside The Last Stand than it was outside. I heard the faint buzzing of what sounded like an air conditioner, but the air inside the bar was still and hot. There were three ceiling fans above me, but none were spinning.

Burl continued to stare at me. His right cheek was fatter than his left. Now and then he chewed a few times and moved what I guessed might be a wad of chewing tobacco in his right cheek to his left jaw. Then he spit a thick black liquid onto the floor behind the bar.

"Can I get a bottle of beer, please?" I asked breaking the silence. I figured Burl wasn't going to say anything, and I didn't want to just sit there all afternoon with him and me staring at each other.

"What the hell you want?" Burl growled and spit once again.

"I'm sorry. Maybe I mumbled. I want a bottle of beer, please. A cold one. It's really hot outside."

"Get out," he said.

"Hey Burl," I said. "All I want is to quench my thirst . . . And ask a couple of questions about the night Edward Hands died, of course."

"Who told you my name?" he asked.

"Nobody," I said. "Your name is on the police reports. And the names of the five guys who were here dancing with that little girl that night were on the reports, too. And oh, by the way. That little girl was underage at the time . . . Only fifteen. And somebody was serving her beers. Tsk – tsk. That wasn't you, was it? Were you tending bar at The Mustang that night? The reports didn't mention who was behind the bar that night, and I have a hunch it was you. The State's gonna' hear about that one if they don't already have a file open on you, Burl."

Burl didn't move. He said, "Prove it som'bitch." He spit once more.

"OK, Burl," I said. "Those five guys, they're regulars here, right? I've been here twice now and I haven't seen The Mustang open yet. My guess is this place is the local hangout."

"Edgy was a good friend a'mine," Burl said. "All's you want is t'get that murderin' bitch off."

"Edgy?" I said. "Edgy is Edward Hands? That's what you call him?"

Burl said nothing. He spit.

I heard someone walk into the saloon behind me. I heard the clicking of heavy cowboy boot heals. I didn't turn around, and I didn't look into the cracked, dirty mirror behind the bar . . . Mainly because I was scared. No one knew I was in that isolated little desert town. Hell, I could be buried under six feet of sand in the next hour, and no one would know.

"What's he want?" It was Sheriff Kronk's voice. I

turned slowly. He was wearing a pistol at his side this time.

Burl said, "Says he wants t'talk to some'a the boys."

I said, "I don't think there's a law against me talking to some of your citizens, is there?"

"There's a law against . . . Interferin' . . . In a police investigation," Sheriff Kronk said. He had trouble with the words, having to hunt around in his head for them. I wondered if he knew what the words meant.

I wasn't about to start an argument with a man with a gun. And I was finally coming to believe that I was just wasting my time there, anyway. So I pushed myself off the barstool and started for the door. Sheriff Kronk stood in my way. He said, "Ain't you gonna' pay for the beer?"

"I didn't have a beer," I said and smiled what I hoped was a friendly smile that would hide the fact that I was scared.

Sheriff Kronk said, "Burl, you give this man a beer?"

"Yeah, two in fact," he said. "They're ten bucks a piece, too."

All I wanted to do was get out of there in one piece and alive. So I pulled out my money clip and found a twenty. I crushed it up into a ball and tossed it towards Burl. Without moving, he let it fall to the floor behind the bar. I hoped it landed in one of his piles of tobacco juice.

Sheriff Kronk stepped aside and let me walk out. I started the long drive back to El Paso, but I wasn't about to give up. I spent some time turning the radio dial but found nothing out in the middle of nowhere. I wished the damn car had satellite radio, which it didn't.

I found the sign at the turnoff to Balling and started down the dusty, thin road. Three miles further on I saw an open flatbed truck parked at the side of the road. Its hood was up. I slowed to see if I could offer the driver a ride somewhere. The driver was a tall, lanky cowboy type, wearing worn jeans, a plaid shirt and a blue baseball cap. He waived me down and I stopped. When I rolled down the passenger side window, before I could say anything, he pulled a big chromed revolver from his belt and pointed it at me.

"Whoa! Wait a minute!" I said. "You can have my money and my car. No problems, OK?"

"Get out," he said. It is my habit to always obey the man with the gun.

As I opened the door a pickup truck pulled to a stop behind me. Three men got out and joined the man with the gun. The four of them stood me in the middle of the circle they formed. These were young men, all in good shape. If not for the clothes they wore – ranch hand type work clothes of blue jeans and rough cowboy boots – I would suspect they could be military types. What led me to that conclusion was the assault rifles two of them carried. Not exactly cowboy guns.

They were all in good physical shape and all sported military haircuts – close cropped - and they were all clean shaven.

I'm pretty good at talking my way out of trouble. I've been told quite often that I am blessed with the Irish gift of gab. I hoped I could be good then, too.

"Hey, fellas," I said. I held my arms up and smiled even though it was a weak smile. "I don't want any trouble. In fact, I'm on my way home."

"That's right," one of them said. He was the shortest and smallest of the four but he had that aura of leader around him. Although he wore the standard jeans, his shirt was a dark blue pocket t-shirt that fit tightly over his muscled arms and chest. He wasn't wearing a hat, and his hair was cut short and tight, military style.

He said, "You are on your way home, Mr. Crew . . . And we're going to make sure you get home quickly." He spoke without the Texas cowboy drawl I was getting used to hearing everywhere I went.

The first punch came from behind me. It was a well

trained, well aimed, professional and well practiced punch to my kidneys, and it knocked me to the ground. It hurt like hell. Very soon, as I lay in the dust, I couldn't tell the difference between the punches and the kicks. I curled into as a tight fetal ball as I could but it didn't help much. The beating seemed to go on forever, until blackness fell all around me. Time drifted away as I drifted into a place where pain disappeared.

I don't know how long I lay in the dirt at the side of the road. Eventually the beating ended. I was hurt . . . Badly . . . But the four young men who had worked me over were professional. They could have murdered me out there in the middle of nowhere, buried me in the desert, and no one would have known.

I thought I was dreaming about someone talking to me softly, calling me by name. Maybe it was Sandy, I hoped. But it wasn't. I tried to open my eyes and immediately the bright sun light caused pain to shoot through my head. Gradually, I started to come around and wake up. I tried to move but there was pain everywhere. A voice told me not to move. I could feel a hand touching me, and where it touched, I hurt.

"I don't think anything's broken," the voice said. "I'll get some water." The words were clouded and seemed to be far away. But they were also welcoming to me. At least whoever it was, was not adding to the pain.

I felt cool water on my lips but swallowing it was very hard and painful. Then there was a cool touch of water on my forehead and across my eyes.

"Don't try to open your eyes, Mr. Crew. You've been hurt really bad," the voice said. "I'm going to get you into my truck. It's going to hurt, but I've got to get you some help. There's a small hospital in Balling. I'm going to take you there."

Whoever it was, as he lifted me off the ground, it caused a tide of pain to shoot up my back and across my stomach. A dark sheet of unconsciousness covered me once again. When I woke I was in a hospital bed. I struggled to open my eyes just enough to see, but the pain was like red hot irons. I reached slowly up, trying to ignore the pain, to touch my face. What I felt was wet and swollen. My eyes were shut and puffy. As I lowered my arm, hot pain shot across my chest.

Squinting as much as I could, I saw a doctor in a white coat writing on a chart. A nurse in a pale blue uniform was at his side. And Jose from the little Mexican restaurant in San Juan de Cristo was there.

The nurse saw my movements and my eyes open just a little and heard me moan at the pain. She said, "He's awake Doctor."

The two started working on me; moving a light across the slits of my eyes as the Doctor forced open my eyelids. The pain was awful. I twisted my head to the side. The nurse checked the machines hooked up to me. She said something to the doctor, but the words were masked by the pain racking through my body.

I opened my eyes a slit again and looked across the room at Jose. I tried to talk but it really hurt. I could feel a couple of cuts across my lips that stung like hot irons. I managed to whisper, "Why?"

The Doctor said, "Agent Perez found you. He brought you here." His voice was waving in and out, from normal to twisted, like an electronic version of some foreign tongue.

"Agent?" I mumbled through my cut and swollen lips. Maybe, I thought, my hearing was damaged . . . Or maybe I was still unconscious and dreaming.

The Doctor looked at Jose, and I think I heard him say, "He doesn't know?"

Jose shook his head and took a step or two closer to me. He held onto the metal rail of the bed and bent down close to my ear. He said, speaking slowly and softly, "Mr. Crew, I'm with ATF. Do you know who kicked the crap out of you?"

"ATF?" I remember saying before I fell into an ocean of blackness once again. I have had nightmares of demons attacking me before. Once again the demons appeared, tearing at me and pulling me deeper into their kingdom devoid of all light and sense.

I don't know how long I was asleep . . . Or maybe unconscious . . . But when I did wake up there was a different nurse at my bedside. This one was dressed in a pink uniform, and she was very young.

"You're awake," she said a little nervously. "That's good."

"How long?" I struggled to say.

"How long have you been asleep?" she asked as she straightened the white sheet covering me, pulling it up to cover my arms and chest. "Almost three days. But you needed it. You've been hurt really bad, you know."

"Jose," I said.

She looked questioningly at me and asked, "Jose? Who's that?"

"Guy . . . Found me . . . ATF," I said.

"Oh, him. His name is Jorge Santos. Someone will contact him. He wants to talk to you," she said. She had a wonderful smile; it was kind, and I could feel the caring coming from her. "But we have to be careful. There's only three of us know who he is."

She left the room and, I began to feel sleep overcoming me again. But before it did, a Doctor walked into the room with the nurse in pink. He read through the chart hanging at the foot of the bed. They spoke quietly for a moment or two, and then the Doctor stepped to my side.

"I think you need to stay awake, Mr. Crew, he said, speaking slowly and a little too loudly. "At least for awhile. We're going to run some tests, x-rays and things. We want to take some pictures of your brain and do a full body MRI. You can't be too careful. You've been badly injured."

"Jose," I said in a bare mumble. My lips still hurt when I moved them but I found I could open my eyes almost all the way without too much pain. "ATF . . . Contact him."

"That's been done," The Doctor said as if speaking to a child. He patted my shoulder gently, I guess maybe trying to comfort me a little. "Is there someone else I should get in touch with? Family? Anybody?"

My mind was still foggy, but I knew Sandy would be frantic about where I was. She had to have left San Marcos and be waiting for me at the Ironwood Mansion Resort. She would have no way of knowing I was in a hospital. No one would know she was in El Paso.

I said. "When can I get out of here?"

"Not for a few days," the Doctor said.

"My wife . . . Ironwood Mansion . . . El Paso," I managed.

The Doctor nodded to the young nurse who left the room to phone Sandy. He followed her, and two orderlies took his place. I spent the next few hours either in machines or hooked up to machines. It was mid-afternoon when I was wheeled back on a gurney to the two-bed hospital room that I shared with no one. A meal – the first since I had been brought to the hospital – was brought in. The tray held a small glass of apple juice, a small plastic dish of green Jell-O, and a small bowl of brown colored broth.

As the nurse - this one a guy in a pale green uniform - placed the tray in front of me I asked, "Is that it? I'm hungry."

"Doctor's orders," he said. "You lost a couple of teeth, and your jaw was dislocated. You're lucky it wasn't broken."

I ran my tongue around my teeth and found an empty spot at the back on the left side. My jaw did hurt, but not any more than 90% of the rest of me. Whoever beat me did a good, professional job on me. It was meant to scare me away, to influence me to go home; to keep me from sticking my nose into what I knew wasn't right. And it would have worked really well on somebody else. But all they did, besides hurt me, was to piss me off. And they had no idea what I do when I got really pissed off.

I was almost asleep when an ambulance crew walked into the room. They had a gurney, and without saying anything, they carefully lifted me onto it, belted me down onto it, and wheeled me out a side door of the hospital. I tried to say something, to tell them to stop. I tried to yell for help but the yell came out too weakly to be heard by anyone. I was quickly put inside a red and white ambulance with the doors closed tightly behind me. I was alone in the back of the ambulance but strapped down and even the slightest movement trying to get myself free caused excruciating pain to shoot through me with electric intensity.

The ambulance we were in drove slowly, obeying traffic laws, and kept the siren off. I couldn't see where we were going, and I was in no physical condition to demand to know. But the ambulance made a lot of turns, stopped at what I assumed were traffic lights, and by the sounds from outside, I knew we weren't in a heavy traffic area. "Got to be someplace rural, maybe suburbs" I thought. I was being kidnapped and taken to someplace without a lot of people around.

The ambulance stopped, and the engine was shut off. The doors opened, and the two men carefully and gently pulled the gurney and me out onto the sidewalk. I was right about suburbs. The houses weren't new but they were in good condition, and the neighborhood was clean.

I was wheeled into a house and carefully lifted off the gurney – they were trying to be gentle but I winced in pain – onto a hospital bed with a soft mattress, much more comfortable than the hard, thin mattress of the hospital. I was left alone, wondering where the hell I was and what the hell was happening. There was no way I was going to be able to defend myself. Whoever took me could kill me at their leisure without any resistance from me.

Two men in dark grey suits walked into the room. I'd

seen the type before - dark suits of medium quality, white shirts well starched, blue ties neatly knotted, and a slight bulge under the jacket where a gun was holstered.

"Mr. Crew," the shorter of the two men said. "I am Federal Marshall Tom Sonner. This is Marshall Marcus Tyner. We're here to protect you until you can return to California." Sonner, even though shorter, bald, and younger than Tyner, had an aura of "I'm in charge around here" surrounding him. Tyner was obviously the muscles of the duo. He was quiet, intense, taking everything in and waiting for his chance to do something to get himself noticed.

"Where am I?" I asked.

"This is a safe house. You'll be OK here," Sonner said.

It was still painful to talk but I managed to say, "Gee, thanks. But I really don't need your help."

"Then you're going home today?" Sonner asked.

"I'm not going home until I get Betsy Concanon out of jail."

"That's an unfortunate and stupid decision," Sonner said. "I'm afraid we're going to have to put you on a plane and send you home . . . In handcuffs if we have to."

"How long will it be before I can travel?' I asked.

"The Doctors say maybe three days," Sonner answered.

I said, "Good. That'll give me time to get my lawyers and a bunch of news media people here."

The two Marshalls looked at each other, Sonner looking up at the six inch taller Tyner, and they left me alone in the room. I was hungry, but I was confused even more so. A dishwasher in a little Mexican restaurant turns out to be an ATF agent. Three cowboy looking guys and a tough son of a bitch who looked military beat me nearly to death. Federal Marshalls want to "protect" me. And Betsy sits in jail for something I was convinced she didn't do. Too many people wanted her to stay in jail.

Time was slipping by. I was in a hospital gown. I could see my clothes hanging in a partially open closet, and a small black plastic bag was on a table on the other side of the room. That had to be all my things - my wallet, watch and money clip. I tried to get out of bed, but the movement caused lightning strikes of pain to shoot from my feet, up my spine, to my brain. I lay back and waited.

I don't know how long I waited, but Jose . . . or was it Jorge . . . Santos . . . Touched my shoulder and spoke softly, "Mr. Crew . . . Mr. Crew. Wake up, Mr. Crew."

I opened my eyes as much as I could. Although the pain had subsided considerably, my left eye must have been swollen badly because I could not open it completely. I said, "Who the hell are you?"

"Mr. Crew," he said. "You've got to go home."

"Why?"

"I can't explain. Just go home," he said.

"What about Betsy Concanon?" I asked.

"What about her?" he asked, and I believe he really didn't know.

"She didn't kill anybody," I managed to say through a sore jaw. "I want her out of jail. You're Feds. You can get her out of jail."

"That can't happen," Jose or Jorge or whatever said.

I again asked, "Why?"

"I can't explain," he said again.

Over the years, I have gotten used to telling authorities where they can go. And I decided to do the same then. I said simply, "If you can't explain . . . Then you can go to hell."

A woman walked into the room. She was dressed casually, neatly. She had a stethoscope hanging around her neck, which told me she was either a doctor or a nurse. She carried a manila folder under her arm.

Standing next to the bed, she said, "I'm Dr. Sobel. I'm going to take care of you."

"That sounds threatening," I said. "You're going to take care of me how?"

She looked at Jose – or Jorge – who shook his head. "Mr. Crew," she said to me. "I'm a doctor. You've been badly hurt. I'm not going to hurt you any more than you've already been hurt. You've got a couple of cracked ribs. That's the worst. Your kidneys are bruised, and of course there are the two lost teeth. You can take care of that when you get home. Implants . . . You know."

"Tell him when he can go home," Jose or Jorge or whatever said.

"As I already told you Agent Santos," Dr. Sobel said. "At least two days, maybe three."

"And what happens if I decide not to go home?" I asked. My throat was dry but it was less painful to talk than it had been hours before. Dr. Sobel glanced at Jose. He shrugged his shoulders and left the room. Dr. Sobel used her stethoscope on my chest and tried to get me to sit up a little, but my cracked ribs ended that quickly.

CHAPTER EIGHT – How did you find me?

Two days later I was up and walking, maybe a little stiffly, maybe bent slightly, and very uncomfortably, but walking anyway. There was some pain that I tried to ignore, but I was able to get around slowly using a metal cane. I was bruised almost everywhere. I was, in fact, a rainbow of red, black and blue. My chest had been wrapped in tight bandages. My left arm was in a sling due to the cracked ribs. I had small bandages keeping a lot of cuts closed. I took a look in a mirror over a dresser and flinched when I saw myself. I was intent on getting out of wherever I was as soon as I could manage.

After eating a fairly good breakfast – my jaw still hurt badly and I missed the two teeth I had lost on the left side – I managed, with great trouble, to dress myself in my clothes. They had been cleaned, and the torn pants and shirt had been replaced with new shirt and pants. When Dr. Sobel saw that I had dressed, she tsk-tsked and told me I should stay in bed.

The house I was in was a federal safe-house, run by the U. S. Marshall's Service. It was comfortable. There was a big screen TV hooked up to a good cable service. The kitchen was a fully stocked, and food that I asked for was never refused. I was even given a bottle of Wild Turkey 101 bourbon.   I never heard anyone say 'No' to anything I wanted, except when I asked to go outside.   There was a single phone hanging near the kitchen.

I was in the living room, having carefully lowered myself into a soft stuffed armchair, reading the morning's local newspaper and drinking too much coffee, when Gandalf Finch walked in.

I was surprised, of course.   "What the hell!" was all I could think of saying.

He laughed as he bent down to clear the doorway.   "I smelled the coffee," he said.   "I could use a cup."

Gandalf was wearing his usual flamboyantly colored clothes, this time a bright royal purple and white pinstriped suit over an equally bright red silk shirt and a starkly yellow tie.   My immediate thought was to have Sandy take him out for a day of shopping.

"Why are you here?" I asked.

"That's not the question I thought you'd ask," he said. "I thought you'd be wondering how I knew where you were hiding."

"OK," I said.   "How did you find me?"

"I told you I know people," he said.   He pulled a pack of his Gauloises cigarettes from his jacket pocket.   Without asking, he lit one and drew the strong smoke in deeply. Through a cloud of acrid smoke he said, "I've been talking to people in El Paso and DC about the murder.   They couldn't be specific, but there's a Federal investigation in process centered around San Juan de Cristo."

"About what?" I asked, almost wishing I could have one of his cigarettes.

After another cloud of smoke filled the room, he said, "I don't know.   But it must be big, or you wouldn't be here."

Out of the corner of my eye I saw the two Marshalls standing at the archway to the kitchen.   They were doing nothing.   They seemed to have been expecting Gandalf.

"Alright," I said.   "I guess I can accept that.   So tell me why you're here?"

"Are you going home, Mr. Crew?" he asked and smiled knowingly.

I looked at the two Marshalls, standing off to the side casually. Both were leaning against a wall. They didn't smile.

I told Gandalf, "No. I think I'll stick around for awhile."

"You know if you do, those guys who attacked you will probably kill you the next time."

He was right, of course. It seems my life's purpose is to risk my own life for someone else's benefit. How many times has that happened in my adult life? And did the future look different right then? I doubted it. So I said, "You're right, of course. But my alternative is to walk away and allow Betsy to spend the rest of her life in prison for something she didn't do."

Gandalf nodded, looked at me squarely in the eye, smiled and said, "Then you need someone like me to protect you."

"Are you offering your services?" I asked him, already knowing the answer but I wanted him to make that offer.

"Well," he said. "I lost the bounty on your Betsy. It doesn't look like I'm going to get anything out of Harry Perkins. I'm 6' 7" tall and I weigh 299 pounds. Besides that, I'm one mean son of a bitch . . . Meaning no disrespect to my mother, of course. It's just the reputation I have."

"How much?" I asked.

He answered, "Fifteen hundred a day . . . Three thousand a day if I save your life."

"Done," I said. "You're hired."

Gandalf crushed out his cigarette in a small potted ivy plant on a table next to his chair. "By the way," he began, "Your wife is in El Paso. She was raising hell at the hospital in Balling."

"Where is she now?"

"She's at that suite of yours at The Ironwood Mansion

Resort. She's mad as hell and giving everyone a hard time.
She raised hell at the hospital. She's been yelling at the
local police and stormed through the Federal Building. I just
left her, as a matter of fact. That little baby of yours is very
pretty. She's going to be a real heartbreaker someday."
        "You were with her?" I said. "You saw her?"
        "Yes . . . I hope that's alright with you?"
        "Why didn't you bring her here with you?" I felt that
temper of mine start to boil. I tried pushing myself out of the
chair but my chest was still bandaged tightly. I let myself fall
back into the soft cushions. And besides, if I could have
gotten out of the chair, what would I have done?
        "I told you I have friends," Gandalf said and grinned
slyly. "I can pretty much do whatever I like because
everybody knows I only break the rules that need to be
broken. But if I had brought your wife here . . . To a high
security Safe House . . . I'd lose a lot of those friends. She
knows you're safe, and she's waiting . . . I wish I could say
she's waiting patiently . . . But she is waiting for you to go to
her."
        I thought about that, but it only took a couple of
seconds to understand the sense of what he was saying and
realize he was right. Bringing Sandy here would not only
blow the cover off a Federal Safe House, it would put her
more deeply into this whole mess than I wanted her to be in.
And there was Caroline to think about, too. So I told
Gandalf, loud enough for the two Marshalls to hear, "I'm
going to leave here after I finish my coffee. Come on into
the kitchen and I'll get you a cup."

                    ****

        A cup of coffee to Gandalf meant scrambling a half
dozen eggs, frying up half a pound of bacon, and toasting
eight slices of bread which were lathered thickly with butter
and mounded with sweet strawberry jam. I watched him as

he ate this.   The two Marshalls also watched from the kitchen doorway, both with arms crossed across their chests.

He was eating the food provided by the Marshall's Service, but I guessed the two watching him weren't about to tell him he shouldn't help himself. I would have liked to put him up against Sandy in an eating match. Sandy can eat as much as she wants and never seems to gain an ounce.

When he had finished, he leaned back in the kitchen chair that barely held his bulk, lit another Gauloises, and blew the smoke slowly up towards the ceiling. The two Marshalls still didn't move.

"So, boss," Gandalf asked. "What do you want to do now?"

Now that was a good question. I didn't want to admit it to anyone, but I had absolutely no idea what to do next. Going back to San Juan de Cristo would be a waste of time and probably dangerous. What would be accomplished by going back to the Bar H Ranch?

My silence and probably the frown on my forehead caused Gandalf to suggest, "I guess if I were you, I'd phone my wife and tell her you're OK. I'd hate to be in your shoes, if you just let her sit back there steaming."

Now that was a good idea, and I could have kicked myself for not thinking of it myself. There was a yellow phone hanging on the wall near the doorway of the kitchen, where the two Marshalls were standing. I struggled to my feet and limped to it. They moved aside, and I got the operator to connect me with the Ironwood Mansion Resort.

What Gandalf and the two Marshalls heard was me saying, "Yes . . . I'm OK . . . Yes dear . . . No dear . . . Of course dear . . . Yes dear . . . No dear . . . But . . . Yes dear . . . No dear . . ." and on it went. She was, well, angry doesn't describe it. But soon her rage faded into sounds of sobbing. "Sandy," I said. "I'm OK. Stay where you are. I'll be there soon."

I hated to leave her like that, but I knew it was for the

best. She and Caroline would be safe . . . For the time being anyway. I hung up and turned to Gandalf. He and the Marshalls were red faced and doing their best to hold back laughter. Gandalf straightened and tried to wipe the smile from his face. "Look," he said, "there were men at the bar that night. May I suggest you talk to them?"

"That's a good idea," I said. "Do you know how I can find them?"

"I know where one of them is," Gandalf said. He slowly, over dramatically, lit another cigarette. He raised his head and artistically blew a stream of blue-grey smoke leisurely towards the ceiling. He said, still looking up at the kitchen ceiling, "Thomas Rocker is in the county jail in El Paso. He's serving six months for DUI and possession of marijuana."

"OK, let's go," I said.

But the two Marshalls had a different idea. They moved from leaning against their walls and stood blocking the archway between the kitchen and living room. "You can't leave here," one of them said very seriously and a bit officiously, his hands on his hips, pushing his dark suit jacket aside so that his side arm was visible to us.

The other said, with arms still folded across his chest "We can't protect you if you leave."

I said, "Thank you for all you've done for me. But the fact that you've done what you've done tells me there's more to all this then a few cowboys assaulting me on a lonely back road. You've got an ATF Agent working undercover. My friend is in jail for a murder she didn't commit. I'm going to have to take my chances out there. I can't just go home."

Except for the clothes I wore, I left the clothes that the Marshall's Service had given me at the safe house. Gandalf and I left the two Marshalls standing at the front door. They had made several phone calls while we were leaving. I don't know who they spoke to, but my gut told me that I now had several Federal Agencies to look out for, too.

I left my rental car that had been towed from the desert road, in the driveway of the safe house. I knew I was in no condition to drive. Gandalf drove his big, red Cadillac Biarritz with the top down. I had tried as best I could to ignore the pain and ease my way down into the front passenger seat. I held on tight as he drove too fast back to El Paso. As we approached the city limits of El Paso, Gandalf slowed and headed to The Ironwood Mansion Resort where Sandy was waiting for me.

When I opened the door to the suite, Little Caroline screamed in happiness and scampered to me. She hugged me around the knees and rode on my leg, laughing joyously as I walked, with the help of the cane supplied by the Feds, into the suite. I wanted to bend down and pick her up but the cracked ribs and bruises stopped me. Sandy's greeting wasn't so happy.

"What the hell happened to you!" she gasped, her hand covering her mouth. I had wanted her to run into my arms and kiss me.

"Just a little accident," I said.

Gandalf was behind me. He stepped around me and picked Caroline up, tossing her into the air to her delight, catching her and stepping aside. He held her in his big arms and looked at Sandy, "He's going to need some comforting, Mrs. Crew."

"Just a little accident!" I said again. "I'll be OK. Nothing to worry about. I've been worse. But I could use a big kiss right now."

I managed to walk to Sandy. I was limping and bent over because standing up straight was too painful on my injured ribs. Gandalf tossed Caroline into the air once again. She laughed uproariously at being up so high, near the room's ceiling. Sandy grabbed onto me; I didn't tell her how much that hurt, but I did wince, and she noticed that. Her hug eased up and she looked up at me. My left eye was still swollen and almost shut, and my jaw was still puffy on the left where the two teeth were missing. My lip was swollen, the cut closed but still raw. She kissed me lightly while tears ran down her cheeks.

Sandy took my arm and helped me as best she could to a soft chair. I lowered myself into it, and Sandy took a couple of steps back away from me. She wiped the tears from her eyes and said, "OK. Now tell me what the hell happened."

I couldn't find the words because I didn't want to scare her. Gandalf, carrying the giggling Caroline, stood beside Sandy and said, "A couple of guys didn't like the questions he was asking."

"And where the hell were you?" she demanded of Gandalf. She looked up at the towering figure in front of her. I saw her hands ball into fists. "Did you just stand around and let this happen?"

I stopped Gandalf from saying anything by telling her, "I just hired him today. He's now our bodyguard. He wasn't a couple of days ago. I was alone."

She took Caroline from Gandalf's arms, hugged her, walked across the room, and turned back to him. "You'd better be damn good at your damn job," she said. "If anything else happens to him . . . I'm gonna' come after you . . . And you don't want that to happen." She walked into the next room and got Caroline ready for an afternoon nap.

The three of us spent the rest of that day and the evening in the suite, trying to agree on what to do next. Sandy wanted to let the attorneys handle Betsy's case and get on the next plane back to San Marcos. I wanted to talk to Thomas Rocker and then go back to San Juan de Cristo . . . With Gandalf, of course. But Gandalf had the sensible suggestion.

"Mrs. Crew," he said. "I get the impression your husband isn't going to just walk away. Tomorrow you go visit Betsy. Do that every day. Keep her hopes up and keep her from getting depressed. If her attorney has showed up, talk to him and work with him. Make sure he knows how important this case is. Make sure he knows that Mr. Crew and I are going to find out what really happened."

"Oh sure," Sandy said. "I'm just going to take Caroline to jail to see Betsy every day. I'm sure she'll enjoy all the murderers and kidnappers and child molesters there. Maybe . . . If we're lucky . . . We can watch a jail break or a riot."

Gandalf grinned and said, "I'll have someone here in the morning to babysit. Someone you can trust. Mr. Crew, you and I are going to the jail, also. But we're going to talk to Tom Rocker. There's nothing like a captive witness to get to the truth."

Sandy asked, "Who's that?"

"He was at The Mustang that night. He's in the El Paso County Jail right now."

We agreed that what Gandalf suggested was the right thing to do. And with that agreement we also agreed that we were all hungry. Caroline had awakened from her nap hours before and was beginning to get grouchy, which we knew was a sign that she was hungry, too. I was in no condition to go to a restaurant, so we ordered shrimp and big steaks and baked potatoes and salads and three bottles of a good California Cabernet. Caroline seemed to enjoy little jars of smashed carrots, smashed peas, and a bottle of warm milk, after which she fell asleep on the couch.

CHAPTER NINE – Rocker And Edgy

The next morning as Sandy was ordering a breakfast of yogurt, fruit, and wheat toast for her and unfortunately the same for me, too, Gandalf knocked on the door of our suite. There was a woman with him. To say she was fat would be a gross understatement.

"This is Abena Ekundayo," he said, introducing the woman. "She's the woman I said will babysit for you."

Neither Sandy nor I said anything. I'm certain we were both thinking the same thing. Gandalf saw that and he said, "Miss Ekundayo is a registered pediatric nurse. She manages one of the child day care centers I own. I trust her absolutely."

"You own a child care center?" Sandy asked.

"Actually, I own five of them," Gandalf said. "El Paso isn't all oil companies and rich people. There are poor neighborhoods here, just as there are in every city. We have children whose lives aren't very good and whose futures are even worse. At my places, they have a safe place to play and they eat well. They learn to read and to deal with others without violence. I hire people very carefully. Miss Ekundayo is the best employee I have."

And so we left Caroline sleeping peacefully in a crib and in the care of Abena Ekundayo. We climbed into Gandalf's bright red Cadillac. Sandy slid into the rear seat easily but it was difficult and very painful for me to get into the front. Gandalf had the convertible top up which caused me to have to bend uncomfortably to get in. My body seemed like one very large and very painful source of torture. Every inch of me hurt, but I tried as best I could to hide it.

We drove to the El Paso County Jail. Gandalf knew where he was going. He pulled into a parking lot clearly marked 'County Personnel Only' and parked in a vacant spot with a painted 'RESERVED' on the curb. I was about to ask until he said, "They know me here." He had to help me out of the car and Sandy held her breath, hands covering her mouth as I got to my feet. Sandy took my arm as we walked across the pavement.

Inside the building, Gandalf led the way to the jail. He held a double glass door open for Sandy and me. He smiled.

"Hey, Gandalf," a jail guard behind a pale green counter said. He seemed pleased to see the big man. "How ya'll doin', man?"

"Fine, Murray. Just fine. How's your wife doing? Is she feeling better?"

The guard said, "The doctor thinks she may have some kind of allergy to somethin'. She got your card and flowers though. Made her feel really good. Thanks."

"You tell her I said I hope she's feeling better real soon," Gandalf said. "If there's anything I can do, you know how to reach me."

"Hey, thanks man," the guard said. "Who you come t'see today?"

Gandalf took Sandy's arm and they took a step or two to the counter. "This is Mrs. Crew," he said. "She wants to see Elizabeth Concanon. I'm afraid she hasn't filled out the visitor's paper work, though. But she's OK. Can she get in?"

"No problem, Gandalf," the guard said. "I'll have the

girl brought to the outside meeting area, OK?"

"That's fine," Gandalf said. "This guy behind me is Mr. Crew. He and I want to see Thomas Rocker. Mr. Crew hasn't filed the paperwork either."

The guard looked at me and my bruised face and swollen left eye. I was bent over slightly and hugging my arms at my chest. "You do that to him, Gandalf?" he asked.

Gandalf laughed loudly and said, "Hey Murray, if I'd hit him he wouldn't be standing right now."

After Gandalf and the guard finished laughing . . . And I didn't find it humorous at all . . . Gandalf pulled a big .45 from its shoulder holster, a small .32 semi-auto from an ankle holster, an angry looking black switchblade knife from his back pocket, and a small spray bottle of mace from a leather holder on his belt. Murray took everything and put them under the counter. "I ain't gonna' lock them up, Gandalf. But if anybody asks I put them in a lock box, OK?"

Sandy had to turn over her purse, and I had to hand over my keys and wallet. These things were locked in a keyed box and the key handed to Gandalf. We each walked through a metal detector, and Gandalf led us down a narrow hallway, making a couple of turns into other narrow hallways, and finally out a door to a small, fully enclosed, concrete paved, outside area. There were a half dozen metal tables and four metal chairs at each table, all bolted down to the concrete. Two of them were under plastic umbrellas. Both of these were occupied by prisoners who were smoking and talking.

When Betsy was brought out, Gandalf walked over to the prisoners and told the men under one of the canopies to leave. They left immediately. Sandy rushed to Betsy and they hugged and cried and hugged some more. They sat in the shade of the vacated table.

A door opened nearby, and a prisoner walked out. A guard next to him pointed to us and Rocker started walking towards us. He stopped halfway and lit a Marlboro cigarette, and then he continued walking.

Tommy Rocker didn't look like a cowboy from some out of the way little dusty town in west Texas. He was tall, broad shouldered and slim. He was wearing the typical orange jump suit that all inmates wore. He had rolled the sleeves up, showing off a tattoo and muscled arms. As he got closer, I saw that the tattoo was a spread wing eagle with USMC written under it.

He stopped about six feet from us, took a deep drag off the cigarette, and looked up at Gandalf. He asked, "You wanted to see me?"

"Let's sit over there," Gandalf said, pointing to the other shaded table. He stepped up to it and told the inmate and his girlfriend, who were sitting there, to leave. She wanted to argue but her boyfriend looked up at Gandalf and pulled her up to her feet. They walked away quickly, the woman looking back angrily over her shoulder.

I struggled to sit, and Tom Rocker joined us. Gandalf lit one of his Gauloises. The smoke from both cigarettes made me choke.

"You get hit by a truck?" Rocker asked, looking at my beat-up face.

My hand went to my swollen eye but I didn't say anything. Gandalf blew some acrid smoke in the air over Rocker's head.

"So? . . . What?" Rocker asked.

I began, "You were at The Mustang the night Edward Hands was killed."

Rocker took in more of the cigarette smoke, blew it towards my face, and said, "So what."

"Tell me what happened," I said.

"Suck my cock," he said.

Gandalf said in a soft but very threatening voice, "Watch your language, Tommy. Answer the man's questions."

Rocker stared at me, smoked the cigarette down to a

stub, crushed it out under his foot, and said, "Put a thousand bucks in my jail account. Then I'll talk to you."

I started to reach for my money clip before I remembered that it, plus everything else I had with me, was locked up at the front desk. Gandalf put a hand on my arm, and said to Tom Rocker, "Tell you what I'm going to do. I'm going to put two thousand dollars in the account of the biggest, baddest son of a bitch they have in here. Then I'm going to tell that son of a bitch to marry you and take your virginity away. How's that?"

Rocker smoked through another cigarette. We all sat silently as he thought, waiting for him to say something. He looked at Gandalf, then at me, then back at Gandalf. Gandalf's threat worked . . . Although I still have doubts that it was really just a threat. I think he really meant what he had said.

When he had crushed out the latest Marlboro, Tom Rocker said in a defeated voice, "OK, I was there."

I asked, "Did you know Edward Hands?"

"Edgy?" he asked. "Yeah, Edgy and me were friends. He wasn't too smart but he was a good guy."

"Edgy," I said. That's what Burl Evans had called him back at The Last Stand. "Is that what everyone called him?"

"Yeah," was all he said.

Gandalf asked, "Why Edgy?"

"He liked to live sort of on the edge . . . Always taking stupid chances . . . And he was always nervous, too."

"You were a Marine," I said. "Do you like to take chances, too?"

Rocker looked down at the tattoo on his arm then smiled, understanding how I had known he was a Marine. "Me?" he said and smiled. "No, I'm too smart. Why?"

"The guys who were with you that night," I asked. "You all knew each other, right?"

"Yeah, sure," he said. "Why?"

"You and your friends spend a lot of time in San Juan

de Cristo, I'll bet," I asked. "You probably spend time at The Last Stand."

"Not much else around out there," Rocker said. "Why?"

"How about The Mustang?" I asked. "You guys like that place, too?" He didn't answer, he didn't smile, he just smoked his Marlboro.

There was thunder cracking inside my head and I was having some trouble breathing deeply. My chest felt like it was about to explode. But I managed to ask, "Do you live out there? There's not much out that way, like you said."

"Yeah," Rocker said. "Why?"

"Where do you live?" I asked him. "Do you live at Harry Perkins' place?"

"Mr. Perkins? That's stupid. I got my own place."

"That's great," I said. "Where?"

"I got a RV. Out in the desert. I like it out there. It's quiet."

My jaw where my teeth were missing began to throb. It was beginning to be difficult to talk. The heat, even sitting in the shade of the steel umbrella, was getting to me. My head was spinning, but I said, "I'm going to take a wild stab in the dark here. You and your friends all work out at the Bar H Ranch, don't you?"

Tom Rocker didn't answer right away. He took the time to crush out his cigarette and light yet another one. I realized his chain smoking was a nervous reaction to being asked piercing questions.

Gandalf's patience was beginning to run short. He said, not even trying to hide the threat, "Answer the man, Tommy."

Rocker said, "Not full time . . . Sort of when they need somethin' done . . . I'm not a cowboy. Why?"

Gandalf asked, "What kind of somethin' are you talking about, Tommy? What kind of work do you do out there?"

Rocker said, "Don't call me Tommy. My name is Thomas. You can call me Tom if you want, but not Tommy. That's a child's name and I'm not a child."

"OK, Tom," Gandalf said smiling. "So what kind of work do you do at the ranch?"

"They pay me to protect the cattle," he said. "Why?"

"Protect the cattle?" I asked. "What the hell does that mean?" The world was beginning to spin around me. I could feel beads of sweat across my forehead. I felt like I might be spun off the hard metal chair. I took a firm grasp on the table.

"Big cats . . . Wolves . . . Coyotes . . . Anything that kills cattle."

"So you're a hunter?" I asked and wiped at my forehead. "That's OK. How about the other guys who were there that night? Are they cattle guards also?"

The joke slipped by Tom Rocker. He said, "I don't know. You gotta' ask them."

"How do I find them?" I asked. "I do want to talk with them."

"I don't know," he answered. I didn't believe him but I was feeling too sick to argue the point. I told myself I'd get back to that later.

"So you were at The Mustang when Edgy was murdered," I said. "The young lady was there . . . The girl who was arrested for Edgy's murder. Did you dance with her?"

"Sure," he said and smiled, leaning back in the chair. He pulled another Marlboro from the crushed pack and lit it. "You don't look so good," he said grinning.

"Tell me about her," I said, ignoring him.

"What's to tell? She was there. She was pretty good looking."

"How old did you think she was?" I asked.

"Hell, I don't know. There aren't enough women out there to care how old they are. She was there, and she was having fun."

"Do you know why she was there?" I asked.

"Hell, that punk Jimmy Perkins brought her. Go ask him."

"Was it just a coincidence that you and your buddies were there the night Jimmy brought her to the saloon?" I asked.

"Hell, I guess so. Why?"

"It was midweek," I said. "Do you guys usually go drinking in the middle of the week? I would think Saturday night would be party night around here."

"Yeah . . . So what? . . . What's your point?"

I wanted to go on but my head was about to explode, my left eye was throbbing. My chest, under the tight bandage, hurt with every breath I took. My stomach was turning at the clouds of cigarette smoke from both Gandalf and Tom Rocker. I put my hands over my eyes and for a minute. I thought I was going to pass out. Gandalf said, "Are you OK, Mr. Crew?"

I didn't say anything, in fact I barely heard him. Gandalf called to a guard and within seconds I had a cold bottle of water in my shaking hand that I managed to drink half way down. Gandalf took the remaining water and poured it over my head. It felt good. I could feel the sweat pouring from me, soaking my clothes. The sky above me and the air around me suddenly became dark and cold. A mind numbing roar filled my head, and my ears were filled with a throbbing electric buzz.

Sandy and Betsy were at my side, both saying something, but it was all too fuzzy. Gandalf pulled me to my feet and all but carried me out of the jail yard. The next thing I remembered was waking up in bed at the Ironwood Mansion suite.

CHAPTER TEN – To Save Betsy Concanon

I spent the next five days in bed. Not that I did so voluntarily. Gandalf's friend and nurse-employee, Abena Ekundayo, took over. When I woke up the day we had gone to the City jail, she was standing at my bedside, along with Sandy, who was holding Caroline. Gandalf stood behind them, looking over their heads and shoulders at me. I tried to push the sheet aside but even that little motion sent pain through my whole body and up into my brain. I groaned and winced at the shock.

"Now, you just have to stay in bed, Mr. Crew," Abena said as she gently pushed me down and pulled the sheet up to my shoulders. I was wearing soft cotton pajamas, and I felt clean. Abena said, "Your wife went shopping, and I gave you a nice sponge bath. You'll feel better soon."

"She's a nurse, Morgan," Sandy said. "She's agreed to stay here and take care of you for awhile."

"Take care of me? I don't need to be taken care of." Even the words hurt as I tried to speak. All I could manage was a weak whisper, and moving my jaw seemed impossible.

Sandy stepped closer to the bed, Caroline in her arms. The baby was looking very serious and worried. Sandy said, "You were badly hurt, Morgan. Worse than we thought. You need to rest and heal."

"Who said so?" I asked. "I was released from the damn hospital, wasn't I?"

"I say so," Abena said in a very authoritative voice. "I say you're going to stay in bed." I could imagine that voice controlling tough street kids who were used to doing whatever they wanted to do. But I'm not a street kid, and I wasn't about to let her control me. Although I imagine she would sit on me if she had to.

"You," I said, "are a baby nurse. You are not a doctor."

She grinned broadly and said, "Well, baby. I'm gonna' be your damn nurse for just about a week. Then we'll see if you can go out and play."

In the end, I stayed in bed for five straight days. Sandy took Abena's side in the argument, and when that happened I knew I had lost. There is never a chance of me winning when Sandy tells me to do something I don't want to do.

But – silently – I was glad they made me stay in bed. I was in a lot of pain. The four guys who met me out in the desert did a professional job on me. They beat me to hurt me, to cause injury, to frighten me away from something. They knew what they were doing - they were experienced at what they did, because they could have gone just a little bit further, and I would be dead. Although they hurt me, they didn't and wouldn't frighten me away.

It was a warning. I've been warned before. I know what a warning is. I have been a target before. I have been shot and almost killed before. To be perfectly honest, I was scared, as I had been many times in the past. I am not your typical hero; I'm scared of almost everything. When my life is in danger, all I want to do is run. That damn little voice in the back of my head screams, telling me to run when I'm in trouble. But I know I can't. People depend on me, and I am somehow able to push past the fear and do what is necessary to help the people I must help.

In the little West Texas town of San Juan de Cristo, there were people who would not warn me a second time. The next time they would kill me, or at least they would try to kill me. I knew I would do whatever I had to do . . . In spite of my fear . . . Both to not let them hurt me or my family, and to help Betsy Concanon. That I was sure of.

So I said to Sandy and Gandalf, "OK, if I'm locked up here, what do I do about Betsy?"

"I'll take care of Betsy," Sandy said. "I'll see her every day. She won't feel alone or abandoned. I saw her while you were in the hospital."

"How is she?" I asked her. "What did she say?"

"She's scared," Sandy said. She let Caroline climb down onto the floor. The baby ran to my bedside, hugged the bed sheets, and looked up at me, worried of course. Sandy went on, "She saw you talking to that inmate. She recognized the man as one of the men at the bar that night. She's scared that he'll hurt her in jail."

Gandalf spoke up, "I told the guards. They put Rocker in solitary, and he'll stay there until this is all over or until his six months are up. He won't get to her."

"You've got that kind of influence?" Sandy asked.

Abena laughed, and Gandalf, grinning slyly, tried not to laugh. He said, "I've got friends." I was beginning to believe that Gandalf Finch really was one of those special people who skirted the boundary between legal and illegal. Most of the time these people did good things, but they did them in ways that most people would, at least, frown at. They 'bent' the law when they had to. They'd hurt people if they had to. But they were respected by most and feared by those who should be frightened of him. I'd met these people before.

I asked Sandy, "What about the lawyer? Has he seen Betsy yet?"

"Yes, twice. Betsy said she liked him. His name is

Christopher Talbot.   He's got an office here in El Paso.
Betsy said he's reading all the police and court records. He
told her he'd never seen anything like it before. Apparently
he's confident he can win at trial."

"OK," I said, speaking as best I could through the
pain. "Go see him tomorrow. Get all you can from him, but
don't tell him yet about what we're doing. Don't let him know
we're looking for the real killer. I want him to feel he has to
work hard. If he knows what we're doing, he might wait it
out. If Betsy has to go to trial, I want her to win."

"And what else can be done?" Sandy asked. "Can we
afford to wait until you can get around?"

Gandalf spoke up. "Tell me what you want me to do,"
he said.

"I don't get it," I said.

"Hey, you're paying me. I want to earn the money. If
I sit around here and stare at your lily white face, I wouldn't
be earning what you're paying me. Tell me what you'd do,
and I'll do it."

I looked at Sandy.   She smiled and nodded her
approval. So I said, "OK, Mr. Finch. I need to talk to the four
other men who were at the bar the night Edgy Hands was
killed. We know their names but nothing else about them.
See if you can find them and talk to them. My gut tells me
there's some kind of connection between them. Bring them
here if you can't get anything out of them . . . Although I think
you know how to get the truth from them. Talk to them one
at a time but don't let them talk to each other. They might
work up a story between them. Don't hurt them too hard."

Gandalf started to pull one of his French cigarettes
out of the pack. Sandy cleared her throat loudly and shook
her head. He relented and put the pack back in his pocket.
He said, "You said there were four guys who beat the crap
out of you. There are four guys who were at the bar out
there you want to talk to. You think maybe they're the same
people?"

"That's what my gut tells me.   Maybe . . . I don't know," I said.

"So tell me what your gut says is going on here," Gandalf asked.

"I think Edgy was killed by one of the five guys he was with. I think Betsy was set up. I think Jimmy Perkins was either too scared to stop it or he was in on it. I have no idea why Edgy was killed.   That's what we need to find out. When we know why, we'll know who killed him."

Gandalf turned and went to the phone on the small desk in the bedroom. He punched in the number for his office, waited, and said, "Hi, Estelle . . . How are you today? . . . Good, look, I'm going to be out all day . . . Don't bring up the damn cell phone thing again. You know I don't like them. Estelle, just pull the file on the Concanon girl. There are five men listed as being at the bar the night of the murder. Do a complete public records check on each of them. Don't leave anything out, and make sure we get driver's license records and auto ownership, too . . . OK, I'll check back later today or tomorrow morning . . . What? . . . You tell Izzy that I'm going to make the damn collections. He needs to stop buggin' me."

Gandalf walked back to us. I just had to ask, "Who's Izzy?" I had a hunch who Izzy was but curiosity was killing me.

"I do some collections for him," he said.

"What kind of collections?"

Gandalf looked at Abena, and she smiled and shrugged her shoulders. He told me, "Izzy makes loans. I collect what's owed to him."

"Look, Mr. Finch," I said. "I don't like violence. While you're working for this Izzy fella' you do what you have to do. While you're working for me I don't want anyone hurt."

"Mr. Crew," he said. "I don't make a habit of hurting people. Look at me. Do you really think someone is going to take me on or say 'no' to me? Oh, there was this biker once. He was big, but I'm bigger. He wound up in the hospital for three months. But most of the time people do what I tell them to do."

****

I spent the next two days in bed, being waited on by Abena and Sandy, and trying not to let Caroline know that her playing on the bed . . . And me . . . Was not at all pain free. Sandy ordered "good, healthy" food for me to eat in bed. I didn't complain about the salads and soups and turkey sandwiches and stuff like that, even though what I really wanted was a fat, greasy hamburger or a thick, juicy steak. Even my Wild Turkey 101 bourbon was withheld from me in favor of glass after glass of unsweetened ice tea, and lots of different fruit juices.

Abena wanted to give me a sponge bath but Sandy took that job on herself, after ushering Abena with Caroline out of the bedroom and locking the door. It was the very best sponge bath I could ever imagine enjoying, and it took a couple of hours. I was sore and in pain when I tried to move, so Sandy did all the work. Ahhh, the very thought of it is still fantastic and still stirs up those special juices.

Sandy did go to see Christopher Talbot at his office in El Paso. He said he had never seen anything like what was in the police report. San Juan de Cristo's Sheriff Kronk had hand written, scribbled really, a one page report of his arrest of Betsy. Kronk had listed Benny Newsinger, Ted Soller, Murray Allott, Thomas Rocker, and Greg West as witnesses but hadn't included any address or contact information on the men. He arrested Betsy and kept her in his ramshackle jail overnight before driving her to El Paso County Jail, Harry Perkins going along for the ride I guess.

After Sandy had told me all this, she said, "There's no way she's going to be found guilty. There's no evidence at all. Kronk didn't do any investigation. And why the hell is she still in jail? The D.A. must have seen the file on her. Why are they keeping her there?"

"Politics," I said. "Someone is pulling some weight. Look, Sandy, we can wait for a trial and then take her home. I doubt a whole jury can be bought. But she won't be safe. I think she's being framed, and I think the people who killed Edgy are the Sheriff's witnesses. They're not going to let her walk away because she might know something that will hang them."

"You're right, of course," Sandy said. She slumped down in a chair near my bed. Her beautiful face was frozen in deep thought. She looked up at me and asked, "Do we break her out of jail?"

I laughed, but then I realized she might actually be serious. Sandy is like that. There is very little she will not do to help a friend. So I had to keep an eye on her. She might actually go and break Betsy out of the El Paso County jail.

****

I was having a breakfast of whole wheat raisin bran cereal, grapefruit juice and whole wheat toast – a menu specially ordered by my dear Sandy who is in constant worry of my weight and waist line – when Gandalf walked into the suite without knocking first.

I was propped up in bed, three pillows under my head, which was causing me some discomfort, but I knew better than to complain. If I had, I would be spoon fed baby food while lying flat on my back. Gandalf looked down at the tray of what Sandy insisted was food, and he said, "Damn! I'm glad I had breakfast before coming here."

"You wouldn't by chance have smuggled some eggs, sausage, and hotcakes in for me, would you?"

Sandy didn't find the joke funny. She took the tray away and asked, "Mr. Finch, would you like some coffee? Morgan and I are going to have some."

"That would be fine. I need to talk with both of you."

He sounded and looked very serious. He pulled a big upholstered chair closer to my bed, sat and leaned back. He and I said nothing while Sandy went for the coffee. It took no more than a minute or two, but it seemed like an eternity. Gandalf couldn't look at me. His eyes kept shifting around the floor and out the window, and then back at the floor. Something bad had happened; I had gotten used to expecting something bad to happen because it always does. People who commit murder will do anything to keep from paying for their crime. They usually do more bad things and more bad things after that, to keep justice from their door.

Sandy returned with a thermos and three big mugs. She filled each, handed two to Gandalf and me, and sat in a chair not too far away cupping her mug in both hands.

Gandalf drank some of the hot coffee, ignoring how it burnt his tongue and lips. His eyes were down, focused on the carpet under his feet. He was drinking the coffee nervously. His hands were shaking as he took one more drink and began, "I ran a records check on the five guys who were at the bar that night. They have a lot in common. Their DMV driver's license records each show the same PO Box back in San Juan de Cristo. None of them own any cars or trucks, at least none registered in Texas. They each receive their mail at the same PO Box shown on their driver's license. And they each have a military service record; two in the Marines, two in the Army, and one Navy."

He went back to drinking the coffee and seemed unable, or maybe unwilling, to look at us. I said, "What's wrong Gandalf?" It was the first time I had called the big man by his first name.

He hesitated a little but finally looked up, first at me and then at Sandy. He said, "I went back to the jail to talk to Rocker again. I thought he might be able to give me a lead to the other four."

He stopped talking and again looked down.

Something had happened, something obviously bad had happened. I said, "Tell me."

"I didn't call ahead," he said slowly. "I don't need to . . . They all know me there. Anyway, when I walked in, one of the guys I know pretty well was working the desk."

Gandalf hesitated again and kept his eyes averted from us. I pushed myself up in bed and ignored the pain. "Gandalf," I said. "What the hell happened?"

He looked up again, from Sandy to me, and said, "Betsy was stabbed. She's hurt very bad."

Sandy dropped the mug of coffee she had been holding; it crashed to the floor and broke, spilling coffee all over the rug. I tried to sit up too quickly but the pain stopped me. Sandy's hands were covering her mouth to stop a scream that wanted to burst from her. Tears flooded from her eyes; I thought for a second or two that she was going to collapse. I wanted to run to her. I pushed the sheets off of me, and ignoring the pain, I threw my legs over the side of the bed. Gandalf quickly reached my bedside and helped me to my feet. I stumbled to Sandy. I tried to lift her but couldn't. She stood, and I took her in my arms. She was crying, sobbing uncontrollably.

I looked over her shoulder and asked Gandalf, "What the hell happened?"

"She was working in the jail's mess hall. She was serving dinner. She was behind the serving line. A fight broke out on the far side of the room. Chaos everywhere. All the guards went to break up the fight and restore order. Someone came up from behind Betsy and stabbed her with a homemade knife . . . Made out of a tooth brush. It pierced a kidney. No one found her on the floor until they had restored order in the mess hall. She had lost a lot of blood. They were able to stop the bleeding but they don't know yet if she's going to lose the kidney. And there's a lot of infection. She's unconscious."

Through her tears Sandy said, "Oh my God! Morgan,

what are we going to do? Betsy can't die."

"She's not going to die," I said. "I'm not going to let her die." I asked Gandalf, "Where is she? What Hospital?"

"She's at El Paso County General.   It's a good facility."

"Sandy," I said. "I need to talk to her attorney. Get him on the phone and get him over here right now."

Sandy ran for the phone; I turned to Gandalf. "You have some contacts inside the jail. I want to know what they're doing to find out who stabbed her." He turned without a word and rushed from the suite.

The few minutes I was on my feet tired me. Abena took my arm and led me back to the bed. I wanted to fall onto the sheets but I knew that would hurt, so I let the nurse help me under the clover slowly. "Abena," I said as she pulled the soft sheet up over me. "I need to find the best private hospital in the area. Can you help me with that?"

"Will they let her leave?" she asked. "I mean, she's still supposed to be in jail."

"Let me worry about that," I said. "Just find out what the best private hospital in the area is. Someplace that's probably very expensive. Someplace where the doctors are the best."

I had seen too many close friends and people I cared about die violent deaths. They were all good people. Their deaths were senseless and useless.   Nothing was accomplished by their deaths. The world is less for their deaths. I wasn't going to sit back and let another person die a useless death.   I would do everything . . . Anything. Whatever had to be done I would do to keep Betsy alive. If that meant getting every damn attorney belonging to Harper, Harper, Jascro and Nettles out of their offices and cubicles and drag them to El Paso, I would do that.

The Crew Family's vast fortune – the money, the banks, the corporations, the shipping companies, the portfolios of stocks and bonds, and all the other things we own and control – has power attached to it. I use that power reluctantly and miserly, but I use it to its fullest when it means saving a friend or relative. I was intent on using every power I could access to save Betsy Concanon.

And then it occurred to me. Betsy really had become part of the family . . . A very important part.

Caroline had walked all by herself to my bedside. She had a long, sad look on her face. She touched my arm and gave me a "Da-Da" in a very concerned little voice. Da-Da was one of a couple dozen words she had learned.

CHAPTER ELEVEN – More Guns Than People

It took a day and a half for Betsy's attorney – Christopher Talbot – to have her transferred to The Stephen H. Maxwell Clinic. The Maxwell Clinic is a very, very, very private hospital for the very, very, very rich, located in a very, very, very wealthy area on the remote outskirts of El Paso. They do a lot of plastic surgery for aging wives of rich men. They do the same for young ladies of marriageable age who want to attract rich men of any age. But they are also renowned for treating those same very, very, very rich people for cancer and heart disease and every other serious illness the very, very, very rich are afflicted with.

She settled in to an elegantly decorated and very large private room quickly. There was a County Cop from the County jail stationed at the door, and standing across the hallway from him were two armed and licensed private security guards I had hired to protect Betsy. The County Cop and the two security guards didn't speak – the County Cop was angry that a couple of rent-a-cops were there, and the security guards were jealous that the County Cop was in charge and standing between them and their client.

Sandy stayed at Betsy's bedside all day for the first three days, returning to our suite late into each evening. She arranged for the outrageous bill to be sent to Harper,

Harper, Jascro and Nettles. And she made sure only the best doctors were there to treat our little biker chick nanny.

Betsy was operated on the second day. A team of three doctors and four nurses, plus several technicians, managed to save her kidney and repair the damage done by the dirty, jail-made knife. She would live and she would not go back to the jail, I had made up my mind to that.

Christopher Talbot and a staff of assistants from Harper, Harper, Jascro and Nettles started flooding the County Courthouse with papers and motions, and a big dollar suit against the County for not protecting Betsy while in their custody. It would take months for everything to be sorted out and in the meantime the doctors would not release her from their hospital. I made sure there was always a good medical reason for her not to be moved.

Caroline was as concerned as everyone even if she couldn't understand what was happening. She could sense our worry and several times she said, "Bets" which is her name for Betsy. She knew something was wrong. Betsy hadn't been around for weeks and Caroline . . . C that is . . . Missed her. It hurt to stretch but I pulled her up, onto my bed, and sat her on my lap. I said softly, "Betsy will be back. She misses you. Don't worry." She smiled. I think, even at her age, she understood.

Now, I realize I may be just a little bit biased here, but little Caroline is sure to be extremely smart and as beautiful as her mother.

****

Three days later it was time for me to get out of bed and get Betsy released permanently. She was doing well, by all reports, but the doctors were convinced – via a huge donation to the hospital – that she needed to stay there rather than return to the County jail.

Truth be told, although I objected to all that time in

bed being taken care of by Sandy and Abena, it did me a lot of good. The pain had subsided into discomfort. I could get in and out of bed myself, and I could walk fairly well with the help of the cane. My left eye wasn't swollen anymore, but I still sported a multi-colored black eye. My lip had pretty well healed

Sandy and Abena both tried to dissuade me from getting on my feet, but I ignored them. Gandalf was in the room, smiling but saying nothing, as I struggled to get my feet on the floor. My chest reminded me that cracked ribs take a long time to heal, but I grinned through it. Neither woman needed to help me get to my clothes or help me dress; I managed on my own and was proud of the effort. It was virtually impossible for me to bend to tie my shoes, so I slipped into an old, raggedy pair of canvass loafers.

When I was dressed I stood proudly, but throwing out my 'very, very manly chest' only hurt, so I walked as best I could across the room to Gandalf.

"I'm gonna' need you to drive me around," I said to him. "Are you OK with that? I don't think I could drive right now."

"No problem, Mr. Crew. I have a suggestion, though."

"What's that?" I asked.

"Look," he began. He glanced over my shoulder towards Sandy who was standing on the other side of the room, her arms folded across her chest, and glaring at us. She wasn't happy. He said, "You were beaten badly and left to die . . . Which you would have had you not been found out there. Your Miss Concanon was almost murdered. Do you get the idea someone doesn't want you folks here sticking your nose into something they want hidden? I get that idea if you don't."

"I've had people try to kill me before," I said. "So far I'm still alive."

"Yeah, well you're in Texas now. There are more guns than people and more crazy cowboys who carry guns than people out here. I carry a gun." He pulled his very well cut grey suit jacket to the side to expose the shoulder holster that held a big Colt .45 semi-auto. "I think you need one, too."

Gandalf stepped to the side and took one long step to a chair nearby that held a black canvass bag he had brought with him. He unzipped it and pulled it open. His bear claw hand was halfway inside the bag when he stopped and looked back at me. He smiled and quickly took a pistol from the bag. He turned, holding it out towards me.

"This is a Smith and Wesson 9mm semi-automatic pistol. It holds eight rounds in the clip . . . The clip is lodged inside the handle." He pointed at the gun's handle and grinned mischievously. "The bullets come out this end," he said, pointing at the barrel. "If you have to shoot it, make sure I'm nowhere near you."

Anger had melted away and Sandy was trying hard not to laugh. She was holding Caroline and the baby sensed the humor and laughed along with her.

I took the big, black pistol from him and said, "Gandalf . . . Can I call you Gandalf?"

"That's my name."

"Good," I said. "Please call me Morgan. Gandalf, I want Sandy to have a gun, too. I want to know she and the baby are protected."

The big man went back to his bag and from it he took a small Smith and Wesson revolver. "This is a .38 Police Special," he said. "It's the smallest thing I have with me." He handed it to Sandy and asked, "Have you ever shot a gun?"

"Once or twice," Sandy said and smiled. She let Caroline slip to the floor. She flipped open the gun's cylinder and spun it like a TV cowboy. She was showing off, of course, but that's OK. I knew she knew what she was doing.

I said, "Sandy, I want you to stay here. Order food delivered . . . Don't go out."

"What about Betsy?" she asked.

"It would be best if you and the baby just stayed here. If the hospital calls and there's a problem . . . Go . . . But take the pistol with you. Gandalf's right. Somebody out there doesn't want us sticking our collective noses into the murder Betsy is charged with. I don't want you and the baby hurt. Just be careful and take care. Gandalf and I will be gone for a couple of days."

"Where are we going?" Gandalf asked. "Should I pack a bag?"

"We'll get what we need when we know where we're going," I said.

"Just where *are* you going, Morgan dear?" Sandy asked. She was worried of course. She and I have been together for enough years for her to know I rush in where angels fear to go. As was usual, she wanted to pull me back from the danger she figured I was about to rush toward.

I knew I couldn't put off Sandy about what I wanted to do, as I could put off Gandalf. She wouldn't allow me to do that. So, I took a moment to think and then I said, "You got addresses on the four guys who were at the bar, Gandalf?"

"Sure," he said. "It was easy. Like I said, they all have the same address on everything I looked at. It's a P.O. Box back in San Juan de Cristo. There are a couple dozen guys using that same box. Everybody's driver's license uses that box. Everything they have uses that same box."

"That doesn't make sense," Sandy said. "Can dozens of people use the same P.O. Box? Is that legal?"

Gandalf smiled maybe a little shyly and said, "Mrs. Crew. Out in these little, isolated, desert towns, there's not much in the way of law . . . Not like you and I know it, anyway. People turn a blind eye to little things like the postal laws and stuff like that."

"Can you find out who owns the box?" I asked.

"I already know."

I waited and Gandalf smiled.

"OK," I said. "So how about telling me . . . Or do I have to buy it from you?"

"No! Of course not," he said. "The name on the P. O. box is . . . Wait for it . . . Mr. John Smith."

"You're kidding," Sandy said.

"No, that's the name and the residence address is a piece of vacant land about twenty miles outside of San Juan de Cristo."

That little bit of fact convinced me there was something going on among the people at the bar the night Edgy Hands was killed. There had to be a conspiracy . . . A vast and big conspiracy of some kind. And Betsy was the victim, not the killer.

I asked Gandalf, "Did you get that information from the Post Office in San Juan?"

"No," he answered. "They don't like my kind there. I'm too dark for them. I have some people who are computer literate."

"You hacked into the Post Office computer?" Sandy asked and laughed.

"Of course," Gandalf said. "Does that kind of thing offend you?"

"Only if you get caught," she said. She laughed and Caroline laughed along with her. Gandalf grinned and Abena chuckled. I didn't laugh. Sandy can best be described as a street fighter who chooses her fights very carefully. She liked it when she or people working with her thumb their noses at authority. I did the same, but I don't take the chances others do.

I interrupted the good times by saying, "Gandalf, we've got only one place to start. That fella at the Mexican restaurant who's really an undercover ATF agent."

"You mean Jose?" Gandalf asked.

"Jose or Jorge," I said. "Whatever his name is."

"He's not ATF. He's a freelancer . . . He's on contract sometimes, when he can get one . . . He pretends to be a lot of things. He gets involved in stuff and then sells what he knows to whoever will buy it. I honestly don't know who he's working for today. I don't know if he's working for anyone. He goes around telling people he's really important and most people believe him. Chances are he's a dishwasher and nothing more."

"OK," I said. "Regardless of who he is, I think we need to go talk to him."

"I told you, I'm not very welcome out there."

"Ok," I said. "If you're afraid, I can understand that. I'll try driving myself . . . You can stay here with the women and children." I said it intentionally trying to work on his manhood. I knew what I said would get to him. I also knew I wasn't going to drive out into the desert alone.

"That's a load of crap, Morgan!" he said. He took a step towards me. Maybe I had really said the wrong thing. "If you wanna' go back there, I'll take you. But I'm not takin' any racist shit from those idiots."

"Good," I said. "Let's go."

CHAPTER TWELVE – I'm Not Sure What I'm Looking For

San Juan de Cristo was just a dark spot on the tan desert horizon as we drove a little too fast down the dusty road. The sunburned, cloudless sky of mid-afternoon reflected off the sand making waves of ocean-like heat rise and distort the horizon. It was impossible not to squint against the glare as we bounced along the dead straight unpaved road. As the little town got closer, it didn't look any better than the last time I was there.

We were on a slight rise – I hesitate to say hill because it really wasn't – that gave me a better view of the surrounding desert. San Juan de Cristo is isolated in the middle of nowhere. I could see nothing but sand, sage, cactus, and a few ugly trees that fought for life in the harsh environment. In the distance I could see the dark black paved streets inside the small town reflecting the heat and looking like streets of water. Gandalf brought his Cadillac to a slow stop at the top of the rise but kept the engine running for the sake of the air conditioner he had installed years before upon arriving in Texas. We were about two miles outside of town.

We sat in silence looking straight ahead. Finally, Gandalf asked, "So what do we do now? You want I should just drive into town and park in front of that Mexicano taco shop? Kind of obvious, isn't it?"

"You're right," I said. "There's no sense in confronting that Sheriff in broad daylight." I wish I had thought of that and waited a few hours before driving to Kronk's little town. "How about we go out to where the Bar H Ranch is."

"You think that Perkins guy has something to do with this?"

"Gandalf, my gut tells me he's right dead square in the middle of it."

Gandalf thought about that for a moment or two, and then asked, "Why?"

I answered, "Money. It's always money, Gandalf. Murders are always for personal gain . . . Almost always for money . . . Most often to hide money gotten illegally. And Harry Perkins appears to be the only one with money around here. I wish I had thought to hire an airplane. I keep forgetting how big this State is."

Gandalf suddenly threw the car into drive, floored the gas pedal, and turned the car suddenly to the left as he spun the big car in a 180. He slid off the side of the hard scrapple road, onto the desert sand, and back onto the road. I was holding on as tight as I could, wishing I hadn't unbuckled my seat belt when he had stopped the car. The Cadillac's tires screeched and kicked up a cloud of sand and stones as he took off back to where we had come from.

"What the hell are you doing?" I said, trying not to scream.

"You said you wanted an airplane. So we're gonna' get an airplane. OK?"

I managed to pull my seat belt around me and I held on as best I could as we bounced along the unpaved road. The speedometer was reading 80 MPH and then 90 MPH. The big car was fishtailing back and forth across the pot-holed, sand covered road. Gandalf slammed on the brakes to avoid a scrawny rabbit that had dashed across the road in front of us. It sent me forward. Violent pain shot across my chest as the seat belt tore into me. Then he floored the gas pedal again and the car approached 100 MPH. The road, thankfully, was straight and but not flat.

"What the hell are you doing!" I screamed. "Are you trying to kill us?"

He smiled but he said nothing. I glanced at the dashboard's odometer. One mile, then two. Five miles sped by before he eased his foot up and the car began to slow as he took a sharp right turn onto what was not more than two parallel ruts in the weed filled, hard packed desert. In the distance I saw a rusty Quonset hut . . . sitting alone in the middle of the brown nowhere we were racing through.

Gandalf let the car slow and he braked as he turned onto a rutted, gravel and weed filled path that led to the Quonset hut. He pulled to a stop at the side of the beat up, rust eaten, pile of metal. It had been patched with various materials, cloth, old metal signs, cardboard, and the patches had been patched over. There was an old gas pump in front of us. It once had been red but now showed only a vague suggestion of the color.

Gandalf grinned at me as he pulled himself from the Cadillac. He walked to an old hand-pumped water well that at one time was painted bright red but that day was more rust than metal. He pumped the handle hard and then splashed the grey water on his face and the back of his head. "I wouldn't drink this stuff if I were you, Morgan." He said. "But it will cool you off a little."

It hurt to get out of the car, the seat belt had irritated my bruised ribs. I decided to pass on the water. "Why are we here?" I asked.

Before Gandalf could answer, a beaten up, over-weathered wooden door at the front of the hut creaked loudly on old hinges as it opened. From inside, a woman, short and fat with dark skin like cracked leather, and thick black hair with gray dusted through it, stepped into the bright sun light. She was short and fatter at her stomach and the hips than at her shoulders. She wore faded jeans that were patched at the knees and torn in several places. Her shirt was bright red and looked as if it might have been sewn from hand woven wool. It hung loose over her waist. She stood in the doorway with an aged Winchester lever action 30-30 held, hammer cocked and ready to shoot.

The woman smiled as she recognized Gandalf, laid the rifle against the side of the building and opened her arms for him. Gandalf ran to her, grabbed her up and spun with her off the ground as she hugged him tightly. She was laughing, screeching like a crazy person.

Gandalf held her bulk up off the ground as he turned to me and said, "Morgan, this is the love of my life. This is Margaret Autumn Leaf. Maggie is a full blooded Comanche. She's the daughter of a chief and great-granddaughter of a war chief who took a whole lotta' scalps. Maggie, this is my good friend, Morgan Crew."

He carefully put the big woman back on her feet and said to her, "Morgan needs an airplane. You got one?"

The Indian woman laughed out loud in an ear splitting, high pitched screech. Her whole body, every inch of her huge body, was shaking and quaking with laughter. She shouted, "I got a fuckin' airplane? I got a fuckin' airplane? . . . Gandalf baby, you know I got a fuckin' airplane!"

She turned and stepped inside the old Quonset hut with Gandalf grinning like a kid on Christmas morning. He waived to me and I followed. Inside it took a moment for my eyes to adjust to the grey, dusty light. The smell of garbage and mold and mildew was overwhelming.

When Maggie flipped a switch on the wall three florescent tubes hanging from the ceiling struggled to turn on. They threw off enough light for me to see a ramshackle collection of paper and sticks and wire that someone, somewhere, at one time, might have called an airplane. It was a biplane, that was obvious. Nothing else was obvious about it.

The wings were patched together bits and pieces of cloth of every imaginable color and pattern, sort of a drunken grandmother's crazy quilt. Some pieces were stitched, others glued to the wings. The fuselauge of the plane looked as if it were brown paper stretched over wooden slats. There were rips in the paper but probably nothing that would be serious. There were two wheels under the wings, one larger than the other that caused the plane to tilt to the left.

Maggie laughed a shaking laugh again and asked, "You wonderin' what the fuck it is, huh? It's a bastard plane, huh? Little bit a' that and a little bit a' that an' who the hell was the momma and poppa? But it gonna fly you anywhere you wanna' go . . . 'bout forty miles there and forty back, huh? No more'an that or we go down in fuckin' flames!" And she screeched again so loud it reverberated against the metal of the hut.

Gandalf was laughing with Maggie. He slowed it down long enough to say, "Maggie made it herself . . . Took a lot of years . . . She started with a wreck of a World War I Sopwith Camel. There wasn't much left of it when she found it. She collected parts from here and there . . . from half a dozen different kinds of airplanes. Maggie's a terrific mechanic. She built the engine from scratch."

"And you're suggesting that I get in that . . . Thing . . . And make believe it's an airplane?" I said.

"Well." Gandalf said, laughing again. "I'm sure as hell not getting in it."

"Yeah, well I may not be a brain surgeon but I'm not stupid, either."

"Morgan, you want an airplane. This is the only airplane in a hundred miles that won't draw attention to you and what you're doing. Maggie is the only pilot who isn't going to ask questions." He turned to the fat Indian and asked, "Maggie, are you going to tell anyone about Morgan taking a ride in your airplane?"

"How I gonna' do that, Gandalf? You know I ain't got no registration for this plane."

"This . . . This pile of junk . . . It isn't registered?" I asked.

"Course not!" she said and screeched in laughter again. "Built the damn thing myself! Got parts from junk yards all over . . . Little bit a'this, little bit a'that. But it goes up really good."

"And I'll bet it comes down really good, too," I said.

****

In the end I strapped myself in the front seat as best I could, using a stiff, weathered, leather seatbelt as old as Maggie herself that I was sure would crumble and break before holding me into the seat. It was bolted to a hard wooden seat that I hoped was bolted down to the airplane itself. Maggie Autumn Leaf screeched in laughter as she throttled back and moved the ramshackle pile of assembled trash down a potholed and rocky stretch of dirt that was the closest thing to a runway there was.

The airplane, as Maggie called it, finally did leave the ground after bumping and bouncing and creaking and shaking and took to the air. I held on tight. Maggie turned and held a pair of ancient earphones up for me to see. I looked down and at my feet and I saw its twin. I put them on and I could hear Maggie over the roar of the engine. "Where you wanna' go?"

I held a small microphone close to my mouth and yelled into it to be heard over the loud and sputtering engine. "Make circles," I said. "Go further out each time. I'm not sure what I'm looking for, but I'll know it when I see it."

We spent the better part of an hour circling above the desert. And then, off in the distance, I saw something dark against the desert tan all around me. "Over there," I said into the microphone. I pointed to my left hoping Maggie would know what I wanted. But she saw what I had seen and banked the biplane to the left and I heard the engine being throttled up. We sped off.

As we got closer I saw a collection of buildings, lined up like barracks on a military base, in the middle of the barren desert. It was surrounded on all sides by a double row of chain link fence, making it a compound of some sort. There were trucks parked neatly to one side. It was in the center of a horse shoe shaped valley walled by rocky hills on three sides. A paved road led from the south into the valley and to the gates of the compound. And then I saw some flashes of light from the ground. I could hear the bullets as they flashed by all around us. The lower wing on the right side of the biplane was hit, tearing the paper.

Maggie pulled back on the stick and her ancient craft pulled up quickly. She turned the plane to the right, pulled back on the stick and rose into the few wispy clouds that broke up the hot blue of the Texas sky. We sped away from what we had found.

****

On the ground Maggie brought her biplane to a bumpy stop, kicking up a cloud of dust behind the biplane, at the front of her Quonset hut. The old, graying woman jumped from the back seat and landed on the ground like a twenty year old. She let spew a string of obscenities like I hadn't heard before as she examined the damage to the paper covered wing.

Gandalf walked close to me and helped me, all but picked me up and carried me, out of the biplane. My chest was throbbing and my head was spinning, but I made it to the ground. He held onto me and whispered, "You better give her some money . . . For the damage."

I peeled three one hundred dollar bills from my money clip, Gandalf nodded approval, and I handed them to

Maggie.   She took them but the string of obscenities continued.

Gandalf took my arm to keep me from falling face down into the dust. He walked me to his Cadillac and all but picked me up and put me in the passenger seat.

CHAPTER THIRTEEN – Fight Fire With Fire

Gandalf drove much slower than when we were on our way there as we drove away from Maggie's little, illegal airport and unlicensed patchwork biplane. My bruised ribs were throbbing again; my head was spinning. I tasted blood inside my mouth where I had lost the teeth. But I had to put it behind me. I had to go on. I had found, I was sure, what I was looking for.

The reason that Edgy Hands was murdered in such a violent manner was unanswered as far as I was concerned. I knew that Betsy had not killed Edgy. She would have run, as she had run for years before. I know Betsy's background as a thief and pickpocket, but I didn't believe she had murder in her heart. There is always a reason for murder and if Betsy had not killed the boy, than I had found the reason. I have learned over the years that Dr. Freud was right when he postulated that nothing is a coincidence. The money in that part of Texas lay with the Perkins. The compound was, I was sure, on the property of the Bar H Ranch. The young men I had met and learned about were all military types. The compound looked military to me. Connecting Edgy Hands to the compound hidden in the desert valley was what I had to do.

Gandalf was quiet as I thought and he concentrated on maneuvering the big car, trying to avoid most of the rocks and pot holes. He recognized that I was in pain and tried as best as he could to make the drive as easy as he could for me. After twenty minutes he finally asked, "OK, are you going to tell me what the hell that was all about?"

"I was looking for something. I think I found it."

"Yeah, you found a bunch of bullet holes in Maggie's plane."

That was true of course. And the bullets told me what I had found was, indeed, what I needed to find. "There's some kind of compound out there. Buildings . . . Trucks . . . All fenced . . . Like a military base."

"Yeah," Gandalf said. "So what? There's army bases all over the friggin' place."

"Would they shoot at a ragged biplane? That place wasn't a U.S. military base."

He thought about that. It didn't take long for him to say, "OK, so you're right. What now?"

"I want a closer look at whatever is there," I said.

Gandalf said very simply, "Why?"

It seemed simple enough to me, and I had to believe it was as simple to Gandalf. He was testing, of course. He wanted to be sure of what he was getting involved in. He wanted to be sure I knew what I was doing.

"Because," I explained, "all this is connected in some way. There's no good reason for a dusty little remote town to set up a murder except to cover something up. This place is too isolated and dirty to have a compound that shoots at rickety old biplanes . . . except to cover something up. I've learned over the years that money is always somehow involved in the bad things that happen. The only money around here is at the Bar H Ranch. That money belongs to the Perkin's family and Jimmy Perkins set up Betsy Concanon for the murder . . . To cover something up. Why cover up nothing? I believe it has to be what Maggie and I found out there in that valley. It's all connected. It has to be."

Gandalf smiled, satisfied, and asked, "OK, where's

this compound?"

"That's a problem. I'm not sure. We were flying in expanding circles, maybe a little short of an hour, when we were shot at. I'm not really sure where it is."

"What was around it? What was the ground like?"

"Desert," I said and felt stupid for it. "I mean . . . I guess it was pretty flat where the compound was . . . But there were hills on either side now that I think of it. Not tall hills, but hills anyway. Sort of long . . . It formed sort of a valley I suppose. And inside the compound . . . I mean inside what I think was a fence, were buildings lined up like military barracks. And there were several trees. I remember thinking . . . Before we were shot at . . . That they were unusual. I mean, they were the only trees around. Everything was brown and barren except for those trees. And there was what I think was a river . . . Maybe a stream, I'm not sure. I mean, there just wasn't a whole lot to see out there. But we were shot at and that means whoever was down didn't want us there, they wanted whatever it is kept a secret."

Gandalf thought for a minute or two. He let is big foot slide off the gas pedal letting the car slow to a crawl. He said, "That's not much to go on. But I'm going to take a stab in the dark." He was quiet again and then said, "Look, if this place is some kind of hideout . . . Or something secret . . . It's got to be further south . . . And maybe near the border. There aren't too many hills and streams down there . . . In fact there's not a lot of anything except a lot of cactus and snakes. But if you saw a valley with a stream running through it I think I can find that. As a matter of fact, if I were going to set up some secret compound, that's where it would be."

"OK, let's go find it," I said.

****

Gandalf's bright red Cadillac Biarritz convertible would not make it across the desert where the best roads are not more than rutted tracks in the sand. So we headed back to El Paso where he borrowed a 4 X 4 Land Rover that had been converted and customized to handle just about any off-road condition. It had huge wheels and was raised up so much I had trouble climbing into it. Gandalf had to lift me into the cab.

At his suggestion and with his help, I bought a couple of backpacks and filled them with MREs and bottled water. We outfitted ourselves with desert camo fatigues and hats, as well as military desert boots. We bought a lightweight nylon tent and Gandalf suggested warm, down sleeping bags, saying, "It gets pretty damn cold out there at night.

And finally, we stopped at a warehouse, owned by Gandalf as it turned out, and from inside we added to what we would carry. He pulled from a rack of several dozen pistols and rifles, a couple of Berretta 9mm pistols with webbing and holsters, and four spare clips of ammo each. Gandalf also took from the rack of rifles, an H&K MP5 submachine gun. He packed a dozen extended clips of ammo into our backpacks, grinned like a kid on Christmas morning, and said, "I think we have everything, Morgan."

"Are we going to need to look like an army?" I asked. "I don't intend to make a frontal assault on that place."

"Whoever's out there shot at a patched up biplane. I doubt they would hesitate to kill us and bury us in the desert. If you really want to find out what's out there . . . And if I'm going to go with you . . . Then we're going to go heavy. You fight fire with fire, Morgan," he said as he led me back to the Land Rover.

****

I convinced Gandalf that we needed to go back to the hotel and let Sandy know we would be gone for a few days.

Sandy is the strongest, most centered women I have ever known, but she also worries about me. I'm not sure if it's because she loves me or because she knows I can screw up everything I touch. Oh well.

In any case, I didn't tell her what we had done or what we were going to do. No need to worry her needlessly. I told her we were going out to find the young men who worked at the Bar H, which I thought was in all likely hood the truth. I had a feeling deep in my gut that they were more members of whatever was inside the compound than ranch hands at the Bar H. I hoped she was curious enough to look in the back of the big Land Rover to find all our equipment. The guns would be hard to explain.

Sandy kissed me on the cheek and told me to be careful. Caroline was taking a nap so I was careful not to wake her when I kissed her on the forehead and pulled her blanket up around her.

We drove off, leaving Sandy standing in the parking lot, arms folded, and looking very worried. It took a couple of hours but soon we were in some of the most desolate country I'd ever seen. The overriding color was sand, with a few patches of green cactus and the rare Joshua tree struggling to survive in the heat.

We had left paved roads behind and were bouncing across the desert. I didn't ask Gandalf where we were going; I could only hope he had some kind of hunch. I played nervously with the Berretta; Gandalf glanced at me regularly and said, "Be careful with that thing. Don't shoot me, OK?"

It was blazingly hot and the Land Rover didn't have an air conditioner. The rolled down windows didn't help except to send streams of heat and dust into the cab. We drove for what seemed like endless hours not seeing anything. I was starting to nod off when Gandalf brought the car to a slow stop. I looked up and saw a short, rocky hillside about fifty yards in front of us. "From here we walk,"

Gandalf said. And walk we did.

My chest was throbbing; I wished I had wrapped it tighter. We started up the rocky rise; Gandalf had to stop often, look back, and wait for me to catch up. I stumbled and slid down the slope a few feet, but I hid the pain and quickly caught up with the big man. He took my backpack from me, carrying both his and mine and all our equipment and guns without saying anything and we continued up.

At the top of the hill we stopped. Gandalf laid the two backpacks, the tent and the guns down and I sat quickly to take in quick mouthfuls of air. I took a bottle of water from one of the backpacks and drank deeply. It was warm but I didn't care. Gandalf was standing with his back to me, looking out onto the desert below. Without turning he said, "I think we may have found it, Morgan."

I stood and walk to stand next to him. Shielding my eyes from the flames of the Texas sun, I looked where he was looking. There, off in the distance, was I was sure it was the fenced compound I had seen from Maggie Autumn Leaf's old biplane. It was surrounded by the valley I had seen from above. The hills on either side and to the north were surrounded by the colorless desert, but it was what I had seen. I could make out the few trees, the only color anywhere to be seen. And I could see the faint image of the stream I had seen from far above. The twisting snakelike stream was more brown than blue water, but I could see it moved, slowly but still moving south,

On the far side of the compound and behind what we saw were more rocky hills and cliffs that formed the horseshoe shaped valley I had seen with Maggie Autumn Leaf. There, straight as an arrow, was the imprint of the road running across the desert into the compound. It was paved in black inside the compound and for some distance outside, past the tall gates that were closed as I looked down upon them. "So," Gandalf asked. "Is that what you saw?"

"Yes. It looks even stranger from the ground than it

did from above."

"And what do we do now?" he asked.

"We get closer," I answered as I picked up my backpack. "I want to stay in the hills and I don't want anyone to know where here. But I want a closer look. Can we do that?"

"I can do it. You look like a pile of shit that's been hit by a truck. Can you do it?"

I smiled as best I could and we started off, clambering across the rocks. I tripped and stumbled now and then, but with Gandalf's help we went on. We stayed to the side of the hill away from the eyes inside the compound. The sun was falling into the west and the air started to cool. A breeze arose without warning. Before long it was dark and I was getting cold. Above me the black sky was crowded with stars, and below me, not more than a mile away now, was the compound, brightly lit by tall flood lights and busy with people milling around.

We found a place not far further on where the ground was fairly level and surrounded by big rocks. It was a place we could stay hidden and observe what was going on below us. Gandalf tossed the nylon tent aside and unrolled the two sleeping bags. He opened a couple of MREs and two bottles of water. "It's cold rations," he said. I watched him tear open a foil package of food and pour some water into it. I copied what he was doing. "This stuff tastes better when it's hot," he said. "But we can't risk a fire."

The 'stuff' was awful, but I ate it anyway. I could have used a cup of coffee, but Gandalf was right, a fire would just draw attention and the smell of coffee . . . Or any other cooked food for that matter . . . Would spread across the clear desert air to draw attention.

After eating, Gandalf pulled himself into a sleeping bag. He almost fit when he curled himself into eat. But he pulled it as best he could around himself and was asleep almost immediately.

I stretched out on the rough ground between two boulders. Using the Steiner binoculars I had bought I gazed down into the compound. It was fenced as I had thought, but it was more fence than I had imagined. It was at least eight feet tall, chain link, with coils of barbed wire fastened across the top. The inside of the fence was lined with tall poles that held lights bright enough to make the place look like mid-day.

There was a line of big trucks inside, maybe ton and a half or bigger. Three were canvassed covered over the beds and two open beds without covering.

Six buildings, long and single story, painted a dull brown, were lined up barrack style in parallel. Another building stood off to the side of these, longer but not taller. On the far end of the compound, was what appeared to be a warehouse; at least it looked like a warehouse. It was bigger than the other buildings and taller. "What the hell could that place be?" I remember wondering.

I looked at my watch; it was early, only slightly past nine PM. Gandalf was snoring away but inside the compound men were awake and moving, sitting and talking, and a few were cleaning big, mean looking rifles. These were not hunting rifles, they were military. There was no mistake about that. And the men weren't in uniform. I could see various colors of shirts and a few wore big cowboy hats.

The desert night was getting colder. I reached behind me and pulled my sleeping bag over me, but sleep evaded me. I held the binoculars and watched the compound for . . . I don't know for how long . . . Until only the fence lights remained on and all the men had retreated into the barracks buildings, locking the tall gates for the night. I wanted to go down there, to get a close look at whatever it was, but I knew that I had to climb down the side of the cliffs and cross open desert to get there. And my chest was throbbing after the days hike.

Eventually sleep covered me and I dreamed of

holding Sandy tight and making love to her. The dream was broken by Gandalf's bear claw hand shaking my shoulder. "You've been dreaming," he said, grinning. "Must have been a good one."

It was bright daylight. The sun was a quarter of the way above the eastern horizon. Gandalf was chewing on a piece of beef jerky and a granola bar. He tossed me one of each and said, "Breakfast. Enjoy it."

I told him what I had seen down at the compound. "That's weird," he said. "There's not any military base around here . . . At least none I've ever heard of."

"I really wanted to go down there," I said. "But my chest was . . ."

He interrupted me. "Good thinking. You'd probably get yourself killed. I'll go tonight, after dark, after they've all gone to bed. Are you sure there weren't any guards posted?"

"I watched for hours," I said. "There was nobody moving. There are two towers, maybe guard towers, but I couldn't see anybody up in them . . . Maybe cameras, but I couldn't see any."

"OK. I'll go after dark."

We spent the day laying among the rocks and passing the binoculars back and forth. There was a lot of activity below us. We counted perhaps twenty-five men working various tasks inside and outside the compound. Men were raking and sweeping the dirt grounds; others were doing work on several of the big trucks; and just outside the fence a group of men were firing various weapons at a professional looking gun range. After half an hour of practice, three light machine guns – M240s as I learned later – were set up and one by one, a dozen men took turns raking the targets with blasts of bullets.

There was a double gate crossing the road that led into the compound. It lay open, two men with what appeared to be AK47s stood guard. The sun was almost directly above us when a small pickup truck bounced along the dirt road, onto the pavement and into the compound. Four men approached as the driver got out. He stood talking to three of them as the fourth drove the pickup into the warehouse. Minutes later it was driven out. A small attaché case was handed to the man who had driven the truck in; he shook hands with the four around him, got back in the truck and drove off.

"What the hell was that all about?" I asked Gandalf.

"Drugs," he answered. "Gotta' be drugs . . . Couldn't be anything else."

That made sense, I thought. Money . . . It was always money. I took a broad leap and felt assured there was a connection between Edgy Hands' murder and the compound. There was nothing else in these hundred square miles of desert that was worth a conspiracy to cover up a murder. And young Jimmy Perkins made the connection to the Bar H Ranch. All I needed to do was prove that connection.

The afternoon passed slowly; I tried to ignore its heat. As we hid amongst the boulders Gandalf ate two more cold MREs; I settled for several granola bars and a few pieces of jerky. Gandalf rationed the water. "Hey, it has to last as long as we're here. There aren't any 7-11 stores around to buy more," he said and laughed. The sun began to set behind the hills to the west. Dusk settled in and the air began to cool once again.

Night darkness surrounded us and Gandalf stripped off his webbing, leaving everything lying at his feet. "I'm going down there now," he said kneeling beside me. 'I'm going to get inside and take a look inside that warehouse. If it's what I think it is . . . I've got some friends in the DEA that'll owe me a big favor."

"You're not going to go armed?" I asked.

"I want to get in and out without anyone knowing I was there. A gun would only alert everyone . . . And to paraphrase, you don't take a 9 MM pistol to a machine gun fight."

CHAPTER FOURTEEN – Fish

During the heat of the day and into the night the flies, the sand fleas, and ants were a torment to us. They buzzed around our heads and crawled up my sleeves and pants legs. I swatted them away and scratched where the ants bit. They didn't seem to annoy Gandalf as much as they did me. I said nothing, but I wished I had brought along a large bottle of insect repellant.

The insects were big and some were small. They were black, they were grey, but when Gandalf stood, turned to smile encouragingly down at me, and took the first few steps toward the edge of the hillside to start down the rocky cliff. For the first time he rose above the boulders. The red insect that settled on his forehead was a new one, one I hadn't seen before. And then it occurred to me that it wasn't an insect . . . I had seen this bug before. This bug was the target of a laser.

The back of Gandalf's head was blown away as I tried to get to him and pull him down to the ground. He lay on his back in the dust, eyes wide in surprise, blood and brains spilling from under his head. I started to crawl backwards. Fear kept my eyes locked on Gandalf. I wanted to get up and run but I seemed to be frozen to the ground and the world was spinning wildly around me.

The air filled with a howling that fell on me hard and hurt like hell. A blindingly bright light from above surrounded me. The dust and sand was stirred up and blacked out my last vision of Gandalf Finch.   Out of the blinding cloud something hit me hard in my lower back as I fought to crawl away. The pain was like a red hot rod slicing up my spine.

"Git' the hell up, som'bitch!" someone screamed. I couldn't see anything through the sand being kicked up. "Git up, I said!" and then I was kicked again this time in my stomach. I pushed myself to my feet, doubled over, trying to ignore the pain. When I was on my feet, trying to block the blowing sand with my hands, I realized for the first time that a helicopter was above me. As I looked up at it, the man who was yelling at me struck out with the butt of the rifle he carried.   His target was my head and he hit his target squarely. When I woke up, I was lying on a cold concrete floor in a dark room, my hands and feet tied tightly behind me.

****

Sandy passed the time at our suite in El Paso nervously.   She played with Caroline; she read the newspapers; she watched some TV, she tried to start reading a book, but her mind kept wandering from it. She took our baby to the zoo twice. But what she did more than anything was worry.   Five days passed and she heard nothing.

Abena went back to her day care job. She sent one of her employees to babysit every time Sandy went to the hospital to visit Betsy. Other than that . . . The days passed slowly.

On the hot afternoon of the sixth day, Sandy was sitting under an umbrella on the resort's patio watching Caroline splash in the kid's pool. C laughed and Sandy laughed with her. She cooled herself with a tall iced tea.

A liveried bellman walked – uncomfortably – to Sandy. "Excuse me, Mrs. Crew," he said uneasily. "There is a . . . A young man here to see you." He looked to the rear and pointed to a short black man, young and dressed like a street gang drug dealer. "Shall I phone the police? He asked for you by name."

Sandy looked at him. He swayed back and forth from his right foot to his left and back again. He wore black jeans, hung low on his hips exposing the top two inches of bright red plaid undershorts. He wore a black sweat shirt, called a 'hoodie', hanging open and pulled over his head. Big Nikes were on his feet, unlaced.

"No," Sandy said. "No police. Not yet. It depends on what he wants. Stay nearby, please and ask him to come here."

The boy walked in a streetwise dance across the big patio drawing the attention and ire of the well-heeled patrons enjoying their afternoon cocktails. He stopped at Sandy's umbrella shaded table and said, "Hey, mama. You Sandy Crew?"

"I am," she answered. "Please sit down. Would you like something? Something to drink?"

The boy sat and slouched down in the padded metal chair. "No," he said, grinning dangerously. "I ain't thirsty or nothin'. I gotta talk to you, mama."

"I'm not your mama," Sandy said. "My name is Mrs. Crew. Now sit up straight and pull the damn hood off your head. You're drawing unwanted attention. I don't want the police rushing in here."

He smiled again, took a moment or two but pulled himself upright sitting tall in the chair. When he pulled the black sweatshirt hood off his head he revealed short cropped hair died a very bright and very unnatural yellow. And big diamond earrings gleamed from his earlobes.

He said nothing, but he stared sharply at Sandy. Finally, she asked, "What do you want?"

"You know Gandy?" the boy asked.

"Gandy? I don't know anyone named Gandy."

"Gandalf Finch," the boy said, nasty annoyance in his

deep voice. "I call him Gandy."

Sandy was unsure of where this was going. She looked behind the boy and felt better seeing the bellman and two hotel security guards standing nearby. "Yes, I know Gandalf Finch," she said. "Why?"

"Cause he dead," the boy said harshly. "An' I wanna' know why."

"Dead! Gandalf's Dead? Why? How?"

Abena Ekundayo walked towards them. She was crying, holding a big handkerchief to her face, wiping her eyes. She went to Caroline and lifted her from the water. "I'll take her to your room, Mrs. Crew. You and Fish should talk there."

The boy – Fish as Abena called him – stood and motioned for Sandy to follow him and Abena. Sandy stood, stopped to ask the two security guards to wait outside the suite, and followed Abena and Fish into the sitting room of the suite. Inside, Abena took Caroline into a bedroom to dry and dress her. Fish slumped into an over-stuffed wing chair and Sandy pulled the chair from the telephone desk near him. She sat and asked, "Gandalf is dead? That can't be."

"They pulled his body from the Rio Grande. The Mexi' side. Floatin' face down in the mud. His fuckin' head was blown off."

Abena opened the bedroom door and said sharply, "You watch your language, young man. I won't have any of that."

Fish sat up straight in the chair again and said, "I'm sorry, Abena. I'm just really pissed off."

Abena shut the bedroom door behind her and left Sandy and the young man alone. Sandy worked her way through the shock of the death of Gandalf Finch and into worry about me. "What about my husband? He was with Gandalf," she asked.

"I don't know nothin' 'bout him. Gandy was alone . . . When the Mexi's found him. I wanna' know why he's dead."

Sandy was suspicious about this young man's motives. Abena seemed to know him and seemed to have some relationship with him, maybe family, maybe not. She asked, "Who are you?"

"Told you," he said, sounding annoyed again. "I'm Fish."

"That's your street name. What's your real name?"

He glared at her, that street anger look that seems to be ever so common. Sandy repeated, "What's your name?"

"Robert Finch," he said. "They call me Fish."

"Finch? You're related to Gandalf somehow?"

He shifted uncomfortably, trying to make faces that looked mean, trying to intimidate. He didn't know Sandy. If he had he would have known that she can be as angry as anyone and when she gets angry, it would be best to clear the room and leave her alone.

"He's my ol' man," Fish said.

"Gandalf is your father? I didn't know he had a family."

"Yeah, well f'get that," Fish said. "I wanna' know who killed him. If your ol' man did that . . . He's dead, unner'stand?" He shifted again in the chair. Sandy was beginning to see that he was more uncomfortable, upset, and ill at ease than dangerous.

"Morgan wouldn't do that," Sandy said softly. "He's not the kind to do that."

"Gandy was out with your ol' man. What were they doin'?"

"What did your father tell you he was doing?" Sandy asked.

"F'get that!" he said sharply. "Yo mama. I ask the damn questions."

"I told you I'm not your mama. Address me as Mrs. Crew or get out. I know you're upset . . . I'm getting upset, too. Your father was our friend. He was helping us. You have my deepest sympathy. Now if you want my help, tell me what Gandalf told you."

Fish's eyes locked on Sandy's. She didn't flinch, she stared back. She had to show this boy that she was stronger than he was. Finally he said, "Me and Gandy didn't talk much. He was always on my case, ya' know? Wanted me t'go to school and all that shit, ya'know? Didn't want me hangin' with my homies, ya' know?"

"Hanging with your homies," Sandy asked. "That means you're in a gang, right?"

"That's whitey talkin' lady. Me and my home boys just hang, ya' know? We family, ya' know?" He was making gang signs with his hands that were meaningless to Sandy.

"Yes, I think I know," Sandy said. She called to Abena and asked her to come into the sitting room.

"Can you stay with Caroline for an hour or two?" she asked her. "I need to go out with Mr. Fish."

"Hey! I ain't goin' nowhere with you, mama," Fish said in trying to sound tough and threatening..

Abena said sternly, "Young man. You are going to do what this lady says to do. She can do things you can't. If you want to find out what happened to your father, you listen to her, understand? And you speak respectfully, too. I will drag your tight little ass into Pastor Lanton's church gym again. And you know what happens when he puts the gloves on and steps into the ring with you."

"OK, OK," he said. "I'll go along for a little while. But when I getting' played, ya' know, me and my home boys are gonna' take over."

Sandy checked on Caroline and found her sleeping soundly in her crib. Abena smiled, Sandy whispered a thank you, and she led Fish from the suite. She rented a car, a Buick sedan at the Hertz office in the lobby. "Can you drive?" she asked Fish.

"Can I drive? You trying to dis' me? 'Course I can drive."

"And do you have a driver's license?" she asked,

smiling, knowing the answer.

"What driver's license?" he said. "That's whitey tellin' folks what they can do and what they can't do, ya' know."

"Yeah, that's what I figured," Sandy said. "Look, I don't know my way around this city. I'm going to let you drive. But if you get stopped by the police or get in an accident, I'm going to say you kidnapped me and hang you out to dry. Understand?"

"Yo' mama . . . I mean Mrs. Crew . . . I'm used to whitey hangin' us black folks out t'dry."

"And stop calling me whitey, too. I find that offensive. I haven't used offensive racial terms on you, have I?" Sandy said and handed Fish the keys to the rental.

Fish slid behind the wheel of the car and looked to his right. Sandy was standing at the passenger side of the car. He rolled the power window down and asked, "You comin'?"

"I'm used to gentlemen opening doors for me," she said.

"You kiddin' me?" he said and laughed uneasily.

Sandy stood waiting. Fish asked, "And what happens if I just drive off and leave you standing there?"

"Then I call the police and report you stole my car. That's grand theft auto. You want that or do you get out of the car, come around here and open this damn door for me."

Fish did get out and walked, slowly, trying to look dangerous, around the rear of the car. He opened the door and Sandy got in. She said, "You slam the door and you'll open it and close it until you get it right." Fish didn't slam the door, even though he wanted to.

Behind the wheel once again Fish started the engine and asked, "Where to, madam?"

"Do you know where The Stephen H. Maxwell Clinic is?" Sandy asked.

"That rich white folk place?" Fish asked. "Yeah, some a'my homeboys does business with them, ya' know."

"Business?" Sandy asked. "What kind of business?"

"You don't wanna' know, Ms. Crew. Leave it like that."

And Sandy decided to leave it like that. She figured that if she knew too much about the young man, she would lose any help he may be able to give her. He pulled out of the parking lot and reached over to the radio, finding a station that broadcast Rap and nothing else. He turned the volume up; Sandy reached over and switched off the radio. "We need to think," she said. "That won't help."

As they drove across town she asked, "Why Fish? How did you get that name?"

"My name's Finch, ya'know? My homeboys calls me Fish . . . Like Finch but not, ya'know?"

That made sense to her. Street names were important to street kids. But she had an idea that she might be able to teach Fish something about being socially . . . Normal, but then what was normal? She tried to decide if that was the correct phrase. It didn't matter really, she had started with the car's door. Lesson number one.

Fish found a parking spot at the clinic under a tree, out of the Texas sun and as far from the front entrance as there was. "You want I should come wit' you?"

Lesson number two. Sandy said, "I would like you to get out of the car and open my door for me . . . Like a gentleman."

"Hey lady! How long you gonna' keep this shit up, huh?"

"Watch your language. I don't appreciate it. And I will keep this shit up until I feel comfortable with you being near me," she said. "Now get out . . . Quickly . . . Walk around the car . . . Open the door and hold it open for me. That's how a gentleman treats a lady."

"You a lady, Ms. Crew?"

"Any woman who expects to be treated like a lady is a lady. A woman who wants to be treated like a slut . . . Like a whore . . . Like anything but a lady, is not a lady. Now get out."

Fish chuckled and got out of the car. He was grinning like a kid when he opened the passenger side door and bowed extravagantly as Sandy got out. "That's good," she said. "But skip the bow from now on."

Fish was two steps behind Sandy as she walked to the front entrance of the clinic. She stopped at the closed door and waited. Fish laughed again and reached around to open the door for her. "Thank you, Robert," she said, calling him by his given name.

"It's Fish," he said simply.

"While you're with me, your name is Robert," Sandy said as she walked into the clinic's lobby. "Get used to it."

The nurses at the front desk were used to seeing Sandy as she had been visiting Betsy every day without missing a day. She normally had Caroline with her. The nurses looked suspiciously at the black dressed street thug who was with her that day.

Betsy was sitting in a chair in her room, reading a book and listening to some music on a CD player Sandy had brought her. She smiled welcomingly at Sandy and looked wonderingly at Fish. She started to push herself out of the chair, but Sandy told her to stay seated. Sandy gave her a welcome kiss on her cheek and introduced Fish.

"This is Robert Finch. He is Gandalf's son," she said. "Something terrible has happened. Gandalf has been murdered . . . We don't know by whom."

Betsy, without standing, said to Fish, "I'm so sorry. That's just awful. Your Father?"

"Yeah, young babe. Me and him wasn't very close . . . But I'm gonna' find out who killed him. And you can call me Fish, ya'know?"

Sandy added, "We're all very upset and we offer our sympathy and condolences to Robert. But to add to our grief, Morgan is missing. I don't know where he is."

"What!", Betsy said. She pushed herself out of the

chair, obviously still in some discomfort. "Missing? You don't think . . ."

"I don't want to think about that," Sandy said. "But I need to find out what happened. And I need your help."

"Anything," Betsy said. "You know that."

"Can you get out of here without anyone knowing you're gone?"

"Yes . . . I guess so . . . Maybe tonight . . . After dark," Betsy said.

"Fine. Robert will be waiting for you in the parking lot. Let's make it about 1 AM? Can you do that? Are you feeling well enough to do that?"

"Sure, no problem," Betsy said. "I may not be able to run, but I can walk . . . And most of the staff here sleep on duty after midnight anyway."

"Fine," Sandy said. "I'm going to buy a car for you to use . . . Nothing flashy . . . But I don't want you traced on airplanes or trains."

"You want me to take C again, right?"

Fish asked, "Who's this C?"

"My daughter, Caroline. Betsy calls her C."

"Yo, mama. That's cool," Fish said with a broad smile and nodding head.

Sandy said turning her attention to Betsy, "Anyway. Yes, I want you to take Caroline and disappear . . . Like you did last time. I'll have a cell phone for you to keep on, but don't make calls on it and only answer my calls. Can you drive a car?"

Betsy answered, "Yes, sure. I might have to stop a lot . . . But I can do that."

"Where you gonna' go, mama?" Fish asked.

Betsy answered, "You don't want to know. Last time I just vanished. No one will find me . . . and C will be safe."

Sandy smiled and hugged Betsy. Betsy appreciated the faith placed in her, but she flinched at her unhealed wound.

****

At five minutes past one in the morning, Betsy was dressed in clothes Sandy had smuggled in for her and started from her room. The hallway was dimly lit and the only sound was the faint buzzing of fluorescent tubes along the ceiling. The still air carried the faint odors of hospital cleansers and cigarette smoke from a break room where the night security guard was drinking stale coffee, reading old magazines, and smoking. Betsy stepped into the hall and eased the door closed behind her. Glancing right and then left, and then right again she walked barefoot, shoes held in her hands, toward the hospital lobby and the main entrance.

She knew that an exit door was very near her room but she also knew it was alarmed. The night security guard would not leave the break room until four that morning when the day staff began to arrive. The alarm would get him moving. The main entrance was unlocked and not alarmed 24/7. But the lobby also had an office and desk where a nurse sat throughout the night shift. Betsy had made a move earlier the evening, as dinner was brought to her room, to overcome this obstacle.

The night nurse, Filetta, had befriended Betsy. More than once she had told Betsy, giggling like a High School girl, that she thought Corretto, a night attendant, was "lindo estupendo" – super cute. That evening, when Corretto brought her dinner, Betsy told him what Filetta had said. "I think tonight you should make your play for her," Betsy whispered with a suggestive wink and sly grin. And Corretto did just that.

As Betsy reached the lobby she hugged the wall and carefully looked around the corner. Half the ceiling lights in the lobby were turned off bringing an eerie grey to the empty room. Filetta was nowhere to be seen. The door to a file room behind the reception desk was closed. She heard giggling and whispering from inside.   Corretto was doing what she hoped he would do.   Betsy smiled and walked silently out the front doors.

The parking lot was lit by several tall flood lights.   The night air was cold and a breeze moved the leaves on the trees lining the parking lot.   There were only three cars parked in the lot that night and none of them had Fish waiting for her.   Betsy's first thought was that he had chickened out.   Then she heard a soft whistle and looked to her left.   In the shadows, at the side of the lot near a big garbage dumpster, away from the lot's lights, Fish stood, waving at her to get her attention.

She couldn't run, but she walked as quickly as she could.   Fish had the passenger side door open and she stiffly slid into the car.   When he was behind the wheel and they were leaving the clinic, he said, "Yo mama, thought you flaked out on me."

"I think Sandy would say that I ain't your mama," Betsy said.   "And I thought you had chickened out on me.   I guess we were both wrong."

By the time the sun was up that morning, Betsy was almost two hundred miles away from El Paso. Caroline was soundly asleep in a car seat strapped into the rear of the Toyota Sandy had provided.   There was $10,000 in cash and a brand new cell phone in her purse.   The small .38 that Gandalf had given Sandy was in the glove box.   Betsy would disappear and wait for Sandy . . . Or me . . . To phone her and tell her to come home.

CHAPTER FIFTEEN – Rosita

The phone on the nightstand next to the bed woke Sandy. She had waited until she thought Betsy and the baby were safely away before retiring to bed. She had sent Fish home, telling him he needed to get better clothes if he were going to be with her and help her. "I've got people to talk to, and I don't want them frightened of you." When Fish left, shaking his head and mumbling something to himself, Sandy showered and crawled into the big bed, pulling the comforter over her. Sleep evaded her but finally flooded over her. It was 6 AM when the phone rang.

She was half awake when she answered. "This is Fish," he said. "You there?"

"Yes . . . Robert . . . I was asleep. What time is it?"

"Straight up six," he said. "I been waiting for you to phone. What we gonna' do? You plannin' on sleepin' the damn day away?"

"Don't curse, Robert. Where are you?"

"I been sittin' in the lobby fo' long enough fo' the rent-a-cops to tell me I gotta' go."

"OK," Sandy said as she rubbed the sleep from her eyes. "Come to the suite. I'll leave the door unlocked. Wait in the sitting room. I'll have some coffee sent up from room service. I'll be out in twenty minutes."

And when Sandy opened the bedroom door a half hour later, Fish was sitting cross legged in a chair, holding a large Starbucks coffee. "I got you a big latte'. That stuff out of room service ain't no good." He pointed to a tall paper cup on the room's desk. Sandy thanked him and reached for the hot coffee.

Fish was dressed in blue jeans, not new, well faded, but clean. He wore a white shirt, open at the collar, that was a size too big for him, but it too was clean. He wore black leather, laced shoes that were clean and polished. His hair was no longer bright yellow. And it was freshly cut close. The diamond earrings he had worn the day before were gone.

Sandy stood across the room from him, drinking the coffee, and looking at him. He smiled and asked, "So how I look? You can take me with you?"

"You look good," she said, smiling appreciatively.

"Yo, Mama . . . I mean Mrs. Crew . . . This ain't me. I just doin' this 'cause I wanna' kill whoever killed my ol' man. An' I figure you gonna' help me do that."

"The idea is to find out what's going on without having to kill anyone. Dead people usually don't talk." Sandy drank some coffee and asked, "Are you carrying a gun?"

"No. 'Course not," he said. "I figured you wouldn't like that. But I got me a gun back in the car. It a big friggin' Beretta. Scare the hell outta' people, ya'know? That OK with you?"

"Some rules," Sandy said. She pulled the leather chair away from the room's desk and sat facing Fish. "I decide what we do, and you do what I tell you to do. That gun will stay in the car. It will be used only to keep you and me . . . And Morgan, of course . . . from being killed. Do you have a problem with any of that?"

"No prob', lady. Just un'nerstan' that when I finds out who iced Gandy, I'm gonna' kill the bastard."

Sandy drank the last of the latte' and tossed the empty cup in the trashcan. She looked deeply at Fish and asked, "Why? I thought you and Gandalf didn't get along? I don't get it."

"Ms. Crew," Fish said. "Gandy was my ol' man. He wanted me to do stuff I didn't wanna' do, ya' know. He wanted me off the streets and like away from my homeboys. My boys, they my brothers, they my family, ya' know. Gandy didn't stick around when I was a kid . . . That pissed me off. But there's somethin' I ain't gonna admit to no one but you. Gandy always took care of me. I needed somethin', like clothes and stuff like that . . . He was always there. He gave me this great red bike when I was a kid. I wouldn't wear the stupid clothes he gave me, though. This stuff I got on now is from him. Gandy took me to ball games, ya know . . . Like baseball and football, ya' know? But he was always on my damn case 'bout hangin' with my homeboys and stuff like that." Fish paused; Sandy saw the gleam of a tear form on the edge of his eyes. "I never liked Gandy . . . But I loved the man. Can you figure that, lady?"

"Yes," she answered in a soft voice. "Yes, I can understand that."

They looked at each other, eye to eye, for a long time. Fish broke the silence. "So what we gonna' do? Sit here and bullshit all day?"

"Watch your language," Sandy said and tried not to grin. "We are going to start at the beginning. Where Morgan and Gandalf started. Whoever did this will then be after us, too. But we will be expecting them. We will be watching for them."

"Then we get t'kill them?" Fish asked.

"My goal is to find out who killed your father and turn them over to the police. Secondly, if Morgan is still alive, I want to find him and keep him alive. But no one gets killed by us unless we are protecting ourselves. Is that clear?"

Fish stood, tossed his empty coffee cup in the trash, and asked, "Where to, lady?"

"San Juan de Cristo," she said. "I hope you know where that is."

"Yo' Mama . . . I mean Mrs. Crew . . . I can find it."

****

The moon was full and straight above them as they approached San Juan de Cristo. Sandy glanced at her watch. It was fifteen minutes past nine. Outside the car the black night was made darker by the dust that was thick as they drove along the bumpy road. Fish slowed the car as they entered the little town.

"There's a Mexican restaurant somewhere," Sandy told him. "There's a guy working there I need to talk to."

Fish drove very slowly down Main Street. He pushed the button on the door to roll down the front windows of the car and suggested, "Smell. If there's a good Mexi place anywhere 'round, you'll know it."

And in fact, they did smell the odors of the food that led them to the edge of town and the old adobe building without a sign on it advertising it as a restaurant. Fish pulled the car to a stop in front of the building, parking at the edge of the wood plank sidewalk. Two young boys were sitting there, young enough to have been in school earlier that day and in bed at that time of night.

Sandy got out of the car and walked past the two boys, into the small restaurant. Fish waited in the car, leaving the engine running, thinking for some reason that they might need a fast get away. At two of the four tables inside, old men with leathery dark skin sat. There was no food on either table, but both tables held a bottle of Tequila and several empty beer bottles. They watched as Sandy walked past them, through an open door, into the kitchen.

A short, fat woman and a young man who was washing the last of the dinner dishes stopped their work to look questioningly at her. "I'm looking for Jose," Sandy said.

The young man took two steps toward Sandy and said, "I'm Jose."

Sandy looked to her right and saw a partially open door. "What's out there?" she asked.

"Garbage cans," Jose said. "Nothing much."

"Good. Let's talk out there."

Outside, Sandy and Jose stood in the middle of what she considered to be a dumping ground. There were broken chairs, a table with three legs, and five beat up aluminum trash cans that were overflowing with very ripe garbage. There was a rusting refrigerator standing with the door open, and next to it was a cracked and filthy toilet without a lid. In between everything were weeds and a few desert flowers. Sandy saw three lizards lounging in the night air, and a rat ran away from the scene.

"Is this place acceptable, Mrs. Crew?" Jose asked.

"You know who I am?"

"Sure. Who else would you be? You're looking for Morgan Crew, right?"

Sandy was speechless. Jose went on, "I found him out in the desert when they kicked the shit out of him. I took him to the hospital."

"How did you know . . . ?"

"I was following him, of course," Jose said. He sat on a chair with three legs, balancing carefully, and lit a cigarette. He offered one to Sandy; she shook her head.

"Why were you following him?" she asked.

"Because he's interfering in an investigation."

"What investigation? What the hell's going on here?" she asked, wishing now that she did smoke cigarettes. She needed something. A martini would be good, she thought.

"Well, Mrs. Crew," Jose said, sending a thick cloud of smoke into the air. "I can't tell you that."

"Why not? I want to find my husband."

"Go home, Mrs. Crew . . . If he's not dead, you'll hear from them," he said. He crushed out the barely smoked cigarette and stood. "Go home . . . Or at least back to El Paso." Jose walked past her, into the restaurant, leaving her alone in the garbage.

Sandy waited a full minute, thinking of what Jose had said, and then walked quickly through the kitchen, through the small room that was the restaurant, and out onto the wooden sidewalk. Fish was in the car, the engine still running, and Sheriff Kronk had both hands against the car's door, leaning down to talk to Fish through the open window.

Sandy spoke for him, "Who are you?"

Kronk turned slowly, stood up, and looked at the attractive woman standing a few feet from him, arms crossed across her chest. "I'm the sheriff here. I want this boy outta' my town. You with him, lady? You gotta' go, too."

"Now wait a minute, Sheriff . . ." Sandy started.

Fish interrupted, "Ms. Crew. Get in the car. Let's get out . . . Like the man says."

She looked at Fish, he nodded knowingly, and Sandy stepped quickly down onto the dirty street. She didn't wait for Fish to open her door. Before she could close the door Fish floored the gas pedal and the car screeched down the street, leaving a cloud of dusty desert sand behind them.

"What the hell was that all about?" Sandy said, holding on tight as they sped out of town onto County Road 8 and the rutted, unpaved road that led nowhere.

"That Sheriff guy says t'leave," Fish said. "So we left."

"Cut it out, Robert. Tell me what happened."

Fish grinned slyly and pulled a folded piece of paper from inside his shirt. He handed it to Sandy. She opened it and read:

"We have your husband, Mrs. Crew. He's safe for now, and he's not too badly hurt. You can have him back for one million dollars in cash.

We will contact you tomorrow to tell you where to bring it. Morgan will be waiting for you."

The note was neatly typed on undistinguished white paper.

"Where did you get this?" Sandy asked. She was astonished, and she was scared. She now knew that I was still alive, and she was determined to keep me that way. A million dollars was cheap, she thought. But it also answered a question for her. Someone thought a million dollars was a lot of money. What they didn't know was that the Crew family was one of the wealthiest families in the world. They could have asked for a hundred million . . . They could have asked for more and gotten it. So Sandy knew that whoever wrote the note wasn't very smart. A million dollars was a lot of money to them.

Fish said, "I was just sittin' there, ya' know? This cowboy lookin' dude walks by and tosses the damn note into the car . . . Right past me . . . An' the guy runs off. Had these damn cowboy boots on . . . Ya' know, with the big heals. Guy looked funny tryin' t'run with them on."

"OK. They said to wait for a phone call. The only place they can call is my cell and the hotel. Let's go back there and wait."

Fish slammed on the brakes and spun the car 180 degrees, and then floored the gas pedal. Tires screeched on the black top streets of the little town. He grinned and glanced at Sandy who was holding on for dear life. "You wanna' go back to El Paso, we gotta go back through Kronk's town. You wanna' risk getting' a speeding ticket . . . Or should I slow down and make us a good target?"

"Slow down," Sandy said. "Please. I want to be alive long enough to get the phone call."

Fish eased up, letting the car slow to forty. When they reached the edge of San Juan de Cristo, he slowed the car to twenty-five as they left the black top and bounced onto the unpaved road.

It took what seemed like an eternity to drive the two blocks that were Main Street. Sheriff Kronk stood on the wooden sidewalk outside his office, arms folded across his chest, watching. People, cowboys for the most part, from The Last Stand Bar walked outside, holding their beers, smoking, and watching them pass by. When Sandy and Fish reached the far edge of town, Fish once again floored the gas for a few seconds, just for the show, and spun tires loudly as they raced along the last one hundred feet of pavement.

****

I was dragged from the hillside, across a couple hundred yards of desert and into the fenced compound. I tried several times to get to my feet, but the men holding onto my arms – too tightly – walked too fast pulling me along with them. All of them were bigger than me, younger than me, and in much better shape than me. I tried to tell them about my ribs, but they ignored me.

I was brought into the biggest of the buildings inside the compound. I had seen it from the hills and assumed it was some kind of warehouse. Inside, it was dark without any lights turned on, but it was cool enough to be a pleasant change from the hot desert. I could see stacks of boxes of all sizes; most of them wood, but a few cardboard boxes also. There were burlap bags stuffed fat and laid on top of one another. The floor was concrete and slick. The air was stale but without any particular odor, save perhaps for the smell of damp paper or cardboard.

They sat me into a bare metal chair, straight backed with arms. I was strapped into leather restraints that were bolted onto the arms. Another leather strap was buckled too tightly across my chest causing even more pain. And my ankles were strapped down onto the legs of the chair.

The two men who had dragged me there turned and left me alone in the dark, closing the big doors behind them.

My eyes adjusted quickly to the dark. I looked around and saw a small office about twenty feet to my left, the door standing wide open. There was a dim light on from a small lamp sitting on a desk inside. I could see filing cabinets and a heavy safe.

The chair was bolted to the concrete floor. As much as I tried to move the chair, it was impossible. So, without much choice left to me, I waited for something to happen. I could see my wristwatch that told me it took about fifteen minutes for the doors to open and the two men who had dragged me into the warehouse to walk in. One of them pulled a black cloth bag over my head and tightened the pull strings around my neck a little too tight. I gagged and they loosened it just a bit.

I couldn't see through the black bag and I found it hard to breathe, although there seemed to be just enough fresh air to keep me alive. I waited again. Time passed slowly. Then I heard footsteps across the concrete floor. It sounded like two, maybe three men in heavy boots, and a lighter step that I guessed was a woman.

"Yeah, that's him." It was clearly a woman's voice but it was muffled, mumbled, and she was forcing a false bass tone.

"What you want t'do with him?" a man asked. His voice was deep and had a commanding tone to it.

I couldn't hear the rest of the conversation. I guessed whoever was there had turned and started back for the door. But I had a bad feeling of what was going to happen.

Suddenly the black bag was ripped off, and I found the two big men who strapped me into the chair standing in front of me, neither looking very happy or friendly. The one on my right said, "They told me I can't hurt you too bad . . . But they didn't say I couldn't hurt you just a little."

"What do you want?" I asked.

"I'm told you're Morgan Crew," the man said. He spoke well, without a definable accent. He was big and obviously spent a lot of time hefting heavy weights to build up his arms and chest and neck. His hair was light brown in color and cropped very short. He wore a light weight plaid cowboy type shirt, the long sleeves rolled up above his elbows. His jeans were faded but clean. He wore military type, tall, laced boots that were highly polished.

"Yes, that's right," I said quickly so as not to piss the guy off. "What do you want?" I repeated.

"Who was the big black guy?"

"My friend," I answered.

"Don't fuck with me, Crew," he snarled. "Who was he?"

I answered, "Gandalf Finch. As I said, he was my friend. Why did you kill him? There wasn't any reason for that."

The man to my left laughed. My interrogator said snidely, "He was the wrong color. His type ain't welcomed around here."

"Where's here? Where am I?" I asked.

"You're fucking with me again, Crew," he said. He took a couple of steps away from me to a small table too far behind me to see. He came back with a four foot long section of green lawn hose. He stood in front of me, smiled, and raised the hose above his head. He brought it down hard across my right forearm. It hurt like hell, and I yelled like hell.

"Now," he said, slapping the hose into his palm several times. "That's just a warning. I can hurt you more than that without hurting you too bad. So don't fuck with me. I ask the questions and you answer."

"OK, OK," I said. "I learn fast. What do you want to know?"

"Why were the two of you up in the hills?" he asked, still slapping the hose in his hand.

I considered quickly whether or not to be absolutely truthful. If I told them the truth, and the people inside the compound were involved in Edgy Hands' death . . . They would probably kill me. If I came up with a story . . . Quickly . . . that I hoped might keep me alive, and these people had something to do with Edgy's death, they would know I was lying and . . . They would probably kill me. So I decided to go with the truth. If I had to die I would die showing these people they weren't as smart as they thought they were.

"You know who I am," I started. "I think you know that a friend of mine is in jail, accused of killing Edgy Hands. I'm trying to find the person who did kill him and get my friend out of jail."

"And you think we killed the son of a bitch?" the man asked.

"I don't know who killed Edgy," I started but when the man swung the rubber hose hard and slashed it across my left shin all I could do was scream in pain. It hurt like hell.

"I said don't fuck with me, Crew."

"I'm telling you the truth," I said, pleading with him. "Christ! You've got me tied down . . . Why the hell wouldn't I tell you the truth? I don't know who killed him."

He slashed the hose across my shin again. It hurt even worse than the last. "Please! Please!" I was moaning more than speaking. The pain was excruciating. "I'm telling you the truth. I came across this place by accident. I was curious, that's all. I figured there was a reason Edgy had to be killed. I just thought . . ." He stopped me again by hitting my other leg with the hose, even harder than the other hits I had taken.

"Why are you here then?"

"I was looking for the guys who were at The Last Stand the night Edgy was killed. I found this place . . . It just looked out of place . . . It got my curiosity up . . . That's all."

I tried to control myself but the pain was furious. I couldn't stop the tears that were flowing across my cheeks. The two men looked down at me, maybe a little sorry for me. I hoped the tears and my crying in pain would do some good, and it appeared it was working. The man with the hose nodded and the two of them walked out of the warehouse, leaving me alone, strapped into the chair, and hurting like the devil had been after me.

****

San Juan de Cristo was miles behind them when Sandy turned to Fish and said, "Do you know where the Bar H Ranch is?" They had left the little desert town an hour before and had ridden in silence. Sandy was thinking, trying to figure out what she could do to find me . . . Or, as the thought rampaged around in the back of her head, to find out if I was alive or dead. She decided she could not just go back to El Paso and wait.

"Not really," Fish answered. "But there ain't much out here. It may take some time but I can probably find it. Why?"

"I learned a long time ago that money is always the thing. People . . . Some people . . . Will do anything for money. They will kill and steal . . . And they will kidnap people. Money . . . Avarice and greed . . . controls people like that. Morgan knew . . . I mean he knows . . . that the only money in this God forsaken place is at the Bar H Ranch. It seems likely that everything leads back there. I want to go there before going back to the hotel."

They drove for hours, first west, then east, then down to the Rio Grande. They took rutted, unpaved roads that led nowhere, turned and retraced where they had come from. Finally they found a dirt road that led to a better road, rutted still, but seemingly more used, with a barbed wire fence on either side. They turned onto it and a half hour later they saw the big house that was the Bar H Ranch sitting on the horizon. Evening was beginning to close in around them; the daylight was dim and would soon be gone altogether.

The house was ablaze with lights shone brightly in every window. The covered porch held a few small tables and wooden chairs.

Fish pulled the car to a stop at the tall front porch of the house. As he and Sandy got out of the car, the front door opened and Harry Perkins stepped outside. He was holding a glass of whiskey in one hand and a long cigar in the other.

"Can I help you folks?" he asked. He made no effort to approach them or to smile. He was suspicious, as he always was when strangers showed up at his door.

Sandy took the first two of the five steps leading up to the covered porch. "I hope so," she said, smiling that wonderful and disarming smile of hers. "I think my husband was here some time ago . . . Morgan Crew."

"Yeah? So what?" Perkins said. He drew on the big cigar, blew out a cloud of smoke and finished the whiskey in his glass in one long swallow.

Sandy took another step and said, "I'm trying to find him. I was just wondering if you've seen him in the last day or two."

"Hell, you think he may have some little girly on the side? Maybe he's takin' a little vacation with a little babe? Maybe he's run off from ya'll? Maybe you need a good attorney? I can't help you, lady."

The door behind Harry opened, and Mary Lou Perkins stepped outside, standing next to her husband but two feet away from him. She looked disparagingly at him and shook her head.

"Harry," she said. "You're being rude again, dear."

She looked at Sandy, smiled and said in a very distinctly southern, courtly accent, "Mrs. Crew. I do apologize for my husband. He can be . . . Well, rude when he's had too much to drink. We don't get many visitors way out here. Now, you and your driver, please come inside. We've finished our supper but please join us for coffee."

"He's not my driver," Sandy said. "Robert is my friend."

Mary Lou stepped aside and opened the door grandly, still smiling.

Harry didn't move. He looked down at Fish who was standing at the bottom of the steps and said, "You gonna' let this boy sit at our table?"

"Harry!" Mary Lou said sharply. "I've told you before I don't appreciate that language."

She looked at Fish, an apologetic frown on her face, and said, "I am sorry, young man. Please come in and have coffee with us. You're very welcome in my home."

Fish followed Sandy into the house, not looking at Harry Perkins as he walked by him. He was suspicious of these people. He'd seen people before who put on a good smile and talked nice . . . Just before they stabbed you in the back.

Inside the Perkins' big ranch house, they found a classically and formally furnished home. Expensive furnishings were expertly placed. Old master paintings hung next to expensive modern art in each room. And each room held, in a prominent position, a large American flag on a tall staff.

Mary Lou led Sandy and Fish through the entry hall and into the dining room. Two ladies, Mexicans, were clearing away the dishes from the family's meal. "Rosita," Mary Lou said with a smile in her words. "We'll have coffee in here, please. And maybe some of those wonderful little butter cookies you make so well." She turned to Sandy and said, "Rosita is just a little darlin'. She bakes the most delicious things for us. I just wouldn't know what to do without her."

Mary Lou waved with a delicate gesture to chairs for Sandy and Fish. The three sat and Mary Lou asked, "Now, my dear. Do I understand that your husband has gone missing?"

"Well, maybe not missing," Sandy said. "I just don't know where he is, and I guess I'm just the worrying type. He was here, I understand. Can you tell me what he spoke with you about?"

Rosita returned to the room, carrying a brightly painted wooden tray with a thermos and four clay, hand painted mugs.

"Oh, Rosita, dear," Mary Lou said kindly, in a voice she might use on favored grandchildren. "Please. These are special guests. Would you bring the good china cups? You're a sweet thing. Thank you."

Sandy watched Rosita carefully. Her expression was one of fear; her dark face paled; her hands were shaking. She curtsied slightly and quickly turned back through the door she had entered through, almost spilling the tray as she ran out of the room.

"I am so sorry," Mary Lou said with an embarrassed and apologetic look on her face. She was a middle aged woman who did her best to keep her young beauty. She was not slim, but she managed to keep excessive weight off with a fully equipped gym in the basement of her house. Her hair showed no signs of graying, perhaps because of the coloring that converted her hair to an almost natural blond. Her makeup was perfect; her clothes not expensive but stylish; her jewelry was gold but not overdone.

Rosita came back into the dining room, this time carrying a large silver tray. On it was an elaborate silver coffee pot, matching silver sugar and cream bowls, and three fine china cups and saucers, so delicate they were almost transparent. Each was decorated with tiny red roses and more suitable to a formal treat than coffee. She placed it gently and carefully on the table and asked, "Shall I pour, señorita Perkins?"

"No, thank you Rosita. And thank you so much for the coffee. Now please go have your supper. You can have the rest of the evening off, my dear."

Mary Lou stood and poured dark coffee into the cups. She handed cups to Sandy and Fish and said, "Please help yourself to sugar and cream."

Sandy asked, "Will your husband be joining us?"

"Oh, my!" Mary Lou said and laughed. "That man will not give up those smelly cigars. I just won't let him smoke the horrible things in the house. He'll stay outside until he's smoked the damn thing down to where it burns his fingers!"

Sandy sipped at the good coffee and then asked, "Again, Mrs. Perkins. Why was my husband here?"

"Oh yes, of course," she said and carefully laid her cup on the table in front of her. "He asked about that poor young thing who's in jail for that terrible murder. We knew her, did you know that? What's her name? I've completely forgotten."

"Betsy," Sandy answered simply.

"That's right! That's her name! She and my son Jimmy were . . . Involved, you know? I can't say that young people are right doing what they do, but . . . Mary Lou shrugged her shoulders and lowered her eyes in an embarrassed gesture. "Anyway, we were devastated that she was arrested for that murder. I just can't believe that sweet young thing could do that. How is she, by the way? Have you seen her lately?"

"Yes," Sandy said. She wasn't about to tell anyone that Betsy had left the State and was in hiding with our daughter. "And that's all you and Morgan spoke about?"

"I'm afraid so, dear. You think your husband might have disappeared? How terrible. I do hope nothing terrible has happened to him."

"Well, I guess I won't take anymore of your time," Sandy said. She and Fish stood. Mary Lou stood and reached out to shake Sandy's hand.

"Please do come back, Mrs. Crew. We don't get many visitors out here. And I do hope you will find out where your husband is. I'm sure he's alright. Maybe car trouble or something. It's so desolate out here that one might stand on the side of the road for days before anyone passes by. I'll say a prayer, anyway," she smiled in sympathy.

Sandy and Fish left the house, walking past Harry Perkins who was still out on the porch, sitting in a rocking chair, smoking his cigar and drinking from a freshened glass of whiskey. When they had driven away, Mary Lou's smile fell quickly and suddenly from her face. She stormed back into the house, slamming the door behind her, kicking open the kitchen, pushing the young girl who was washing dishes against the sink, causing her to drop a plate that shattered on the linoleum floor. She pushed the screen door open at the back of the kitchen so hard, it was torn from the top of its two hinges. She pushed it aside, tearing the screen.

Outside she walked, furious, to the second of six small adobe huts that were lined up perpendicular to the big ranch house. Each was not more than ten by twenty feet in size. She pounded on the weather beaten door. Rosita started to open the door. Mary Lou kicked at it, cracking the thin and weather dried wood. Rosita screamed and stepped backwards, tripping over a thatch basket and falling onto the old mattress on the floor that was her bed.

Mary Lou stood over her and slapped Rosita hard across her face. "You fuckin' filthy Mexican bitch!" she screamed. "You fuckin' embarrassed me with those filthy Mexican crap mugs! You stupid bitch!"

Mary Lou hit Rosita again, this time with a closed fist. Rosita fell to the floor, screaming and crying, blood streaming from the side of her mouth. She rolled herself into a ball as Mary Lou started kicking the woman, over and over until Rosita was barely conscious.

"You filthy fuckin' dirty Mexican bitch!" Mary Lou screamed and spat on the woman. "You get your filthy, crappy poncho and your filthy crappy sandals and get the hell off my property, you bitch! Now! I don't wanna' see your filthy God damn Mexican face anywhere around here five fuckin' minutes from now! Do you understand?"

Mary Lou ripped one of Rosita's blouses from the back of a chair and wiped her bloody hands, throwing the blouse on the dirt floor when she was done.

CHAPTER SIXTEEN – Colonel Max

Fish and Sandy were quiet as they bounced along the unpaved desert road away from the Bar H Ranch. Night darkness was heavy around them. The car's headlights barely broke through the blackness in front of them.

Fish drove slowly, trying not to run off the unlit dirt road. He made a slight turn to the left to follow a bend in the road. Then, in front of them, a figure appeared in the headlights. As they approached, they saw it was a young man, standing at the side of the road, holding the reins of a tall horse with a bright white muzzle and white socks. I had taken Sandy to thoroughbred races often enough for her to recognize a prize horse when she saw one. The man was waving them down.

"Ya' think the horse got engine trouble?" Fish joked.

Sandy said, "Maybe a flat tire?"

Fish stopped the car, and Sandy rolled down her window. The young man bent and looked inside. "Are you Mrs. Crew?" he asked.

"Yes. Who are you?"

The young man looked across at Fish. "Is he with you?" he asked.

"Of course," Sandy answered. "He's driving the car, isn't he?"

"Look," he began. "I want to tell you I'm sorry."

"Sorry for what?"

"Betsy," he said, shame in his voice and on his face. "I set her up . . . She didn't kill nobody."

"What! Who are you?" Sandy asked, shocked and bewildered at what the young man had said.

"I'm Jimmy Perkins," he said. "I picked up Betsy and brought her here. It was all planned to cover Edgy's murder. I didn't want to do it . . . They made me do it . . . I'm so sorry . . . Tell Betsy that, will you?"

Before Sandy could say anything a Jeep painted drab olive green, dented and dirty, the kind of jeep used for years by the military before Humvees took over, came to a quick stop behind them, headlights off, and frightening Jimmy's horse. The horse whinnied and rose up on its hind legs. Jimmy spoke softly to the big horse, calmed it and turned back to the man driving the jeep.

A tall man, dressed in pressed and starched green military fatigues, with close cropped dark hair, pants bloused over polished black military jump boots, climbed out of the Jeep and walked slowly to them.

"Jimmy," he said. "What the hell are you doin'?"

"Nothin', Flynn. I ain't doin' nothin'", Jimmy was clearly frightened. He was having a hard time calming his horse, but was having an even more difficult time calming himself.

"If you ain't doin' nothin'", Flynn said. "Then go home. Your mother ain't gonna like this."

"I didn't say nothin', Flynn. I swear it. I wouldn't say nothin'."

"Then do what I say and go home."

Jimmy quickly climbed up onto the saddle, and Flynn walked back to his Jeep. Jimmy leaned down while Flynn's back was turned and whispered to Sandy through the open window, "Hidden Horse Canyon."

He kicked the horse's flanks and road off as fast as the big horse could run, back towards his house. Flynn turned the Jeep around and followed him.

"What the hell was that all about?" Fish asked.

"I'm not really sure," Sandy answered. "I mean, I knew Betsy was framed. But Jimmy Perkins admitting it? Why?"

"Hell lady," Fish said as he started the car back on the dirt road. "I'm a city boy. All this cowboy crap is weird t'me."

"Robert," Sandy said. "I'd tell you to watch your language . . . But I feel the same way. All this cowboy crap is weird to me, too. Have you ever heard of Hidden Horse Canyon?"

"Sounds like somethin' outta' one of those friggin' old John Wayne movies. But I know somebody who might know. You up to stayin' up all night?"

"Before I answer that," Sandy said. "Who do you know?"

"There's this old Comanche Indian broad that Gandy knows . . . I mean knew. If anybody knows anything about this damn desert, she does. I mean, don't Indians know all that stuff?"

It took hours for them to find Margaret Autumn Leaf's old Quonset hut in the dark of the nearly moonless night. It was almost midnight when Fish pulled the car to a stop. The building was dark; the night desert air was bitterly cold, and a chilly wind was blowing from the north. They pulled themselves from the car and stood in front of the Quonset. Fish knocked on the door, softly at first, then harder. Then, from behind them, came the chilling sound of a gun being cocked. Maggie had stepped around from the back of the building, a long double barreled shotgun in her hands.

"Who the hell you?" she growled. "What you want? I gonna shoot you dead."

"Maggie, it's me . . . Fish . . . Robert, you know. Gandy's kid."

"You Gandy's boy?" Margaret asked, peering at Robert trying to remember what the boy looked like. "It's been too many years," she said. "If you Gandy's boy, you

grown now. Sure, you look a little like him . . . But how I
know you Robert?"

"On my fifteenth birthday . . . Remember? Gandy
brought me here . . . You took me up in your plane and
scared me silly . . . Remember?"

"Ha!" Maggie laughed. She un-cocked the shotgun
and started to lean it against the side of the Quonset. "Sure,
I remember you. You shit your damn pants and puked all
over your damn shoes when I took you up!"

She dropped the big shotgun onto the ground and
opened her fat arms and rushed at Fish, taking him off his
feet and spinning him around. They were both laughing.
Finally she put him back on his feet and said loudly, "You
two come inside . . . Outta' the damn cold. You hungry?
You want somethin'?"

Inside, it was warmer than outside, but still cold.
Maggie flipped a couple of switches, and lights came on
revealing the patched together biplane. "What the hell is
that?" Sandy asked, starring at it.

Fish laughed and said, "That's Maggie's airplane.
She built it herself. And it really works, too."

"You actually got in that thing and left the ground?"

Maggie shrieked her cackling laugh and said, "He left
the damn ground but his damn stomach didn't go with him!
He scared to hell!"

"Yeah, well, anyway," Sandy began. "I'm Sandy Crew
. . ."

"You that Morgan fella's woman?" Maggie interrupted.
She had stopped laughing suddenly and become very
serious.

"You know Morgan?" Sandy asked.

"Sure I know that good lookin' fella'. He went up in
my God damn plane, too."

"He did? When . . . Where?"

Maggie laughed again, the shrieking reverberating
against the metal walls of the building. She took an old pipe

from her pocket. She stuck it in her mouth and lit it with a wooden match she struck on the seat of her blue jeans. Drawing deeply, she blew out a cloud. "I don't keep days like you whites do," she said and drew on the pipe again. "He here some time ago."

"And he flew in your airplane?" Sandy asked.

"Sure he did," Maggie laughed again. "He scared but he do it anyway. Flew him all over. He saw that Hidden Horse Canyon place and we come home. He excited I guess. Then him and Gandy drove off."

Fish looked at Sandy who looked back at him. "That's it," he said. To Maggie he asked, "Where is it?"

"Sorta' that way," she said, flicking her thumb over her shoulder.

Fish said, "I've got a map. Can you find it on the map, Maggie?"

"Sure . . . Maybe . . . I guess so. Why this so damn important?"

Sandy nodded at Fish and he said, "Gandy . . . My dad . . . He's dead. Somebody killed him . . . Dumped him in the mud on the Mexi said of the Rio Grande."

"Gandy's dead?" Maggie said, not really believing what she had heard. She let the pipe slip from her lips and fall to the concrete floor where it shattered. "That can't be. That big fella', he too damn tough. He too damn big." A silvery tear crept from the corner of her eye and ran down her fat, dark cheek. She brushed it away with the back of her hand. "Fish," she said. "You find out who did this . . . You and me, we stretch the som'bitch out in the sun and let the damn ants kill him, OK?"

Fish ran outside to get the map from the car. He slammed the door behind him as he ran back into the Quonset. There was a work bench at one side of the room. It was covered with trash, junk and tools. Fish swept everything off, onto the floor, with one swipe of his arm and spread the map open on the bench top.

"Maggie, show me where this place is," Fish said.

The old Comanche woman bent over the map. She took it all in and ran her finger over the paper. Then she pointed and said, "That's it. Right there. That's Hidden Horse Canyon."

Fish grabbed up the map and said, "OK, Lady Crew, let's go."

"Robert," Sandy answered. "It's late . . . It's dark out. We need to find a motel or something and go when it's light."

Maggie laughed her screeching laugh again. "There ain't no hotels or nothin' 'round here! Maybe you find a bed over there in San Juan de Cristo . . . But ain't no hotels 'round here."

"So what you wanna' do, Lady Crew?"

Maggie turned and walked to the back of the Quonset. She came back with an armful of old, patched blankets and tossed them on the floor under her biplane. "You sleep here," she said. "I fix you some rabbit and onion for breakfast. Good night now." She walked away, leaving Sandy and Fish alone.

"OK, Lady Crew," Fish said. "It's up to you. We sleep here or outside."

Sandy took two of the blankets and walked away. They blankets smelled of age and dirt, but she had little choice. She said, "You sleep here . . . I'll sleep back there."

****

In the morning, Sandy drank something Maggie Autumn Leaf called coffee. She tried to eat some of the rabbit stew Maggie spooned from a big iron pot onto a paper plate, but decided hunger was better than the food. Fish drank some coffee, turned down the stew, and paced back and forth across the big room.

"Hey, lady," he said to Sandy. "When we gonna' go?"

"Be patient, Robert," she answered. "We need

patience. If there's one thing Morgan has taught me, it's that only fools rush in. Now, how's the gas in the car? Don't you think you should fill it up? That is if Maggie will let you use her pump outside."

"You bet," Maggie said. She stood and walked outside with Fish. Sandy tried to down a second cup of the hot brown liquid Maggie had brewed. Some people might call it coffee, but it had only a faint relationship to what Sandy and I love to drink in the morning.

They came back as Sandy drank the last few drops from the cup. "Ok," Fish demanded. "Let's go now, can we?"

"Wait a minute, Robert," Sandy said. She looked at Maggie and asked, "Do you have any guns around here?"

"Do I got guns!" she exclaimed. "'Course I got guns." She waived to Sandy to follow her. At the far back of the Quonset, in a dark corner, she stopped at an unpainted wooden cabinet that stood from the floor to the tall ceiling. It was padlocked, and Maggie unlocked it quickly. Opening the double doors, she stood back and let Sandy see the array of pistols, rifles, sub-machine guns, and shotguns hanging inside. There were four drawers that held flares and fragmentation grenades. Sandy saw dozens of sticks of dynamite, sweating dangerously, and old enough for her to want to leave them lay where they were.

"You take whatever you need," Maggie said. "Plenty of bullets, too. But when you find who killed Gandy, you bring him here to me, OK?"

Sandy took a 9mm Glock. She told me later that she took it because it was light and she had fired one before. Maggie handed her three magazines of ammunition. Sandy put one in the Glock and the other two in her back pants pocket.

"Robert," She said. "You've got a pistol. If you've ever fired one of the small rifles here, take it."

Without hesitation Fish grabbed an H&K MP5.

Maggie took four long clips for the submachine gun from a drawer under the cabinet and handed them to Fish.

"We'll need water, Maggie. I don't suppose you keep bottled water here, do you?"

"Noooo," Maggie said and laughed again. "I get you a couple water bags. They better. No damn plastic, you know?"

Maggie disappeared, leaving Sandy and Fish to check their weapons. "Robert," Sandy said. "These are for defense, understand? You don't get to kill anyone except in self-defense, right?"

"Sure, Mama," Fish said, smiling slyly. "Anything you say."

"I'm not your mama," Sandy reminded him softly with a gentle smile on her face. She didn't want to be too hard on him. She knew they were probably walking into danger. It wasn't the right time to correct him.

Maggie returned with two big desert water bags; Sandy silently hoped they were some kind of fabric and not the stomach of some animal. Maggie also had an old flour sack filled with cans of food. "You might need this," she said.

Fish carried everything out to the car. He started to walk around to the driver's side, stopped and made a show of walking back to the passenger side. He opened the door and bowed. Maggie screeched again and said, "Lady, you gotta' be damn good t'get Fish t'do that!"

An hour later they were bouncing slowly along a rutted path that maybe a hundred years ago some horse drawn wagons would have driven over. It was blazing hot outside; the air conditioner inside did little to ease the heat. Fish pulled the map in front of him without stopping the car. He studied it and then tossed it over his shoulder into the rear.

"If we're where I think we are, there's a paved road up ahead," he said. "The map says it goes north and south.

Could be it leads into the canyon. You wanna' go there?"

"Yes, but take it easy. I want to stop a mile or two before we get into the canyon."

"You got it," Fish said. And when they reached a two lane blacktop road, he turned right and started north. Twenty-five minutes later they saw the canyon walls ahead of them in the distance. He pulled the car to a stop.

"Good," Sandy said. "Do you know how to drain the fluid from the coolant system?"

"Why you wanna' do that?" Fish asked. "The car ain't gonna go far if it overheats."

"That's the idea," she said. "Whatever is in the canyon, I want them to see us in trouble."

"OK," Fish said as he got out of the car. He crawled under the car and found the fluid drain. He opened it and got back in the car. They drove away, leaving a trail of coolant behind them.

Five miles further on, the red dashboard light was flashing, and the car was sputtering and slowing. The engine died, and Fish pulled the car to the side of the road.

"Now what?" he asked.

"Now we walk," Sandy said. "Take your pistol . . . Leave the big gun . . . Leave all your ID and wallet. And when we find someone, you let me do the talking." Sandy slid her purse under the car's seat and got out of the car. She tucked the Glock into the waist band of her pants and pulled her white blouse out to hang loosely over her waist and the gun.

They walked for ten miles through the heat of the West Texas desert. Fish carried the water bag Maggie had given them, and his Berretta which was tucked in his belt behind his back.

"How much further we gonna' walk?" he asked.

Sandy didn't answer. They started up a slight rise in the road and when they had reached the top, they saw off in the distance a tall chain link fence with a double gate closed across the road. Sandy stopped and said, "I think we found what we're looking for."

A hundred yards from the gate, they saw it swing open and a pickup truck drove out, towards them. It moved slowly, cautiously. It was not new; it was dented and dull and once may have been red in color. As it got closer Sandy saw there was only one person inside. The driver pulled to a stop next to them. The window was rolled down; the driver rested his arm on the open window. He wasn't smiling. He said, "This here's a private road. What'er you doin' here?"

Sandy smiled her beautifully disarming smile and said, "Our car over heated . . . Back there . . . We hoped to find some help."

A slow smile drifted onto the driver's face. He was a middle aged man, perhaps 45 years old. His face, unshaven for several days, didn't hide the fact that he had seen hard times. There was a scar on his left cheek, four inches long and deep. His arm was muscled, tanned and covered with sun bleached hair. Another scar crossed his forearm deep and diagonally. He wore a faded T-shirt that once carried a camouflage print, now faded after a couple of years of wear.

"Well," he said. "Hop in and we'll go get some help."

Fish opened the door, Sandy got in, and Fish followed. They saw the driver wore blue jeans, not new, and a military web-belt onto which was fastened a holster holding a big semi-auto pistol with a well worn handle.

Sandy said, smiling still, "You always carry a gun?"

He answered, "Yeah . . . Coyotes . . . Snakes . . . Stuff like that."

He turned the pickup around and started back towards the gate and fence. As they passed through, the gate closed automatically. The truck came to a stop in the middle of what was a compound of some sort. Sandy took it all in quickly - barracks-like buildings and what seemed to be a fairly good sized warehouse. There were two rows of seven separate small outbuildings each and towards the back of the compound what might be a garage with a gas pump in front. At each corner of the rectangle was a tall watch tower, but none of the four had anyone standing guard. At the front of the outbuildings, in the middle of a large open area between the gates and the buildings, was a tall flagpole with an American flag draped lazily in the still air. And to the side of the compound, outside the fence, was a firing range. The whole compound was situated at the end of the canyon, which walled the compound with brown and barren rock on three sides.

The driver of the pickup truck opened his door and climbed out. "Wait here," he said. He walked away, leaving Fish and Sandy alone, inside the truck, in the middle of the fenced compound, watched only by a few men who lounged around, smoking and talking.

"So what now?" Fish asked.

"Be patient," Sandy said. "We're going to find out what's going on very soon."

The driver walked past two of the small buildings, knocked on the door of the third, and entered. Three minutes later, he walked out again with another man at his side. The second man was in his mid-forties, lean and dressed in desert camo-fatigue pants and a black T-shirt. The T-shirt fit like a second skin over his muscular arms and chest, and tapered down to tight abs and a narrow waist. He wore a military sidearm also. He walked with a lot of authority, and his tanned face reflected a demand for that authority. He wore a black eye patch over his left eye, giving him the look of a pirate.

At the pickup, the driver opened the passenger door and said, "Please get out." They did and stood in front of the two men.

The driver said, "This is Colonel Max. I am Captain Freeman. Why are you here?"

"Is this a military base?" Sandy asked. She was acting like a somewhat naïve woman, someone who had honestly come looking for help, and she was doing it very well. She put on a nervous smile and looked around the compound. She also looked hard at Colonel Max, eyeing his muscles lasciviously.

Colonel Max pulled a cigarette from the crumpled pack he had in one of the pockets of his fatigue pants. He lit the cigarette with the practiced and dramatic flip of a lighter and said, "This is my camp. Why are you here?"

"Like I said. Our car overheated. We were looking for help."

"That's a load of prime bullshit lady," Max said harshly. His smile had a vicious threat behind it. "You're carrying a water bag that looks full. Why not use that in your car?"

"Gosh, I don't know," Sandy said innocently. "I guess I never thought of that."

"How about you, boy. You ever thought of that?" Max asked Fish.

"I ain't no boy," Fish answered. He wasn't putting on an act like Sandy was. His face was twisted in a mean-street scowl.

"He's my driver," Sandy said.

"Let me see some ID," Colonel Max demanded.

"Oh shit, man," Fish said. "Left it back in the car. Ain't that somethin'?"

"How about you, lady?"

"Now that I think of it, I probably should have taken my purse with me. Sorry."

The Colonel turned to Captain Freeman and said, "Stay here with them. I'm gonna' make a phone call."

Colonel Max walked away, back to the building he had come out of. Freeman leaned against the fender of the pickup truck and lit a cigarette. Sandy took a couple of steps closer to him and said, "You know, I'll bet you'd like to see something."

"What?" Freeman asked. He pushed himself off of

the pick-up, smiled a little, flipped the cigarette away, maybe hoping Sandy was going to open her blouse for him. Instead she pulled the Glock from under her blouse.

CHAPTER SEVENTEEN – I'm Sick Of All The Lies

"Now," she said. "If any of those men lounging around out here start shooting, you're the first one to die. Do you understand that?" She held the pistol close to her, hoping the men standing around the compound couldn't see it.

Freemen nodded his head, his eyes locked on the Glock just inches from his stomach.

"Answer me truthfully," Sandy whispered. "Do you have someone here . . . Morgan Crew?"

Freeman didn't say anything, but beads of sweat were forming on his forehead.

Sandy jabbed the pistol into Freeman's stomach and said, "One more time, Captain . . . Or whatever the hell you are. Is Morgan Crew here?"

"Yes," he said.

"Where?"

"In building E."

"And where the hell is building E?"

"Back that way," Freeman said, flicking his thumb in the direction of the buildings lined up towards the rear of the compound.

"OK," Sandy said. "You lead the way. Walk slowly, casually, and smile. Robert, keep your gun in your belt but be prepared. Follow three or four steps behind us. If anybody starts shooting . . . Run and shoot. Get away if you can. Don't wait for me."

"You got it. But I gonna' kill some of these mothers before I go."

They walked towards the series of barracks-like buildings, Freeman in front feeling Sandy's gun at his lower back. Sandy nudged him once and said, "I said smile." And he did.

They passed buildings marked A, B, C, and D. At building E, which turned out to be what Sandy assumed was a warehouse, Freeman stopped.

"Open the door," Sandy ordered and he did. When the door was open Sandy pushed him inside the dark building. "Lights," she demanded. Freeman found a light switch and flooded the small room with a dozen bright bare bulbs hanging from the ceiling. At the center of the room, twenty feet away, she saw me, strapped down to a hard metal chair.

"Well," I said with a forced, dry voice through cracked lips. "Took you long enough to get here."

"Don't press your luck, dear," she said. "I could just leave you here, you know."

Fish quickly took the pistol from Freeman's holster and held it at the man's back.

As Sandy walked closer to me she saw the ugly, bruises on my arm and leg. My wrists were so tightly bound by the leather straps that my hands were swollen and discolored. Sandy rushed to me, knelt, and gently touched my face. Her hands were shaking as she unbuckled the thick leather at my wrists and ankles. Tears were welling up in her eyes. She was mumbling swear words and threats of mayhem and murder.

"Who's with you?" I asked, nodding towards Fish who was holding his pistol at Freeman's back.

Sandy wiped her eyes with the back of her hand and said, "This is Robert Finch. He's Gandalf's son. I trust him explicitly. He even opens doors for me," she said, trying to laugh. "What did they do to you?"

"Nothing much," I managed.

When the straps were removed, I tried to stand, but after uncounted days of sitting in the hard chair, added to the huge bruise and swelling on my left leg, my legs were nearly useless. I was beginning to get used to being in pain. The memory of the beating I had taken out in the desert was still sharp every time my cracked ribs sent hot pain up my back, and my arm and leg throbbed from being the target of the rubber hose. With Sandy's help, I managed to get to my feet. I took a few steps, trying to ignore the pain and found I could move if I let my anger grow stronger than the throbbing pain.

While Sandy was freeing me from the chair, Fish had stepped forward, closed the door behind him, punched the Captain's big semi-auto into the small of Freeman's back and pushed the man to the floor, face down on the cold concrete. He put his foot on the small of the man's back, held his gun close to Freeman's head and asked, "You the bastard killed Gandy?"

"Robert! Not now," Sandy said.

"'Nuff of the bullshit, lady. I'm gonna start killing these damn white folks 'til I find out who killed Gandy."

"Robert, think. If you fire one shot, there'll be dozens of people here to kill us. Think. Let's do this the right way."

It took a moment or two for Fish to understand the good sense of not starting a shooting war he would certainly lose. He took his foot off of Freeman, took a deep breath and stepped away from the man who decided to stay prostrate on the floor. "OK, lady Crew," he said. "Your way. For awhile, anyway. But if these sons a'bitches done killed Gandy I gonna kill'em. I hope you understand that."

I could take a few steps if I leaned my weight on Sandy. She told Captain Freeman, "Get up and help us." He pushed himself to his feet slowly, maybe a little arrogantly, and helped Sandy to hold me upright. "You know you can't get out of here," Freeman said. "The minute you step outside you're going to get blown apart."

I managed to say, "I have a feeling . . . If we don't get out . . . You're going to die. Right dear?"

"I'm afraid so," Sandy said. "I wouldn't have it any other way, dear." She stood back, holding her Glock pointed at Freeman. "Now, you will help Morgan outside. We're going to go back to your pickup truck and drive away from here."

Freeman said, "There are probably twenty-five men waiting out there for you. You're all going to die. Why not just give me your guns and you won't be hurt."

"And they'll kill you, too?" I suggested.

"No. All my men are expert shots. They'll blow your fuckin' heads off, and I'll walk away."

Sandy asked me, "Morgan, can you stand by yourself?"

"Let me lean against the wall," I said. My voice was still raspy, but knowing that I would be OK helped me regain some of my voice.

Sandy waved Freeman to help me to a wall. He stepped back when I could stand against the wall on my own. She handed her Glock to me and asked, "Can you shoot this man if you have to?" I said I could and held the gun pointed at Freeman who was standing a few feet away. I managed to push the pain away, but my head was spinning. I leaned hard against the wall to keep from falling on my face. My hand was shaking a little, and my fingers felt a little weak, but I had enough strength to pull the trigger if I had to, and Freemen was so close that I couldn't miss.

Then Sandy said, "Robert, come with me. I want to talk to you."

She and Fish walked to the furthest corner of the room, out of earshot of both Freeman and me. "Robert, can you . . . As quietly as possible . . . Get out of the room without being seen?"

"Hey Mama," he said, smiling. "If I can break into buildings, I can break out, too. But ain't that guy gonna' see me?"

"How would you get out without being seen?"

Fish looked around the warehouse taking everything in. There were no windows and the only door was at the front, where we all had come in. The ceiling was too tall, more than fifteen feet above us, so breaking through one of the roof vents was out of the question.

"I think I can get through the wall in the back. I done that a couple a'times, ya'know. 'Cept of course I was breaking in, not breaking out."

"OK, don't tell me about that," Sandy said. "Do you think you can break through the wall without anyone hearing you?"

"Yeah, lady Crew. These walls are all just drywall . . . Nothin' much, cheap shit, ya'know. And the whole damn building ain't nothin' but plywood. I got me a good knife. I can cut my way through if I can have some time. You gotta keep these white sons a'bitches busy."

"Morgan and I can do that, but not forever."

He handed Freeman's gun to Sandy and turned quickly towards the rear of the warehouse. Sandy told him to wait. "When you get out, go get help. Don't get caught. Get back to the car if you can and drive as fast as you can. Use the water bag to fill the radiator. Find some police somewhere. We aren't going to last long here. Maybe overnight but not much longer than that."

Fish started for the back of the warehouse and found a place behind stacks of boxes where he wouldn't be seen. Sandy walked back to the door, opening it a crack. Afternoon had turned to dusk. Nightfall would soon cover the compound. There were a dozen men gathered outside the warehouse. All were armed and all looked really pissed off. Sandy shouted out, "If you come in here, Captain

Freeman dies!" She slammed the door hard and turned off the lights leaving the windowless room in pitch blackness.

Fish took the signal and began to use his pocket knife to cut through the drywall and exterior plywood of the building. It took more than an hour but he was able to cut a hole large enough for him to crawl through. The chain link fence was only five feet from the back of the building. Flood lights were filling the compound, but the space between the small buildings and the fence were dimly lit. Fish looked left and right; he could see no one.

Fish made a quick dash for the fence, climbed it and swung over the barbed wire catching his shirt and ripping a long piece of fabric, leaving it hanging on the wire. On the ground, he ran.

****

Sandy took her Glock from me. I slid down the wall and sat on the floor. My eyes were quickly used to the dark, since I had been held in the dark for most of the time they had me as their prisoner. Freeman was standing now ten feet away. I could see he was inching slowly towards the closed door.

"Sandy," I said. "Stand with your back next to the door . . . Not in front of the door . . . Captain Freeman wants to make a break for it. Will you shoot him if he tries that?"

"Of course," she answered. Freeman stopped moving. "But he won't go anywhere if he's strapped into the chair he had you in." She waived the gun towards the chair, and Freeman walked to it without complaining. He sat and Sandy told him, "Strap your ankles . . . Tight." When he had done this she said, "Now strap your right wrist down . . . Tight again." When he had finished, Sandy stepped to his left side, held the gun against his temple, and with her left hand, strapped his left wrist down.

When she was satisfied that Captain Freemen wasn't

going anywhere, she walked back to me and sat on the floor close to me. She wrapped an arm around my shoulder and asked, "Morgan, what did they do to you?"

"Oh, they roughed me up pretty well. Not so bad . . . I've had worse."

"What did they use on you? You leg looks nearly broken."

"Just a little piece of rubber hose," I said. "Nothing lethal."

"Jesus Christ! I'm so sorry," she whispered. Tears filled her eyes once again.

"Nothing to worry about," I said and smiled, trying to make her feel better.

"What do they want?"

"They wanted to know why Gandalf and I were here," I answered and shot a glare at Freeman. "They killed Gandalf. They shot him in the head for no damn reason. We were up in the hills . . . Gandalf stood up and a sniper got him."

She turned to Freeman and asked, "Who the hell are you people?"

"We are the American Freedom Army," he said proudly. He sat up straight and threw out his chest.

"What the hell is the American Freedom Party," I asked.

He said, "We are a movement of free white men who will return this nation to its founding principles. This whole damn Country's being overrun by Mexis and blacks. White folks found this Country, and we want it back."

"So you're some kind of racist militia group?" I asked.

"If sticking up for the white race makes us racist . . . Then have it your way. And we're not some kind of militia. We are an army . . . Equipped, trained, and ready. When the time comes, we will take over. "

"Take over what?" I asked.

"We will take over the free nation of Texas. Our

brothers-in-arms up north will take over free nations along the Canadian border. We're spreading into Arizona and New Mexico."

"And what will you do once you've done that?"

"We will return this nation to free white people. We will get rid of coloreds . . . Mexicans and blacks and all those chinks from Asia."

"How do you get rid of them?" Sandy asked.

"Plans are being made," he said in a secretive voice, grinning proudly.

"Sounds a lot like Nazis, don't you think, Morgan?"

"Could be," I answered. "That type of thing is easy to do if you find the right people. They all start with really stupid people. Sounds like this place might be full of stupid people."

Sandy asked, "I'll bet Freeman isn't your real name, is it?"

"Freeman is my new American name. My Christian name is different."

"Your Christian name?" Sandy said. "I'm surprised you know anything about Christianity."

Nothing more was said. An hour past, then two. I knew what Sandy was doing; she was listening. She was listening for gun fire, or shouting, or any other disturbance. If there was none, then Fish had escaped.

Time slipped away and still nothing from outside. I was worried about that. Something had to be brewing outside. My mind ran through pictures of a couple dozen armed men breaking in and shooting everything. We wouldn't stand a chance.

Sandy had moved from next to me and stood next to the door. She pressed her ear to the door and listened. She watched Freeman as she listened. He was smiling a nasty, knowing smile. I hoped he didn't know something I didn't know.

There were no sounds outside, which gave hope to us

that at least Fish had gotten away safely. If anyone had seen him there would be shooting. Sandy returned to my side and sat close to me. She spoke softly, "I need to go to the back of the warehouse. If Robert made it out, he left a hole in the wall back there. If someone finds that hole . . . We're in trouble."

"Good thought," I said. "Can you move enough boxes to cover the whole?" I asked. I wanted to get up and help, but I knew I wasn't in any physical condition to do that.

"I think so," she said. "Can you take Freeman's gun and watch him?"

I nodded, hoping without speaking that I would not pass out. Sandy got to her feet and disappeared to the far back of the warehouse. The little desk lamp in the office couldn't send light more than ten feet from the desk. At the back of the warehouse it was darker than night. But she found the hole Fish had cut in the wall. It wasn't very big, but if anyone from outside walked to the rear of the building it would be easily found. She knelt and looked outside. It was dark but she saw the rag of Fish's shirt hanging from the barbed wire, blowing in the night breeze.

The hole had to be covered and blocked. It was an easy access for any of Freeman's good buddies to get inside and kill us. There were many dozens of boxes and crates filling half of the warehouse. Some were just too big and too heavy for her to move, but she found eight wooden crates that she could slide in front of the hole. She was satisfied that it would be difficult, if not impossible, for anyone to get inside using the hole in the wall.

One of the crates she had moved had a loose top, the nails having come loose. Curiosity got the best of her. She managed to pull open the wooden top, looked inside, and wasn't surprised to find plastic wrapped packages, the size of large bricks, of white powder.

Back with me, she sat on the floor next to me and said, "I think I found a bunch of drugs back there." She told me what she had done and what she had found.

"I figured there was more to this place than just a bunch of gun nuts talking revolution."

"Do you think that's why that boy was killed?"

"I think it's a better than even bet that drugs and money had a lot to do with it. And I'd bet my last million that this damn place has more to do with drugs and money than with revolution."

It was cold inside the big warehouse, and I was in pain. My head was spinning, and my stomach was twisting. I moaned a little when I tried to straighten out my left leg, the one that was the target for Max's slashing garden hose.

"Are you really OK," she whispered, hearing the moan.

"I'll live," I said. My throat was raw and even to whisper hurt. I had been chained to the chair and in the dark for what seemed like weeks, but was in fact only days. Time when you are confined in the dark either stands still or spins crazily out of control. I wasn't given water or food, and it seemed whoever these people were, they seemed to enjoy taking turns slapping me around. It wasn't as bad as the beating I'd taken in the desert, and no one used the rubber hose on me again. But it was bad enough.

They kept asking me the same question, "Who are you working for?" Not being a hero, I tried to tell them the truth, over and over again, that all I wanted was to find out why Betsy Concanon was in jail. But they seemed to believe I was working for some ultra secret government agency and that I was infiltrating their little corner of the world. Paranoid stuff, but I learned quickly these people weren't the brightest lights on the ol' chandelier.

I knew that Fish had escaped because there wasn't any noise that would have occurred if anyone had seen him or caught him. We were just waiting for him to have enough time to safely get away. And enough time had gone by. If Fish had made it out safely, he would be at the car and well on his way to find help. I said to Sandy, "It's time. Are you ready? I don't think they'll kill us, but they may hurt you."

"Don't you think we should wait?" she asked. "I don't think they'll rush us as long as we have Captain America over there."

"He's not coming back tonight," I said. "It'll take at least a full day. They'll only wait so long. Pretty soon they're going to rush this place."

Then we heard some commotion outside; loud talk, arguing. "Stay where you are Morgan," Sandy said. "This may be it. Don't try to stand, but shoot when you have to."

She quickly went to Freeman, unbuckled the straps holding him in the chair and told him to stand. She walked behind him to ten feet from the closed door, looping her left arm around his neck and holding her Glock to the right side of his head.

From outside we heard a woman's voice. "Mrs. Crew! Mrs. Crew! Can you hear me?"

It was Mary Lou Perkins. I looked at Sandy, and she looked at me. I shrugged my shoulders in disbelief. Sandy called out, "I can hear you, Mrs. Perkins."

"May I come inside and speak with you and your husband?"

"Come in alone," Sandy answered. "I have a gun on Captain Freeman and he'll be the first to die. Morgan has a gun and I promise you, you'll be the second one to die if you try anything stupid."

The door swung open, very slowly. Light from the flood lights surrounding the compound flooded into the room, hurting my dark adjusted eyes. Mary Lou stepped carefully into the little room, leaving the door open behind her. She held a Coleman lamp that was bright enough to light the immediate area. She held it high and looked around. She smiled and nodded at me, sitting on the floor, holding Freeman's pistol pointed at her. Sandy remained standing behind Freeman, who was as tall as she.

"My, my!" Mary Lou said sweetly with all the old southern charm she could muster. "What have we here? My dear Mrs. Crew, just what in the world are ya'll doin'?"

"Trying to stay alive," Sandy said. "Just what the hell are you doing?"

"Well, I am hopin' to straighten out this terrible mess. I'm just so upset that this has all happened. Ya'll just can't imagine. Now, ya'll come outside with me . . . Ya'll will be very safe. Let me get some people to help your good husband. Let's go have some food, some coffee, maybe a little bourbon? How's that sound Mr. Crew? Ya'll like bourbon, don't ya'll? An' I've got just the best bourbon ya'll ever tasted. Let's just get this terrible mess all over with, is that agreeable?"

"How can we trust anything around here," I asked.

"No one here will want me to be hurt," Mary Lou answered with a sweet little smile on her face. "You let the Captain go and I'll stay with you. There's this here little mess hall just a few steps away. The food's not what I'd serve at home, but ya'll look like ya'll could do with some food. We'll go there, is that alright?"

"You tied up my husband and beat him," Sandy said. "How do we trust you now?"

"My dear," she said, as sweetly as she could manage. "I'm so very sorry about all that. I'm just sick about it. Mrs. Crew, I have some . . . How do you say it? . . . Some pull around here. These boys, they listen t'me. They respect women . . . Like in the old days. Now let me help you."

Sandy looked questioningly at me. I shrugged my shoulders once again. I mean, what did we have to lose? We had two pistols and no spare ammo to hold off a dozen or more men with military weapons. Sooner or later, Fish would be back with help. How long could we wait?

So Sandy pushed Freeman away, towards the door and said, "Get out." He walked slowly, trying to look tough and defiant, leaving the door open behind him as he went out of our sight.

"Now, my dear," Mary Lou said. "Why don't ya'll just come with me? You can keep your gun if you want. I'll have a couple of the boys come help Mr. Crew. All this is just so embarrassing t'me."

She smiled again and half turned towards the open door. "Max!" she called out. "Max! Please send in two men to help Mr. Crew. And tell them to be very, very careful and respectful. I just don't know . . ."

Two men walked into the room; one was short, built like a bear and bearded. The other was tall, wiry thin, and with a shaved-bald head. They were dressed in camo colored pants and dirty tan T-shirts that should have been washed several days ago.

Mary Lou directed them to me. Between the two of them, they lifted me off the floor like I was a bag of feathers. They grabbed me under my arms; I hurt just about everywhere by that time, but I didn't complain.

Mary Lou told them, "Please help Mr. Crew to the mess hall. We're gonna' get these good folks some food and water. And let's have that medic fella' . . . What's his name? Bruno or something? . . . Let's get him to look after Mr. Crew. It's just terrible. I'm just mortified at all this."

Mary Lou led the way across the compound. The two men helped me, although I thought I might be able to walk by myself. Sandy followed a few steps behind, making it obvious she still held a gun level at Mary Lou's back.

It was deep into the night, yet the compound was brightly lit from the surrounding flood lamps. We walked across hard packed dirt, through a gauntlet of well armed men; I counted eighteen. Colonel Max and Captain Freeman stood off to the side. Freeman's empty holster had been filled with a pistol. He didn't look very happy; I wondered if he was just pissed off at me and Sandy or was he contemplating some discipline at having been caught by Sandy and Fish.

Mary Lou stopped at the double doors to a long, rectangular building. She stood starring at the doors waiting for something. Finally a young man came running. He strapped his M16 rifle over his shoulder and opened the doors, a little frightened and a little apologetic in his subservient bow. Mary Lou walked into the building without saying a word and turned on a series of ceiling lights.

Inside, it was in fact a mess hall, with two rows of four wooden tables each. Benches were lined up on either side of each table. The smell of coffee permeated the big room. I motioned to the two men at my side towards a table which they took me to. I sat on the nearest bench and rested my elbows behind me on the table top trying to look casual and not give the impression of being in pain. Mary Lou told the two men who had walked with me to leave. They did, and they moved quickly. Her voice didn't hold the southern charm it did when she spoke to us.

Mary Lou waited until the three of us were alone. Sandy sat on the bench next to me, and we waited to see our fates. Mary Lou turned to us, smiling as sweetly as she always did, and said, "Now, first I want to apologize for all this. I am so very ashamed. Mr. Crew, I do hope ya'll aren't too angry with me."

"You run this place?" I asked her.

"Like I said, these boys are all good boys. They respect ladies. I just don't know why all this happened to ya'll."

Harry Perkins stormed into the mess hall. He was staggeringly drunk and holding a big, black cigar in the fingers of his right hand. "Where's that black boy you was with!" he shouted.

"Harry!" Mary Lou said. "I thought I told you to wait outside!"

"Screw that shit!" he slurred and stumbled forward, almost tripping over his own feet. "They had some black bastard with them, and now he's gone!"

Mary Lou looked at us menacingly and angry. "Is that true?" she asked.

We said nothing. She told her husband to go get Colonel Max and Captain Freeman. "And don't come back with them! You're drunk again!"

Harry turned and stormed from the mess hall. He said, under his breath, something that sounded like, "Truck you, witch."

Max and Freeman came running. They stopped and stood sort of like at attention in front of Mary Lou. She smiled that sweet, southern lady smile again, and asked, "Was there someone else with them when they arrived unannounced?"

Max answered, "She had a driver, a young black guy. He came with a big black guy. That one's dead."

Mary Lou turned to us, pure red-faced anger having taken over; all the old world charm drained from her. "Where is he?" she demanded.

Sandy answered, "I'm sure I don't know. He told me he was going to go for a pack of cigarettes. He never came back. That happens with men. They're so damn unreliable."

Freeman said, "There's a hole in the back of the wall in the warehouse."

She turned her back to us and faced Max and Freeman. They both were big men, men I wouldn't want to tangle with, even if I were in good shape. But they were frightened; they were visibly shaking.

"Why wasn't I told of this?" Mary Lou asked. Seconds ago she was a sweet southern belle with a ready smile. Now, she was a deep voiced, angry person to be really, really scared of. At least, I was scared.

"I was going to tell you . . ." Freeman began but she interrupted him.

"Bullshit! You withheld important information! I need all available intelligence in order to command around here! You fucked up, Captain! You too, Colonel!"

"I'm sorry . . ."

"Shut up! Get out!"

Freeman turned and ran outside. Colonel Max followed, only he didn't run. Mary Lou took a deep breath and turned to us once again. "I guess I'm gonna' need that there gun, Mrs. Crew. And yours too, Mr. Crew." she said and walked to us, her hand held out for Sandy's Glock.

She raised the gun and pointed it at Mary Lou. She said, "Suppose I just kill you instead?"

"Well, I don't think a sweet young thing like ya'll would have the guts to do that," she said, smiling that sweet southern lady smile again. "And if you did, there'd be twenty guns in here filling the two a'you with more lead than ya'll certainly would like."

"That makes sense," Sandy said. "Except you'd be dead and you wouldn't know if we were killed or not. Think about it, Mary Lou."

And she did think about it. I could see in her face the question spinning around inside her brain: 'Can this woman really kill me?'

Sandy interrupted her thoughts. She said, "What we have here is what they call a Mexican standoff. We're going to talk, and while we talk, I want you to get Morgan some water . . . And I think some food, too. I know my husband has been without food and water for a couple of days now . . . And I'm hungry, too."

I guess Mary Lou finished her thinking and decided to stay alive for awhile. Without turning, she yelled over her shoulder, "Sammy! Get some food and water in here! Now!"

A tall, thin man with a three day stubble on his face, wearing blue jeans, a rumpled white shirt, open collared and sleeves rolled up to his elbows, and a long white but stained apron, ran into the mess hall. Without stopping, he ran into a back room and reappeared within seconds with a wooden tray filled with six bottles of water. He laid the tray on the table near us and started back to what must have been a kitchen. Sandy stopped him, "Scrambled eggs," she called out. "Soft scrambled . . . And a glass of milk." The man nodded and ran off.

Sandy handed me a bottle which I managed to open with weak and shaking hands, even though it was difficult. I knew Sandy had to keep the Glock pointed at Mary Lou, and with only one hand, she could not have opened the bottle. The water was good; they had withheld water from me for however many days they had held me in the dark. Immediately, my head started to clear and I felt a little strength begin to return.

"So, anyway," Sandy said. "Tell me who the hell you people are."

Mary Lou smiled again, but this time it was a nervous smile, not the sweet, southern lady thing. "We are The Real American Army," she said arching her shoulders back proudly, trying to fain pride, but I could see she was faking that.

"And just what is The Real American Army?" I asked. The water had helped; my dry, parched throat didn't hurt as much, and I found my voice was beginning to return.

"We are preparing for the takeover of this great nation," Mary Lou said.

"What great nation?" I asked her.

Mary Lou hesitated; she was shifting back and forth from foot to foot. She couldn't look at me and her face was reddening. She was lying to me.

"We want a nation for white Christians . . . Like it used to be," she said.

Sandy looked at me, and she smiled knowingly. The cook brought a plate of eggs, a couple slices of toast and a tall glass of milk. Sandy told him, "Get out," and he ran through the open doorway.

"Morgan dear," she said smiling that beautiful smile of hers that I love so much, "You eat up while I smack this li'l ol' southern belle up 'side her li'l ol' southern head with this li'l ol' pistol of mine."

She stood and took a couple of steps towards Mary Lou. Mary Lou backed up, holding her hands up in front of her, until her back was against the wooden wall of the mess hall. "You . . . You . . . You can't hit me . . ." she stammered.

"Don't you believe that," I said. "Sandy's got this mean streak inside of her. Hell, she beats the crap outta' me all the time."

"No . . . No, please . . ."

"Mary Lou," Sandy said as she moved closer to the woman. "I'm sick of all the lies. Now tell me what the hell's going on around here. I found the drugs back in the warehouse. A little truth right now will go a long way."

The woman said nothing, but she was shaking with fear. Sandy raised the Glock, and I wondered if she really was going to pistol-whip the woman. Mary Lou raised her arms over her head and fell to her knees.

From outside, Max called into the mess hall, "Mrs. Perkins! Mrs. Perkins! Barterimo is here! What do you want me to do?"

CHAPTER EIGHTEEN – The Killings

"Who's Barterimo?" I asked. The eggs were good; the milk helped. The toast began to steady my stomach. I drank another bottle of water. My head had stopped spinning, and I felt a little strength returning. I pushed myself to my feet. My bruised leg hurt. I had been tied down to the chair for days. I smelled bad – they hadn't let me up even to urinate - and I felt worse. But the food and water was helping, and I felt anger returning.

When Mary Lou didn't tell me who Barterimo was, I said to Sandy, "Let me have a few minutes with her."

"Sit down, Morgan. I can beat her if that's necessary."

"I'm not going to hit her, Dear. I'm going to put one bullet in either of her feet and one bullet in either of her knees. Then either of her elbows and either of her hands. She'll be a friggin' vegetable when I get done with her."

Sandy smiled as she stepped away from Mary Lou. I walked slowly and stood close to Mary Lou. I looked her in the eyes and pointed the gun at her left foot. "Ordinarily I'd say I was sorry," I said. "But in your case, it'll be a pleasure."

"Wait!" she screamed. "Barterimo is a driver . . . He delivers stuff . . . That's all."

"Delivers what?"

"I can't . . . I can't . . ."

I was steady enough on my feet to suggest, "Sandy, dear. Why don't we take Mary Lou here outside so she can sign for whatever Barterimo delivers? We both know it's a shipment of drugs."

I carried the bottle of water in one hand and Freeman's semi-auto in the other. Sandy carried her Glock. Mary Lou didn't want to, but she led the way outside, her hands raised well above her head. It was rapidly approaching early morning, pre-dawn grey daylight. The men in the compound's yard were all grouped in one place, near the tall flag pole. All were well armed and looking more uncertain than mean. Behind them was a bright red pickup truck; a man was standing next to it with arms folded and looking mean, also. He was bald headed and muscular, and sported tattooed arms, neck, and bald head. His dark mustache hung long, below his chin.

I wasn't sure what to do next, but the buzzing coming from the east attracted everyone's attention. The sun was just beginning to edge itself over the top of the canyon wall. From out of the sun, I immediately recognized Maggie Autumn Leaf's rickety old biplane, the engine sputtering and missing loudly. It was flying nose down, skimming the side of the cliffs, heading straight for the compound. I looked around me and saw everyone looking at the biplane, all obviously wondering just what the hell they were looking at.

I took Sandy's arm, and we quietly started backwards without anyone noticing. Mary Lou stood frozen, her arms still up straight over her head, staring at what was coming right for her. Maggie kept coming, nose angled down, the nose of the bi-plane pointed right at the crowd of people in the compound. Sandy and I had walked backwards to the entrance to the warehouse, the biggest building in the fenced compound. The door was still hanging open, but before we could step inside, Maggie pulled the biplane's nose up and she tossed three hand grenades out onto the crowd. Bodies flew everywhere, and those not hit ran in every direction.

She was close enough to the ground for me to see – if not hear her screeching laughter above the roar of the un-muffled engine – Maggie cackling madly as she flew up and pulled her biplane into a barrel roll. On the way down, she tossed four more grenades from a higher altitude. Then some of the men, those not killed by the grenades, started firing at her. Pistols and rifles and M-16s and AK47s, all firing madly.

Maggie pulled up and to the left, returning again and started firing an old machine gun she had attached to the upper wing of her biplane. It raked across the compound's yard, hitting two of the men and the red pickup Barterimo had been driving. The gas tank exploded into a ball of flame taking more of the armed men with it. When she was over the compound, she once again tossed grenades out, this time aiming for groups of men trying to hide behind trucks and buildings.

As she started to pull up and turn a third time, smoke started to spew from the engine. The biplane slowed as Maggie pulled back on the stick to get altitude, and then I saw flames burst from the smoke. The old, raggedy biplane was nose straight up towards the sky, a couple of hundred feet up. Then it stopped and hung in the sky like a kite. I couldn't see Maggie who was hidden inside the smoke and flame as her biplane spun slowly to the left and fell to ground, nose down, and exploded in a ball of flame outside the compound but close enough to the fence for it to be blown down by the explosion.

"My God!" was all I could think of saying. Sandy was holding onto me, her face buried against my chest.

Outside, all around us, were fires and vehicles exploding. Many of the wooden buildings were on fire, and lying on the dirt of the compound were bodies everywhere. And from their hiding places, the few remaining alive walked into the death site, aimless, wondering what to do. They went from body to body; they were looking for someone to tell them what they should do now.

I saw the pickup truck that Barterimo had driven into the compound. It had been blown apart, and the distinctive odor of burning cocaine permeated the air all around it. Barterimo lay on his back on the ground near his truck. He had no face left, and his chest was only red blood and torn flesh. Four other men lay nearby, one of them trying to get to his feet. He was bleeding badly and gave up, crumpling down onto the dirt.

We stepped outside, Sandy hanging onto my arm. Neither of us noticed when the Glock slipped from Sandy's hand and fell to the dusty ground. She was crying; and whispered, "Let's get the hell out of here."

We walked around the carnage, the few men who had survived the attack wandered without taking notice of us. I stopped and picked up an AK-47. I said to Sandy, "We need to find Mary Lou . . . If she's still alive."

We found Harry Perkins lying face up in a pool of his own blood, a five foot long shard of wood piercing his chest. I heard a voice, at first thinking it was just something I was imagining. I turned and looked all around the warzone. Through a cloud of smoke, Mary Lou stumbled over a body, regained her footing and kept walking; calling out in a weak, faint voice, "Help! Someone help me! Help!"

Her dress was in tatters, blood covered her face running from a gash across the top of her scalp. Her right arm hung lifeless at her side, blood flowing from her shoulder. Sandy went to her and gently took her by her left arm. "Come with me," she said. She led Mary Lou back to the warehouse where she found a first aid kit.

All I wanted to do was get out of there and go home. I'd been beat up and tortured, and for what? I really didn't know. As I walked around the battleground, looking for a vehicle that wasn't damaged, the realization came to me that only Mary Lou knew why I had been held captive. So I gave up looking for a car and followed Sandy to the Warehouse.

As she treated Mary Lou's wounds, I asked, "Enough of the bullshit, Mary Lou. Tell me what this is all about. That truck load of drugs out there . . . Is that the real business you're in?"

Sandy was wiping Mary Lou's blood from her face. She had wrapped a tight cotton bandage around the gash on her shoulder. Mary Lou looked at me with contempt in her eyes. She said, "Go to hell."

Sandy smiled and asked her, "Where is your son?"

"My son?" Mary Lou answered.

"You know . . . Jimmy . . . Your son."

"Go to hell," Mary Lou repeated.

As Sandy put pressure on the gash across Mary Lou's scalp she said, "I think you set our child's nanny . . . Betsy . . . Up for a murder. I think you had to kill Edgy Hands . . . Maybe because he was talking too much . . . Maybe because he just pissed you off. Anyway, everybody knows everybody out here, so you had to import someone to take the fall. Your son, Jimmy, was sent out to do that."

"Go to hell," Mary Lou said once again.

I said, "This whole thing has to do with drugs . . . Don't deny it, Mary Lou. This whole militia crap thing is just a cover. All your militia thugs do is provide protection . . . and distribution probably. I know that, Mary Lou . . . And you're going to pay for it. You're going to answer for the murders . . . You're going to answer for the smuggling."

Mary Lou flinched when Sandy placed an alcohol dampened piece of cotton on the scalp gash. But it didn't hurt enough to stop her from repeating, "Go to hell."

Before I could say anything else in this waste of time, Colonel Max called from outside, "Mrs. Perkins! You OK?"

Mary Lou pushed Sandy's hand away and yelled, "Get in here and kill these bastards!"

I quickly moved to a corner, leaving the door to my left. I waived at Sandy to run to the rear of the warehouse.

She took Mary Lou's arm, but she shook Sandy off and ran, staggering, for the door. We let her go, and when she reached the door, as she had her hand on the knob, the door burst open, pushing her back. Shots from a half dozen automatic weapons were fired that nearly ripped Mary Lou in half. She collapsed to the floor and bled out quickly.

Outside, people were shouting and swearing. That's good, I thought. Keep them arguing amongst themselves. One shot . . . Then two more. That's even better, I said to myself. More shouting and a few more gun shots. Maybe they'll kill themselves off.

Then someone burst into the warehouse and sprayed bullets from an M-16 in front of him. I shouldered my AK-47 and fired one shot hitting the man in the ribs and killing him. Another man rushed in, stopped, looked around for me but I took two shots and killed him, also.

Killing is not an easy thing for me. I've had to kill before . . . To save my life . . . To save Sandy's life. The nightmares of the killings will be with me forever. But I knew, pushing myself into the corner, that I would kill anyone coming into the warehouse, at least as long as my AK's bullets held out.

Colonel Max called to me again. "Morgan! Morgan! Can you hear me?"

"I can hear you Max!"

"Let's stop all this! We can all walk away! All I want is the cocaine!"

"Well, that's nice," I answered. "I don't have any particular use for illegal drugs, so why don't you come inside and get it!"

"I don't wanna' die, Morgan!"

"I don't want to die either!" I said and shouldered the AK again. I had a hunch someone was going to come through the open door again.

I could hear some muffled talk from outside. It sounded like arguing again, but there were no more gunshots.

Max called out again, "Morgan! Both the Perkins are dead! I've got three men left! This whole operation's dead and gone! Look, in the back of the warehouse is a safe! It's got a quarter million bucks in it! You take it, and I'll take the cocaine! Is that a deal?"

"I don't want the money!" I yelled back.

"So what the fuck do you want?" he yelled angrily.

"I want answers! Everybody out there! Drop whatever guns and knives you're carrying, and come inside with your hands on top of your head!" I called out. "If you want to live long enough to get out of here, do what I say! I've killed two of your men and I'll kill you too if I have to!"

I waited, and while I waited, Sandy came to me and stood at my side. I didn't want the love of my life to get hurt, but hiding in the back of the warehouse wouldn't keep her alive if Max decided to come in shooting. If we were to die, I wanted to die with her.

But Max surprised me and took tentative steps into the warehouse, his hands on the top of his head. "Stop where you are," I said. "Turn around slowly."

He did as I said and stopped, facing me. "Close the door behind you," I ordered. He did without saying anything and returned his hands to the top of his head. "Take three steps towards me . . . Face the wall . . . Stand against the wall . . . Press your nose against the wall, and keep your hands on your head." Max did as he was told.

Sandy followed close behind me as we walked to Colonel Max. I pressed the barrel of the AK against Max's temple and told Sandy to pat him down. She found nothing. We stepped away from him, to what I thought was a safe distance – far enough that Max couldn't jump on us but close enough for me not to miss if I had to shoot him.

"OK, Max," I said. "You can put your hands down and step away from the wall."

He was very slow and careful to do as I said. When

he faced us he asked, "So what the hell do you want?"

CHAPTER NINETEEN – Come Home With Us

"Tell me about Edgy Hands," I said.

"Edgy?" Max questioned. "Is that what all this shit's about? You killed a couple dozen people and ruined this operation because of a dumb, friggin' loud mouth idiot?"

"Is that who Edgy was?" I asked. "Edgy was killed because he was talking to much?"

"Edgy Hands was a waste of time. I didn't want him here. He put too much shit up his nose, and he drank too much. He was a loud mouth ass hole and a lazy son of a bitch. I need men . . . Not friggin' idiots."

"Who was he talking to?" Sandy asked.

"Anybody who would listen . . . Anybody who would buy him a damn bottle of beer."

I asked, "He spent a lot of time in San Juan de Cristo, right? He spent a lot of time at The Last Stand?"

"That's the best thing Edgy could do. He was an expert at hangin' out, drinking, and bullshitting." Max said derisively.

"I've been to The Last Stand," I said. "The guys who hang out there are cowboys who work at the Bar H and are probably your own people. Who was Edgy talking to? There aren't a whole lot of other people out here."

"You know that already," Max said. "There ain't but one person Mary Lou worries about. That friggin' Mexi who

201

thinks he's some kind of James Bond spy."

"You mean Jose Santos?" I asked.

"That's one of the names he goes by."

"He's an ATF agent," Sandy said. "You knew that? You knew that, and you just let him hang out back in that rat trap little town?"

"He's nothin' near being an ATF Agent. He's a load of bull crap," Max said. "He tries to sell stuff to the Feds. He's nothing."

"He's not a Federal Agent?" I asked. "But Edgy was talking to him, so you killed Edgy?"

"Who said I killed him?" Max said smiling. "That girl killed him, right?"

Sandy took a step forward; my hand on her arm stopped her. She said, "Betsy didn't kill anyone. I think she was set up for the murder. I think you and Mary Lou Perkins were responsible for killing Edgy Hands."

"Speculation, Mrs. Crew. Nothing more. Now, you may leave here . . . Alive . . . Now. There's a truck out there . . . One of three left undamaged by that crazy bitch Indian. Take the rifle with you . . . Take whatever you want . . . Go now. If you choose to stay, you will die."

"We'll go," I said. "Just tell me where I can find Jimmy Perkins."

"Hah! That punk kid! He's probably hiding in some closet back at the ranch, peeing his pants. He ain't worth rattlesnake shit. Do what you want with him."

I looked at Sandy; she nodded, and we left. We stepped around the dead, avoided the fires, and didn't look at the three men left of Mary Lou's fake 'Real American Army'. As we walked past them, they ran into the warehouse, anxious to get their hands on the money and cocaine.

Near the gate that was hanging open as the result of one of Maggie's hand grenades, we found a Nissan pickup truck. Keys were in the ignition. We looked to the wreckage of Maggie's biplane. She had to know she would be killed, but she took a lot of these people with her.

We got in the pickup truck and drove through the gate, Sandy driving as I tried to find a position in the small cab that didn't hurt. The dirt of the compound was potholed from Maggie's attack. We bounced along slowly, even slower as we passed close to the burnt wreckage of Maggie Autumn Leaf's patched together biplane. Little was left but charred wood, ash, and twisted wire. Maggie's twisted and lifeless body lay under what was left of a wing. She had worn a full dress that had been stitched with Comanche religious symbols. It was burning.

We drove for two miles without speaking. Too many people had died, and for what? Greed and money. How many times in my life have I had to battle greed? My family has everything; money, power, everything. And how often have I wondered just how we got to where we are today? Did greed . . . Murder . . . Crimes . . . Did anything of these things have anything to do with it? I don't know. But I know that my life has a purpose, whether I liked it or not. My life is meant to help others do what they cannot do for themselves. Putting my life at risk is necessary.

Over a rise in the road we saw lights flashing - red lights, blue lights, white lights. They were miles away but recognizable as police cars. Sandy pulled the pickup to a stop in the middle of the road, and we waited.

As they got near us, we got out of the truck and stood in front of it. The line of eleven cars slowed and eventually stopped. There were several different kinds of Texas State cops, ATF cops, DEA cops, and FBI cops. And in the middle of the line was the rental car Sandy and Fish had arrived in. Fish got out of it and joined the police approaching us.

One of the cops, in some kind of uniform that I really didn't care about, asked, "Are you Morgan and Sandy Crew?"

I told him we were, and he said, "My orders are to get

you out of here, but I see you've done that already. Will you wait here for us?"

Sandy said, "No. We want to get as far away from here as possible."

I added, "There are four of them left alive."

"Alive! What the hell happened? Don't tell me you two killed them all."

"You'll see when you get there," I said. "It's only a couple of miles up the road. The four of them are in the biggest building, loading cocaine onto a truck. It's a warehouse of sorts and filled with stuff you'll be interested in. This is the only road out. You can't miss them . . . But be careful. Even though there are only four of them, they're well armed."

They started back to their cars. Sandy and I pulled Fish to the side. Sandy said, "Robert, come with us. There's nothing for you to do back there."

"Yo' Mama. They killed Gandy. I got stuff t'do, ya'know?" Fish said. He smiled, and in that smile I could see the respect, maybe even some love, he felt for Sandy.

"You can't do anything, Robert. They're all dead. Both the Perkins people are dead . . . Almost all the people back there are dead. The police will arrest the others. And Maggie's dead, too."

"Maggie!" Fish said. "Maggie's dead?"

"She attacked the compound," I said. "She flew that biplane of hers. She blew up the place and killed a lot of people. They shot her plane up. She crashed."

"That's shit, man," he said. Tears welled up in his eyes. "Christ! I stopped there and filled the damn car with gas. I told her . . . I told her who killed Gandy . . . Shit! I didn't know she was goin' after'em! Shit man!"

"It's not your fault, Robert," Sandy said. She touched his shoulder but he pulled away quickly.

"I got stuff t'do, Lady Crew," he said. He wiped his eyes and stood up straight, throwing his shoulders back and his chest out.

"Come with us. Come home with us," Sandy said.

"Hey Lady Crew," Fish said. "You think I could make it in your world? I ain't even close to fittin' in there . . . No more than you could fit in on my streets with my homeboys, ya' know? Gandy, he tried to get me off the streets. He couldn't, and you can't either. I don't mean no disrespect, ya' know. I just know where I belong."

He started to walk back to the car. I stopped him and told him, "Hang back in the compound. Stay out of sight if you can. Don't mention this to the police. Inside the warehouse there's a safe. Find it. Wait until everyone is gone. If the safe is still closed and locked, there's a quarter million dollars in that safe. Do some good with it, OK?"

Fish smiled and nodded knowingly. He held out his hand, and I took it. We shook hands, man to man, sharing respect. Fish got back in the car. He drove away, catching up with the line of police cars. Sandy asked, "Do you think he'll return the rental car?"

I laughed, "Are you kidding? He'll strip it and sell it piece by piece."

****

We drove on, aimlessly, silently. Finally Sandy said, "Let's go to the ranch. We still have to find Jimmy Perkins. He's the only one who can get Betsy back to us."

"And Tommy Rocker," I said. "He's still in jail. When he finds out what happened, he may decide to talk."

"You're right, of course," Sandy said. "We can offer him a good attorney and get him a deal. But he's not going anywhere. Let's go find Jimmy first."

There weren't enough roads for us to get lost in the desert wilderness. It took a couple of hours, but we found the long road leading up to the Bar H Ranch. We took the couple of miles slowly, watching for anyone who might be expecting us and who would stop us. But we saw no one.

The big house came into view, and still no one was to be seen. Sandy parked the pickup at the front steps. She said, "Maybe you should yell . . . Or maybe I should hit the horn?"

"Let's try the doorbell," I said. Sandy got out from behind the wheel and helped me out of the pickup. I was walking better, although my left leg was still bruised and sore from the rubber hose.

At the door, I rang the bell three times and knocked loudly on the door a couple of times. No answer. I tried the doorknob but found the door locked. We walked around to the back of the house. Behind the house, hidden from the front and anyone who drove up the long road, we found six small adobe huts lined up perpendicular to the house. A very dead oak tree wasted away at the rear of the huts.

There were steps leading up to a back door of the house. A wooden screen door, the screen torn, hung broken from one of its hinges. We stepped into the kitchen and walked through the doorway into the dining room. We searched through all the rooms of the house, upstairs and downstairs and found no one. We unlocked the front door and stepped out onto the covered porch.

Outside, we walked to the small huts behind the house and found them all empty of people. The stables and barn were empty of people and animals. There was no one anywhere. We returned to the house and sat in wooden rockers on the porch.

"There's got to be some ranch hands somewhere," I said. "And the cooks and maids? Where are they?"

"Could they all have heard that the Perkins were dead?" Sandy asked. "Could they all have just left?"

"Could be," I said. "Didn't Colonel Max say Jimmy was probably hiding in the basement? Maybe that was a hint? Did you see a door to a basement?"

Sandy said she hadn't. "Let's see if we can find it."

Retracing our steps through the ground floor of the house, looking in closets and behind tall furniture, we found nothing. "So what now?" I asked.

Sandy started pulling rugs up off the floor. Together we were able to rip the bigger rugs up, and in a back room that was the ranch office, under a thick rug woven with pictures of buffalos and Indians, we found a heavy trap door. With Sandy's help, we pulled it open and dodged a bullet that came from the dark end of the stairs below.

"Jimmy! Jimmy! It's Sandy Crew!" she called out. "There are no police here! Just my husband and me! All we want is to talk to you!"

"No! I know Conner Blake's there! I'll kill you! Go away!"

"Who's Conner Blake?" Sandy asked.

From behind us came the voice, "Ah'm Conner Blake. Who're ya'll?" He spoke in a slow, heavy Southern drawl. He was an athletically built man, maybe forty years old. His close cropped hair had the promise of grey showing around the edges. His face was wrinkled and tanned dark, an indication of a hard life that kept hard memories of murders spinning in his head. He wore a red plaid shirt, sleeves rolled up to expose a tattoo that had blurred over twenty years. His blue jeans were faded but clean, tight fitting and rolled at the bottom over healed and worn square toed boots that were meant for work rather than show.

From below Jimmy screamed, "Told you! Told you! He ain't comin' down here!"

I turned to Blake and asked, "What do you want?"

"Don't matter what I want," he said. He took a step or two to a tall backed leather chair that sat at a small, expensive looking desk. He sat, pulled a long, thin cigar from a humidor sitting on top of the desk, lit it with a wooden match he took from the drawer of the desk, and blew smoke towards the ceiling. "What matters is what the hell ya'll want."

"We want to speak with Jimmy," I said. "He seems to think you're going to hurt him."

"Hurt him?" Blake said and laughed. "I ain't gonna' hurt the boy . . . 'Less he keeps shootin' off his fuckin' mouth like he been doin'.'."

From below, through the open trap door, Jimmy yelled, "See! Told you so!"

Sandy said, "Mr. Blake. I don't know who you are. But Jimmy Perkins has evidence that will free a young girl from prison. She has been wrongly accused of murder. Jimmy knows the truth."

"And ya'll . . . The two of ya'll . . . Ya'll know the truth, too?" Blake asked.

I answered, "Yes. All we want is to get our friend released from jail. All the rest of whatever this is, is none of our business, and we don't really care about it."

"Released from jail, ya'll say?" Blake asked. "Ah' think ya'll know she ain't in no jail no more. Ah' think ya'll know Betsy Colcannon's on the run right now. So why ya'll wanna' do more than ya'll already done?"

"We don't want her to be on the run the rest of her life," Sandy answered.

"An' if that girl gets her charges dropped . . . What's gonna happen to the boy that got killed? Who ya'll think will pay for that?"

From below Jimmy yelled up, "He done it! He done it!"

"You killed Edgy Hands?" I asked.

"That there's a real good name for that loud mouth som'bitch," Blake said. "Couldn't keep his damn mouth shut 'round nobody. Som'bitch deserved t'die."

"So you killed him," I said. It wasn't a question. I think I knew the answer but I had to be sure.

"Nah, I didn't kill the som'bitch," Blake said, grinning. He drew deeply on the cigar and filled the room with more smoke.

"But you arranged it," I said. Making a statement and still not questioning. Blake grinned almost proudly but he didn't say anything. He laid the burning cigar on the edge of the desk and slowly sat forward in the chair. He reached behind him and pulled a shiny, chrome plated colt revolver from behind him. It was a modern version of the old 'Peacemaker' revolvers cowboys used to carry.

"Now," he said, pointing the gun back and forth from Sandy to me and back to Sandy. "Now, ah'm gonna' kill ya'll and then I'm gonna' go down in that there hole and kill little Jimmy."

"Wait a minute, wait a minute," I said. I turned to Sandy and asked, "Look, babe. It looks like we're going to die here. It's been a fun ride. I do love you and respect you. But before I die, I really would like one of those cigars. You know I've never really gotten away from smoking."

"Morgan Crew! I've told you how many times I don't want you smoking."

"Sandy, my dear. What can it hurt? He's going to kill us anyway."

"Well," Sandy said with a scowl on her face. "I guess if you have to."

I turned to Blake and asked, "How about it? Can I have a smoke before you kill us?"

"My mama raised me t'be polite," he said. "Ya'll go ahead. There ain't no rush. I can wait."

I stepped to the desk and opened the humidor. The cigar was cheap, hard, dry, and the wrapper was flaking. I'd had better . . . Without Sandy knowing about it, of course.

I bit off the end and spit it to the side. "Hand me one of those matches, will you, please?" I asked.

As Blake reached around to open the drawer, Sandy and I moved together. I fell on him and grabbed the gun, pushing it away. Sandy grabbed his gun arm with one hand and his throat with other. We all fell to the floor and rolled across the room. The gun fired once, harming only a wall.

We wound up on top of Conner Blake; I was punching him any place I could, as hard as I could, considering my damaged ribs, while Sandy was biting his gun hand. He yelled and dropped the gun, Sandy grabbed it up, cocked the hammer, pointed it at Blake and said, "OK, enough of all this."

I pushed Blake away and got to my feet. Sandy handed the pistol to me. It was a pretty gun, mother of pearl grips and very shiny, but it was heavy and had only five rounds left in it. We each carried pistols that were tucked under our belts at our waists. We each pulled them out; Blake's eyes opened wide, and his jaw fell open.

Blake started to get up off the floor. I stopped him, "Stay where you are, Conner. You can tell me what I want to know from down there."

"I ain't gonna' say nothin'. Ya'll go t'hell."

I said, "Conner, I've had great results shooting people a little bit at a time. I'm going to tell you the same thing I told Mary Lou back at her compound. I've got five rounds left here in your gun and nine in my semi-auto. That means, if I use only your gun, I can put one bullet through either of your feet . . . One in either of your knees . . . And still have one left for one of your elbows. Then I can use a few of the bullets from my own gun. Now, you're not going to die . . . But you'll need someone to push you around in a wheelchair for the rest of your unnatural life and feed you through a tube, too. How does the sound to you?"

"You ain't got the balls."

I cocked the hammer and touched the pistol to Blake's right foot. "Try me," I said.

He tried to spit but his dry mouth found little spittle. I pulled the trigger, and his cowboy boot filled with blood as he screamed.

"Morgan!" Sandy said in a surprised whisper.

"Conner," I said. "How about the other foot?"

"No! No! Wait! Ah'll tell you what ya'll want!"

"What I want is you and Jimmy back in El Paso. I know that Edgy Hands was talking about the drug operation back at the compound. He had to be shut up. I think somebody . . . Maybe you . . . Was ordered to kill Edgy. San Juan de Cristo is too small a town. Everybody knows everybody. So Jimmy brought an out of town girl to take the fall. You're going to talk to the police and give them complete and truthful statements. Do you do that, or will you lose your left foot, too?"

I didn't notice that Jimmy Perkins had climbed out of his hole and was standing behind us. He held a well used .22 semi-auto rifle. I heard him but not in time to stop him from firing six quick rounds into Conner Blake's chest. The man slumped on the floor, dead.

Sandy screamed as the shots rang out. I wasn't fast enough to stop him, but I did manage to grab the rifle from him after he had killed Conner. I pushed him backwards. He fell over a stack of cardboard boxes and dropped to the floor. He was crying like a child, sobbing, and he rolled himself into a ball.

I tossed the rifle away and checked Conner for a pulse, finding none. "He's dead," I told Sandy. "Now what?"

"We've got to call in the police," Sandy said. She was backing away from the dead Conner Blake, covering her mouth with her hand, and unable to take her eyes off the body.

"What police?" I asked. "Do we call in Sheriff Kronk? How about all those Feds back at Mary Lou's compound? There's been so many killings . . . Who do we call?"

Sandy could not answer. I said, "Our only purpose here is to get Betsy out of trouble. Frankly Sandy, I couldn't care less how many of these idiots kill each other. We'd all be better off if they kill each other off until they're all dead. Let's get back to why we're here."

Sandy turned away from the body on the floor. "We've got Jimmy," she answered. "He can tell us the truth.

He can tell the attorneys back in El Paso the truth. - I doubt he's going to give us much trouble."

Jimmy was lying on the floor where I had pushed him. He was crying like a baby, sobbing, crying out for "mommy". I tried pulling him to his feet but my ribs were really hurting. Sandy grabbed one arm and I took the other pulling him from the floor to his unsteady feet. But what do we do next? I asked Sandy.

She said, "Look Morgan, I'm tired and hungry, and I know you are, too. I think Jimmy here could use some coffee . . . Maybe something stronger. We need to calm him down so we can talk to him. Let's go to the kitchen. We can talk to him there."

We sat Jimmy on a chair at the kitchen's small, old, wooden table that was out of place in the expensive kitchen. I imagined that in the Perkins house, only the help ate at that table. Mary Lou wouldn't have allowed family or friends to sit at such a table. Jimmy had stopped crying finally; he was wiping his runny nose on the sleeve of his blue plaid shirt. Sandy found a tin of ground coffee and a stove top coffee pot. In short order, the kitchen was filled with the smell of fresh coffee. I found a bottle of cheap tequila under the sink; that would have to do. Sandy found some cheap brown clay cups in a cupboard.

By the time Sandy put a cup of coffee in front of Jimmy, and I had added a splash of tequila, he had calmed down and was ready to talk. He drank from the cup, coughed, and drank some more.

"What happened out there?" he asked.

"You mean the compound?" I asked.

"The training camp," he corrected me. "My mom's training camp . . . Where her army is. When I got home, most of the ranch hands were packing up and leaving. They said there was a slaughter out there. Only Conner Blake stayed."

"So who was Conner Blake?" I asked.

"He's my mom's ranch foreman around here. He's a real bastard. He hates me and pushes me around all the time. My mom always lets him get away with it. Said it would make a man outta' me. I hate him. I hate him."

"He's dead, you know," Sandy said softly.

"Good," Jimmy said and smiled. "Who killed him?"

I looked at Sandy wondering if this boy was sane or had he slipped into some other reality. Sandy touched the boy's arm gently and said, "You killed him. Do you remember?"

He grinned strangely. It took a few seconds before he said, "I did? Good. He deserves to be dead. How's my mom? Where is she?"

"Jimmy," Sandy began, speaking softly, trying for some compassion that must have been hard to come by. "The camp . . . There was a gun battle back there . . . Your father is dead."

"Good!" Jimmy said brightly, smiling brightly and sitting up straighter in the chair. "I hate him, too. Always drinking. All he could do was slap me around when he was drunk. I'm glad he's dead. But where's my mom? I wanna' see her."

Sandy looked at me, I sensed unable to go on. So I told him, "It's all gone. Most of the men there are dead. The rest have been arrested. The drugs have been confiscated."

"Drugs? What drugs?" Jimmy asked. I honestly believed he didn't know. "She was running some stupid militia thing . . . She thought she was gonna' take over the whole damn Country. That's so friggin' stupid. I mean, what the hell is she thinking? Where is she, anyway?"

Sandy pulled a chair close to Jimmy and sat. She took his hand in hers and said softly, "Your parents . . . Both of them . . . They're dead, Jimmy. I'm so sorry."

At first Jimmy tried to smile, not believing what Sandy had said. Then the smile washed from his face as tears started once again. "My Mom? She's dead?"

"I'm so sorry, Jimmy," Sandy said.

Jimmy looked up, wiped the tears from his eyes, and said, "I don't give a damn about that son of a bitch Dad of mine. If he's dead, he's burning in hell. That's where he belongs. But my Mom, she loved me I think. She hated everything . . . But she loved me. I wanted her to love me anyway. My Dad, he stayed drunk to hide from her an' everything. I'm glad he's dead . . . But I'm gonna' miss my Mom." There were no more tears. Jimmy looked down into his cup of coffee and tequila, took another long drink, placed the cup carefully on the table, and sat back, his eyes looking at something far away that only he could see.

There was nothing I could say that would make any sense. I couldn't understand the life Jimmy Perkins must have led to bring him to the point of wishing his father to be in hell. But we were there for other matters - getting Betsy Concanon freed from a charge of murder. So I said, "Look, Jimmy. You have to come back to El Paso with us."

"What for?"

"Our friend has been charged with a murder you know she didn't commit."

Jimmy wiped the back of his hand across his face, wiping away tears that weren't there, pushed himself to sit up straight, and smiled a little. "I ain't goin' nowhere," he said. "I own the Bar H now. It's mine. I'm the boss. This is my land. So you two get off my land. Get off . . . Or I'm gonna' call some of my employees . . . Some of my ranch hands that'll beat you up. Understand?"

"Please Jimmy . . ." Sandy began. But my temper was starting to rise again. My ribs were aching, and I was at that point where I really didn't give a damn any more. Too much had happened to me to really care. I stood quickly, grabbed Jimmy by his shirt collar and pulled him to his feet. I still held Conner Blake's cowboy pistol. I held it close to his face.

"Shut your mouth!" I hissed. "You're coming with us

and you're going to tell the truth about Edgy Hands' murder. Now get out!" I pushed him towards the kitchen door, and then I pushed him through the living room, and through the front door onto the covered porch. Sandy went down the steps first and opened the passenger side door of the pickup truck.

I grabbed Jimmy's arm and started down the steps when a shot rang out. Wood splintered to my left. Another shot hit the front door behind us. The third hit Jimmy squarely in the chest. He fell backwards against the house and slumped to the porch.

It didn't take much for me to fall to the porch next to Jimmy. He was screaming for his mother again, clutching his chest where his blood was pouring between his fingers. He was kicking and rolling around. I tried to stop him to no avail. I couldn't stand up, and I didn't want to put myself in the line of fire.

Gradually Jimmy slowed his kicking and rolling; his words were slurred from the blood streaming from his mouth. He rolled once more and stopped, facing me. I was only a few inches from his face. He stared at me, eyes wide eyed, his mouth open and filled with blood. He was dead.

Sandy had jumped to the ground and crawled under the pickup truck. When no more shots were fired, she eased her way out and got to her feet, crouching behind the truck and looked over the hood. There was no one within sight.

"Morgan!" she yelled. "Morgan! Are you OK?"

"Stay where you are! I'll come down to you!"

"Be careful!" she called back. "I can't see anybody but . . ."

"I know. There's only one way to find out."

I stood up quickly and ran, limping still, across the steps to the railing on the other side and fell to the floor. Nothing. So I jumped up again and stood still this time, for only two or three seconds, and then fell to the floor again. Still Nothing.

"Sandy," I said. "I think it's OK. Stay where you are."

I stood slowly and walked down the steps, looking as I stepped cautiously. I reached down and helped Sandy to her feet. "I think he's gone," I said. "I guess only Jimmy was the target."

****

Sandy and I were sitting on the steps of the front porch. "Now what do we do?" Sandy asked. Jimmy's body lay lifeless to our right. Each of us in turn felt compelled to look down at Jimmy.

"If I had some bourbon, I'd get drunk," I answered.

"I'd be there before you if I could get my hands on some vodka."

We looked at each other and stood together. Inside the house we started looking around. "There's gotta' be some booze around here somewhere," I said. I opened cupboards in the living room and dining room as Sandy searched through the office where Jimmy's trap door hiding place was. She called out to me, "Morgan! Come in here! I found something!"

My immediate thought was booze of some kind. Cheap or rare, anything would be good. When I walked into the office, Sandy was standing in front of a four drawer black metal filing cabinet. The top drawer was open, bent and twisted as the result of her forcing the locked drawer open. Sandy was flipping through the papers inside.

"There are files on everybody," she said. "Colonel Max . . . Captain Freeman . . . Probably everybody out at the compound. Here's one on that stupid Sheriff out in San Juan de Cristo. There's one on Betsy. Oh my God! Here's a file on you and me!"

The top drawer, the second and the third were filled with files on close to one hundred people. I imagined there was a file on every person anywhere near San Juan de Cristo. There were files on Mexicans from across the border. There were files on people who, according to the information in the files, lived as far away as Chicago, Los Angeles, Miami, and New York. And there was a file on the late Henry Perkins, too. Only Mary Lou didn't have a file. It seems she liked to know everything about everyone. The files were complete life's records, every detail of everyone's life that she could get her hands on.

"Mary Lou not only didn't like people," I suggested. "She didn't trust anyone . . . Including her husband. This is the stuff of blackmail."

"We need to take this stuff with us," Sandy said. "There's got to be somebody outside of San Juan de Cristo who would love to see all this."

We found a few boxes in the back of a closet. They were stuffed with clothes that should have been disposed of a long time ago. We dumped the clothes and filled the boxes with the files. As we were carrying them out to the pickup truck, we had to walk past Jimmy Perkins, lying in the sun. "We can't leave him here," Sandy said.

"You're right, of course. And Conner Blake is still inside."

"We should call the police," Sandy said.

"What police? How about Sheriff Kronk? Should we go see if anybody's left at the compound? I don't know who to trust. Who killed Jimmy Perkins? When will the Feds get tired of us being around dead people? I'm not sure how much longer the Crew family name will get us out of trouble. And we still have to find a way to clear Betsy's name."

"So what do we do?"

"We could try the FBI, I guess," I suggested. "Maybe the State Police. We can't just drive away and leave them here."

"I guess you're right. There's a phone inside. Let's start with the State Police." Sandy said and led the way into the house.

Three hours later we watched as an old ambulance drove away with Jimmy Perkins and Conner Blake in the back, to be taken somewhere. They wouldn't tell us where. A dozen cops from the El Paso State Police office, all wearing broad brimmed white Stetson cowboy hats, beige uniforms, and big guns on their hips, remained. They took a hundred photos and measured everything and tagged what they considered evidence.

The man in charge, Michael Oberez, wearing gold Captain's bars on his shoulders, sat on the porch in front of us. He kept asking the same questions over and over again, keeping eye contact with us. I didn't mind. I'd been through that before, and I knew he was just doing his job. We told him everything, leaving out no detail of the killings at Mary Lou's ranch house.

In the end he took Jimmy's .22 rifle, bagged neatly in plastic, with him. It had been dusted for finger prints. Two deputies climbed down into the cellar hole beneath the house, where Jimmy had been hiding. They found spiders; a few cockroaches, and a puddle Jimmy had left when he couldn't wait to find a bathroom.

Oberez admitted that Jimmy was shot from long range. The first bullets that had missed Jimmy were carefully removed from the wood of the porch. They were, I was told, .556 MM military ammunition. He wanted to take us in too, until he phoned El Paso and spoke to someone he showed some deference to. I imagine he was told to let us go. When Oberez told us we were free to go, I smiled slyly at Sandy and thanked Oberez for all he had done. We stayed in the shade of the front porch while Oberez and his dozen Deputies drove away.

****

I had found a large brown clay pitcher in a cabinet under the sink in the kitchen. It looked clean enough, so I filled it with ice and water. Sandy pulled a couple of glasses from an upper cabinet. Back on the front porch we drank our fill and wondered what we were going to do next. We had the files in the bed of the pickup, but who do we take them to? And how was that going to help Betsy? Our conversation was interrupted when we saw the dust cloud of a vehicle coming towards us along the long, flat road that approached the ranch house.

It was barely thirty minutes since Captain Oberez had driven off. We stood and waited. I was worried about who was coming to see us. Too many people have died. Too many murders. And when people are murdered, more murders follow in attempts to cover up the crimes.

The car, a grey, nondescript four door sedan, pulled to a stop, and Jose Santos, the dishwasher from San Juan de Cristo's Mexican restaurant and who had found me in the desert and took me to a hospital after I had been worked over by four of Mary Lou's men, stepped out from the passenger side. From the driver's side, Colonel Max got out.

It was him, there was no mistaking that. It was Colonel Max. Although this time he wore a nice grey suit of medium value, a crisp white shirt with an old school type striped tie, both the shirt and tie loosened at the collar in respect of the Texas heat. He was clean shaven and the eye patch was missing.

"Who the hell *are* you?" I asked him as he walked towards us.

He reached inside his suit jacket. Sandy and I both flinched and took a step backward anticipating a gun. My hand searched for Captain Freeman's pistol that was still tucked inside my belt at my back. He took out a leather encased ID card holder and showed it to us. I held out my hand for the ID. He took two of the stairs up to me and I took it from him, looked at it and showed it to Sandy. The man was Karl Oberman, FBI Special Agent.

I handed the ID back to him and said, "I don't get it. You're FBI? I don't get it."

"You screwed up an investigation that has been two years in the making, Mr. Crew. Just what the hell were you thinking?"

"What the hell do you mean, what was I thinking? I've got a good friend who's been framed for a murder. All this crap . . . All the deaths including another friend of mine, Gandalf Finch, are related to that one frame-up. So don't come to me and start throwing your FBI weight around."

CHAPTER TWENTY – Santos

We sat on chairs on the Perkin's covered front porch. The heat had eased slightly in the shade of the porch and by a breeze blowing from the north. Inside the house was hotter than outside. The air conditioner system did little to cool the 100 degree heat of the day. Jose Santos refilled the pitcher I had with ice and water in the kitchen, and found two more glasses, as Sandy and I talked with Agent Oberman. Oberman had calmed down when he realized that I wasn't going to be pushed around. He actually became a little friendly.

"What the hell was all that about back at the compound?" I asked, trying to sound as friendly as Oberman seemed to be, but it was hard. I was angry and I felt like revenge would be a good thing. "Are you playing both ends of the stick? How the hell could you run a place like that and be a Federal Agent at the same time? How the hell could you let them tie me up and beat the crap outta' me?"

"I had to get you out of there alive," Oberman explained. "You screwed up the whole thing, and if I had any sense, I would have let them kill you. Mary Lou wanted to kill you after she got the million dollars ransom. But I couldn't do that. When that damn Indian squaw blew up the whole damn place, I had hopes of picking up the pieces . . . Of finishing the job of finding out who Mary Lou was selling drugs to . . . Before that damn army of cops showed up. You really screwed up. I was about to bust open one of the biggest drug smuggling operations in the last ten years. Mary Lou was beginning to trust me. She promoted me and she was about to let me in on her distribution network."

"Our friend, Betsy Concanon, was set up for the murder of Edgy Hands," I explained. "I'm sorry that your investigation was affected. All we want is to set her free. Then we'll go home and you can have all the rest of this."

"All the rest of what? It's all been blown to hell." He apologized nicely to Sandy for the language and then said, "What makes you think your girl is innocent?" he smiled like he knew something I didn't know.

Sandy said, "Because we know her . . . And because she told us she didn't kill that boy."

Oberman was laughing when Santos brought the cold water to us on an old tray. He had heard our conversation with Oberman. "Where is she?" Santos asked.

"I honestly don't know," I said. "And that's the way it's going to be until we find out who did kill Edgy Hands."

"And that brought you to Mary Lou's operation?" Oberman asked.

"It was the trail we followed," Sandy said. "We had no idea the Perkins' were running drugs."

"Hell, they had me tied up back there," I said. "They wanted a million dollars to set me free. And they murdered Gandalf Finch. All that doesn't bother you?"

"The ransom was actually Jose's idea," Oberman said; Jose smiled proudly. "We needed some way to keep you alive. He suggested it to me, and I suggested it to Mary Lou. That crazy bitch wanted to kill you without even knowing who the hell you were. She was a greedy old lady, so the idea of getting a million dollars appealed to her. It kept you alive."

"And you and Jose were working together on all this?" Sandy asked.

Jose said, "I'm with I.C.E. I've been in San Juan de

Cristo for three years . . . Washing dishes," he said derisively.

I sat forward in the chair and asked, "So you know who killed Edgy Hands, then?"

"Sure I do," Jose said. "Your girl . . . Concanon . . . Least ways that's what I heard. I wasn't there . . . They don't let Mexicans in the bars back there. And I really don't care. Your girl's been a real wild one . . . But you know that. I've seen her file. It's about time she paid the price for all the crap she's done."

There was little else to talk about. I have found attitudes like that all too common amongst hardened cops who have seen too much bad stuff in their careers. It becomes an attitude quickly learned and espoused. Hang the bad guy for anything because the bad guy must have done something wrong somewhere, sometime.

No, there was no point in continuing. I asked Oberman if he was going to arrest us, although I knew the answer already.

"Hell," he said angrily, "If I had my way, I put a damn bullet in your damn head and then throw you in jail. But you got pull; people want you left alone. So I've got to leave you alone." Oberman drained his glass and carefully laid it on a small table at his side.

We had four cardboard boxes of files in the back of the pickup truck. Sandy wondered silently if we should give them to Agent Oberman. I got up and said our goodbyes to the two men. Not mentioning the files told Sandy we were going to keep them for awhile at least. Trust has always been a difficult thing to come by for me. I have a hard time trusting people . . . Anyone . . . When I'm in trouble, that is. I didn't trust Oberman and Santos. There was something wrong there. Maybe it was just their attitudes, maybe it was something else. They'd been telling lies and working too many angles for too long. People who do that for too many years often fall into the whirlpool of lies they tell until they can't tell the lies from the truth. So I'd keep the files until I found someone important enough to occupy a big, major corner office with lots of windows in some tall Federal Building somewhere.

As I started for the steps, Agent Oberman stood, saw Captain Freeman's big semi-auto tucked in my belt, and yelled, "Hey! Where'd you get that gun? Hand it over!"

"Why," I asked simply.

"Because you're not supposed to be carrying a gun."

"Who told you that?" I asked. "How do you know I'm not supposed to have a gun? Hell, I've been shot at, kidnapped, tortured, and almost killed. I think I'll keep this gun for awhile."

I started down the stairs, Sandy a step or two behind me, for the pickup truck.

He yelled again, "Where do you think you're going?"

"Back to El Paso," I said, as I opened the passenger door for Sandy.

"I don't think so. I changed my mind. I think it best that you come with me. There's a bunch of questions you need to answer."

"About what?" I asked.

"We're going to start with how you arranged for that damn Indian to kill everyone," Oberman said. "I think you've got something to do with that."

"That's crazy," Sandy said. "We were inside the compound. You had my husband tied up and beaten. You used a rubber hose on him. How's that going to sound to whoever you work for?"

I started walking back towards the house and stopped close enough to Oberman to be too close to him. "Do you know who I am?" I asked Oberman, maybe a little too braggadocio in the way I said it, with my hands on my hips a little too dramatically, but I was beginning to lose my temper. "Do you know how many lawyers are going to meet you wherever you think you're going to take us? Do you have any idea what the lawsuits will do to your career?"

"That sounds like a threat," Oberman said.

"It's not a threat," Sandy said, more calmly than I could. She was leaning against the pickup truck, arms folded in front of her and smiling that wonderfully beautiful and sweet smile of hers that could make any man melt like ice in August. "My husband is in the habit of promising exactly what he says."

I added, "Do yourself a favor. Get out your cell phone and call your bosses back in D.C. Tell them what you want to do."

"There's no cell service out here," Oberman said.

"Then go inside and use Mary Lou's phone. Geez! Do I have to tell you everything?"

Oberman hesitated but he did go inside, almost running and swearing under his breath. Sandy, Jose, and I waited on the porch. I had another glass of cold water and rubbed my side where my ribs still ached. It took a few minutes, I didn't keep track because I knew the outcome. Oberman returned to the porch and said, "You can go."

As we started towards the pickup truck, Sandy laughed and said softly, whispering in my ear, "I can't get enough of you, Morgan dear."

"Well that's nice to hear," I said. "But physically, I might not be able to perform in the magnificent way I normally do. My ribs still hurt really bad. And we should wait until we're alone, anyway."

"I don't mean that, you idiot," she said, laughing and slapping my shoulder. "I mean I can't get over what your damn name does. All the way into Washington! My God!"

"Hey, it's your name, too."

I opened the truck's door for her and stopped. Sandy stopped, looked at my face, my wrinkled forehead, twisted in thought, and asked, "Now what?"

"Where are we going?" I asked.

"What do you mean?" Sandy asked. "Back to El

Paso. Tommy Rocker is the only lead we have left. And we need to find someone to give the files to."

"Think about it. Oberman phoned someone then comes and tells us we can go. They want us to go back to El Paso. They want us spending time with Tommy. They want us away from here. Right here is where it all happened. Not back in El Paso."

"So, it's not your family's influence this time? They want us to go away? That's why Oberman said we can go?"

"I think so," I said. "At least my gut is telling me that." I closed the truck's door before Sandy could slide in and said, "Let's go try something."

Sandy followed me back to the front porch. Oberman and Santos were standing there, watching us. I started up the steps and Oberman said, "I thought I told you that you could go?"

"Yeah," I said. "I changed my mind. I thought we might stay awhile."

"What the hell you mean? I told you to leave."

"No you didn't," I said. Sandy followed me onto the porch. We sat comfortably in the same couple of chairs we had left. "You said we *could* leave. Not we *had* to leave."

"OK," Oberman said. He was starting to lose his temper. That was a good thing, I thought. When people get angry, they don't think quickly or rationally. "OK, now I'm telling you to get the hell outta' here."

I looked at Sandy, she looked at me, and we smiled. We knew we had him.

"No," Sandy said to Agent Oberman. "We're going to hang around here for awhile. Why don't you go call whoever it was you called and see if they say that's OK with them?"

Oberman sat down in a chair next to mine, pulled a pack of Marlboros from his shirt pocket and lit one. Sandy was about to make one of her speeches about the harmful effects of cigarettes, but I touched her arm gently, and she sat back, grasped her hands on her lap so tightly the

knuckles turned white, and said nothing. We waited for
Oberman to decide what he was going to do. I knew, and I
knew that Sandy also knew, that Oberman was a dangerous
man. OK, he was maybe working undercover to break up
Mary Lou's drug business. But he crossed the line when he
used violence to get where he was with her. What did he do
to become her confidant? We were sitting on Mary Lou's
front porch with him, out in the middle of nowhere. What
would he do to us without anyone ever knowing about it?

He smoked the cigarette down almost to the point
where it burnt his fingers, while he paced back and forth
across the porch. He flicked the stub out onto the brown
grass in front of the house and said, "Let's go Santos." He
stood and headed for the stairs down to his car.

Santos started to follow him. I stopped them and
said, "Jose . . . Or Jorge . . . Whatever the hell your name is.
I want to talk to you. You stay . . . Agent Oberman . . . You
go."

Santos looked at Oberman, waiting for his OK to stay
or go. Oberman got in the car he and Santos had arrived in,
said nothing, slammed the door hard, and drove away,
kicking up a cloud of dust, sand, and rocks behind him.
Santos walked back to us and pulled a chair closer to where
we were sitting. He sat, leaned back, crossed his legs, and
asked, "So what the hell you want?"

"Let's start with your name," I said. "Jose . . . Jorge . .
. What?"

Santos hesitated then answered, "I work undercover.
You know that. My name is not for the public . . . And
definitely not for you."

"So what do we call you?" Sandy asked.

"Jose . . . Jorge . . . I don't care. Call me anything you
want."

"OK, Santos," I said, deciding that's what we would
call him whether it was his name or not. "Now that that's
settled, I want information from you."

"Well, that's nice for you," he said. He sat forward in his chair, leaning his elbows on his knees, and snarled, "But I ain't gonna' tell you nothin'"

"We'll see about that," I said. "But tell me who you work for. Are you FBI . . . DEA . . . What? I don't believe for a second you're actually with ICE."

He leaned back in the chair, crossed his legs again, and thought about that for a moment. I could see the wheels inside his head working out the math of whether or not I should know any part of the truth. Finally he said, "Look, I'm a contract agent. At one time another I've worked for almost every Federal Agency there is. I like the independent life. And I get paid well, too."

"And right now, you're independent?" I asked.

"Yeah," he said and sat back in the chair, a proud and confident smile crossing his face.

"So you've been in San Juan de Cristo . . . For how long, exactly?"

Santos grinned. I think he knew where this was going, so he opened up and told me what I wanted to know. "I been there almost ten months now. Washing damn dishes. And you wanna' know if I been paid by the Feds all that time? They paid me for a couple of months. Now they pay me for information only. I give'em what I can, but it's tough back there. They hate Mexicans."

"So the truth is," I said, "You're working for pennies and eating tacos and frijoles. You don't give the Feds a whole lot, and they don't give you a whole lot of money. But you want to stay independent. Are you independent enough to work for me?"

"Whata'ya mean?" Santos suddenly was interested. I could almost see the dollar signs in his eyes. He uncrossed his legs and sat forward.

"How much do the Feds pay you?" I asked.

"Depends," he said. His forehead frowned, and he looked down at his feet. He was either going to lie, or he was embarrassed. Either way, I didn't care. "Five hundred a day, if it's a dangerous job," he said. "If I give them something, an' they think it's good stuff, they might give me a couple hundred." I could see he sensed where this was going, and he had his hopes up.

"OK," I said. "I want to hire you for $1000 a day."

Santos thought about that, but he should never play serious poker. He was almost licking his lips at the thought of making that kind of money. He shot up straight in his chair and I could almost see the greed sweating from his forehead. He tried bargaining.

"I'm still on the books here with the Feds," he said.

"And you can stay on their books. I don't care about what they're doing. All I want is to find out who killed Edgy Hands. If you want to help me do that, I'll pay you $1000 a day. Do we have a deal?"

Santos restrained himself from jumping out of his chair. He tried to look like he was considering and thinking about it, but it was easy enough to see he wanted the money. His face was blushed red at the anticipation of getting his hands on that kind of cash. It took only a few seconds for him to reach out his hand to me and say, "You got a deal."

I shook his hand, but before I could say anything, he said, "I don't know nothing about Edgy Hands. I wasn't there that night. So you owe me a thousand bucks for today. Pay me and I'll get outta' here."

"Santos, my friend," I said. "You just started. You know the people back in San Juan de Cristo. You are going back there with us, and we're going to find out what the hell's happening back there."

"I can't go back with you. It'll blow my cover."

"OK," I said. "Then tell me about that sheriff . . . What's his name? I forgot."

"Kronk," Santos answered, almost spitting the name out of his mouth. "He's a son'a'bitch. He hates the

Mexicans. Give's 'em a really hard time. Beats the crap outta' them whenever he can . . . Old men and women, too. For whatever he can come up with."

"Was he involved with Mary Lou Perkins?"

"Mary Lou owned everybody out here," Santos said. "Just about everybody was on her payroll. I'll bet a lot of people are wondering if the money is gonna' keep flowing. She's the one paid to have the dirt roads in town paved. She keeps the shops open. I have a suspicion Kronk is somehow involved in the transport of drugs outta' here. Maybe other stuff. But it's just a suspicion. There's stuff that goes on back there that the whites keep really secret. I've tried, but I can't get close so long as my skin is dark as it is. I've seen trucks drive into town late at night, but I haven't been able to figure out what the hell they do."

"How about those two cowboy bars?"

"The Mustang and The Last Stand," Santos reminded me. "Mary Lou Perkins owns them and the whole damn town, the jail included. I checked on filed deeds at the County Court House. Everything is in her name . . . Even the cockroach infested frijoles shack I work at. The strange thing is, Mary Lou never collected any rents on anything. I think all she wanted was control and a place to handle the shipment of drugs out of . . . And maybe other stuff, too."

"One thing has me wondering," I said. "That small town can't have a population of more than 20 or 25 people. Why did Mary Lou support two bars?"

"The Last Stand is where everybody hangs out. I've been watching The Mustang. Hardly nobody goes in there. Maybe Kronk once in awhile. It's locked up tight most of the time."

"But The Mustang is where Edgy Hands was killed." I said, starting to get confused. But I knew that confusion meant I was getting close to the truth.

"Yeah, I know," Santos said. "That's strange."

Sandy asked, "So if The Last Stand is where

everyone hangs out . . . But the murder happened in The Mustang . . . Why do you think everybody was there that night instead of The Last Stand?"

Santos thought about that but said nothing. I asked, "Do you think maybe the murder was planned, and Betsy was set up to take the fall? Sounds like it to me." I could see the idea had germinated, but he still said nothing. I felt he was withholding something. He wanted the money, but he wasn't willing to be completely open with me. I needed to bait the hook in order to real Santos in and find out what he knew. "We found a bunch of files in the house," I told him. "Files on just about everybody, I think."

Santos suddenly looked worried. His brown face reddened. He sat forward once again and asked, "One on me, too?"

"I'm afraid so," I said. "I haven't looked through it, but it's got your name on it."

"I wanna' see that," Santos demanded.

Sandy said, "First things first, Mr. Santos. Who killed Edgy Hands?"

"How the hell should I know?"

"You know the people who are involved," Sandy said. "The ranch hands here . . . You know them . . . You know the people at the compound. You know they were involved in all this, and one of them probably killed Jimmy."

"Yeah, I know them all. But they're a bunch of racist bastards. They don't talk to me, and I'm not allowed in either of those damn cowboy bars. Like I said, they don't like the color of my skin."

"There were people here at the ranch. You know them, too?" Sandy asked.

"There were four guys who were only workers here at the ranch. They took care of the place, that's all. The ranch never did a whole lot. I mean, they run a few cattle and Mary Lou's horses, of course. She liked Appaloosas and kept a couple of 'em here. They weren't involved in the drug operation. They hardly ever left the Bar H. I seen them at The Last Stand once in awhile, on a Saturday night, but that's all."

"What about the other men who were at The Mustang when Edgy was killed?" I asked.

I couldn't remember their names so Sandy helped. "Benny Newsinger, Ted Soller, Murray Allott, Greg West and Tommy Rocker. Tommy Rocker's in jail."

Santos said, "Newsinger and Allott were at Mary Lou's base when that crazy Indian blew up the place. They're both dead. I don't know where Soller and West are. Hell, they could be hiding in the shadows anyplace around here. They're both military trained, and they know what they're doing."

"Could either one of them have killed Jimmy?" I asked. "It was a long range shot with a military rifle."

"Hell yes," Santos said. "Everybody out there was ex-military of some kind. And Mary Lou made them practice with all kinds of guns. Soller and West were as good as anybody out there. Yeah, either one could have killed him."

"What about Rocker?" I asked.

"That punk is a dope head. He likes to stay high. But he likes to hurt people, too. That's why Mary Lou kept him around I think. Strong arm stuff, ya' know? They're all military trained, like I said. Rocker too."

It became obvious to both of us that we weren't getting anywhere. Santos knew about Mary Lou's people, and it was all very interesting, but it wasn't leading anywhere. Sandy decided to change the subject and maybe learn something. She said, "So Mary Lou Perkins was importing drugs from Mexico. She must have had a distribution system. Tell us about that."

"Yeah, that's a tough one. I don't know much about how she sells that crap. Oberman was working on that. He might know."

"Come on, Santos," I said. "You've been at this for

almost a year. If you want that thousand bucks, you've got to be straight with us."

"Hey! All I do is look and report. They never tell me nothin'."

I looked at Sandy, and she looked at me. We, as usual, each thought the same thing. Santos wasn't as much help as we hoped he would be. But one thing was certain, all this spun around San Juan de Cristo. We had to go there.

CHAPTER TWENTY ONE – The Truck

"You expect me to go into San Juan de Cristo with you and burn my cover?" Santos argued. "Well, that ain't about to happen."

"You're right, of course," I said. "We'll go in after dark and drop you off outside of town. Tomorrow morning we're going into town and find out what the hell is happening in The Last Stand and The Mustang. I want you to start asking around. I don't care who you talk to. Talk to any cowboys or townspeople who will talk to you. There's got to be a couple customers in your restaurant that know something. If you want your thousand dollars you'll do it."

"And how do I get in touch with you?" he asked snidely. "You want me to meet you in Sheriff Kronk's office or somethin'?"

Sandy spoke up, "I think we're going to stay right here at the ranch for a few days. It's closer to San Juan than going back to El Paso. I don't think Mary Lou will mind. The phone's still working. Phone us here every night at ten PM. That's every night, understood? Until we tell you to stop. Miss a day and you miss your thousand dollars for that day."

Santos looked at me, maybe looking for the man of the house to make a better decision. Instead I said, "Sounds like a plan to me." But that didn't seem to be a great plan to Santos. He shook his head and mumbled a few swear words under his breath.

While we waited for dark to surround us, Sandy rooted around the kitchen looking for something we could use for dinner. I stayed out on the porch, slouching back in a chair, while Santos walked back and forth, kicking dirt up as he paced at the bottom of the stairs.

I watched him for twenty minutes, and when I couldn't take it anymore, I sat up straight and asked him, "Santos, what the hell's bothering you?"

"Bothering me? What the hell's bothering me? And you ain't worried about nothin' I suppose?"

"Come on up out of the sun," I said. "Sit down and give it a rest."

"Give it a damn rest? Is that all you can think of?"

"You think I'm not worried?" I said. "You think I'm not scared? I've got my wife in there who's been a target more than once. She's been shot and almost killed. I've been shot. Every day we're out here, we stand a chance of being murdered. That man I was with . . . Gandalf Finch . . . He was killed, and I could easily have been killed with him. I've got a kid out there somewhere I'm trying to protect. I want her to grow up with a mother and father. So, yes I'm friggin' worried, and I'm friggin' scared. I'm always scared because I have to do what I'm doing, and I'd rather be back home playing golf and enjoying life. Now stop feeling sorry for yourself, and come up here, and sit down, and cool off. You're not helping yourself or me."

Santos stomped loudly up the stairs and sat down hard in a chair as far from me as he could. He crossed his legs and folded his arms tightly across his chest. He spat over the porch rail but would not look at me.

Sandy had found a couple of cans of corned beef hash and fried up some eggs. When Santos and I walked into the kitchen I said, "That's all you could find?"

"Tell you what," she said. "You cook from now on."

****

It was half past two in the morning when we dropped Santos off a good mile outside of town. I reminded him of what he needed to do to get his $1000 per day. We watched as Santos walked away into the dark toward San Juan de Cristo. Sandy and I shared a thought that it was possible we would not hear from him at all.

I drove us back to the Bar H, and we found a bedroom on the second floor that looked like it hadn't been used recently. There was a bathroom next to the bedroom. We found some clean towels, and Sandy was very gentle as she washed the bruises all over my body. "My God!" she spoke softly. "They really did a job on you."

Sleep was fleeting for me. I was worried and not a little scared. We had to go into that little rat hole of a town, and the thought that we would not leave kept spinning around inside my head.

I managed to get a few hours of sleep before getting up at a quarter to six. I crept downstairs and made a pot of coffee in the kitchen. I was sitting at the small kitchen table, when at half past seven Sandy stumbled into the kitchen, rubbing the sleep from her eyes. She said nothing as I filled a big mug with hot coffee and slid it toward her. She sat and let the coffee wake her.

Finally she said, "Are we still going back there?"

"I don't know what else to do. Betsy's an escapee who's been charged with murder. I suppose she can spend the rest of her life on the run . . . She can stay underground . . . There'll always be someone out looking for her. Is that what we want for her? "

"Of course not," Sandy said. "So what are we going to do?"

"I've been thinking about that most of the night," I said. "Mary Lou is dead. Her organization must be falling apart. Whoever is left in San Juan de Cristo must be going crazy trying to figure out what to do. I want to take advantage of that. In confusion there is profit. I heard that somewhere. Anyway, I have a feeling everything revolves around The Mustang. Santos told us that nobody goes in there. The cowboys hang out at The Last Stand. He said trucks pull to the rear of The Mustang. Edgy Hands was murdered in The Mustang. There's got to be something there."

I paused and waited for Sandy to come in synch with my thinking. We are almost attached at the hip in the way we think. This time I saw the beautiful smile rise on her face like the sun on a beautiful morning. I knew she knew what I wanted to do.

"So we're going to sneak into The Mustang?"

"We're going to criminally break and enter The Mustang, dear. We're going to find out what goes on inside there. And we're going to hope no one catches us."

"And if someone does catch us?" Sandy asked as she finished the mug of coffee.

I filled her mug and said, "That's why you're going to wait outside . . . Someplace safe."

"Someplace safe? Someplace safe! Who the hell are you talking to! I've never stayed someplace safe . . . Even before I met you! That's insulting!"

"What about Caroline?" I asked calmly.

Sandy couldn't answer that, of course. We both knew our lives changed when Caroline came into our lives. We both knew that at least one of us had to be there to see Caroline grow up. She said, "OK, I'll wait outside . . . But not too far away. And you take that gun with you. If anything happens, I'm going to come in shooting with my gun."

****

We drove the pickup truck off the hard dirt road onto the desert a couple of miles away from San Juan de Cristo. I kept the truck moving as fast it would go across the sand, knowing that when I put the brakes on, the little truck would probably be stuck in the soft sand. When I did stop, I had found a small outcropping of red-brown sandstone rock to park on. From there we could see the little cross roads town a mile away.

"Stay here," I said. "If you see anything going very wrong, get out of here. Go back to El Paso. Get the County Sheriff or the State Cops or some Feds or anybody you think you can trust and get back here. Take them right into the center of town and tear the place apart if you have to."

"You be careful," Sandy said. She touched my shoulder gently and her eyes filled with tears. "I don't want you to get hurt."

"You know me . . . If I have to, I'll buy my way out," I laughed. As I started to get out of the truck, a thought occurred to me. "Don't trust Santos. Never trust anyone whose loyalty depends on being bought."

I started walking towards the back of the town. There wasn't anything to give me cover but I couldn't see any movement at all inside town. I kept hoping that with Mary Lou's death, everyone had cut and run, and I'd find the town deserted. Half way there, the only movement I had seen was a big lizard that ran for cover under a rock at my approach, and a nasty looking rattle snake that wasn't about to run away. I gave it a wide berth. There was an old yellow dog asleep at the back of the town's gas station, lounging in some late morning shade. I hoped he wouldn't wake up and start barking. He didn't.

I reached the edge of town and started easing my way along the rear of the buildings. After peering through the alleyways between buildings, I quickly passed between them until reaching the back of The Mustang. There were five battered metal trash cans, only three sporting covers.

All were empty. I found the electric meter and saw it wasn't moving at all; no electric was being used inside. I wondered if the bar had refrigerators and what was happening to whatever they held.

Near the meter was a wooden door held closed with a heavy padlock. A small window was nearby. It was covered by a rusted and torn screen. The glass of the window was cracked but in place. I looked inside through the dirt and grime on the glass and found a dark room filled with cardboard boxes and nothing else.

I had to get inside . . . Because I felt inside was where all the answers were. But I didn't want to go around to the front of the building. The window looked promising, but my ribs still ached, and I hadn't recovered from my time at Mary Lou's compound. I figured I wouldn't be able to climb in through the window, so the door was my only way in, if I were to get in at all.

I looked around for something to rip the padlock off its hinge. I tried a rock, smacking it against the padlock, but it was too noisy and didn't work anyway. So I made it carefully back to the town's garage. It was as deserted as everything else appeared to be. The old yellow dog looked up from its sleep, saw me, and laid its head back down, taking no interest in me. The rear door of the garage was closed but not locked. Inside I found a tire iron lying on the oily, dirty floor of the garage and went back to The Mustang with it. And it worked to rip the padlock away from the door, even though it was noisy as hell as it ripped away from the wood.

Inside it was hot, still, and smelled of urine and excrement. I found a swinging door that opened into the bar area. It was dark, and empty, and eerily still. Sunlight filtered in through thin, brown curtains hanging across the windows at the front of the bar. Dust and dirt was layered everywhere. Not even foot prints disturbed the layer of dirt on the wooden floor.

I found the room that Betsy described as the place

where she slept the night of Edgy Hand's murder.   It held only a metal bunk, with a thin dirty mattress lying askew on it, and six cardboard boxes.

It took me a half an hour to root through what little was inside The Mustang.   There simply wasn't anything there. I was about to give up, but I knew that Sandy might have other Ideas. I stepped outside and waved to get her attention and tell her to come to me. She left the pickup truck where it was and walked to me, looking all around her as she walked, looking for anyone who might see her.

When she was at my side, she asked, "What's the matter? Did you find something?"

We were standing in the hot, near mid-day sun, pacing around the rear of The Mustang, kicking at pebbles and wishing we were back home in San Marcos, enjoying a cool breeze coming in off the Pacific, through the harbor, and up the hillside to our home. After I had told her what little I found inside, she said, "Let's go inside and get out of the sun. Let's talk."

Inside Sandy put her hand to her nose and mouth and said, "Christ, this place stinks. Where's it coming from?"

Now that was a good question and an example of why I need to keep Sandy close by. "Damn if I know," I said. "The restrooms are near the front of the bar. And they haven't been used in a long time. It smells like sewage backup, but there's no evidence of that."

I started moving boxes away from the walls in the front of the bar area but found nothing. Then under one of the musty cardboard boxes in the back room, I found a trap door in the floor. I pulled it open, and the room was flooded with putrid dead air from below. My stomach twisted, and I could feel bile rushing up to my throat.   I pulled a handkerchief from my back pocket to cover my nose and mouth. Sandy backed away quickly.

I was about to climb down into whatever it was below, when we heard a truck, by the sound of it a big truck, pull to a stop at the front of the bar. We heard loud talking, angry words, on the street. We quietly walked to the covered front windows and peered out carefully. Sheriff Kronk was there; a man was halfway out of the tractor of the big truck; two other men in blue jeans and cowboy hats stood close by, hands in their back pockets.

"What do you think that is?" Sandy asked.

"Santos said a truck pulls up to The Mustang and then moves to the rear."

"So what's in the truck?"

"That, my dear, is what we need to find out. My gut tells me that whatever is inside that truck is what Edgy Hands was murdered over. And I have a feeling that whatever is inside that truck isn't a load of beer and peanuts."

They were arguing now. Sheriff Kronk told the driver, "Get the hell outta' here. It's all over. Go on back to the pickup point."

"And do what?" the driver asked.

"Dump 'em," the Sheriff growled. "I don't give a shit, but you ain't gonna' leave 'em here."

"I don't like that!" the driver said. "All's I do is drive 'em here. I ain't gonna' do nothin' else. What if the cops see me? You wanna dump 'em . . . You do it."

For a minute I thought Sheriff Kronk was going to pull his pistol out and maybe shoot the truck driver. His hand was hovering over it nervously, when someone walked along the sidewalk to them.

I could just barely see the man through the dirty window, but I recognized the voice. Karl Oberman, the FBI agent who had been working at the compound as Colonel Max, said, "Wait a minute. What's going on here?" Oberman wasn't wearing the suit he had worn the day before; he was back in camo-fatigue pants and a skin tight black T-shirt. There was a military webbed belt slung low around his waist, and hanging from it was a black holster holding a really big pistol.

Sheriff Kronk answered, "Got a load here. Mary Lou's dead. This whole thing is gone t'hell."

"Well Sheriff," Oberman said, "The operation will go on, regardless. You will unload as usual."

"Who said so?" Kronk growled.

"I said," Oberman said. "I'm in charge now."

Through the foggy glass of the window, I saw Kronk staring at Oberman, his hands on his hips and a nasty grin pasted on his face. "So Max," he said. "So you ain't no Colonel no more? What the hell you made yourself? A fuckin' General or somethin'?" He laughed at his little joke. No one else laughed.

Oberman countered, "Watch your language, Sheriff. Don't push too hard, you'll regret it. You wanna' keep your damn job and paycheck, you'll do what I tell you to do. I'm gonna' keep the whole damn operation going, understand?"

I looked at Sandy, and she looked at me. "Either Oberman wasn't an FBI Agent, or he decided to latch onto all the money Mary Lou Perkins has been making," I whispered. Sandy nodded agreement.

Oberman then ordered, "Take the truck around back. Nothing changes."

"Now what?" Sandy asked. "They'll know someone's here."

I put my finger to my lips and whispered, "Wait."

The truck engine started and pulled away from the wooden sidewalk. It was a sixteen wheeler without any markings on it. Oberman and Kronk walked together following it, and the two cowboys followed them. When all had turned the corner, I forced open the locked front door of the bar and we ran across the paved street, into the alley between a locked and shuttered general store and an equally dark and closed-tight little bank.

We hid behind the buildings in the shadows, wondering what to do next.

Sandy said, "We need to get back to the pickup truck."

"You go," I said. "Take a wide swing around the town so no one sees you. I'm going to find out what the hell that truck is dropping off."

"Morgan, if you're going to be stupid . . . I'm going to be stupid with you. Do you understand that if they catch us . . . They'll kill us. And we have no defense. Our two little pistols might not be enough. Are you still determined to be stupid?"

I thought about that for a second or two and then said, "I guess so. You coming with me?" I grinned like a mischievous little boy about to do something he shouldn't do.

We waited in the shadows; we watched and we listened. It came as I thought it would. There was shouting and yelling and swearing and men running out the broken front door of The Mustang. They ran up and down the street, kicking open doors and running into and out of empty buildings.

It took only a minute or two. I prayed to a God I hadn't had much time for over the years that they wouldn't cross the street and find us. Then Sheriff Kronk, Oberman, and the two cowboys gathered together in the middle of the street as the eighteen wheeler truck came out from behind The Mustang as fast as it could move, turned right and sped north away from San Juan de Cristo.

Sheriff Kronk drew his pistol and raised it only to have it grabbed away by Karl Oberman. They argued, swearing at each other, and then all four retreated back into The Mustang.

We waited without moving from the shadows. And we waited some more. Sandy whispered in my ear, "What do we do? The truck's gone."

"Whatever was in that truck is now in The Mustang. I've got to find out what all this about."

It seemed like an eternity, but eventually Kronk and

Oberman and their two companions walked out of The Mustang and down the wooden sidewalk to the Sheriff's office and inside.

"Now," I said and Sandy followed me out of the alley. We ran as fast as we could across the street and into The Mustang. I was breathing hard; Sandy wasn't. "That's all those years of cigarettes," she accused.

Inside, the Mustang hadn't changed. It was as dark, musty, dirty, and dank, and smelled like a backed up sewer, as it had just a short while ago. Whatever was brought in from the truck was not in the bar area. But I was certain there was something there, something that was at the center of Betsy being accused of murder.

I started for the back room and the trap door. I hoped that had to be where whatever would clear Betsy was waiting. A dozen filled and tape-sealed cardboard boxes had been stacked on top of the trap door concealing it. We moved them aside revealing a brand new pad lock securing the trap door closed. Sandy carefully opened the back door and found our tire iron lying in the dust near the trash cans. She handed it to me and nodded. I ripped the hinge from the wood and slowly lifted the trap door open. A flood of voices rose up to us.

CHAPTER TWENTY TWO – Getting Caught

Men, women, and children from down in the hole were yelling, screaming, and crying out for help. It was Spanish. I knew very little Spanish, Sandy knew more. "They say they are being left to die, Morgan," she told me. "For God's sake, what the hell's going on?"

There had been a ladder going down into the below ground room when I had opened the trap door the first time. That ladder was missing. I looked around the small store room; Sandy went out the still open back door. She found the ladder leaning against the building. I carried it in and lowered it down into the dark hole.

The people below began fighting to get to the ladder and climb out of the dark hole. One by one they managed to get out. As they did they got quiet and stood around Sandy and me, staring, perhaps looking for some direction and help. They whispered amongst themselves, but their eyes were locked on us. When they were all out, I counted thirty-six people - most men, some women and even a few children.

They were dirty and dressed in rough clothes, some little more than rags. The men had the appearance of age brought on by a hard life and hard work. A couple of the women were very pregnant. The children, five of them, needed a good meal or two and a good bath.

When they were all out, I slammed the trap door shut in an effort to keep the stench from below from rising up to us. It didn't do much. I turned to the people and asked, "Who are you?"

When no one answered, Sandy asked in Spanish, "Puede alguien habla Inglés?" She said in English, "We want to help you, but we need to know why you're here."

A small, very thin man stepped from the middle of the group. His skin was burnt dark, his hair salted with grey. His face was like leather with creases of age and a hard life, covered with a thick three or four day growth of beard. "I speak a little," he said in a gravelly, heavily accented voice.

"Who are you?" I asked.

"My name Miguel," he answered and tried to smile.

"No, I mean who are all of you? Why are you here?"

Miguel stared, not understanding what I had asked. Sandy said, "Por qué Estás aquí?"

He smiled again and said, "We work farms, yes? We come to work farms, yes?"

Sandy turned to me and said, "I think they're illegals. Could Mary Lou be smuggling people across the border?"

"We know she was smuggling drugs. Why not people? I wonder if these people paid to get here?"

"Pagó para llegar hasta aquí?" she asked. "I think that's how you say it."

"Yes," Miguel answered. "Much money. All we have."

We managed to convince everyone there to stay inside the little storeroom, to stay quiet, not to go outside, and to just wait for us to get them some help. Miguel said he understood and spoke to his people. They all nodded, and there was a round of 'gracias' and other words of thanks.

Sandy and I stepped outside and talked in the sun. "So what do we do now?" she asked.

"I don't think we have a choice," I answered. "We need to get up to Santos and hope they have a phone there. We've got to get ICE here to take care of these people."

"ICE!" Sandy argued. "They'll send them back to Mexico."

"Of course. They're illegals. That word has meaning."

"But Morgan . . ."

"Sandy, this just ain't the time to get into one of your liberal moods. I have a feeling those people were never intended to work on someone's farm."

"You mean . . ."

"Yes, dear. I mean they and all their predecessors pay to cross the border and then they're killed. I think that's been going on for years. They are left down in that stink hole without food and water for as long as it takes to weaken them enough so they can't fight back. Then they're taken out to the desert, murdered and buried."

"Morgan! I can't believe people would do that."

"Not even Mary Lou Perkins?"

We decided that we had to get to the little restaurant where Santos washed dishes. The question was, how do we do that without Kronk and Oberman seeing us. I knew the Sheriff's office was where they were, and that the office was on the same side of Main Street as the Mustang. Santos' little place was on the other side of Main and directly across the street from the Sheriff's office. So we ran across the street and took the alleys back to the other side of town and cautiously made our way, building by building, south along Main to the back of the taco shack.

The rear door was open, the back filled with smelly garbage and junk. I looked in through the open door and saw Santos at a sink filled with dishes and pots and pans. He turned fast and drew a gun from under his shirt when he saw me in the corner of his eye.

"What the hell!" he said, lowering the gun.

"I need a phone," I told him.

"Why?"

I stepped inside and Sandy followed. "You know

those trucks that come and go from the back of the Mustang? They're carrying illegals from Mexico. There's a group of them there know. I need to get them help."

"What! . . . What the hell! . . . What!"

"Forget all the surprise crap, Santos," I said, taking a few threatening steps towards him. "I think you knew all along. If you didn't know for sure, you had a good idea."

"That's bullshit . . ."

"Cut it, Santos," I said. "You knew Mary Lou was running drugs. Did you really believe those huge 18 wheelers were carrying tons of drugs into town? Forget it. Now I need to use a phone. Where is it?"

He didn't say anything for a moment or two. His gaze went from me to Sandy and back again. I would bet my last million that he was trying to calculate the best way to keep his job and my $1000 a day. He said, "There's a pay phone out front . . . But all the phone lines are tapped."

"Then how do I get word out?" I asked.

He thought for a minute then said, "You gotta go. Get to El Paso. People there will help. Go to the Federal Building."

I turned to Sandy and told her, "You have to go. Get to the pickup truck and drive like hell."

"You're going to stay here?" she asked.

"I have to, Babe. If Kronk or Oberman find them . . ."

"Oberman?" Santos interrupted.

"Yes, he's working with Kronk. There's two other guys with them. Cowboy types."

"They both about five foot ten? Lean, military types?"

"That's them," I said.

"That's Ted Soller and Greg West."

"Sandy," I said, "Get going and make it fast."

She kissed me quickly, whispered, "Take care of yourself," and ran out the back door.

"You need to come with me," I told Santos. "Tell your people here to make excuses for you if anybody asks."

"Why?"

"Because I don't speak Spanish and you do. And bring that gun with you."

****

"Jesus Christ!" Santos said when we walked into the back room of The Mustang. "This place stinks!" The thirty-six people were huddled together, obviously afraid. The women held onto the children; the men tried to shelter the women. I'd been there before; I've felt scared like they were feeling; at someone else's mercy . . . Wondering if there would be any mercy. I knew how they felt. "What the hell are they doin' here? Who the hell are they?"

"Mary Lou had more than the drug operation going. She was importing illegal Mexicans into the U. S. I think everybody knew about the drug thing. I think everybody in San Juan de Cristo knew their livelihood depended on the drug money Mary Lou was making. But I don't think everybody knew about the people running thing. I think Mary Lou kept that to a few of her closest people. And I have an idea that's why Edgy Hands was murdered. He wasn't talking too much about the drugs. Mary Lou wouldn't care about that because everyone knew about the drugs. He was talking about the people smuggling, and Mary Lou couldn't have that."

Santos thought about that. He looked at the people crowded into the little room. They were a pitiful looking lot; their clothes were torn and dirty, and they looked hungry. He turned to me and said, "OK, that makes sense. I always thought it was strange that everybody talked so openly about where all the money came from. But what do you intend to do about these people?"

That was a good question. All I could say was, "It'll take hours for Sandy to bring help back."

"And if Kronk decides to walk his fat ass here and finds us standing around with these people? I mean I got only twelve rounds in my gun and no spare clips. You think we can hold them off for a couple of hours?"

"What do you suggest?" I asked.

"I think you and me should get the hell outta' here and run as fast as we can."

"And leave these people here?" I asked. "You know they were scheduled to be killed." I told Santos how we had found the people. Santos was obviously shaken. The stench, even with the trap door closed, was overwhelming. "We can't let them be killed," I said.

"Killed? What the hell you mean?"

I explained my theory that they had paid Mary Lou to bring them into the U. S. to work farms, but they would wind up dead and buried out in the desert. Santos seemed to understand. I think he knew and understood Mary Lou Perkins and that she was capable of anything. "OK," he said when I was done, "so what are you gonna' do?"

I told Santos to tell the people they would have to go back into the hole. He told them that help was on the way, but it would be hours before the police could get there.

"La policia! No! No policia!" They were all talking at once and too loudly. Someone was going to hear them and bring trouble to The Mustang's back room.   Santos told them to be quiet. He explained that they were in danger; that the men who brought them there were going to hurt them. It took some talk but finally they agreed to climb back into the little room beneath the trap door. With Santos' help we managed to replace the hinge and padlock so it looked, without close inspection . . . We could only hope . . . Like it had not been broken.

"Now what?" Santos asked.

"Can I trust you?" I asked him.

"Can I trust you to give me my thousand bucks a day?"

"I said I will."

"Then you can trust me. What ya' want me t'do?"

"Give me your gun . . . Then go back to your job and watch the Sheriff's office. If anybody leaves there, you come running and get here to me before they do . . . Or make some noise . . . Or do something to let me know."

"I ain't giving you my gun."

"Then just go," I said. I was getting frustrated, and I could feel that temper of mine begin to rise.

"You really mean to do this, don't you?" Santos asked.

"Yes, I really mean to do this. Look, if I'm right, they intend to leave those people down there for days, maybe a week. I don't think they're going to come back here very soon. I hope I'm right. But if I'm wrong, I've got to do something until my wife gets back here with help."

"You think you can hold them off for hours? Maybe a day? You're crazy, you know that, man?"

I just smiled, knowing he was probably right.

"OK, look, you hangin' here ain't gonna' accomplish nothin'. Come with me, and wait at the taqueria. They never go there, and we can watch what they're doin' from there. It ain't gonna' do these people any good if you get killed. We'll do what we can for them," Santos said.

It hit me then that he really wanted to help me . . . Maybe for the money I'd promised him. Maybe he thought that if I was dead, he wouldn't get his money. But he wanted to help anyway. What he said seemed to make sense, at least more sense than me fighting off four armed killers. So Santos and I made our way back to his sink and dirty dishes. I was hungry, and while I sat at the lone window, fogged with dirt and grease and dead flies, watching the Sheriff's office, a plate of eggs and beans and tortillas was brought to me. The coffee was strong and slightly bitter, but with spoonfuls of brown sugar in it, it woke me and strengthened my resolve.

Hours passed by. I guessed – maybe I was hoping – Sandy had enough time to get to El Paso, and she was now trying to talk someone into coming back to San Juan de Cristo with her. I was beginning to doze off in the mid-afternoon heat, when the door to the Sherriff's office opened.

Kronk stepped out, looked up at the hot desert sun, put on his sunglasses, adjusted his slightly frayed yellow straw cowboy hat, and looked north along Main Street. Karl Oberman joined Kronk on the wooden sidewalk, wiped the sweat from his brow, and he too looked north, shading the sun from his eyes with his hand. I bent closer to the filthy window to try to see what they were looking at.

A dusty cloud moved off the unpaved highway onto the paved Main Street. It pulled to a stop at the foot of the three wooden steps leading up to the front of the Sheriff's office. It was our little pickup truck, and Sandy was pulled roughly from the bed of the truck by Sheriff Kronk. Her hands were rope-bound behind her, there was a red bandana tied around her mouth, her slacks and blouse were dirty and torn. There was a look of defiance on her face, and blood dripped from the corner of her mouth staining the bandana gag.

While Kronk held her from behind by her arms, Karl Oberman stepped down onto the street. He slowly drew a big, black semi-auto pistol from a holster at his side and put the muzzle against the side of Sandy's head.

He called out loudly, "OK, Morgan! I know you're here! You've got exactly five seconds and then I kill your wife!"

I jumped from the table and ran out the door. "No! NO!" I shouted. "I'm here! Don't!"

CHAPTER TWENTY THREE – Now What

The jail in San Juan de Cristo had two small cells, throwbacks to the old Wild West. They were 10 foot by 10 foot brick rooms with steel bars on the single open window of either cell. Steel bars separated the cells from each other, and doors of steel bars separated the cells from the Sheriff's small office. There was one short metal bunk in each cell, neither with a mattress of any kind, just rusty springs, a few of which were broken and hanging loose. There was a battered toilet in each cell, neither with a seat or cover and both in dire need of a cleaning. There was a faucet protruding from the brick wall above the toilet, the only source of drinking water in the cell. The problem being that the water from it was brown and tasted like nothing like I have ever tasted before.

Sandy was in one cell, and I was in the cell next door. It was still and very hot in the jail.

"Are you OK?" I asked.

"Yeah," Sandy answered, dabbing at her bloody lip. They had untied her, and the gag hung loosely around her neck. "That son of a bitch hit me when I tried to kick him in the nuts."

"What happened?"

"I was only a mile from Interstate 10. I was stupid enough to stop for a car with the hood up. I thought someone might need help. When I got out, this guy grabbed me. I pushed him away and tried to kick him, but he was quick and he hit me."

"Did he do anything else to you?"

"If you mean, did he rape me . . . No. I'm guessing he was under orders to bring me back. That's all. But I'm going to kick that guy in the nuts sooner or later. To make a long story short, he tied me up and tossed me into the back of the pickup. When I wouldn't stop yelling and swearing at him, he put this crappy gag around my mouth." She quickly untied the bandana and tossed it across the cell. "And here we are, dear."

And she was right again, there we were. It was late afternoon and the cell windows faced west, letting the afternoon sun stream in. The small building was closed except for the barred windows. Not a breath of air moved in the cells, and the temperature continued to rise.

Hours passed without anyone but us inside the jail. The heat became oppressive, and all we could do was splash some dirty water from the faucet on us. Sandy started yelling as loud as she could. Either no one heard her, or no one cared.

"Save your voice," I said. "Lie on the floor and out of the sun. I have a feeling we're in the same fix as those Mexican's under The Mustang."

"You mean they're going to keep us here . . . Without food and water?"

"Exactly," I answered. "I think the normal routine is to weaken their victims until they can't fight back . . . And then kill them."

We waited, trying to not move and trying to conserve what little fluids we had left after hours of sweating in the hot-box cells. I watched as the sun streaming into the cells sank and then was gone. Dusk was cooler but not by much. More hours passed and cold darkness finally filled the cells. And cold it was. Bitter cold, as deserts are at night. We tried to huddle together with the steel bars between us, but it did little good - we were shivering cold.

I don't know what time it was. When I surrendered myself to Kronk and Oberman I was searched, and everything, including my Rolex watch, was taken from me. All they left me with were the clothes on my back. It was pitch black inside the cells when I heard something.

"Pssst . . . Pssst."

"What's that?" Sandy whispered.

"I don't know," I said. "I think it's coming from outside."

I pushed myself to my feet and walked to the steel bunk under the window.

"Pssst . . . Pssst."

I stepped up onto the bunk and slowly raised myself to the cell's barred window, holding onto the bars to keep myself from falling. Outside, below, huddled against the wall in the dark was a shadowy figure of a man.

"Hey," the figure spoke in a low voice, almost too quiet for me to hear. "You wanna' get outta' here?"

"Who are you? I can't see you."

"F'get that. You wanna get outta' here or not?"

"Yes . . . Of course we want to get out of here."

The shadow moved slightly and something flew through the bars of the window, just inches from my head. It landed on the concrete floor loudly, metal sparking as it bounced.

"T'marow when Greg West comes t'check on ya' . . . Use the knife. There's a truck waitin' out behind The Mustang. Take it an' get out. Don't come back."

"Who are you? Why are you doing this?" I asked, but whoever it was had disappeared into the night.

Sandy was pressed against the bars separating us. "What is it? Who was that?" she asked.

I stepped down off the bunk, picked up the knife, and stepped closer to her. The knife was big - the blade eight inches long. The handle was well worn, wrapped in stained leather, but the blade was polished and sharp as a razor.

"I don't know who it was," I said. "I couldn't recognize the voice, and I couldn't see who it was. He said that Greg West would come to check on us in the morning. He said to use the knife on him, get out of the cells, and that a truck would be waiting for us behind The Mustang."

"You mean he wants you to kill someone?" Sandy asked.

"I'm guessing, maybe I'm just hoping, that West will have the keys to the cells on him. I need to get them . . . Somehow. We need to get out of here."

"But killing someone like that? Isn't there some other way?"

We agreed to try to get some sleep. It's sometimes hard to believe how cold the desert can get at night. Sandy slept . . . Restlessly but she slept. I found sleep to be far away from me. I spent the night shivering and thinking of sinking the knife into Greg West. Where would I aim for? How would I get him close to the cell? And what if he didn't have keys with him?

Over and over, throughout the long night, I saw in my mind's eye the young man with the knife sticking out of him, bleeding to death on the dirty floor of the Sheriff's office. It was a nightmare, but one I knew I had to make real if Sandy and I were to survive.

Eventually the sun rose, as it always does, and a new day faced us. The bitter cold began to slide away, and the cells warmed. We stood at the bars separating our cells, holding each other as best we could. We said nothing, both knowing what the next few hours held for us. Killing the man was one thing, and maybe even the easiest task ahead of us. We still had to get out of Sheriff's Kronk's jail and office, get to the truck waiting for us, and get away from San Juan de Cristo.

I had no way of knowing the time of day, but I

assumed it was very near noon – the oppressive heat gave me a clue – when the front door to the Sheriff's office opened. I had the knife held tightly in my belt at the small of my back. My hand went there unconsciously just to check that it was still there.

A black silhouette of a man stood in the open doorway against the bright sunlight. He stepped slowly, deliberately, into the office and closed the door behind him. Gregg West wore a big white but dusty Stetson pushed back on his head, a bright red plaid shirt, and worn jeans over dirty cowboy boots. He was grinning callously, while his lips held a cigarette. He stood too far away from our cells and said, "So, how're you folks? Doin' well I hope? Anythin' I can get for ya'll?"

I whispered in a gravelly voice, "Money."

"What?' West said. "You want money? That what ya'll said?"

I said again, this time in even a softer voice, "Money."

West took a couple of steps closer to me. He was curious and, as I hoped, greedy. "What money?" he asked.

I raised my hand weakly and waved him closer to me. I whispered again, "Money".

West came closer but was still out of arm's reach. I waived again and pointed to my throat trying to tell him my voice was weak. Then he took two more steps and was nearly touching the cell's bars. I grabbed his shirt with my left hand and pulled hard, pulling him against the steel cage. The knife was in my hand and pressed against his stomach.

Greg was startled and frightened and tried to pull away, but I held tightly to his shirt and pressed the blade against him. The cigarette fell from his lips to the floor. He started to scream, but I pushed just a little harder with the knife. He looked down, eyes wide in fright, his mouth hanging open, but he didn't make a sound.

"I don't want to kill you," I said. "But I will if I have to. I want the keys."

"What keys, man? I ain't got no keys."

"Don't screw with me boy," I said. "Give me the keys to these cells."

"I'm tellin' ya'll, I ain't got no keys."

I turned to Sandy and questioned with a look. She looked at Greg West and said, "Drop your pants."

West said, "What! I ain't gonna' do that!"

She turned to me and said, sounding like she really meant it, "Go ahead. Stick the son of a bitch."

"Wait a minute," West cried out, as I pushed the point of knife a fraction more at his stomach. He reached down and unfastened the too big silver buckle of his belt, unbuttoned his jeans and let them slide to the floor.

"Kick them over here," Sandy ordered.

Greg had a hard time getting the jeans over his boots, kicking at them nervously, but when they were free, he did kick them across the floor. Sandy reached through the bars and pulled them into her cell. She emptied the pockets onto the floor and found a two inch wide key ring with four big keys on it. She tried each on the lock to her cell, and the third worked. The bars swung open, and she stepped outside. After moving West to the side, while I moved with him, keeping the knife at his stomach, she unlocked the door to my cell. I stepped outside quickly, holding onto to West, and pushed him back against the brick wall of the jail.

"Wait there a minute," she said. She went to the Sheriff's office at the front of the jail and searched through his small desk, then around the rest of the room. When she came back, she said, "No handcuffs. But I found a tool box with a roll of duct tape."

She pulled Greg's arms behind his back and taped them heavily. Then she wrapped tape four times around his head, over his mouth. When she was done, I pulled West into the cell, pushing him to the floor. I took the tape and wrapped his ankles together. He lay quietly and unmoving on the cell's floor, as I closed and locked the bars. His eyes were locked on us.

Sandy and I stood outside the cell, looking down at Greg West. Without looking at me she asked, "Now what?"

CHAPTER TWENTY FOUR – You Kill Him, I Can't

We needed to get out of Kronk's office and get to the rear of The Mustang. How we did that was the question. There wasn't a back door in the jail so the only way out appeared to be the front door. But somewhere outside the front door were Sheriff Kronk, Karl Oberman, and the others.

"Should we just make a run for it?" Sandy asked.

"You know the old saying," I said. "Don't take a knife to a gun fight. They'll shoot us down before we get ten feet away."

"Somebody out there wants to help us," she said. "Do you think it was Santos?"

"I doubt it," I answered. "I couldn't see who it was, but it wasn't Santos' voice. I've never heard whoever it was before."

"But who then? And how do we get more help?"

I couldn't answer that. And so, once again we waited. "Dark is our best hope," I said.

There wasn't much in Sheriff Kronk's office, except a lot of dirt and sand on the wood floor. There was a battered old desk and a hard wooden chair, kept from loneliness by a single four drawer file cabinet. Five Playboy centerfolds decorated one unpainted wooden wall. A framed photo of Mary Lou Perkins hung lopsided on the opposite wall. There was a short table under her picture that held a single burner hotplate. A blue coffee pot sat on it. It was empty.

The file cabinet was locked, but it took only a little effort to break the lock with the knife. I searched through the drawers, finding little of interest, except for an unopened bag of beef jerky. I tore it opened and offered a piece to Sandy.

"I wish there was some water to go with this," she said. She was right once again, of course. And I had an idea . . . Maybe more of a hope than anything else. I went to Greg West, who was still lying quietly on the cell floor. Using the knife, I cut his shirt off and folded it several times.

"Bring that coffee pot over here," I said to Sandy.

Using the layers of shirt as a filter, I ran water from one of the faucets inside a cell into the coffee pot. The water in the pot was still brown, but the shirt had filtered out a lot of disgusting solids.

"You want to drink that?" Sandy asked.

I put the pot to my lips and drank. "It tastes like crap, but it's water. You should drink some. This heat will dehydrate us fast."

Sandy sipped from the coffee pot, coughed and choked, but she did manage to swallow the warm, brown water. "That's enough of that," she said. "Now what do we do?"

I didn't have an answer for that. But there was one thing I was sure of, and I told Sandy, "Look, sooner or later someone is going to wonder where Greg West is. They're going to come looking for him. I don't think we can wait around here any longer."

Sandy nodded reluctant agreement. We went to the grimy window of Sheriff Kronk's office and peered out. North and South along Main Street seemed deserted. Only that same old yellow dog was outside, and he was asleep across the street in front of Santos' taqueria, in the shade under a sad looking bench.

The Last Stand, where I assumed Kronk, Oberman, and the others were waiting, was to our right and across the street. I hoped they were drinking beer and a lot of it. To our left was the town's shabby garage and gas station.

I whispered, even though we were alone, "I'll go first. Out and to the left. When I reach the garage, you come and run fast. Be as quiet as you can. If we can make it into the garage, we might just be able to skirt behind the buildings and get to The Mustang."

I handed the knife to Sandy and said, "Use it if you have to."

My chest was still hurting, and I could still feel bruises from the beatings I had taken at the compound. But I ducked low out the door and ran as fast as I could to the garage maybe a hundred feet away. The sliding door of the garage into the work area was open. Inside was dark but actually a little cooler than outside. Sandy ran seconds behind me. I was breathing hard; she wasn't, but I didn't need a lecture on all those years of smoking and the extra weight I carried.

I took a minute to catch my breath, and then we glanced quickly out the rear door. We saw nothing but trash, bits and pieces of cars and trucks, and hot desert. "Slow," I said. "If we get caught, I want you to run. At least try to get away. I'll try to keep them busy as long as I can."

We walked slowly, stopping where buildings weren't connected before running across the open space between them. I saw the truck waiting for us less than a hundred yards away, behind The Mustang. But the distance seemed like miles. So far so good.

Then I heard the truck's engine start and it moved towards us. We froze in our tracks. I reached for the knife Sandy was still carrying, although I was still trying to convince myself I could do something with it to protect her and me.

We pressed ourselves against a building; it was useless to run or try to hide. The truck, a late model Ford double cab pick-up, slowed and pulled to a stop next to us.

"Who are you?" I asked the man behind the wheel.

"Ted Soller," he said. "Now ya'll get the hell in, and let's get the hell outta' here."

I opened the passenger side door and before Sandy could get in, I noticed that Soller had an empty knife scabbard hanging from his belt.

Ted Soller was one of the five men who were at The Mustang the night Edgy Hands was killed. Benny Newsinger and Murray Allott were killed back at the compound when Maggie Autumn Leaf attacked it. Thomas Rocker was in jail back in El Paso. Greg West was still taped up . . . I hoped . . . Back at Kronk's little jail. I was confident that one of the five killed Edgy Hands. But why was Ted Soller helping us?

I got in after Sandy and closed the door. Soller floored the gas pedal, turned the wheel sharply to the left and we sped away, kicking up a big cloud of dust as we bounced along across the desert. I reached across Sandy and handed the knife to Soller. "Thanks," I said. He took it and slid it back into his empty scabbard, then smiled at me.

We bounced roughly for a minute or two and then Sandy asked simply, "Why?"

"I got this thing my momma called a Christian conscience. I ain't gonna' see two white folks killed f'nothin', ya' know?"

"But what about those poor people down in that stink hole under The Mustang?" she asked him.

"They ain't white folks," he said glancing at us quickly. He said it like he was surprised we didn't know that.

"But . . ." Sandy started but I elbowed her and shook my head just enough for her to know not to say anything more. If we were going to get away from San Juan de Cristo, we would need Ted Soller's help. There was no sense in pissing the guy off.

After five more minutes I asked him, "Did you really want me to kill Greg West back there?"

"Hey, man," he said. "That som'bitch needed t'die. I

hate that som'bitch, ya' know?"

"Is he that bad?" Sandy asked.

"Hey lady, that som'bitch hates me, so I hate him. There ain't nothin' I can do that som'bitch don't laugh at."

I said, "Well, I can understand that. I know people who are like that."

"I'm glad he's dead," he said. He turned to look at me and asked, "He is dead, ain't he?"

"You wanted him dead, didn't you?" I said evasively. He smiled.

We drove on, skidding across sand and then jumping across rocks but without further talk. We reached a well worn dirt road and turned north. "This here road'll get ya'll to Inner'state 10. From there, ya'll can hitch hike . . . But don't ya'll come back to town, unner'stand?"

"We need some water," Sandy said.

"Yeah, well maybe whoever picks ya'll up will have some."

We reached Interstate 10, and Soller pulled the truck to a slow stop along the dirt road, a couple hundred yards from the highway. He looked at us, waiting for us to get out.

"I need to talk to you," I said. "I need to know what happened at The Mustang the night Edgy Hands died."

Soller looked suspiciously, angrily at me. "What the hell ya'll talkin' 'bout? That som'bitch was killed. That girl done it. Ever'body knows that."

"You were there, right?" I asked.

"Sure . . . Me an' the guys was all there."

"Do you remember the girl who was there?"

"Sure . . . Pretty little thing. I danced a couple times with her," he said grinning salaciously.

"She was drinking a lot wasn't she?" I asked.

"Sure, we all was. Lot of beer and whiskey."

"I understand Edgy liked to talk . . . To brag I guess," I said.

"That som'bitch was always shootin' off his big mouth

'bout sum'thin'. Never could shut him up."

"What kind of stuff did he like to talk about?"

"You tryin' to trick me, ain't you?" Soller said trying to sound smart. "I ain't gonna talk 'bout security stuff."

"Well, I can understand that," I said. "You're former military, aren't you? You know how important secrets are."

"You bet," he said proudly. "I know stuff ain't nobody knows . . . Least ways not too many people."

Sandy nudged me just enough for me to follow her lead. "Hey, can we get out of the truck for a minute? I need to stretch my legs." She smiled that wonderful smile of hers and looked him in the eye.

"Yeah," he said. "I could use a smoke."

We all got out of the truck and walked to the front. Soller lit a Marlboro. I wanted one, but I knew what Sandy's reaction would be, so I didn't ask for one. He leaned back against the truck's grill, putting one cowboy booted foot on the bumper. Sandy joined him, standing very close, elbow to elbow, one foot on the truck's bumper also.

"So you were in the military?" she asked.

"Yeah. I was in the Army."

"I thought so," she said, smiling at him suggestively. "You look like a military man. I'll bet you can handle yourself."

"Hell, lady. I can handle lots of stuff. If your old man wasn't here I'd show ya'. Know what I mean?"

"I'll bet," Sandy said. She pushed herself off the truck and stood in front of Soller. "Can you handle this?" she said and kicked him hard in his shin. He spit the cigarette out of his mouth, yelled and bent forward. I hit him hard on his jaw with an upper cut. He flew backwards, bounced off the truck and fell face down onto the sand.

"You did that well," Sandy said.

"I think I broke my hand!" I said.

****

Ted Soller woke up in the bed of the pickup. He was in his undershorts and socks, his toes sticking out from the holes in them, and nothing else. His hands were tightly bound behind his back with strips I had cut from his blue jeans. His feet were wrapped in his leather belt and secure. When he could see, he twisted and turned and grunted and growled, but he could not free himself.

"God damn it!" he spit out. "Get me outta' here!"

Sandy had torn Ted's shirt in half and had fashioned a funny looking head scarf from it. I didn't tell her it looked funny, but I think she knew that. It was keeping the hot desert sun off her head. She had offered me the other half of the shirt, but I turned it down. One of us looking funny was enough.

"Now, now, Teddy," I said patting his skinny, hairy leg. "We're going to talk, and you're going to tell me what I want to know. And then we're going to drive into El Paso and talk to the police there."

"I ain't telling you shit!"

"Oh, I think you will . . . Eventually. Can you sit up enough to see that patch of thorny cactus over there? Well, I'm going to toss you right into the middle of those thorns. How does that sound?"

"You ain't got the balls," he said and tried to spit at me.

I grabbed his belt bound ankles and dragged him from the bed of the truck. He landed hard on the dirt road and grunted in pain. Holding onto the belt, I dragged him across the dirt and sand to the cactus. He was kicking and swearing, but he was tied tightly.

"Now," I said. "I can pick up your skinny little ass and toss you into these bushes. Or you can tell me what I want to know."

"Fuck you man!"

Sandy had joined us. She said, "OK Morgan. You take his feet, I'll take his shoulders and we toss him on three, OK?"

She bent and took him by his shoulders; I lifted him by his ankles. "Wait a minute!" he yelled. "Wait a damn minute!"

We laid him down and I said, "Are we going to talk?"

"Depends on what you wanna' know."

"I want to know who killed Edgy Hands."

"That bitch girl. I done tol' you that already."

"OK, Sandy," I said. "I guess he wants the thorn bushes. Let's pick him up."

"No! Wait a minute!" he screamed again.

"Then damn it, Ted, who killed Edgy Hands," I demanded.

"If I tell ya', I ain't gonna' go back there t'town. They'll kill me, too."

"That I can promise you," I said. Once I knew the truth of Edgy Hand's murder, I intended to get back to El Paso, breaking every speed law I could find. Ted Soller would be coming with me.

"OK," he said, resigned to the fact that he would have to tell me the truth. "Get me outta' the damn sun. Then I'll tell ya'll what I know."

Sandy and I each grabbed an arm and pulled Ted back to the pickup truck. It was getting into the late afternoon; the east side of the truck bore a little shade. We sat him on the running board.

"Now talk," I ordered. "From the beginning. And I warn you, I know what really happened. If you lie, I'm going to know it."

****

Ted Soller's Story

"Mary Lou . . . You know, the Perkins woman . . . She got this big operation goin'. Started years ago. San Juan de Cristo was dead. Mary Lou, she kept the town goin' with the money she made off her ranch. But then everything went t'hell, ya'know?"

"You mean when the economy collapsed?" Sandy asked.

"Yeah, I don't know nothing 'bout that shit," he said. "Cattle prices went t'hell. The town started t'fall apart. Mary Lou, she had this side business goin'. Runnin' Mexicans up for farm workers up north. Even that went t'hell. So she started runnin' drugs . . . Just a little at first t'cover expenses. It got bigger and bigger. She hired on guys like me could use a gun. And she opened that fort of hers. Big shit, ya'know?"

"You mean her compound . . . Where I was held?" I asked.

"Yeah, that place was a joke. We was supposed to tell everybody we was training like an army. But it was nothin' but a warehouse for her drugs. We all laughed real good when she wasn't around.

"An' she wanted more, ya'know?" he went on. I started feeling as if he wanted to talk about it, maybe to get it off his chest. "She was a greedy bitch. It was too damn expensive for her to actually run them Mexi's up north. It was cheaper just to bring'em across the damn boarder. Me and the others were paid t'kill Mexi's she got paid t'bring up. Easier than shippin'em north, ya'know? Anyway, one of us guys, Edgy, he couldn't keep his damn mouth shut. Always hinting around, braggin' like, and joking 'bout what we was doin'. Mary Lou found out that the ATF was out t'talk to him 'bout runnin' guns into her training camp. She was afraid he was gonna' talk about everything, the drugs an' Mexi's an' especially the killin'.   She was real scared 'bout that, ya'know."''

"So Mary Lou had Edgy Hands killed?" I asked.

"Yeah. An' he was wisin' off t'her all the damn time, too. Mary Lou don't take no shit off nobody. But he had family who was gonna' miss him, and questions was gonna' be asked. So Mary Lou, she sent that punk son o'hers out to find a sucker. Someone we could pin the killin' on. He come back with that little girl.

"So's we took her into The Mustang. Just us, nobody else. We poured our own beer and danced a lot. We get her drunk, and then Jimmy Perkins put somethin' in her beer. She was out quick. Mary Lou come in, an' a couple of us, we drag her into the back room. Mary Lou tol' all of us . . . 'cept for Jimmy that is . . . She says to get out so we did. You know the rest."

"So you're saying Mary Lou killed Edgy Hands?" Sandy asked.

"Either her or Jimmy," Soller said. "I'd put my money on Mary Lou 'cause Jimmy ain't got the balls."

"Who killed Jimmy back at the ranch?" I asked.

"I don't know," he said. "Maybe Greg West. He likes to hurt people and kill people. I kinda' liked Jimmy . . . Even though he was a punk. He never said nothin' bad t'nobody. But Mary Lou rode the kid hard. She wanted him to be tough . . . Like her. But Jimmy could never be tough and mean."

"What about Harry Perkins?" Sandy asked. "How was he involved?"

"Ol' Harry?" Ted said and laughed. "That ol' man was a drunk an' nothin' else. But if I was married to Mary Lou, I'd stay drunk, too. You know she changed the name of her ranch from The Angus Cattle Company to The Bar H? Harry was sayin' he was leavin' her. She gave him a new name for the ranch . . . H for Harry. She told him to run the ranch, but us guys did all the work without him, 'cause he was always drunk."

"So Mary Lou framed Betsy," I said. "Then she gave her money to run away. But she lost a quarter of a million dollars in the bond she put up to get Betsy out of jail. That doesn't make sense."

"It does if you knew how much damn money she was makin'. God damn millions, ya'know. That two fifty was nothin' to her. She'd make that back in less than a month if she could keep the Feds away."

"Did Mary Lou ever talk about this with you?"

"Nah, she never talked to any of us face t'face," he said. He moved around a little, stretching, but just in case I said, "Forget about trying to get loose. I will kill you, if I have to. I don't want to, but I will if you force me." He stopped struggling and relaxed back on the running board.

"How did you get your orders?" I asked.

"Colonel Max," Ted answered. "He ran the camp and the operations. Him and Mary Lou was tight."

"Colonel Max?" I asked. "That's Karl Oberman, right?"

"Who?" Ted asked. "Don't know nobody called that."

"OK, Ted," I began. "Now we're going to drive into El Paso, and you're going to tell the police and D.A. what you told us."

He frowned and asked, "I gotta' do that?"

"Your choice," I said. "We can leave you here . . . Or we can drop you off back in town . . . Or you can come with us and get this whole thing straightened out."

It didn't take long for Ted to understand that his choice was life or death. "OK, let's get goin'. But do I gotta go in my undershorts?"

We pulled Ted to his feet and started to help him into the pickup truck, when we heard the engine and saw the cloud of dust kicked up by the speeding car headed towards us from the south, on the dirt road. It was too close for us to try to run away.

A big, open bed truck came to a loud, short stop behind the pickup. Karl Oberman stepped from the truck. He walked with his hands on his hips and a big gun holstered at his waist. He looked unhappy.

"Just what the hell do you two think you're doing?" he barked at us. "Are you two really trying to fuck up my investigation?"

"Investigation?" Ted said. "Hey Colonel Max! What the hell ya'll mean?"

"Shut your mouth, Ted. You're in enough trouble."

"But . . ."

"I said shut your damn mouth," Oberman ordered.

He turned to look back and forth from me to Sandy and back to me. "Why couldn't you leave well enough alone? You weren't going to get hurt. I would have seen to that. Now you've screwed everything up."

"All we want to do is clear Betsy Concanon," I said. "Ted here has agreed to testify. He will testify that Mary Lou Perkins killed Edgy Hands. And that will clear up Edgy's murder. That's all we want to do. All the rest of it is your business."

Oberman looked at Ted Soller, tied up and in his underwear. "Are you really going to testify?" he asked him.

"I gotta, Colonel," he said in a pleading voice, almost at the point of tears. "They know everythin'. It was me got'em outta' jail back there. I gave'em the knife they used to kill Greg."

"You think they killed Greg? They didn't kill Greg. We found Greg tied up and in jail."

"You mean he's alive?" Ted was both surprised and scared. He wasn't the brightest light in the chandelier. I could almost see the rusty wheels spinning around inside his head, as he tried to delve out what exactly was happening. I guessed he thought that if I lied to him once – telling him I had killed Greg West when I hadn't – I might be lying to him about other things, too. But Oberman cleared it all up for him very quickly.

He said, "No, they didn't kill your buddy Greg. He's alive, and you're alive, and I have to figure out some way of salvaging my investigation."

I asked, "You're investigation? You mean all this crap is part of your investigation?"

Sandy added, "And those poor people down in the hole . . . They're all part of your investigation?"

"Yes," he said. "I know what it looks like, but I want to find the end of the line. We already know who is supplying the drugs from across the border. We need to know who they're going to. And we need to find out who is receiving the Mexicans."

"Receiving?" I said. I was amazed that Karl Oberman was telling us that the Mexicans weren't meant to be killed.

"Of course. What the hell did you think?"

I said, "Ted told us he and the others were hired by Mary Lou Perkins to kill the Mexicans. That's not true?"

"He told you that? Ted, did you tell them that you killed the Mexicans Mary Lou brought up?"

"I had to, Colonel. Hell, what would happen to me if they brought me back to town? I'd be killed; Kronk'll kill me. Ya'll know that."

Oberman nodded, looked down at the ground, kicked some sand with the toe of his boot, put his hands on his hips, and then looked up at Ted Soller, standing there in his underwear, tied up, and leaning against the door of the truck. He quickly drew the big semi-auto from the holster at his waist and shot Ted, blowing the top of his head off. Ted slumped to the ground a vacant stare across his face.

Sandy screamed, turned and fell to her knees in the dirt. She covered her eyes and screamed again. I took a couple of steps backward, the world spinning away in slow motion in front of my eyes. I felt wet and looked up to see the rain before I realized it wasn't rain, I was covered in Ted Soller's blood.

When I regained vision, I wiped Ted's blood from my face and saw Oberman who had stepped to Sandy's side as she knelt in the dirt. His big gun was pointed against her head. I ran the few steps to Sandy and yelled, "NO! WAIT! PLEASE!"

Oberman lowered his gun. I pulled Sandy to her feet and hugged her tightly to me. She was crying uncontrollably. I had never seen her in such an emotional state before. She was near hysteria, pounding her fists onto my chest and screaming. She twisted and turned, and I kept her close to me.

Oberman seemed confused at least. He took a step closer to us. That let Sandy push away from me and lash out at him. She grabbed his gun and pulled it easily from his hand, tossing it away, as she pushed him backwards. They fell, tripping over Ted Soller's body, and rolled in the dirt. I jumped on top of him, and as Sandy held his arms, I pummeled him wildly with both hands.

He was bleeding from his mouth, nose, and his right eye when Sandy got to her feet and picked up his gun. "Let him up, Morgan," she said. She wasn't crying now. She was cool and calm, and I realized that she had been acting, and acting very well.

When we were on our feet, she handed the big pistol to me. "I can't shoot him, Morgan," she said. "You do it."

And I felt the urge to do exactly that. But I needed information. Another dead person wouldn't help us at all. So I held the gun, pointed at Oberman, and said in as threatening a voice as I could manage, "You have one chance to stay alive."

He pushed himself to his feet and swaggered arrogantly, hooking his thumbs in his belt, and said, "You don't have the balls to kill me."

"You're probably right," I said. "I'm not a cold blooded killer. Oh, I've killed people before, but in self-defense. People like you . . . Who can kill so easily . . . You're different than I am. But I have absolutely no compunction about hurting you badly. My guess is there are enough bullets in this gun to cripple you badly. I will do that, if you don't tell me what I want to know."

"Shit! You think you can prove anything? You're even holding the gun that killed stupid Ted Soller. Your finger prints are all over it. You shoot me, and there'll be residue all over your hands. The best thing you can do is trade my gun for this pickup truck. Drive away and forget this whole damn thing."

"First answer a few questions," I demanded. "Why? I mean, what the hell are you doing? Whose side are you on anyway?"

Oberman pulled a pack of cigarettes from his shirt pocket, drew one out and put it to his lips. He lit it with a gold lighter, drew the smoke in deeply and exhaled it up towards the sky. He said, "Do you have any idea how much money the Perkins bitch was making? I mean, she was pocketing ten, twenty million a year from the drugs. She was so damn greedy that she was making a couple hundred thousand a year taking money from Mexicans to smuggle them in and then killing them."

"So you want that money?" Sandy asked. "You want to take over Mary Lou's operation?"

"Well, lady. I guess you've got to figure that one out. Am I investigating the whole operation? Trying to find out who her contacts are?" He paused and took a deep drag off the cigarette and then said, "Or am I taking over for the money? You figure it out."

"You killed Ted Soller in cold blood," Sandy said.

"And who told the dumb ass that I wasn't Colonel Max? You two did. If you hadn't, he'd be alive today. But if he ever got back to San Juan de Cristo and told everyone who I really am, then either my investigation is blown, or my taking over from Mary Lou is blown. So he had to die, and you two are responsible for Soller's death. This thing is bigger than Ted Soller."

I looked at Sandy. She shrugged her shoulders. I agreed. What was the truth, and was it our job to get to the truth? I had to bring us back to what Sandy and I were in the West Texas desert for. So I asked Oberman, "Tell me what you know about Edgy Hands' death."

"I wasn't there," he said as he crushed his cigarette out in the dirt under his boot.

"So tell me what you know," I demanded.

"Edgy was a punk. He liked to brag to anybody who was nearby. He was always chasing the couple women we got out here. He even went after the Mexican women. The damn ATF had a warrant out for him because he talked too much. He was constantly pissing Mary Lou off. He had to die. For all I know, your little girl killed him. Or maybe it was Mary Lou. I wouldn't put it past her. She was a cold blooded bitch if I ever saw one. I don't know who killed him."

"OK," I said. "Then I want a trade. You for Greg West. He was there that night. He can testify and get Betsy Concanon out of jail."

"And if I say no?"

"Then we take you back to El Paso, turn you over to whatever Federal Agency will want you, and you can explain everything to them."

Oberman lit another cigarette, quickly smoked it halfway down, and tossed it away. "OK," he said. "And if you get Greg West and take him to El Paso, do you screw up my investigation, too?"

"Frankly, Mr. Oberman, I've had enough of you people. I don't give a damn about your investigation. All I want is to clear Betsy Concanon of the murder charge. Greg West is the only person left who knows that Mary Lou Perkins killed Edgy Hands. I need him . . . That's all I care about."

Sandy asked Oberman, "And what about those people in the hole under The Mustang? Do you kill them?"

"Think about it," he said as he lit yet another cigarette. He was beginning to show some nervousness. "If I'm really running a Federal investigation . . . Those people are safe. If I'm not . . . And you know they're down there . . . Would I kill them while you're alive to tell about it? No, they'll live. I'll either send them home or send them north . . . But they'll live."

Sandy looked at me and nodded her approval. Oberman saw this, crushed out the cigarette and said, "OK, we got a deal. Do we leave now?"

CHAPTER TWENTY FIVE - Hogtied

Sandy sat behind the wheel of Oberman's truck. I sat in the middle, holding the pistol tight against Oberman's side. There was a quart size plastic bottle of water on the floor of the truck. It was warm, but Sandy and I each drank our fill, emptying the bottle. My head had been spinning from the last couple of days with only a mouthful of dirty water back in the jail cell. But it cleared quickly with the water. And what we had to do in the next hour or so was also clear.

My hope, and maybe even my prayer, was that Oberman, or Colonel Max as the people in San Juan de Cristo knew him, was important enough to keep us alive. If he was that important, we would be able to trade him for Greg West. If not . . . Well, I tried not to think about that.

As we approached the outskirts of town, Sandy brought the big truck to a stop. The town looked deserted, only that old yellow dog was out, still asleep in the shade of the raised wooden sidewalk. I thought that maybe Santos would be there to protect our backs. But then I saw the grey smoke of a dying fire at the far end of town. Santos' taqueria had been burnt to the ground. I gave up any hopes I had of his help.

Sandy put the truck into gear, and we drove into town as slow as the big truck would move. "Where is everybody?" she asked.

I poked the gun into Oberman's rips and he said, "At The Last Stand."

Sandy drove to The Last Stand, did a u-turn and parked across the street from the bar, facing north. I told her, "You wait here. Keep the engine running. Blow the horn if anybody approaches you. If I'm not back in fifteen minutes, get the hell out of here, and do the best you can to get to El Paso."

I nudged Oberman again and he opened the door. We slid out, and we walked across the street, me behind him with the gun in the small of his back. At the door to The Last Stand, he stopped and said over his shoulder, "You sure you want to walk in there with that gun in my back?"

I tucked the big semi-auto under my belt, and we stepped inside the bar. Sheriff Kronk was there. There was a short, fat man there behind the bar, who I recognized as the bartender from my last visit there. And two other cowboy types were there. A sawed off, double barreled shotgun was on the bar next to Burl.

Sheriff Kronk stood. "You got'em, Colonel." He said. "Where's the woman?"

"Shut up and sit down Kronk," Oberman said. "Mr. Crew here wants Greg West. He thinks West will tell the cops about Edgy Hands. Who here thinks we should give him West?"

Apparently no one there thought giving Greg West to me was a very good idea. Oberman turned to face me and said, "Well, I guess you just lost, Mr. Crew." He waived his arm to call to the people behind him. Everyone, Kronk and Evans, and the two cowboys, stood and started moving towards me very slowly. The fat bartender had walked from behind his bar, leaving the shotgun there. Oberman was smiling viciously. I pulled the gun from my belt and raised and fired a shot into the ceiling but that didn't stop them.

Sandy had come in, using the back door of the bar, having ignored as usual what I had asked her to do. Sandy grabbed the shotgun from the bar and fired a shot over everyone's head. The sound reverberated through the room and made everyone duck and cover on the sawdust covered floor. Only Oberman and I didn't move.

Sandy called out, "Now, I've done some trap shooting at my husband's screwed up, phony, too rich country club so I can handle a shotgun. I've got one round left here, and I will use it if I have to."

I love that babe!

Anyway, I told everyone to get to their feet and then find the nearest chair and sit in it. When they were down, I shoved Oberman to an empty chair and he sat. Sandy and I stood in front of them. I went to Kronk and pulled his pistol from its holster. None of the others appeared to be armed.

"Now that I have your attention," I said, sounding very satisfied once again. "I want Greg West, and I want to take him to El Paso. All I want him to do is clear Betsy Concanon, and he'll be back home in no time at all. Although I think you folks are all insane and a bunch of real bastards, I'm going to leave you alone . . . If I take Greg West with me. Do we have a deal?"

No one answered immediately, but then Sheriff Kronk said, "That there's gonna' to be difficult. Greg is dead."

Oberman swung around to face Kronk and said, "What the hell do you mean? Who killed him?"

"I killed him," Kronk said proudly. "When we found him all cow-tied in my jail, he was mouthin' off t'me. He got rough, and I shot the som'bitch dead. He had it comin'."

Well, I thought, that put the nail in the damn coffin. Everyone who was at The Mustang when Edgy Hands was murdered was dead. Everyone who knew that Mary Lou killed Edgy was dead. Except for Tommy Rocker who was safe in jail in El Paso. But Tommy was smart, perhaps the smartest one involved in all this crap. I wasn't sure he would cooperate and face a conspiracy to commit murder charge. Without someone to tell the truth, what could I do?

On the other hand, Sheriff Kronk was still on the witness list. He didn't witness the murder, nor was he at The

Mustang before the murder. He was in town when Mary Lou killed Edgy. He had to be in on the plan to frame Betsy. The only chance I had left was to bring Kronk . . . And Oberman . . . Back to El Paso with me. By blowing this whole mess, the entire Mary Lou Perkins operation to kingdom come, the D.A. might just believe that Betsy was innocent.

One of the two cowboys stood slowly, his hands over his head. His voice was shaky and weak when he said, "Look mister, me an' Ben here, we ain't got nothin' to do with all this. We was just workin' out at the ranch. The Sheriff here said he was deputizin' us. We ain't done nothin'."

The other cowboy stood just as slowly and said, "That's right mister. Joey's right. We haven't done anything except be afraid of Kronk over there."

I turned to Oberman and asked, "Are they telling the truth? Are they ranch hands and nothing more?"

"Yes, I guess so," he answered. "At least I've never seen them before."

"OK," I said. "You two sit down and stay out of this, and you'll be OK."

I stepped close to Sandy without taking my eyes off of the group sitting in front of us. I whispered close to her ear, "I think we need to take Kronk with us. And it might help if we take Oberman, too. What do you think?"

"I think we should tie them all up, get in the truck and get the hell outta' here," she whispered.

"What about Betsy? Do we tell her to spend the rest of her life on the run?"

"You're right, of course," she said, resigned to the fact. "But just how do we get the two of them back to El Paso? You think they're going to come willingly? And what about the other three?"

I told Joey to get up and come to me. I held up my hand to tell him to stop when he was a couple of feet in front of me. "Turn around," I told him. "I'm going to pat you down. Are you armed with anything?"

"I got me a pocket knife," he said. "In my back pocket. But my daddy gave it to me, so please don't take it from me. It's all I got from him."

I handed the pistol to Sandy and patted Joey down from head to foot. I had seen my good friend San Marcos Police Detective Bob Sommers do the same a few times, so I knew pretty well what to do. I found nothing but the small bone handled pocket knife which I left in the boy's pocket. I told Joey to go stand at the bar, facing the bar, hands on the bar, back to me. He did so quickly.

"Ben," I said. "Come on over here. I'm going to search you, too."

But Ben didn't stand. He asked, "Why?"

"Because normally the man with the gun calls the rules of the game. My gun . . . My rules. Now do you want to come over here or not?"

"Look, I told you I've got nothing to do with anything here. The only reason I'm here at all is because Kronk said he'd kill me if I tried to leave. Whatever you've got in mind, just leave me out of it, OK?"

"You sound like an educated young man," I said. "I mean, there aren't any ya'lls and all that when you speak."

"Don't butter me up, please. I just want to be left out of everything. If you want to do something for me, let me walk out of here. You have my word; you'll never see me again."

"Sorry," I said. "You'll have to stay."

I turned to Joey who was still standing with his back to me. "Joey, is there any rope anywhere in the bar?"

"Morgan," Sandy said softly and looked around the walls of the tavern. "There are lariats all over the place."

I looked around, and sure enough the bar was decorated with animal heads, mounted fish, a saddle or two, a few old west rifles, and three wound lariat ropes. Kronk was laughing.

"Joey," I said, a little embarrassed, but what the hell, I

still held the guns. "Get one of those ropes, and tie Ben to the bartender, whatever his name is. Tie them back to back, and tie them tight."

Joey moved quickly, and in a minute or two, the two men were tied up. "Now get another rope," I told Joey. "Use that pocket knife of yours to cut enough to tie Kronk's hands behind him. Then do the same for Oberman over there."

"Oberman?" Joey asked. "Who's Oberman?"

"Oh that's just great," Karl Oberman said disgustedly.

Sheriff Kronk looked at Karl Oberman and asked, "So that's your real name? I was wonderin' when we'd get t'know who you are."

I looked at Oberman. I was honestly sorry I spoke without thinking. He looked hard at me and said, "Get on with it, and keep your mouth shut."

Kronk was curious. He asked, "What else don't we know 'sides your name, Colonel?"

Karl said nothing.

Joey finished tying Kronk and Oberman, their hands behind their backs. I asked, "Did you tie them tight?"

He stepped aside, obviously nervous and maybe a little frightened of what would happen next. He answered, "Best I could, sir."

"Do you want to get out of here, Joey?" I asked.

"Yes, sir. That would be real good."

"Do you want to go to El Paso with us?"

"Good as any place I reckon," he said and smiled for the first time.

"OK," I said. "Sheriff Kronk and your Colonel are coming with us. Pick up what's left of that rope, and come with us."

I told Kronk and Oberman to get on their feet, and the three of us followed them outside to the big truck. I had Kronk and Oberman scramble up into the bed of the truck and sit there.

I told Joey, "I think they call it hogtie, Joey. Am I

right?"

He smiled again and said, "Yes sir. I guess that'll keep them right there."

Joey rolled the two men over onto their stomachs. As he was tying their feet and looping the rope up to the hands, bending their legs backward, Sandy asked me, "What about those Mexicans?"

"We can't take them all with us. We'll have to send someone back for them. They'll be OK for another day."

When Joey was done, he stood to the side, a few feet away from us, waiting. "Joey," I said. "Are you coming with us?"

"What's gonna' happen when we get t'El Paso?"

"You go your way, and we'll go ours," I said. "If you need money, I can advance you some . . . Enough to get you where you want to go."

"I guess I can do that," he said, smiled again and started for the cab of the truck.

I stopped him and said, "Joey, I need to hold onto your pocket knife until we get to El Paso. I promise to give it back to you."

I think he understood. He didn't hesitate to reach into his jeans pocket and handed me his knife. In the truck, he sat in the rear of the double cabin. Sandy sat next to me, as I drove away, north out of San Juan de Cristo.

CHAPTER TWENTY SIX – We'll Go To Trial

We drove north off the paved road that Mary Lou Perkins had paid for and onto County Road 8. It was late in the afternoon. The sun was nearing the western horizon. Exhaustion was starting to set in. It did little to cover the continuing pain in my chest. I did my best to not think about it.

We were three miles outside of town, when we saw the dust cloud in front of us, moving towards us.

"Who do you think it is?" Sandy asked. "Haven't we had enough of this stuff?"

"Can't be anybody bad," I said, hoping I was right. "Maybe just some tourists out for a drive."

"Yeah, count on it," Sandy said. She picked up the shotgun and rested it across her lap. I pulled Oberman's pistol from my waist and laid it on the seat next to me.

Joey asked from the rear seat, "Hey, what's goin' on?"

"Don't worry Joey," Sandy said. "We're always in some kind of trouble . . . And we always get ourselves out of it."

I slowed the truck and pulled to the side of the road. Sandy jumped out and went to the back. She told Kronk and Oberman to stay still and be quiet. I got out with the pistol and told Joey to wait in the truck.

Three big black SUVs with blacked out windows came

to a stop. I held the pistol at my side and waited. The back door of the first SUV opened, and Santos stepped out.

"What the hell you doin', man?" he said and laughed loudly. "You gonna' start a war with that little gun?"

I wasn't sure what to do, start shooting or shake his hand. There were so many people living double lives around San Juan de Cristo, I wasn't sure if I should trust Santos or not. "Who's with you?" I asked.

"Who? Them?" he said and laughed again. "Mainly FBI and a few State cops. When you were dumb enough to walk out of the taqueria, I split and went for help. I bet a couple guys you'd be dead by now. Guess I lost five bucks."

I slowly raised the pistol and pointed it at Santos. That brought the reaction I thought it would. The doors of all three SUVs flew open and a dozen men and women jumped out, all shouting "DROP THE GUN! DROP IT NOW!"

Two or three were in uniform, two or three in suits, the rest had bullet proof vests on. I saw a few badges. I was satisfied that they were cops. I dropped the gun, and Sandy came around from the back of the truck without the shotgun. Joey slid out of the truck and stood next to her.

The third of the three SUVs had a big cooler of bottled water, and a couple bags of peanuts were found in one of the cars. Sandy and I filled up on all the peanuts we could get our hands on and drank a couple bottles of the cold water while we told our story. Joey was about to be handcuffed before I vouched for him. "He helped us," I said. "He's one of the good guys."

When we had finished telling them how we got out of San Juan de Cristo, one of the suits, older than the rest, grey hair and easy to recognize as being in charge, pulled a leather case from his inside coat pocket and showed it to us. He said, "I am FBI Agent In Charge John Harrison. Do you mean to tell me you've got a Town Sheriff and an undercover FBI agent tied up in the back of your truck?"

"Well, I'll tell you," I said. "I really doubt Karl Oberman

is still on your side. I think he saw his chance to take over Mary Lou Perkin's operation. I'd be careful of him, if I were you. And that town Sheriff . . . He is a cold blooded killer."

Agent Harrison waved to a couple of the other suits, who walked quickly to the back of the truck. They came back with Sheriff Kronk and Karl Oberman, untied and walking freely.

Harrison walked up to Oberman and snarled, "Well, Karl. I guess I've finally got you." He spun Oberman around and pushed him against the front of the big truck. He roughly pulled Oberman's hands behind his back and slapped handcuffs on him. "I've been waiting ten years to do that," Harrison said.

Sheriff Kronk was handcuffed, and the two of them were walked back to the third SUV. They were put into the back seat, and the door was slammed on them.

I looked questioningly at Agent Harrison. My look said, 'What the hell's going on?"

Harrison read the look on my face and explained, "Oberman's been dirty for years. I may not be able to prove he's dirty this time, but Kronk may flip on him. Anyway, I'm going to try. Look, I know who you are. We were told you were out here doing what the two of you normally do . . . Getting in trouble," he laughed. "Now get the hell outta' here, will you?"

"I need Kronk and Oberman to clear our friend of murder. They're the closest thing I've got to witnesses who can testify that Mary Lou Perkins killed Edgy Hands."

"Well, you can't have them," he said.

That sounded kind of final. Sandy touched my arm to stop me from losing my temper once again. She spoke softly, "We still have Thomas Rocker. We can make a deal with him."

Harrison asked, "You have who?"

"There's a guy in jail back in El Paso," Sandy explained. "He's the only person left who knows about a murder our employee is accused of. We need him to testify, so we can clear Betsy Concanon."

"Yes, I know about the Concanon girl," Harrison said. "Where is she?"

"I honestly don't know," I said.

"And the person you need . . . That's Thomas Rocker?"

"Yes, he's our last hope."

"Well, you're out of luck again," Harrison said. He tried to hide his satisfied smile but he couldn't completely. Over the years Sandy and I have come to understand that cops of any sort normally don't like us. We interfere in their good work, and all too often we do what they cannot do. The Crew family money and power are the tools we use. But we do good things for people who can't, for whatever reason, help themselves. Our good friend Bob Sommers, back in San Marcos, is the rare exception. He is a cop, a long time friend of mine, and a cop who often turns to Sandy and me for help.

Agent Harrison, on the other hand, had no love for us. We probably did mess up his investigation, and I'd bet my last million he was trying to figure out how he'd write all this up truthfully and honestly, and still make himself look good.

I asked him, "What does that mean? Are you saying we can't have access to Rocker?"

"Oh, you can have access to him. All you have to do is dig down six feet or so."

"What! You mean he's dead?"

Harrison laughed and turned from me, walking back to his SUV. Santos took a couple of steps toward Sandy and me, looked satisfied and happy, and said, "Rocker was in solitary to keep him away from the Concanon girl. When she split, there was no reason to keep him in solitary. He was in the exercise yard, when he picked a fight with the wrong guy. A young black guy associated with the Crips. The next day Rocker was dead . . . Had his throat cut and was stabbed thirty-eight times."

"Now what do we do?" Sandy asked. Tears were filling her beautiful blue eyes. Betsy was a part of our family, an important part. She seemed lost to us.

Santos put his hand on Sandy's shoulder. "I'm sorry," he said. "I've gotta' go. I've gotta' get those poor people out of that hole back in San Juan de Cristo."

"You know about that?" I asked, astonished.

"Yeah, I know. It makes me sick to my stomach, too."

He turned and walked to the first SUV, got in, and closed the door. All the others returned to their cars. The three big, black cars drove away. They left Sandy, Joey, and me staring after them, as they kicked up a cloud of dust, heading back to that damn little town.

Without speaking, the three of us got back in the big truck and drove away.

****

We said good bye to Joey before crossing into El Paso's city limits. I returned his pocket knife to him. He refused our offer of money. I told him to come with us to the nearest ATM, but he just smiled, thanked us, and walked away. I parked the big truck in a strip mall parking lot and found a cab that took Sandy and me to our suite at The Ironwood Mansion.

We shared a long shower, I shaved several days' growth of beard, and Sandy washed her hair. Sandy ordered some dinner from room service - big steaks – a very unusual dinner for Sandy, who has for years denied me the red meat I love – salads, and a bottle of Cristal champagne. While we waited for the dinner to be delivered, Sandy raided the honor bar and mixed a couple of drinks for us. We ate in silence, both wondering what we could do to help Betsy.

Sleep tried to fight its way from us, but exhaustion

was stronger, and we slept for twelve uninterrupted hours. When we woke, we knew we had to talk. Sandy started, "Now what? What the hell can we do?"

As so often has happened over the years, when I was in really deep trouble or when I was confused about what I should do, I talked with Peter Jascro. Peter is a long time friend of my father, and since my father's death he has stood in his place, giving me guidance and help when I needed both. He is the managing partner of Harper, Harper, Jascro, and Nettles, the Crew family's attorneys who oversee our companies, investments, and, when needed, our personal lives.

I phoned his office, put the call on speaker, and interrupted a meeting he was in.

"What is it, Morgan," he said. "I'm in a meeting."

"I need your help, Peter. Betsy's still in trouble. It's even worse than before."

I told him the whole story, from the beginning, leaving out nothing, making it sound as plausible as possible that Mary Lou Perkins killed Edgy Hands. It took a full half hour, and Peter did not object to being pulled from his meeting.

"When I was done, Peter said, "First, Betsy must turn herself in immediately. It was a mistake helping her evade custody. Don't tell me if you can contact her, but do so if you can. Second, I'll have a new attorney from our Dallas office there today. Talbot is in trial for the next week or two. Anyway, I think there's a good chance we can save Betsy."

When I hung up, I asked Sandy, "So, do we call Betsy?"

"I don't see that we have any choice."

She walked to the desk, sat, her hand hovering over the telephone for a moment or two. Finally, she picked up the phone and dialed in Betsy's cell phone number. She held the phone to her ear and waited. It rang four times, five, six. At first I didn't think she would answer and maybe we had lost her . . . And Caroline forever. And then Betsy answered.

"Hey Sandy!" she said brightly. "I was just changing C. What's up?"

"We need you to come to El Paso, Betsy."

She said nothing for a moment, and then asked, "Why? Things are going good here."

"Things aren't going so well here," Sandy said. "We've been speaking with Peter Jascro. He's sending an attorney here. He thinks he can get you released and the charges dropped. But he says you have to be here . . . You have to turn yourself in."

"That doesn't sound like such a good idea."

"Betsy, we need you back in our lives. You're important to us. What would Caroline do without you? Are you going to stay on the run forever?"

Betsy said nothing again. I took the phone and said, "Look, Betsy. You know it took me a long time to like you. But I like you now. I want what's best for you. I want to see you finish college. I want you there to help Caroline with her math homework. I want you to be a part of my family. Please do what we're asking."

She didn't hesitate this time but answered right away, "OK, you want me to drive? It'll take a few days."

"I'll get you plane tickets. What airport?"

****

Abena Ekundayo, Gandalf's friend and nurse, knocked on our door. It was both good and sad seeing her. It brought back the memory of Gandalf Finch being murdered. I still don't know who pulled the trigger that blew my friend's head open. Whoever it was, he's dead now.

Abena was obviously saddened. We sat on the suite's patio and drank iced tea while we talked. Light conversation about little nothings led finally to the reason for

Abena's visit. She asked, "What happened? Why was Gandalf killed?"

I tried to tell her, to make it seem like there was some good purpose to his death. But my words couldn't begin to justify his needless death. "It was a bunch of people who cared nothing for life."

"But why? I just don't understand. Why was he there in the first place? Did you really need him so much that he had to die to get what you wanted?"

"Abena," Sandy started, "I think we both know the kind of man Gandalf was. Sure, Morgan was paying him, but I think Gandalf would have helped even if we couldn't pay him a dime. When he came to our home in California, he told us he didn't believe Betsy was guilty of murder. He offered his help. We accepted his help."

Abena's eyes looked at the red tiled patio deck, thinking about it all, trying to weigh all the positives against the negatives. It became obvious to me that she had loved Gandalf; that she still loved him and probably would always carry that love in her heart.

We spent two hours talking about Gandalf. Abena told us stories of the things he had done, some good and some terrible.

She said, "Yes, he did some things that surprised me and even sickened me. Some very violent things. But in the end, the violence seemed to be with a purpose. I think he believed he was doing more good than harm; that the good outweighed the bad. And I believe that, too.

"I mean, he kept all the day care centers open . . . All by himself. No one ever offered anything to help. All those children . . . All those years . . ."Tears began to flow, and she could not speak about him anymore.

She rose, and wiping the tears away with a small tissue, she said, "I must not keep you any further. Thank you for seeing me. And by the way, thank you for the $200,000. It will help keep Gandalf's day care centers open for awhile longer."

When she had left Sandy asked, "$200,000? Did you send that to her?"

"Not me," I answered. "But I think I know who did. Remember Fish? We told him about that safe at the compound and the quarter million in it. I can just see him now, driving around in his father's red Cadillac, the top down, taking over where Gandalf left off."

****

We were relaxing at the pool, trying to decide what to have for dinner, when Peter's attorney arrived. He was a short, rumpled little man, balding, with eyeglasses askew over a round, red face. His suit needed pressing, the collar was dusted with dandruff, and his shoes needed some polish and care. He carried an old scuffed leather briefcase, maybe the same one he used twenty five years ago when he was in law school.

He walked directly to us and asked, "Are you Mr. & Mrs. Crew?"

I said we were.

"I'm Chester Hobson. Peter Jascro asked me to see you."

We returned to our suite and sat at the small dining table where we could talk in private. Chester pulled a wrinkled pad of yellow paper from his briefcase. He flipped page after page, looking for an unused page. When he found one, he searched through all his pockets for something to write with, finally digging down to the bottom of his briefcase, where he found a short pencil that had been broken in half and was indented with teeth marks. He held the pencil hovering over the pad and said, "OK, tell me everything."

It took nearly two hours to tell Chester the whole

story. He interrupted many, many times, asking what we thought were meaningless questions, asking us to repeat things two or three times. But I knew there was meaning to his seeming lack of attention.

Years ago I would have asked Chester to leave and phoned Peter to ask for a real attorney. But I have learned that the attorneys who work for Peter Jascro are not necessarily the prettiest, but they are always the best. I took Chester calmly and hoped that Peter would be right once again.

When Sandy and I had finished telling him everything in great detail, Chester quietly put his pad of paper back in his old briefcase, stuck the pencil stub in his jacket's breast pocket, stood and said, "When Ms. Concanon's plane arrives, you meet her and take her directly to jail. Let me know when. I will be there."

"Do you believe Betsy is innocent?" I asked him.

"From what you've told me, I believe this Perkins woman is very capable of murder. But we have no evidence of that fact."

He picked up his briefcase, turned and started to leave. "Where are you going?" I asked.

Chester stopped and turned, a confused look on his chubby face. "I'm going. Why?" he answered simply like my question was stupid.

"I guess we'd like to know what you're going to do."

"I'm sorry," he frowned and said, as if he had to explain something that should not need explaining. "I thought you knew that. I'm going to get the charges against Ms. Concanon dropped. Wasn't that made clear to you?" He walked away.

The next morning we rented a car and drove to the airport. We drank too much coffee there, waiting for Betsy's plane to arrive. It was late, of course, but we ran to her when we saw her walking through the security area. She was carrying Caroline in a hand woven canvas baby carrier strapped to her chest. Betsy was dressed in a long, ankle length skirt of bright colors and of what could have been home spun materials. She wore a white, puffy peasant blouse, and her hair was its natural black, tied back in a bun on the top of her head.

Sandy ran to them and took Caroline into her arms. Sandy was crying; Caroline was giggling in joy.

While they were busy loving each other, I pulled Betsy aside. "I guess you weren't with your biker friends in San Francisco?"

"No. There's this family of kids in Montana. I guess you old folks would call them hippies. They have this commune; they live off the land. It was a nice little vacation, and I thought it would be a safe place to hide out."

"We've got things to talk about," I told her.

"I can guess," she answered. Her eyes welled with tears that she tried to fight back. "You want me to turn myself in."

"You have to," I insisted. "Look, everybody who was at the bar that night is dead. I have a good attorney waiting for you. He says he can have the charges dropped. But you have to go back to jail until this is all over."

"What about that Tommy Rocker guy?" she asked. "He tried to kill me once. He's going to try again."

"He's dead, Betsy," I said. "I told you. Everybody who was at the bar is dead. A whole bunch of other people have died in the last couple of days. Gandalf is dead. I think you'll be safe."

"Gandalf, too?" she said. "I liked him. He was cool, you know."

"He was a good man," I said. "But you need to turn yourself in, Betsy."

She nodded and wiped the tears away. "If you say so," she said.

We dropped Sandy and the baby at our suite. Betsy hugged Caroline and kissed Sandy on her cheek. "I'll be back soon . . . Right Morgan?" she asked. Sandy phoned Chester Hobson. She was concerned about Betsy. But at least we had Caroline back. I think Sandy knew, as I knew, that soon all four of us would be home in San Marcos once again.

Chester was waiting for us at the jail as he promised. I warned Betsy ahead of time not to worry about what her attorney looked like. He approached, and Betsy hesitated. "Are you sure?" she whispered.

He introduced himself and told us, "Ms. Concanon, you'll need to spend the night in jail. We have a hearing tomorrow morning at 9 AM at which time the State will drop all charges against you. You should be sleeping in your own bed tomorrow night."

I hugged Betsy tightly and spoke softly close to her ear, "It'll all be alright."

****

Little Chester Hobson was as good as his word. He had met with the District Attorney . . . Not the Deputy D.A. who would handle the case but the El Paso County District Attorney himself. All the witnesses the prosecution had, who would have been more than enough to convict Betsy of murder, were dead. The closest thing the prosecution had to a witness to put on the stand against Betsy was Sheriff Kronk. But he wasn't an eye witness; he wasn't at The Mustang the night Edgy Hands was killed. All he had was his 'investigation report', which was nothing more than a hand written, one page piece of paper that was laughable. He hadn't bothered to take any written witness statements because the whole murder had been planned so well. What could go wrong?

Sheriff Kronk had retained a T.V. lawyer, a man who was always on T.V. seeking auto accident clients. Kronk, advised by his attorney, was refusing to talk to anyone. The D.A.'s office had tried to talk to him, but he refused to even look at them when they were talking to him. His T.V. attorney refused to allow him to testify at Betsy's trial, claiming Fifth Amendment protection.

Chester had met with the FBI the night before going to the D.A.'s office. The FBI had swept Karl Oberman, alias Colonel Max, away during the night. No one knew where he had gone, and I really didn't care. That sealed the casket on the case against Betsy. They had no case at all.

After flipping through Betsy's file and listening to Chester, the District Attorney tossed the file on his desk and looked disgustedly at his deputy. He was resigned to having lost this one. He said, "She needs to spend ninety days in jail for escaping custody. In exchange I'll drop the murder charge."

"I'm very sorry, but we'll decline that offer," Chester said. "We'd like to go to trial as soon as possible."

In the end, all charges were dropped against our little biker chick, and she was able to return to San Marcos with us. Betsy has tried to put the whole nightmare behind her, but I have a feeling the whole episode will be with her forever.

CHAPTER TWENTY SEVEN- The Party

Months had passed, and we had done our best at putting San Juan de Cristo behind us. It became one of those memories that get clouded by fog day by day, but would never escape us in nightmares we all suffered. So many people had died; good people like Gandalf Finch and bad people . . . Very bad people like Mary Lou Perkins. Bad memories and very painful memories.

I had tried to find out what happened to the Mexicans who had been locked up in the hole under The Mustang. I tried ICE, the FBI, the ATF. No one would talk to me. I tried to locate Santos, but no one would admit knowing the man. He seemed to have disappeared into the haze of secret operations.

I was able to find out what Fish was doing, and sure enough, he was, as I thought, driving around in Gandalf's red Cadillac, collecting debts, chasing bale jumpers, and doing whatever was necessary to keep the day care centers open.

We were having a small party at our San Marcos house in the hills. Bob Sommers was there, of course. He had given up on his diet and was back to his normal two hundred fifty pounds. But he hadn't smoked a cigarette in five weeks, which made Sandy very happy. He was in a good mood, enjoying all the catered food but limiting himself to a few bottles of beer.

We had a full house that night. Friends from the San Marcos hills and friends from down in Harborside filled the house for no other reason than they were our friends. The differences in their wealth were left outside when they were at our house. Bankers and fishermen were friends and exchanged jokes.

Sandy, as usual, was the perfect hostess (or maybe I should say 'host' to be politically correct). I kept her happy by limiting myself to two Wild Turkeys with just a splash of club soda the entire night. And I didn't compete with Bob Sommers at the food tables.

Little Caroline was having a ball. She was scampering around the house, from person to person, showing off how well she could walk all by herself and how well she could gurgle and speak the few words she could speak. One person after another picked her up and hugged her, telling her she was as beautiful as her mother, then putting her down to run to the next person.

Betsy had truly become one of the family. No longer did she dress in black, and her hair hadn't seen anything but it's natural color since returning home. She had grown into a lady, and our friends had a difficult time remembering the rebellious child she once was. Weeks ago, she had asked if she could see a doctor who did tattoo removal. While Sandy had just smiled kindly, I had nearly jumped up and down for joy. We found a good doctor in San Francisco, and tonight she was tattoo free.

Darkness fell early in the autumn along the Northern California coast. Caroline was tiring of showing off. She sat on the floor and yawned. Betsy went to her, picked her up and announced, "I think you'll all need to say good night to C," which everyone did in turn. She carried Caroline into her bedroom, bathed her and dressed her, and took her to her brand new child's bed, C having almost outgrown her crib.

As she tucked Caroline into her covers, she said, "OK

C. Now you go to sleep. I'll try to keep the noise down out there."

Caroline laughed, yawned again, and held her arms out to Betsy. Betsy bent and kissed the baby on her forehead. "Oh C," she said as a tear escaped from her eye. "I love you so much. I wonder if I can tell you something? Will you keep it to yourself? I just have to tell someone. I can't keep it in any longer. You won't tell anyone, will you? Back there . . . In that terrible bar . . . That boy tried to rape me. They got me drunk, and I think they tried to drug me, too. I could hardly move. I was terribly dizzy. I felt like I was going to throw up. He dragged me back to that ugly room and tried to rape me. I kicked at him . . . I hit him . . . I scratched his face but I couldn't get him off of me. He was tearing at my clothes. I had to do something.

"I clawed at him and my hand found a knife he was carrying on his belt. I took it and . . . God help me . . . I stabbed that poor boy in the back. He screamed and rolled off of me. I guess I was hysterical. I think I was almost unconscious. I just kept stabbing him and stabbing him. Oh C! I killed that poor boy . . . I killed that poor boy."

THE END

www.ingramcontent.com/pod-product-compliance
Lightning Source LLC
Chambersburg PA
CBHW031553240626
47153CB00002B/491